LOVE UNTIL IT HURTS

Fiona Blakemore

Love Until it Hurts

Fiona Blakemore is a doctor and graduate of the MA Creative Writing programme at Bath Spa University.

Love Until it Hurts, her debut novel, was shortlisted for the Janklow and Nesbit Bath Spa Prize 2018.

Fiona writes under a pseudonym.

www.fionablakemore.com
@WriterFionaB 🐦

For BJFB

'We see only what we know'

Johann Wolfgang von Goethe, 1749–1832

CONTENTS

1

RUTH

Strip lighting plays tricks on the eye. The twitch of a muscle merely the reflected flicker of an overhead bulb. A bloom on his cheeks which fades when she tilts her head for a closer look. She can't be sure.

She reaches into her bag for her stethoscope, actions propelling her faster than thoughts. Her equipment's not there. Why should it be? They haven't asked her here to verify death. Of course not. Her eyes focus on the shiny toecaps of the police constable.

'Please take your time,' he says, shifting his weight from one foot to the other.

She lifts her head. Their eyes level. Mirroring his professional smile she turns to look at the body. The slight parting of his mouth, the depression of his jaw, evidence that rigor mortis has already set in. His hair has been parted to the left of centre, and trained in either direction. It's so uncharacteristic of him that she reaches over and brushes it forward with her fingers. It feels lank. Matted. It dawns on her, in slow motion, the reason why his hair has been fashioned this way. She gags. The rim of a dark, oily crater is visible over his right parietal bone. The boggy depression proof, if she needed it, that death had come instantly.

She bites her lip until she can taste metal in her mouth. Her fingers are greased with congealed blood. Bile bubbles in her throat. Despite the steadying hand on her back, she resists the temptation to sit down. Inhaling deeply she turns to the policeman.

'Just one more thing, please. So that I can be sure.'

The constable remains impassive, studying her face.

Leaning against the cold metal of the trolley, she edges the white sheet further down. He's dressed in a short-sleeved hospital gown. A stained label is attached to his wrist but it's the withered right arm that draws her attention. Her eyes follow its contours. His hand rests across his abdomen like a stiffened claw. If there'd been any thread of doubt, it is now dispelled.

She bends down, her kiss on the back of his hand a warm imprint on a cold waxwork.

'Yes,' she says, her breath curling away from her in the icy night air. 'This is him.'

2

RUTH

FEBRUARY 2005

Birdsong punctuates the dawn, but Ruth is already awake. Insomnia is an unwelcome and constant bedfellow on nights before emergency duty.

'Think of it as pre-match nerves,' Mark used to say. 'Once you get going everything will flow.' That was two years ago. It was never this bad when he was around. She should be used to it by now. Should take everything in her stride. But it's the unpredictability of the day ahead that unsettles her. Every time.

She stretches her leg across the bed, seeking out familiar warmth, but there's none to be found. A gap in the curtains deflects a thin gauze of light onto the carpet. Curious to know the time, she grapples with the switch of the bedside light. The room is cast in a sepia glow. Five thirty. She reaches for the TV remote control. Leaning back against the pillows, she presses the television screen into action.

A young man in a summer jacket is reporting on the test cricket from Melbourne. Ten thousand, four hundred and ninety seven miles away. At least twenty one hours' flight time, depending on stopovers. The familiar skyline pulls her into the screen. Memories of walks along the Yarra. The aroma of fresh coffee on the South Bank. The wheeze of the number 47 tram from Wattle Tree Road to Flinders Street Market.

A springing sensation on the bedclothes makes her jump.

'Ah, Tilly, there you are,' she says, her attention jerked back to the present. 'Did I scare you away last night, my darling?' She glances down at the rumpled throw, cast aside in the hot rage of her dreams. 'Mummy's sorry, sweetie. Another bad night.'

The warm pelt of her tabby cat presses against the arch of her knees. Ruth closes her eyes, wiping her sweaty palms on the bedsheet. She reaches out to stroke the ruff of fur and the cat responds with an ingratiating purr. Damned Monday mornings. Her skin needles with anxiety. Self-doubt can't take control. People are depending on her. She takes a deep breath.

In fourteen hours she can have a swim or a stress-busting gym session on her way home.

With sleep now a futile endeavour, she drags herself into the shower and follows this with a double shot espresso. She leaves the house under a battle grey sky, and by the time she swings her car in to the surgery car park she has a thumping headache.

★

'You're early this morning.' A female voice permeates the damp air. The petite figure of a dark-haired woman in uniform comes into view. She's balancing a couple of boxes on one hand, while she fiddles with the tailgate of her car.

'Priya,' says Ruth, studying the nurse's face. 'Haven't seen you in ages. Thought you'd moved to Byefield.'

The back door of Priya's car springs open, revealing an ordered assortment of equipment: cardboard kidney dishes, a urinal, a sharps bin, bundles of incontinence pads. Priya laughs. 'Ha, the Palliative Care Team is spread even more thinly now. Doubled my workload. I'm covering Tadwick as well.' She places the boxes in the boot and straightens her back. 'Anyway, how are you?'

'Fine, thanks. Gearing myself up for an emergency duty session. Too bad we never have time for a proper chat.'

'I know,' says Priya, clicking the tailgate shut. She hesitates then turns back. 'You should come to the hospice Ball next month. I'm getting a table together with some of the girls from the District team. You're welcome to join us.'

Ruth laughs. 'Thanks.' She can't remember the last time she had a proper night out. The thought of going unaccompanied panics her. 'I'll think about it.'

'Okay. Do. Better get going, I guess.' Priya gets into her car and waves as she reverses out of the car park. Ruth bends down to lift her battered Gladstone bag and a heavy stack of files, and wavers towards the staff entrance.

Ten minutes later, installed in front of her computer screen, a lukewarm mug of tea placed before her, she stares in frustration into the blinking blue void of a frozen computer.

Sod it. So much for her time-saving efficiency. The phone messages will be mounting already. She feels a tensing of the muscles round her neck, reboots the computer and, fifteen minutes later, the onslaught of patients begins.

As a trainee doctor her mentor often spoke to her about risk management. 'Think of the worst case scenario,' he would say. 'If you can't exclude it get another opinion or admit to hospital. If you're satisfied with the diagnosis, treat according to best practice guidelines, whilst managing patients' expectations.

But don't forget safety-netting advice in case things deteriorate.'

Treat. Manage expectations. Safety-net. Simple as that. But that didn't take into account the constant interruptions, always prefaced by the words,

'Sorry to bother you but this won't take long,'

'Could you just sign this prescription?'

'Could you just come and look at this wound?'

'Can you quickly check for me if this throat infection needs antibiotics?'

'Could you issue this repeat medicine?'

'I've had Mrs. Harris's daughter on the phone again, can you ring her back?'

Ruth massages her brow, then calls in her first patient.

Billy's mother enters the room first, tugging her six-year-old son behind her. He's wearing off-white trainers with socks that don't match. He's still in his pyjamas, which have a faint whiff of Marmite and a brown stain down one leg. His eyelashes are dusted with green snot, but most striking is the rasp of his wheeze and the shape of his chest, over-inflated like a taut balloon.

'I'm just going to put a little clip on your finger,' explains Ruth, fixing a pulse oximeter to his outstretched digit. 'It doesn't hurt. It just has some flashing numbers on it.' After a quick listen to his chest, she dispatches him to the practice nurse for a nebuliser to alleviate his asthma. Despite her drumming headache it makes her smile to hear him chatting to the nurse fifteen minutes later, while Ruth explains his steroid medication to his mother. Buoyed by his insouciance she continues with the unabated list of patients and, by mid-morning, manages to ignore the hunger pangs which gnaw away at her stomach.

A woman in her seventies is brought in by her husband. He's worried about her swollen leg. Ruth notices how he interlaces his fingers with his wife's and gives them a reassuring squeeze, causing the gnarled blue veins to contort on his crusty hand. Her milky eyes, distanced through dementia, gaze beyond him. She listens and smiles whilst Ruth explains that she's going to organise a scan and an anticoagulant injection, in case she has a blood clot in her calf.

Next a young guy in his twenties, whose girlfriend had phoned the surgery begging for him to be seen that morning. She'd described his weeks of sleepless nights, poor concentration and panic attacks which had now come to a head when he'd broken down in tears at work. Finally, he'd agreed to see someone about it.

He slumps in front of Ruth now, eyes locked on his shoes. He twists his fingers in his lap, the soft ticking of a clock filling the space between them. Ruth senses his angst. It could so easily be her sitting in the opposite chair. Avoiding eye contact. Wondering where to begin. She wants to reach out to him, to tell him she knows how he feels, but she bites her lip. It's one thing to show empathy, but quite another to lower your professional guard. Eventually he opens up about his father's recent death and his fear of having cancer like his dad. As his words start to flow, his relief is tangible. Sometimes a listening ear is the best recourse.

Sixteen patients seen, twenty seven cases of telephone advice given and still fifteen phone calls to return. With only seven minutes allocated per patient, it's inevitable that she's going to run late. Ten past twelve now and the mug of tea, stone cold and rimmed with scum, remains untouched on her desk. Pinpricks of pain behind both eyes cause her to squint at the computer. Her pace is slowing to a halt.

Her final phone call is to Mrs. Tremayne, a fifty-eight-year-old woman, complaining of upper abdominal pain since the early hours of the morning. Ruth glances at her records and at her watch. Two home visits still to do. No time for a break. It must be Mrs. Tremayne's gallstones playing up again. She picks up the phone, advises her to double up on her painkillers and take an anti-sickness pill.

'I'll ring you later this afternoon,' she promises, 'to see how you're getting on.'

By now the combination of central heating, body odour and stale urine from the samples building up by the sink is stifling her consulting room. Feeling slightly nauseous, Ruth lets reception know she is leaving and, embracing the fresh air, sets off on her rounds.

3

DOMINIC

Plink. Plink. Plink. Plink. Drips hits the base of the tangerine-ringed pan, marking time like a melancholic metronome. Dominic brushes toast crumbs off the kitchen table. A hairball clings to the chair leg, trapping motes of dust which glimmer in an unforgiving draught. A morsel of fish finger pokes out from under the cooker. Perhaps he should leave it there. Maybe, if he leaves it, she'll come back and order will be restored.

'Eurgh, a scratchy kiss,' complained Bella, wriggling out of his grasp, when Courtney arrived earlier to take her to school. No wonder. The stubble on his chin feels like coconut husk, rough with each reverse stroke.

There was a time when he would have welcomed no deadlines. A whole day all to himself? Luxury. No need to sprint for the 7.44 to Waterloo. No requirement to deliver on his portfolios. No more demands. Now? Only emptiness.

He decides to make a list. A list will help.

1. Answer mail.
2. Empty bin.
3. Ring bank.
4. Sort study.

He herds the pile of mail towards him. Quite a few letters, the envelopes handwritten. But who are the wordsmiths of the looped scrolls, the staccato fonts, the hasty scrawls? New best friends? Long lost friends? Of hers? Of his? Of theirs? He pushes them to one side.

There's a flyer advertising family-size pizzas, two for the price of one. He screws it up into a ball. The Indian takeaway menu might come in handy, though. He clips it to the fridge, along with the leaflet on cleaning services.

'Big Apple, the city that never sleeps' taunts the fridge magnet. God, that must have been ten years ago, at least. He'll hang on to it for now. It serves a purpose, holding all this shit together.

He tosses pellets of paper into the bin, then heaves the unwieldy sack out of its container. It splits, extruding its contents over the kitchen floor. A smell of smoked fish and melon juice assaults his nostrils. There is a temptation to sink to his knees and wallow in this rancid magma, but he snaps another black bag off the roll, transfers the rubbish, then lugs it up the steps from the basement and out to the front gate.

Steve the postman makes his way up the street, weaving in and out between green wheelie bins. He's wearing shorts, a defiant badge of office against the morning chill, and he whistles as he sorts envelopes.

A truck, bearing scaffolding planks, draws up, almost level to the house. A man jumps out and runs round the back of the vehicle. He shouts an instruction, then beckons the driver to reverse the beeping truck into a parking slot. The hollow clanking of poles blunts Dominic's senses. He wants to wrestle the steel tubes out of the builder's grasp, to kick the wheels of his vehicle, to berate him for going about his usual business. Instead he bites his lip and retreats.

A glass casserole dish sits by the front step. As Dominic lifts it, a scrap of paper, torn from a notebook, quivers in the breeze. He grasps it and reads, 'Thinking of you both, the Robinsons xx.' As he looks up at the townhouses opposite, he's not sure if he catches the twitch of a curtain from one of the flats.

The frost scissors his breath. He shivers, picks up the dish, and goes inside.

Filling the kettle, he flicks the switch, then picks up the phone. A sequence of jarring noises connect him to a crisp, enunciated message.

'Thank you for calling. In order to direct you to the most appropriate department please state clearly the reason for your call.'

'Probate.'

Pause.

'I'm sorry I didn't catch that. Please state clearly the reason for your call.'

'PROBATE.'

He switches to loudspeaker, drowns a tea bag, then pulps it in the peaty water.

A series of clicks then a low hum.

'Thank you for waiting. Your call is important to us. We are experiencing a high volume of calls at the moment. You are currently eighty-seven in the queue. Please note that you may find the answer to your query on our website www.cavendishbanking. com. Alternatively, please hold.' The irritating sound of Vivaldi's 'Four Seasons.'

'Oh, fuck off!' The phone glances off the granite worktop.

An irksome itch under his wedding ring forces him to scratch at his skin like a rodent. Soon, pink weals spiral across his hands and wrists.

'Enough!' he wails, flinging his arm out and knocking over his tea. An insidious stain creeps over the list, blurring the words. Enough for today. No more. One out of four is an achievement. The rest can wait until tomorrow.

He takes an antihistamine tablet, then stretches out on the sofa. Balancing a cushion behind his head, and working his shoulder blades against the linen ticking, he shifts around from side to side so that his neck curves round one armrest and his smooth, bare feet jut out over the other. Feathery contrails are just visible through the casement windows and he can feel the slanting sun on his face. Shifting shadows migrate across the wall and quilt the carpet, the heat under his skin abates and his eyelids feel heavy.

When he wakes his feet are freezing. The room is a haze of grey. Leaden walls, ashen cabinets, tungsten mirror. The cold breath of the winter afternoon whispers through the cracks in the windowsills, nagging him out of his inertia. Fuzzy outlines become three-dimensional. The hands on the wall clock tell him he has been lying there for at least three hours. Grimacing at the ache in his shoulders and neck, he sits up. Acid sours his palate. He needs a drink and a shower. The bottle of tonic in the fridge door is three-quarters empty so he drains it, the last drops fizzing over his chin, then he drags himself upstairs and runs the taps.

Jets of hot water pepper his chest. He lathers the hair on his arms into soapy meringues. The heat seeps into the atrophied musculature of his right forearm and soothes his tethered scars. His left hand moves in firm, circular movements across his chest, over his thighs, between his legs, coaxing energy back into his body. He emerges from the verbena-scented fug and cocoons himself in a downy bath towel. Gradually the mist clears.

There are three new messages on his voicemail.

'Hi, Dominic, it's Carla. We've been held up a bit. Back by four thirty-ish, thanks.'

'Hi, Mate, it's Mike. Table's booked. Rose and Crown tomorrow. Twelve thirty. That'll fit in with our appointment. Let me know if that's okay. Cheers.'

'Hello, Mr. Peterson? My name is Fleur Kinsman. I'm from the Gazette. We have met before, you may not remember. I hope you don't mind me ringing. It's Multiple Sclerosis Week next week and we're doing a piece to raise awareness. I wondered if you'd be interested in contributing your thoughts. Apologies if you're not up to it and quite understand. But do let me know on this number if you are. Thank you so much.'

He turns on the radio. Someone is talking about the origins of colloquial expressions. The familiar accent makes him smile. 'Don't get mardy with me,' Madeleine would say, deliberately reverting to her northern slang whenever he was feeling moody. They hardly ever had an argument.

The words from the radio flow over him, dispersing at the sound of the doorbell. Its tone is prolonged, intrusive. He wants to ignore it but the buzzing persists, so he descends the stairs two at a time and sees a blotch of blue behind the frosted glass of the front door.

'I hope I didn't wake you up,' says Priya, with a smile that fills her face. Her pristine uniform exudes order and calm. 'I'm off duty soon and I really wanted to catch you today.' She follows him down to the kitchen.

'I'd offer you coffee,' says Dominic, 'but I was just—'

'Thanks for the offer, but I haven't got time today.'

'And before you ask, -shit- that's how I'm feeling.'

'That's okay, Dominic. I wouldn't expect anything else.' Priya deposits her shoulder bag on the floor, bends down to extract something from the pocket, and sits down at the kitchen table. 'What about Bella? How's she doing?'

He shrugs. 'Just the usual coughs and colds. We're managing.'

'Well, look, I just wanted to give you this card from the hospice. It's our twenty-four-hour helpline. Just because we're not going to be popping in to see you anymore, it doesn't mean we've forgotten about you. You know there's plenty of support available to help you through the next stage of your journey.'

Dominic bites his lip. He wants to tell her he's not on a fucking train, admiring the scenery. 'I'm not sure what to say,' he utters, his voice trailing off. 'I guess, in a funny kind of way I'm going to miss you. When I say funny, I don't mean funny. I mean, I'm sorry that you had to come here in the first place. Oh, that sounds awful. It's not that I'm ungrateful or anything. I am really grateful for everything you've done.'

She smiles and leans over to place her hand on top of his. 'That's okay. My privilege. I hope, as time goes on, you'll find strength in knowing that, when the end came, Madeleine was at home, with you by her side.'

Her touch is gentle. It occurs to Dominic that, throughout the course of her frequent visits over the past month, he doesn't know the first thing about Priya, beyond the spotless uniform, the scrubbed nails, the calm efficiency. He wonders if she's ever reached out in the middle of the night to a cold hollow on the opposite side of the bed.

'Well I better be going now,' she says, gathering her notes into a blue plastic wallet. 'Oh, I nearly forgot,' she adds. There's a hesitation in her voice. It occurs to Dominic later that the split-second pause, no doubt, reflected her years of dealing with the bereaved, and was probably the real reason for her visit.

'I can take the rest of the equipment today. I know the OT came to collect the large items, so it's just the small bits and bobs we left behind. Shall I go up to Madeleine's room? I'm happy to do it on my own if it upsets you.'

'No need. The district nurse came last Wednesday.' Priya raises an eyebrow.

'She took three boxes away. The unused drugs we bagged up and I took them to the pharmacist for disposal.'

'The district nurse?'

'Yes. I think she said her name was Pauline.'

'Pauline?'

'Yeah, I hadn't met her before. She said she was one of the agency nurses.'

'Agency?' Priya's expression relaxes. 'Oh, of course, Rosie's on holiday at the moment. That would explain it. Okay, that's fine.' She stumbles as she stands up, the twisted strap of her holdall catching on the chair leg. Dominic stoops to untangle the bag, a light floral scent stopping him momentarily in his tracks.

'Take care, my friend,' she says, giving him a hug, and he feels a genuine warmth in the embrace. 'You know where we are.'

He watches her walking out to her car, then shrinks back against the curtain as he spots Carla Maitland barrelling along the street with two little girls in tow.

Carla breezes past him when he opens the front door, her arms filled with an assortment of kids' paraphernalia: jackets, wellies, plastic containers, all of which she dumps in a heap on the hall floor.

'Show your daddy what we've been making today, Isabella,' she says, looking at his daughter who has followed behind. Bella is clutching a pink plastic container to her chest. A section of her hair has come adrift from her ponytail, and hangs over her face in a matted mess. She sways from side to side and looks at the floor.

The sound of rustling prompts Carla to swing round. 'Chloe, come out of there, please,' she says to her daughter, who has tramped muddy footprints across the hallway, and now has her hand in a large glass vase of dried flowers. 'We've been making gingerbread men haven't we, Isabella,' she continues, 'and we made a special one for your daddy.'

Bella sucks her thumb.

'How have you been today, Dom?' Carla leans forward, and Dom recoils at the smell of chip fat.

'Oh, fine, you know.'

He leaves the front door open, despite the invasion of wintry air.

'Come on then, Chloe, we better get going.' She gathers her things and guides Chloe out of the door with her. 'You know, Bella's no trouble. I'll have her any time. Chloe's having her birthday party on

Saturday. Hopefully, Bella can come. See how you feel.'

'Thanks.'

She marches out, along the short path and onto the street, then turns. 'Just remember, call if you need anything!'

In the kitchen Dominic picks up the gingerbread biscuit, sniffs it and places it back in its pink plastic coffin.

He looks at his daughter, who has followed him downstairs. Her spindly legs, longer than those of most four-year-olds, are splayed as she sits on the kitchen floor. She's picking at a scab on her knee. Her blonde hair is dusted with flour. Spots of cinnamon-coloured dough smatter her corduroy dress like an infectious rash.

'Come here,' he says, pulling her onto his lap. He cradles her, smelling her warm gingery scent. 'I expect you're not hungry now, are you?'

Bella looks up. Dominic finds himself gazing into deep pools of blue.

'Daddy?'

'Yes, love?'

'Can I go to Chloe's party?'

'Let's wait and see, shall we?' He strokes the back of her hair, picking out little pieces of biscuit.

'Daddy?'

'What, darling?'

'Mummy would say yes.'

4

RUTH

It's too late to go to the gym after work, and besides, Ruth feels no inclination. She's exhausted. The house, silent in the darkness, has a rank quality, like water in a vase of wilted flowers. She pushes the remains of the microwaved curry dinner to one side. Topping up her glass of Sauvignon Blanc, she reaches over for her laptop. It blinks into action, raining scarlet shapes across the screen which morph into hearts. Ruth groans. 'Valentine's Day. Of course. How could I forget?' The comforting warmth of Tilly swishes against her legs.

'Well, Tilly,' she says, with an edge of sourness

that she knows borders on sarcasm, 'let's see what delights are on offer tonight.' She scrolls down a cliché-ridden list of potential matches on Likeminds.com. Row upon row of company directors appear, their 'glasses half-full', all brimming with excitement at the prospect of 'curling up in front of a roaring log fire'. None catch her attention. God, this is so tedious. She can't fathom it. Thirty-two-years-old, with a good job. Financially secure yet zero social life. She craves someone to share a meal, a laugh, a bed. Only two encounters since re-joining the dating site six months ago. What's wrong with her? The first resulted in an evening of stilted conversation, the second had potential, until she received a text the following day saying, 'Sorry the chemistry just wasn't there.' Loser. Should she cancel her subscription?

She takes a swig of wine. Perhaps she should bale out of computer dating and be more sociable. Maybe join Priya and her friends at the hospice Ball? She picks at a fingernail. Maybe not. At least web browsing offers her some degree of anonymity.

Ten months she'd been with Mark. The tangle of pain twists tighter in her stomach. It was so unfair. They'd been so good together. If it hadn't been for his careless text messages, how long would it have taken her to realise he was already married? Why hadn't he told her? 'Separated not married, Ruth. There is a difference,' was his riposte. No. Married. With children.

And even when confronted, he still wanted to carry on their relationship. But not with kids. For him that was a deal breaker. She buries her face in her hands, as anxiety knots her emotions. How could she be so naïve? Is she really such a bad judge of character?

She drains the glass. An after-taste sours her mouth. He was a liar. She wasn't to blame, for Christ's sake. He led a double life. She mustn't beat herself up about hitching with such a dud. Tugging at the cuticle of her forefinger, a bead of blood appears. There's still time. Take today, for example. Hadn't she seen someone who was a first-time mum at thirty-nine?

No, she must learn to trust again. Have faith in the opposite sex. To hell with it, she thinks, as she clicks on the computer mouse and sends winky faces to half a dozen potential lovers.

She watches the closing headlines of the midnight news from her bed. Uncurling her toes against the warmth of the electric blanket, she feels relaxed. Despite her misgivings, today had gone well: the grateful mother of the little boy with asthma, the anxious young guy who was able to look her in the eye on leaving, and give her a smile. Suddenly fear spirals in her stomach. Hell. She didn't call back Margaret Tremayne, the gallstone patient, as promised. She runs through her symptoms, recalling the first time she presented with biliary colic, subsequently confirmed on ultrasound. As far as she was aware, Margaret hadn't called back again.

Surely that was good news? She looks at the clock. Ten to one. She can't ring her now. She hesitates, remembering the time she called on a patient at three in the morning just to check they were all right. They'd been grateful, sure, but their bemusement had left her feeling embarrassed. No, it would have to wait until morning surgery. Cursing her forgetfulness she switches off the light. Another sleepless night beckons.

★

The surgery is deserted as Ruth crosses the glass-domed atrium at seven thirty the next morning.

'Ruth, can I have a quick word with you before you start surgery?' says a voice echoing through the empty waiting room.

Paul Franklin, senior partner, stands in the corridor, gesturing her towards the open door of his consulting room. His avuncular smile makes her feel like one of his patients.

She nods and crosses the threshold. It's not often she has the occasion to come into his room. Taking a seat next to the mahogany desk, curiosity gets the better of her as she looks at the framed photographs gracing its embossed leather top. Smiling happy families. Predictable, of course.

He sits opposite, his arms crossed, and leans forward.

'I've had Margaret Tremayne's son on the phone this morning.'

'Margaret Tremayne's son?'

'Yes. Margaret's in Intensive Care.'

Cold shudders through Ruth's taut frame, her heart constricts. She glances at Paul, seeking reassurance. His expression remains calm.

'Apparently she rang in with pain yesterday. You advised her to double her painkillers.'

There's a fluttering in Ruth's chest, like a moth trapped under a lampshade.

'Yes. It was a really busy emergency surgery. What's happened? Is she okay?'

Paul sits back in his chair and studies her. Heat suffuses her cheeks.

'She is now. She was defibrillated twice in the ambulance. Anterior myocardial infarction. Don't worry about it, Ruth. I'm just marking your card in case he rings back later. We'll put in on the agenda for the next practice meeting.'

The words form in her mouth, but are barely audible. 'She's going to be okay though, isn't she?' What a redundant question, she realises. It's probably too early to tell.

'I think so. From what the son was saying it sounds like she was stented shortly after admission. Anyway if I hear any more I'll let you know. Try not to stress about it. I just thought you ought to know in case you see any of the family.' He turns his attention to the pile of unsigned prescriptions on his desk. 'We can talk about it later, if you like.'

Ruth shrinks out of his room, just making it to her desk before she feels her knees give way. She takes a gulp of tea from the mug on her desk. It tastes rancid.

Anterior myocardial infarction? How the hell could she have missed that? Thank God Margaret had survived. She racks her brain for a few minutes, then checks her computer entries for the previous day, conscious of the loud pulsing in her ears. At least she'd done the safety-netting bit. But had she? She hadn't even examined her. And she'd forgotten to ring her back. A heart attack? What an unbelievably stupid mistake to make. She chews on a thumbnail. A near miss. But it could have been worse.

She'd have to think about it later. Soon her waiting room would be full of hopeful patients.

*

Val sounds very upbeat on the phone that evening. The sound of Mike shouting a greeting over the background television noise reminds her that the world hasn't stopped. She feels encouraged.

'Look, Ruth, it goes with the job. Don't be too

hard on yourself, it could happen to any of us. How many times since our house jobs have we said that?'

'But how could I have missed that? It's so obvious when I think of it now.'

'Ah yes, the bloody retrospectoscope, that most useful of surgical instruments,' says Val. 'There but for the grace of God go I. It's going to be okay, Ruth, honestly.'

'Look, I know you're trying to reassure me, Val. Believe me, I'm grateful, but the pressure is really getting to me. I wish I was on maternity leave like you.'

A throaty laugh down the line. 'It's not all plain sailing for me, I can tell you. And the time's flying past so quickly. I can't bear to think about going back to work at the moment. Just don't know how I'm going to cope. Anyway, listen, you and I need to go out on the lash again, before then. What do you say?'

'Yeah.' Even to Ruth's ears her own voice sounds feeble. 'Just let me know when it suits.'

'Well, while I remember,' says Val, her voice breathy with excitement. 'I've got a babysitter for the twenty fifth of March. Mike and I are going to the hospice Ball. He's very keen on getting a table together. I'm not sure about the company he's invited, but it would be a chance for you and I to catch up.'

The hospice Ball. Priya had mentioned it. Ruth sighs inwardly, rehearsing the usual excuses, *I'll be the only single one there, I've nothing to wear, if I drive I won't be able to have a drink,* but her friend is so warm, so non-judgemental that suddenly without warning, or justification, she feels the tears welling up and begins to weep.

Val, measuring the space between sympathy and resolve, waits for her response.

It comes, a full sixty seconds later.

'Okay, count me in.'

'That's my girl. I'll get you a ticket. It'll be just like old times.'

5

DOMINIC

The Rose and Crown, at the top of the High Street, is tucked away behind the Co-op car park.

It's three or four years since Dominic's last visit and, during that time, it's undergone an extensive refurbishment. The snooker table and juke box have gone, replaced instead by distressed oak floor boards, low lighting and exposed beams, in a contrived attempt to make the place look old. This lunchtime the place is packed, full of workers from the nearby trading estate and pensioners enjoying their two-for one deals. The lounge bar smacks of warm beer and fried food. For some, life goes on.

He spots Mike, sitting in the corner, bent over the

crossword, his pint hardly touched. Mike looks up, his face breaking into a broad grin.

'Good to see you, mate,' says Mike.

Dominic places his pint of lime and soda on the table and draws up a chair.

Mike screws up his nose. 'Sorry, I've just realised. You're off the booze. Bit of a crap idea of mine to meet in the pub.'

'Don't be daft. Although one of us will need to stay sober.' Dominic smiles, taking off his single-breasted wool coat and laying it over the back of the chair. He removes a set of keys from his back pocket and places them on the table with his phone. 'Anyway how are you?'

'Yeah, not bad. I should be asking you that. It was a lovely service by the way. Standing room only at the back of the church. Sorry I had to slip off without coming back to the house.' He gives a weak smile. 'Baby duties' he adds, as if an explanation is required. He takes a long swig of his beer, and wipes the froth from his mouth with the back of his hand. Dominic tries to weigh up if that's the real reason why he sloped off from the church without speaking to him. They sit in silence for a few seconds.

'I've made some progress with the portfolios,' says Mike, fidgeting with a beer mat. 'Once you get the Grant of Representation we can meet up again and go through the division of assets. I think you should put some in a trust fund for Isabella, and I've got some ideas on that.' He takes another mouthful of beer then raps his glass down at an angle on the table and foamy liquid swills over the side. 'But I guess you've probably already thought of that. Also, a tip. Lucky Pagoda, emerging Chinese telecoms company. One to watch. Apparently they're looking at buying into Formula One.'

Dominic picks up a plastic cocktail stirrer and swirls the ice cubes round and round in his glass. He thinks about all the friends they used to have. The sicker Madeleine got, the less they wanted to see of her. Towards the end both she and Dom preferred it that way. They didn't want to be reminded of what life might have been for them if fate, and illness, hadn't intervened. He's aware of the lull in conversation.

Mike's eyebrows arch. 'Guess it's a bit too early to even be thinking about that, isn't it?'

Dominic studies his friend's face. He can't decide if the lines which criss-cross his brow are ones of commiseration or impatience.

'Listen, mate,' says Mike, 'there's no hurry to do these things but I'm more than happy to suggest some investments for you when you're ready.' He pulls two menus across the table top. 'Let's order some food, shall we?'

Dominic isn't hungry. He picks the first thing he sees.

'Just like the old days, eh,' says Mike, later, reaching over to spoon tartare sauce over greasy batter, 'when we would nip out to Deacons on Cannon Street?'

It was true, they went back years the two of them. He remembers the first day they met. Amidst the frenetic activity of the Stock Exchange trading floor they mingled like counters on a Ludo board, Mike, in his red trader's jacket and Dominic, wearing the blue jacket of an Exchange official.

'I hear that's closed now,' says Mike, in between mouthfuls.

'Deacons?'

'Yeah. And the College Press. And the City Harvest.'

'Christ, now you're making me feel old.' Dominic tries to remember these eateries but he can't place them.

'Probably turned into noodle bars, or take-away coffee shops.' He swallows a mouthful. 'By the way, Val says she's sorry she couldn't collect Bella later.'

Dominic shrugs. 'Oh, no worries. I managed to sort it with a babysitter. Maybe another time, eh?' He clears his throat. 'How is she, by the way?' Dominic can picture the last time he saw Val, standing outside the library, heavily pregnant and with a two-year-old child in tow. He had slowed down to a stop at the traffic lights and strained to get a better look. Disappointment replaced curiosity as he took in the oversized sweatshirt and leggings, the wayward hair, the distracted look. He'd retracted his head behind the sun visor and she hadn't seen him, being diverted by the toddler who was pulling on her hand. The lights changed and he'd sped away.

Mike pauses his cutlery. A muscle twitches in his cheek. 'Good, thanks. Another five months maternity leave left, then back to the practice. She's hoping to stay on there and maybe get a partnership eventually. There's a few retirements coming up in the next three years or so.' There's a strained silence for a few seconds. Mike shifts in his seat, his eyes now focussed on his plate. 'She's really sorry she didn't make it to the funeral but Ollie was ill. Hope you understand.'

Dom purses his lips and nods. The strains of a familiar Kylie Minogue tune can be heard in the background. Mike may be intuitive with share indices but thank God he was short-sighted in other aspects of his life. Anyway that was all in the past. A mistake. He'd got away with it.

Mike yawns. 'Before I forget, I want you to have this.' He reaches into the inside pocket of his jacket and flicks a card down on the table, then hastily retracts it from the wet table top. 'It's a ticket for the hospice Ball. March the twenty fifth. We're getting a table together. Val told me not to give it to you. Said it was too soon, but I think it would do you the world of good to join us.'

Dominic nods. 'I'll think about it,' he says, scrutinising the ticket, then tucking it in his coat pocket. 'God knows, it's for a good cause.' He glances at his watch and signals to the surly-looking waitress. 'This one's on me,' he says as he taps his PIN into the machine, and they head off to the Probate Registry.

★

Dominic is glad to get home. He shuts the front door behind him, blocking the extraneous noise of traffic. From the wintry gloom of the hallway he trudges upstairs and pushes open the door of the study. Within minutes of switching on the electric heater the smell of singed dust challenges his apathy. He hadn't expected to feel so emotional in the Probate Registry. Cool, calm collected Dominic. Used to overseeing deals worth millions of dollars without as much as the acceleration of a heartbeat or tremor in his voice. Yet when he was invited to place his hand on the Bible and utter the oath it was as if he had a large pebble in his throat.

He picks up a yellowed business card with the words *Dominic Peterson, Senior Pit Official, LIFFE.* He runs it along the line of desiccated flies on the windowsill, flicking them onto the pencil shavings curling in the wastepaper bin.

This used to be Madeleine's room. She would sit

at her desk when she researched and wrote her articles, hoping for a publication in *The Lancet* or *Frontiers of Immunology*. In the early days this was an aspiration she achieved with remarkable regularity, but latterly she was content if her theories and reasoned arguments made it to the Letters page.

Sitting on the floor, and leaning back against the wall, he stretches out his legs on the carpet. A newspaper, its pages unfolded at the obituary notices, lies draped on top of a shoebox brimming with receipts.

'Cancer specialist's life cut short at 38.' *The Guardian*

'Cancer cure setback as top doc loses own battle.' *The Daily Mail*

And there was a wedding photo of them, taken in 1998.

Ironic that the papers wanted to focus on her cancer work when, all these years, she had been hoping for a cure for multiple sclerosis.

He wonders what his own obituary would say about him. That he narrowly escaped an IRA bomb at the London Stock Exchange in 1990? That his great-grandmother fled the Armenian genocide in 1916? 'You're a Petrossian, Dom,' his father used to say, ruffling Dominic's thick, dark hair. 'That's where you get your good looks from.' He remembers recoiling under his father's leathery touch at the time, but he was right. Women seemed to find him attractive.

And at least he could thank his great-grandmother for his strength of character and defiance of authority.

He stands up and adjusts the creases on his trousers. His outline, reflected in the glass of Madeleine's framed certificates, belies someone in his early forties. But, if she was here now, she would be teasing him to have his hair cut, to smarten up a bit.

'Why do you have to be so bloody maudlin all the time, Dom?' she would say.

But she couldn't say that now.

Madeleine was dead.

She died peacefully five weeks, four days and eleven hours earlier. But only the last twenty four hours were peaceful. Or were they? Maybe he's fooling himself. Instead, how many days had been punctuated with misery, as gradually she became more dependent on her walking stick, on her wheelchair, on her feeding tube, on him? His eyes prick with tears at the unfairness of it all.

The enormity of his task overwhelms him. Exhaustion consumes him like an encroaching mould. The heaviness in his chest, present since the day of the funeral, is still there. A leaden weight, which restricts his breathing. His migraines have been getting more frequent too. He knows what to do.

He goes down one flight of stairs to the bathroom. The little shot glass should be at the back of the cupboard. Swinging open the mirrored cabinet door, and taking care not to look at himself in the process, he rummages around impatiently. Pill packets and tablet bottles, which crowd together on the glass shelves like jumbled teeth, now tumble and spill out all over the floor.

Sinking down on to the cold lino he surveys the mess. Blister packs of yellow capsules, white and orange capsules, pale blue tablets, and bottles containing non-descript white discs clatter on the floor looking like a sweet shop's pick and mix selection.

He grabs a smattering of silver strips and sifts them through his hands. The cold enamel of the washbasin pedestal presses against his back, as he reads the labels: Gabapentin, dantrolene, oxybutynin, tizanidine, diazepam, baclofen. It's a cocktail that had kept a diseased body going for several years. How many of them would it take to end a healthy one? But what about Bella? Poor little sod. More importantly what about him? Nobody understands his own pain. The twitch starts in his chest and he fights against it but gradually his shoulders start to convulse and tears ensue.

He hears the clash of the front door and Courtney's shrill voice, 'Hi. We're back!' Dominic scrambles to his feet and goes out onto the landing.

'I'll be down in a minute,' he shouts, from the top of the stairs. Gathering the spilt medicines into a pedal-bin liner, he takes it into his bedroom and secretes it as far as possible out of view, under the bed.

'Daddy!' cries Bella, her arms outstretched, as he descends the stairs.

'Hi, Bella,' Dominic says, scooping her up in his arms. 'Have you had a good day?'

'Look what I made at school.'

'Oh that's lovely, darling,' says Dominic, trying to decipher the slashes of colour on the tracing paper.

'Look,' Bella says, her innocent face bursting with enthusiasm, 'there's the clouds, and there's the sun, and there's Mummy in her stripy top, in heaven.'

He exchanges glances with Courtney, who hunches her shoulders.

'Daddy?'

'Yeah?'

'You see this bit at the bottom? That's a very, really long ladder.'

'That's a lovely picture, darling.'

'Tell Daddy what else you did today, Bella,' says Courtney. 'You went on a nature trail didn't you?'

But Bella isn't listening. She lets go of the picture and it floats, like a feather, to the ground. 'Need a wee wee,' she says and she disappears in the direction of the downstairs loo.

Courtney picks up her bag, inclines her head towards Dominic and lowers her voice. 'Sue Ford asked me to pass on a message.'

'Sue who?'

'Sue Ford. Bella's teacher. She wants to know if

you can go and see her after school collection tomorrow. For a chat.'

'Whatever the hell for?' Dominic can picture the scene. Being summoned into a classroom, by someone nearly twenty years his junior, and being invited to sit on a small chair, whilst she offers advice on parenting. How bloody condescending. The nerve endings in his skin prickle with indignation.

'Well, obviously, she wouldn't say anything to me. But I'm sure she's only trying to help. She said the class were making Mothers' Day cards today, so one of the teaching assistants took Bella on a nature trail instead.'

Dominic takes a pan from one of the kitchen units and strikes it on top of the cooker.

'I'm coping perfectly well. Surely you can see that.'

'I can. Of course I can,' says Courtney, extracting her car keys from her shopper. 'Listen, Dom,' she says, sidling up to him and causing him to lean back against the worktop. 'Don't be offended if I do things sometimes, without being asked. Things aren't easy for you.' She moves forward and gives him a hug, the faint odour of stale tobacco almost disguised by the citrusy smell of her hair. She releases her grasp. The moment is gone. 'Well I better get going. I've still got the supermarket shop to do. Do you need anything?'

He stands back, inwardly congratulating himself at

his self-control, and dismisses her with a light tap on the arm. 'I'm fine. Honestly. Thanks. See you soon.'

After she's gone he slumps in quiet contemplation at the kitchen table. Bella's not been herself recently. But that's hardly a surprise. The poor appetite. The tummy aches. The sickness. It all adds up. She's lost her mother. What the fuck do they expect? He knows how she feels. Is this what's meant by shock?

He was told he had shock after his accident. 'Four pints of blood they gave you, son,' said his father, standing over his hospital bed when he recovered consciousness. 'Four pints. You were in shock.' Somehow this doesn't feel the same.

There's a movement at the corner of his vision. Bella has re-appeared and she's changed into her pyjamas.

'Ready for bed already, darling?'

Her lower lip quivers. She turns and heads back out of the room, quickening her pace, but Dominic is on his feet and catches the tail end of her pyjama top.

'I'm just going to cook some tea, darling. Are you hungry?'

She turns towards him. 'I. Sorry,' she sniffs.

Dominic strains to hear what she is saying.

'Accident, Daddy. Sorry.'

'That's okay, sweetie. You stay here and Daddy will sort it out.' And with teeth clenched and a slight flare of his nostrils he gets on with the next task in hand.

6

DOMINIC

MARCH 2005

Dominic changes his tie for the third time. First the black, then the kingfisher blue. He settles for the peacock print. It complements his Liberty silk waistcoat to perfection.

The theme tune from 'Eastenders' resonates from the living room. He wants to stand at the top of the stairs and shout, 'Turn the fucking noise down,' but resists the urge, as Bella is asleep. Her allergy medicine should settle her for the night. Too bad Courtney couldn't babysit this evening. She'd sounded so irritated when he said he was going to a dinner dance, but at least she'd been able to send this seventeen-year-old substitute instead.

'Don't mind me, Mr. Peterson,' said the plump adolescent, as she humped a large rucksack over the threshold. 'I've brought my course work with me, so I've plenty to do this evening.' Then she collapsed onto the sofa and reached for the remote control. Lazy cow. A nice little earner for her, as she has sod all to do this evening. Bella won't be a problem.

He takes a swig from his hip flask and flicks the switch on his radio. The haunting melody of Khachaturian's Violin Concerto in D minor cloaks him. Memories of ducking the fists that rained down on him, after his father's drink-fuelled evenings. His jaw muscles tighten. His father. That sophisticated, smooth talking, lying bastard. The father who would lavish gifts on him when he returned from his long haul destinations. The toy aeroplane was his favourite. He must have spent hours ramping the wheels along the carpet, before flying it round the room on top-secret missions. Until the day his father walked out, when he crashed it into the wall, crumpling its wings.

'One day you could be a pilot, Dom, just like me,' his father said.

Just like him? His eczema prickles the back of his neck as he recalls the arguments, the phone calls from other women that made his mother cry, the bits of broken glass embedded in the pulps of his fingers that still send shocks through his hands. Of course his father took no responsibility for that. The accident was Dominic's fault.

He pulls up the stiff collar of his dress shirt, until it digs under his chin. Then he passes the bow tie round the back of his neck. Even all those years since the fall, it still makes him wince to raise his right arm behind his head. With slow, careful movements he folds the long side of the tie over the short, then passes the material up through the back and centre, tightening the noose against his Adam's apple.

'You poor devil,' he mouths to his reflection in the wardrobe mirror. He makes a wide smile to check his teeth for stray food particles. Nearly ready. Opening the top drawer of a walnut chest he takes out the bottle of pills nestling on the stack of carefully folded silk squares. He swallows a pink tablet, selects a matching Liberty print handkerchief for his breast pocket, then closes the drawer.

The door-bell rings. He adjusts his gold cufflinks, pats his pockets for his keys and phone, and sweeps down the stairs. Offering a swift 'Bye, see you later,' to the back of the babysitter's head, he climbs into the waiting taxi and disappears into the night.

7

RUTH

The banqueting room of the Town Hall is dimly lit. Ruth peers through the throng of people lining the bar. She tries to avoid catching the hem of her gown on her heels, aware that her teetering gait denotes a woman who is not comfortable in stilettos. She's stopped in her tracks by someone in a multi-coloured wig, who's selling raffle tickets. Ruth scrabbles in her crimson clutch bag for a ten pound note. Warmth bathes her cheeks as she looks around, anxious to spot a familiar face. She exchanges nods with several people who look vaguely familiar, members of the community nursing team perhaps. Priya is nowhere in sight. How long is she going to have to stand here looking awkward?

Mike is visible, at the far end of the bar, trying to grasp two glass tumblers and mixer bottles. His profile, acquired through breaking his nose in a rugby injury many years ago, is instantly recognisable. His face transforms into a kindly symmetry as Ruth approaches.

'Ruth, so glad you could come,' he says, clinking the glasses back down on the bar and embracing her in a warm hug. 'You look stunning. Val won't be long. What can I get you to drink?' He tries to attract the attention of the barman. 'Now,' he says, turning back to Ruth, once he has placed another order. 'I need to tell you about some of the company at our table this evening. I want you to meet–'

Another voice targets her from the periphery and she swirls round to encounter a beacon of shimmering sequins. It takes her a few seconds to process the image, having not seen Val looking so glamorous since her wedding.

'Wow, Val,' counters Ruth. 'Look at you. You look fabulous!'

'You too,' gushes the woman who looks flushed with excitement. 'First proper night out in two years. Let's get the party started!' The gist of Mike's conversation is lost as the two women swap stories on dietary regimes, shoe purchases and the latest news on fellow alumnae.

More guests drift in for the evening's entertainment, and the decibel level starts to climb. A smell of vanilla and stale sweat emerges as the temperature rises.

A gong sounds, the toastmaster instructs everyone to take their seats, and they make their way to their table, past the high-backed chairs decked out in purple and white bows. As they shuffle en masse towards the seating area Val turns to Ruth.

'I've been meaning to ask you,' she says, lowering her voice and leaning in a little closer. 'How's it going on the, er, the dating front? Did you post that profile in the end?' Her mouth curls in a mischievous smile.

'What d'you think? Ha, back on Likeminds.com if you must know. But swear you won't say anything to Mike. Promise? I'd die of embarrassment.'

'I won't. I need to warn you though. Mike has invited one of his friends to join us tonight. I wouldn't be surprised if he was trying to match you up.'

'And? So what, Dr. Armitage? Are you trying to warn me off?'

'No. You're a big girl now. You don't need me to tell you what to do.' Val pauses and raises her eyebrows. 'Just be careful. That's all I'm saying.' She glances around, 'Anyway he may not turn up.' Her dress glints like a sunbeam dancing on a magnifying glass as she turns to find her seat. 'And you and I still need to have a girls' night out soon. I haven't forgotten. It's been too long.'

They find their table. Adorned with a centrepiece

of white roses and purple orchids it seats ten. As she looks for her place name, Ruth catches Mike's whispered aside to Val.

'Where the hell is Dom? Told you this would happen. I hope he hasn't changed his mind.'

She finds her seat along the middle of the table, and polite introductions are made all round. All couples, as Ruth suspected, but the seat next to her is conspicuously empty. This could be an early night. She is about to pull out her chair when a soft voice catches her,

'Here, let me get that for you.'

'Dom, where the devil have you been?' asks Mike. 'We thought you weren't coming.'

The tall man, with thick dark hair and high cheekbones, slides out Ruth's chair. Seemingly impervious to his friend's rebuke he holds her gaze, his eyes crinkling as his smile widens. She notes the sartorial elegance, the corner of a Liberty handkerchief poking out of his top pocket, the thick gold band on his ring finger. Much later she would recall that very moment, how she held her breath for several seconds before giving a soft sigh.

'Damn taxi took the long way round and then we got held up by the roadworks on the by-pass.'

Heads nod, tongues click and the consensus round the table is that the traffic in town at the moment is appalling. Dominic Peterson is introduced to everyone and he's forgiven for being late. They sit down to dinner and the repartee round the table is relaxed.

'So how long have you known Mike?' asks Ruth, addressing the stranger to her right, as they pick their way through the first course of smoked salmon and salad leaves.

Dominic fixes her with a steady look. There is something distanced about his dark brown eyes, as well as an impeccable propriety. The stray hairs which brush his collar and the speck of blood on his chin, where he must have nicked his skin shaving, suggest a vulnerability. She glances across the table but Val is engrossed in conversation with another guest.

'Mike and I go back a long way,' he replies. 'We met on the trading floor.'

'The trading floor?' Ruth says, feeling clueless.

'The London International Financial Futures Exchange,' interjects Mike, leaning in to Ruth's left side, 'or LIFFE, as we used to know it.' Mike and Dominic both laugh, as if it's a well-rehearsed routine, but the joke is lost on Ruth.

'The Stock Exchange,' says Dominic, quietly. 'I worked as an Exchange official and Mike was a trader.'

Ruth nods, trying to digest this information.

'We got to know each other,' Dominic continues, 'from our jostling on the trading floor. Then in

1998, when the market moved to electronic trading we both moved across to the same bank.'

A waiter hovers with red and white wine. Ruth notices that Dominic waves him on and refills his glass of water. She pushes lettuce leaves round her plate. Why hasn't she met this guy before, if he's such good mates with Mike?

'And so you still work together?' she asks, but Dominic has turned his head and the woman on his right throws her head back in laughter.

Feeling piqued Ruth engages in polite conversation with another couple. David, the man opposite, with close-cropped hair and eyes like flint, is a retired detective; his wife Angela, rake thin, with a tinkly laugh, is a criminal lawyer. It transpires that Angela is also a trustee for the hospice, which explains their attendance. 'And we like to do our bit for charity,' David confides, as he leans far enough forward for Ruth to notice a couple of gold fillings, flashing like doubloons.

Dominic seems to be having an entertaining evening, engaging the guests opposite. She is conscious of him pausing to look at her mid-conversations with others. It irks her that he has clocked her looking at him, so whenever their eyes meet she darts her gaze elsewhere. Instead, she looks at Val, who glances back and smiles.

'Who is this guy?' Ruth mouths to her friend.

Val shrugs, her eyes widen and she continues talking to the guest sitting opposite her. The evening drones on and, above the clatter of cutlery, Ruth is brought up to date with the antics of Mike's wonderful children.

★

The jazz quartet strikes up a blues number on stage, as Ruth weaves her way back to the table from the Ladies' cloakroom. She must find Val, to say good bye. She searches in her bag for the taxi number as a hand grasps her arm.

'So you decided to come after all,' says Priya, causing Ruth to start. She looks at her nursing colleague, barely recognisable in her butterscotch halter-neck dress and stylish up-do, then blushes. She'd forgotten she might meet Priya here. 'You must come and join our table.'

'Priya, you must forgive me,' says Ruth, leaning over to peck her on the cheek, 'actually I was just-'

'She was going to accompany me.' The tall man with the Liberty print waistcoat intercepts them. Priya looks startled for a second, as if she recognises Dominic. She smiles at Ruth, her hesitation suggesting she was about to say something, but now thinks better of it.

'Would you excuse us?' says Dominic, steering Ruth round in the direction of the door. 'I was just going for a breather,' he says in a gentle voice. 'I think there's a quieter bar near the foyer. Would you join me for a drink?'

For reasons she can't fathom, Ruth nods in agreement and falls in step with this intriguing stranger. The strains of 'The Girl from Ipanema' dissipate in diminishing spirals as they walk away from the ballroom, towards the emerging glare of the outer bar. Within the confines of the narrow saloon, glass chinks on chrome, and laughter competes with voluble gossip. They perch on barstools, their knees touching. Ruth sits still, anxious not to draw attention to their jarring proximity, although she feels sure that the imprint of her companion's bony edges will be left on her knee caps. The scalloped white lights behind the bar afford Ruth a better look at his face. The peeling skin on his furrowed brow, the broken capillaries on his cheeks and the slight greying of his temples delineate a man much older than she first thought. Strikingly handsome, but careworn. He nods his head and the barman immediately springs to attention.

She settles for a vodka martini, restraining herself from adding 'shaken not stirred,' although it may lighten the mood. He adds a lime and soda to the order. She wonders if he disapproves of her choice.

'So, I hear you're a doctor?' he says, and there is a faint curl of his lip.

'Yes,' replies Ruth. 'Val and I were at Med school together. We've been friends for years and I got in contact with her again when I came back from Aus-'

'Excuse me,' he says, leaning over her to reach for a paper napkin. This time she catches a faint hint of musk. Their knees are wedged so tightly together now that she feels a static electricity from her gown when she shuffles her chair to make more room. 'Sorry,' he says, as he places the napkin under his glass, 'you were saying?'

'Just that I've known Val for a long time. I had a short spell working in Australia, and when I came back nine months ago, and got a job in a local practice, we picked up our friendship again. I guess that's what you do with good friends, isn't it? It was her husband Mike's idea for me to come here tonight.' The vodka martini slides down her throat.

Dominic is stirring the ice cubes round and round in his glass. Left handed. His wedding ring catching the light.

'Anything else, sir?' The barman hovers but is dismissed.

Her cocktail glass is nearly empty.

'So what about you?' she says, eyeing the gold band with every stir of his soda.

She wonders why Mike has asked him along tonight. Maybe his wife is away at a conference. She can picture her, probably a bit older than Ruth, thin, chic, attractive, probably a career woman. She's not going to make that mistake again. 'Family at home tonight?'

Dominic stops mixing his drink and looks at her.

'Yes, the babysitter's in charge this evening.'

Another pause. Strobe lighting reflects in the mirrors behind the bar. The dull thump of a beatbox starts up from next door. Its repetitive throb echoes in Ruth's head.

'Sounds quite lively in there, doesn't it?' She thinks about the early start she's going to have in the morning. It's her turn to do Saturday morning surgery.

Dominic sits back in his chair. For a few seconds he appears to be staring into middle distance. He breaks from his meditation and looks at her.

'Not very conducive to having a conversation, though,' he adds. 'I don't suppose you'd care to have a dance?'

'Listen, Dominic, thanks for the offer,' she says, scraping her chair back. 'It's been really nice meeting you, but I'm going to have to get going. I'm working in the morning.'

For a moment he looks deflated, then retains his composure. 'Of course,' he replies. 'Your duty. I understand. My wife was a doctor.'

It's a reply that halts her momentarily, and she sits back down.

'Your wife?'

'Yes, my wife. Madeleine. She died in January.'

Suddenly it all makes sense. The aloofness. The distracted behaviour. In the space of a heartbeat his pain comes scudding towards her. She rests her hand on top of his, knocking a cocktail stirrer to the floor. Dominic's face crumples and a wave of sympathy washes over her.

'The hospice was very good to us in her final days.'

'I'm so sorry,' she says, 'I hadn't realised.'

In the silence that follows, Ruth's hand lingers. She's worried that if she lifts it too soon it may expose hurt, like a plaster being peeled off a wound. She raises her head slowly until her eyes meet his. It would be okay to let go now, but she doesn't want to.

'You mentioned you had a babysitter?'

'I have a daughter, Isabella. She's four.'

Ruth squeezes his hand.

'My wife was ill for a long time. Multiple sclerosis. She was diagnosed in 1999, two years before Isabella was born. Her health was in gradual decline for the last two years.' He clears his throat. 'But then I guess you'd understand that, as a doctor.' Suddenly he retracts his hand. 'I need to get going too,' says Dominic. 'Mustn't forget the babysitter. And anyway I'm not a great fan of strobe lighting. Where do you live? Maybe we can share a taxi?' He takes his phone out of his pocket and scrolls down the screen.

'Here,' says Ruth, extracting a card from her bag. 'I have a taxi number. I live in Tadwick.'

'Ah. And I live in Byefield. Other side of the by-pass. Opposite direction.' He takes her arm and they walk towards the cloakrooms. Away from the noise of the band, the corridor is quiet and half in shadow. 'Well at least let me call you a cab.' He pauses. 'And allow me one more thing.'

Ruth smiles. 'Which is?'

He looks at her intently. She wonders if he's trying to decipher her moral compass.

'Would you write your number down for me? I'd like to call you.'

'Of course.'

Thinking about this later he must have taken her look of bruised expectancy as his cue. His hands move to either side of her face now, lifting it up to meet his lips. His mouth feels soft, and there's an urgency in his embrace, as his tongue grazes her teeth. Gently he guides her further into the shadows, until her back is pressed against the wall. He touches her chin with his fingertip, then slowly traces the line of her throat, pausing at the notch at the top of her breastbone. A moment so unexpected that she catches her breath. She wants to hold it in freeze-frame. They stand in silence for a few minutes, his peppermint breath warm on her neck. She's unwilling to break away. Then he moves his hands to the top of her arms and steps back to look at her. The subdued lighting in the hallway casts a luminous sheen across one side of his face, and he smiles. They disengage and walk towards the cloakroom to collect their coats. Ruth turns her face away. She has surprised herself at her brazenness and is unable to contain her smile.

8
RUTH

'In nomine patris et filii…'

Sister Immaculata walks towards her, across the tennis court. Her wimple flaps, like an angry crow, revealing the high shuttered windows of the convent over her left shoulder. She has eyes like currants, set in puffy pockets of dough, and she fixes them on Ruth.

'You're going to need to speak louder, my child. You'll need to be heard at the back of the church. Now, when I raise my hands, try again.' She turns back towards the net, and her habit billows around her feet. Ruth sways on the baseline and waits patiently for the signal. The cold seeps through her thin plimsolls, tormenting the chilblains on her toes. Her cheeks are chapped, her throat dry. She wants to reach under her knicker elastic and the scratch of hessian, for a hanky to wipe her nose, but Sister Immaculata is ready, her arms raised in supplication.

'My God, I detest all the sins of my life,' begins Ruth, as the wind teases her voice into diminishing spirals. 'I am truly sorry that I have sinned, because thou art infinitely good, and sin displeases Thee, have mercy......'

The hands are down again. Ruth senses the nun's irritation. Sister Immaculata rustles towards her once more. Her eyes are flashing.

'Contrition, my child, contrition. It's your Holy Communion! The Good Lord needs to hear that you're sorry. So do the people at the back of the church! This is your very last chance to practise. Say it again for the last time.'

Ruth takes a deep breath and studies the nun's face. The thinning eyebrows and the complexion flecked with sun spots belong to another person. A quizzical furrow divides her brow. A corn-coloured frizz circles her face, her lips are dusky blue. Ruth looks for absolution in Margaret Tremayne's face.

'Forgive me, Margaret, for I have sinned!'

★

She sits up in bed. Her shirt is damp with sweat. Her heartbeat pulses in her ears. Nausea swamps her. Why the convent? Why Sister Immaculata? She adjusts to the shadows taking shape around the room, the oak chest by the window, the dressing table cluttered with bottles, the illuminated alarm clock on the bedside table. Six thirty. Saturday. Another hour's respite before getting up for work.

She'd wanted to visit Margaret as soon as she came home, to draw up a chair next to the chintz sofa, to take her hand and say, 'I'm sorry,' but Paul Franklin had advised against it.

'We need to follow proper procedure,' he said, 'now that an official complaint has come through. Need to run your response letter through the medical defence organisation first. There'll be time to apologise after.'

She curses Alan Tremayne for going straight to the Practice Manager the day after his mother's hospital admission. Of course proper procedure had to be followed but taking the official route took time.

She closes her eyes. Poor Margaret lying in her Coronary Care bed, surrounded by bleeping machines and flashing monitors. Margaret, being wheeled into the ED room, as a clogged artery was rodded, under the harsh arc lights. Margaret, levitating between light and darkness. If only she'd had the chance to explain herself, Margaret would have forgiven her.

'It could have happened to anyone.' Isn't that what Val had said to her? 'There's so much pressure to give telephone advice now,' she said, 'when there just isn't enough time to see everybody.'

Time. Precious time. But complaints procedures take even more time, thinks Ruth as she sinks her feet into the Fair Isle boots by the side of the bed, and shuffles over to the window, tripping over a crimson evening dress which lies discarded on the floor. She lifts the curtain a fraction. A pale pink disc rises behind the office blocks in the distance, casting a large bruise across the sky. Across the neighbourhood, lights blink and curtains are drawn back. Ruth imagines scenarios all too familiar to her from her house calls: the octogenarian sitting in urine–soaked pyjamas, waiting for the sound of a key scraping in a frosted lock, the exhausted parent who has nursed a febrile child all night, the pregnant mother unable to settle after another false alarm.

Why did she agree to go in early today? Surely the lab results could wait till Monday? She picks up her dress and, clutching it like a comforter, climbs back into bed. Burying her face in the soft folds of material, she can smell him. And if she closes her eyes she can picture him too. His good looks, his impeccable manners. Even his aloofness had been appealing to a degree, but there was something else. Beneath that veneer of arrogance lay a vulnerability. She recognised it as soon as she asked him about his family. When he looked away she could see the hurt in his eyes.

With a dart of panic she realises he has her number but she doesn't have his. What if she never hears from Dominic again? Casting aside her duvet she eases herself out of bed and hears the hot water pipes clank into action.

★

'Just a couple of messages before you start,' says Ginny, as Ruth arrives at the surgery. The receptionist has left her tea- 'milk, no sugar'- on her desk, with two chocolate biscuits, no doubt by way of sweetener for the requests which follow. 'The District Nurse needs a prescription for liquid morphine for one of her home visits. Oh, and can you ring Mr Hobbs with his INR result? It came through after the surgery closed yesterday and he wants to know how much warfarin to take. They're on the computer. Thanks.'

Ruth flicks biscuit crumbs off her skirt, then a pinging noise alerts her to her phone. She extracts it from her pocket and studies the text message.

Morning. How's the head? Are you free for coffee later? Dom. x

Dominic? Her pulse quickens. She hadn't expected to hear from him so quickly. A brisk knock makes her jump and, before she has a chance to respond, the district nurse pokes her head round the door frame.

'Just thought I'd catch you before you start surgery,' she says. 'I'm on my way to see Mrs. Phillips and I need that prescription for morphine.'

'Yes. Of course. Just doing it now,' Ruth replies, feeling piqued. 'Can you give me two minutes? I'll come down to reception with it.'

The nurse retreats and Ruth glances at her phone. Hastily she taps on it.

Sounds good. Could be in Byefield 2ish. Tell me where and I'll be there. R.

She hesitates, re-reads her message several times, then adds a kiss before pressing 'send.'

Clicking on the record of the palliative care patient she sees the District Nurse's request. She scrolls down the drug formulary on the computer screen until she gets to morphine solution. Her phone goes again. God, he's keen. She looks down and sees that the message is from Val.

Where did you get to last night? Couldn't find you to say goodbye. Hope you've got a good excuse. Ring me later. xx

Quickly Ruth sends back a 'thumbs up' emoji. She switches off her phone. No more interruptions.

Turning back to the computer screen she prints off a prescription, signs it and runs down to reception to hand it over to the nurse. Tick. A quick phone call to Mr Hobbs next who is advised on his dose of warfarin. Great. Then just time to dictate three referrals from yesterday before the appointments start. Sorted.

Her first patient is a four-year-old boy. His anxious mother rolls up his sleeve to reveal a well-demarcated rash. He sits meekly, engulfed by the consulting room chair, his large brown eyes looking at Ruth from under a thick fringe.

'Mrs. Choudhury,' says Ruth, 'would you mind if one of our junior doctors has a look at Sanjay's rash? It's certainly nothing to worry about but it's an interesting presentation.' She calls in the trainee from the adjoining room.

The young doctor takes Sanjay's arm and inspects the dusky pink targets enveloping the little boy's hands and arms. He turns to Ruth with a shake of his head.

'Erythema multiforme,' pronounces Ruth, stroking the little boy's arm, 'It's a common skin disease and it's not serious, but these little target lesions are a classic presentation. Most likely caused by a virus and should settle in time.' The mother's shoulders drop, as she nods her head and smiles at Ruth. The trainee looks suitably impressed.

Ruth is packing her equipment into her battered leather Gladstone bag when Ginny puts through a call from the pharmacist.

'Dr. Cooper? Abbey Pharmacy here. We received your prescription for liquid morphine this morning and just wanted to check the dose with you. You've requested the concentrated solution. That's twenty milligrams per ml. It's usually two milligrams per ml.'

There is silence, measured only by the scudding of Ruth's heartbeat. She hooks the phone under her chin as she scrolls down the formulary list. Usually the commonest items flash up first on the computer screen, but then Ruth realises the list has been changed to alphabetical order. Hadn't there been an e mail about it recently? Morphine concentrated oral solution, hardly ever prescribed, comes before morphine oral solution. Fuck. Alphabetical. Simple as that. Fucking alphabetical, just as 'jail' comes before 'jury.'

'Yes, you're right. Thanks for calling me,' she says, her voice splintering. 'It's the two milligrams per ml solution that's required. I'll drop the new script round to you after surgery. Around one, if that's okay? Yes? Well, thanks again, very grateful to you.'

She slumps over the desk, her head in her hands. Jesus. Ten times the required concentration? My God, how could she do that? Her skin constricts with goose bumps. Another stupid mistake. What's wrong with her? And suddenly Sister Immaculata's dream makes sense. Guilt. Threaded through every fibre of her body since her convent days. Guilt for taking time out of medical school as a student. Guilt that Margaret Tremayne had a heart attack. And now guilt that she's allowed herself to be seduced by a man who's recently bereaved.

Contrition, my child, contrition, she thinks to herself, as she hurries out of the surgery.

9
RUTH

Steam rises from the unfurled umbrellas by the door, fogging the windows of the Cardamom Café. It's packed and a mixed aroma of fried bacon and damp newsprint lingers. Ruth feels a trickle of sweat run down her back, as she spots Dominic signalling to her from a corner table. Taking a deep breath she squeezes through the packed tables. He rises and offers a stilted peck on each cheek.

'Dominic, I'm so sorry I'm late,' she says, brushing matted clumps of hair away from her face. 'I got held up at work.'

'No probs. Hope you managed to save a few lives,' he says, his mouth creasing into a disarming smile.

'Ha, yes,' she says, peeling off her coat, twisting sideways to face the little girl who is sitting at the table.

'Ruth,' says Dominic, 'I want you to meet Bella. Bella say hello.'

Bella has scattered coloured crayons over the table top and is engrossed in her drawing.

'Hiya,' says Ruth. She's caught off guard. She hadn't expected to meet Bella so soon. 'That looks interesting.'

The child looks up through a curtain of blonde hair and stares at her. Her azure eyes are like saucers and remind Ruth of her cat. 'It's a hole,' she says. 'A big, blue hole.'

'I've ordered some food as Bella was getting fidgety,' says Dominic, sliding the pile of coats across the upholstery. 'I hope you don't mind.'

'Of course not,' says Ruth. Mind? It's their first date and he's brought along his four-year-old daughter? But then what was he supposed to do? *Contrition*, nags an inner voice. 'Gosh, it's warm in here' she says, feeling her cheeks colour.

A waitress appears with a dish of ice cream, prompting Bella to drop one of her crayons. 'Banana split?' says the young woman, lowering the confection onto the table and stepping back to look at Dominic with a degree of expectation. 'Can I get you anything else, sir?' Dominic turns to Ruth.

'Just a cappuccino for me, please,' says Ruth.

'Me too,' says Dominic, 'and maybe a jug of water.'

'Daddy, look at that lady's dragon,' pipes up Bella, as the tattooed waitress disappears. 'I'm going to draw a dragon,' she says, picking up a red crayon.

'Later, Bella,' Dominic says, collecting Bella's crayons and placing them to one side. 'So how was this morning?' he says, turning to Ruth. 'Busy, I expect?' He fixes a stray clip in Bella's hair and strokes the top of her head. Something stirs in Ruth's chest.

'Oh, just the usual,' she replies 'Nothing that couldn't be sorted.' She smooths back her hair. She must block out the anxiety of her near-miss this morning. Plenty of time to ruminate over that when she gets home. 'So, I hope the Ball was a success.' They exchange glances and she thinks about their embrace by the cloakroom.

'Yes, let's hope they raised lots of money.'

Dominic leans over and carefully picks bits of banana off Bella's sleeve, transferring them to a napkin, which he screws up into a tight ball. Ruth can't help observing his right hand. Why didn't she notice it last night? A mild deformity, the proximal finger joints hyperextended, the distal ones flexed. She remembers seeing a similar case as a student. Rheumatoid arthritis maybe? She can't be sure but reminds herself to cast off her doctor's hat. She's off duty now. She looks away.

The waitress returns, balancing a tray of coffee

cups and a water jug, and looks at the mess Bella is making. She removes some of the scrunched up paper from the table. 'I'll bring you some more napkins,' she says with a smile.

They sit in silence, watching Bella, until both speak simultaneously. They laugh.

'Go ahead, please,' says Ruth.

'Oh, well, actually, I was going to say is everything okay?' offers Dominic. 'You seem a little pre-occupied.'

His intuition catches her unexpectedly. 'I'm fine. It's just that ... I had a busy morning and I...and I haven't been sleeping well. I've just got a lot on my mind at the-'

'Daddy.' Ruth feels a sharp kick on her knee as Bella wriggles along the seat.

'Not now, Bella, please. Ruth is talking.'

Ruth watches Bella making ice cream swirls with her spoon and silently chides herself for being so selfish. 'Oh gosh, I'm sorry. That's very self-indulgent of me to start talking about my problems. Enough about me. What about you?'

Dominic shifts in his seat. 'Oh, we're muddling along.' He leans over to tuck a napkin into the collar of Bella's dress, carefully lifting her hair out of the way. An endearing gesture. 'Nothing much to say. I'm more interested in hearing about you. You were saying last night that you worked in Australia?' he says, as he twists in his seat to face her.

71

'Yes. I wanted to spread my wings.' She laughs. 'After I graduated from Leeds I did a year in Paediatrics, then a year in Obs and Gynae so I could get an Australian licence. Then off I went. I was in Melbourne for two years.' She pauses and takes a sip of water.

'What made you come back?'

'Good question,' says Ruth. She looks away. There is a man two tables away whose profile bears a close resemblance to Mark's. Blonde hair, broad physique. He's sitting with three kids, and a slim attractive woman, who is probably their mother. He turns to say something to one of the kids, bringing his narrow chin and small eyes into view. Of course it's not him. Mark is in Australia. Ruth looks back at Dominic. 'I guess I'd got tired of travelling. I missed my parents. And my friends.'

'Fair enough,' says Dom, 'a case of the grass isn't always greener.'

She smiles. 'You could say that.'

Bella pushes her plate away.

'Have a bit more, Bella,' says her dad, putting his cup down.

'No! Don't want to!'

'Come on, one more mouthful.' He tries to coax her, but Bella is having none of it. He lifts the toy kangaroo, lying on the seat next to her. 'Watch out, Roo, will finish it if you don't.' Her mouth is clamped shut, her face set in grim determination. 'One more, then we can go to the park and feed the ducks.' He reaches over for the little girl's spoon just as Ruth lifts the water jug to re-fill her glass. The glass is knocked sideways.

'Oh. I'm so sorry,' says Dominic, grasping a paper napkin and dabbing Ruth's soaked thigh. His hand lingers and their eyes meet. Beneath the table she rests her hand on his for a few seconds.

'It's okay it was my fault.'

'Daddy, I need a wee.' Bella's voice pricks at Ruth's conscience like a tack stuck to the sole of her shoe.

Dominic folds his lips. 'Would you excuse us please, Ruth,' he says, sliding Bella out of her seat.

Ruth stirs her coffee as father and daughter criss-cross the room. Blonde curls bounce on Bella's collar as Bella pulls on her father's arm. Poor Dominic. And poor Bella, having to grow up without her mother. She waits until they are out of sight then extracts her phone from her pocket and scrolls down to Val's number.

Call u later. So much to catch up on.

★

By the time they leave the café it's stopped raining, but a chill breeze feathers the water of the boating lake. The boathouse is padlocked, the ice cream kiosk is boarded, its metal sign creaking in the wind. A few people, muffled in thick scarves, walk the perimeter of the lake.

Ruth wishes she'd had time to go home and change instead of coming here straight from work. Her pencil skirt feels tight, her court shoes uncomfortable, as the wind whips round her legs, forcing her to march briskly. Dominic is smiling at her.

'I didn't exactly come dressed for the occasion, I know,' she says, as if reading his thoughts. 'I'd give anything to swap these for my trainers right now.' She lifts her foot and points her shoe in the air.

'Maybe next time,' he replies, raising a quizzical eyebrow. He rummages in his rucksack for a pair of knitted gloves and a woolly hat. 'Come here, Bella,' he says, catching the tail end of Bella's coat. 'Let's put your hat and gloves on. Let me have Roo. We can put him in Daddy's bag so he doesn't get lost.' He squats down beside the little girl, and a gust of wind ruffles his thick locks. He pulls the hat down over her ears. Bella remains rooted to the spot and tight-lipped, but as soon as he's finished she skips away. 'You don't mind if we walk to the other side of the lake, do you?' asks Dominic, 'Only I'd promised Bella we could feed the ducks.'

'Of course, not,' she replies, her breath curling away from her as she shivers in the crisp air. They fall into step together and, as they pick up a steady pace, she feels the blood rushing to her calves, elevating her stride. Bella stops to pick up a stick, then runs after a pigeon, her pink wellies slapping along the uneven tarmac. 'You're doing a great job with Bella, if you don't mind me saying. She's a lovely little girl.'

Dominic casts her a sideways glance. 'She's not been well recently. Something's been bothering me. Tell me, you'll know this as a doctor. Is multiple sclerosis hereditary?'

The question catches her unaware. It's barely twenty four hours since they met and already he's picking her brains as a doctor.

'Why?'

'Bella's had a couple of bladder infections recently. I worry about these things.'

Bella stamps through a puddle and laughs as the muddy water sloshes up her wellies. She's behaving like any normal four-year-old, but concern is mapped across her father's face. Ruth castigates herself. He's probably just anxious, he's recently bereaved after all.

'Urine infections are quite common in little girls,' she says, as they pass an elderly lady walking her dog. 'I'm sure it's nothing to worry about. Maybe she's a bit run down. I'm sure it's not connected to multiple sclerosis.' She lifts her collar, tucking in some stray hairs. They walk on in silence, content to watch Bella zig-zagging across the path. Minutes pass before Ruth feels the need to strike up conversation again.

'You mentioned that your wife was a doctor?' she says, then inwardly chides herself. Of all the questions she could ask why on earth has she chosen one about his late wife, for God's sake? Partly nerves, partly curiosity.

'Madeleine. Yes. She was an immunologist.'

'How did you meet?'

'We were students together at Cambridge. I was studying Maths. We went our separate ways for a while after graduation. Bizarrely we met up again by chance in Hong Kong. I'd gone over for a friend's wedding and she was presenting a paper at a congress, on stem cell transplantation.' His features soften. 'We bumped into each other at a function in the Hong Kong Jockey Club.' He turns to look at her. 'Strange thing, fate, isn't it?'

Ruth digs her hands deeper into her pockets. She can't help but feel sorry for Dominic. The sound of a cycle bell interrupts her train of thought. She's strayed on to the cycle path. As the bicycle flashes past she sidesteps it and brushes Dominic's arm. She grasps it to steady herself.

'Woah,' he says, grabbing hold of her. 'These guys think they have right of way regardless.' He juts his elbow towards her and she links his arm. Neither look at each other. It's an instinctive gesture and it feels right.

10

BELLA

There's a little table in the waiting room. On it are lots of red and blue whirly wires with coloured beads. Bella tries to make the yellow beads go round the wires from one end to the other but then there's a loud buzz above her head.

'That's us,' says her daddy, taking her hand, as they go down the passage. He knocks on one of the doors.

'Come in,' says a voice behind the door.

There's a lady sitting at a table, in front of a big computer. She smiles and asks them to sit down.

'Hello, Isabella,' she says, her eyes flicking between Bella and her daddy. 'How can I help today?'

Bella's daddy puts his hand on her knee. 'Stop swinging your legs when the doctor is talking to us,' he says. He takes a little book out of his pocket and he flicks the pages while he talks to the lady.

Under the lady's table is a box. Bella climbs off the chair and crawls under the table to see what's in it. No-one stops her. It has some books in it and a big cube with holes to post shapes through. Bella thinks that's for babies. She sits on the floor and has a look round. There are lots of drawers with shiny handles. There's a tall bed with a pillow. She wonders if that's where the lady sleeps. There's an orange bin, and a black one, and a yellow one. The room has a lemony smell.

The nice lady's face appears under the table.

'Time to come out now, Isabella,' she says. Bella wonders if she's been naughty. Her daddy calls her Isabella when she's been naughty. And that's a lot.

The lady lifts her onto the bed, then shines the torch. In her ears. In her throat. Prods her belly.

'Everything seems hunky dory,' she says, 'but I think it's worth doing a few tests just to be on the safe side.'

She gives her daddy a little pot. He takes Bella to the loo and tells her to wee in it. Her daddy gets wee on his hand. He goes to the sink to wash it off but now his thumb is bleeding. He knocked it on the jaggedy edge of the sink.

'Silly me,' he says, as he sticks his thumb under the tap. It's an accident.

When they go back in the room the lady puts a stick in the wee then waves the stick round like a little wand.

'Ta-da!' she says, 'A speckle of blood. I think we have the answer. Daddy is going to give you some nice medicine which will make you feel better.'

In the car, on the way home, Daddy tells Bella about when she was a little baby.

'When you were born, Bella, you were such a tiny baby you had to live in a little plastic bubble till you grew stronger. You were just like a little chick waiting to hatch.'

'Did I tap on the shell when I was ready to come out?'

Her daddy laughs.

'Not quite, Bella, but you've always been a little fighter. We need to make sure you stay that way.'

11

DOMINIC

'Sorry to keep you waiting, just putting you through now…..'

A hum on the line, like an annoying bluebottle. Dominic stares out the window. The bird feeder, crammed with seed, sways on its cast iron support by the low garden wall. A finch perches on the wires and pecks at the sunflower hearts and peanuts.

'Hello, is that Mr. Peterson? Yes? It's Dr. Crofton here.'

'Hello, Doctor. Thanks for your time.'

'Not at all. Sorry I wasn't able to speak to you earlier. I have the result of Bella's blood test. It shows she has a mild anaemia. Nothing to worry about. Actually anaemia is fairly common in young children. That could explain why she's had her recent urine infections. I'll do a prescription for iron for you to collect. Is that okay?'

Next door's tortoiseshell cat appears on an adjoining high stone wall. It pads along the top, its fluid musculature supple, precise. It stops. Rigid.

'Yes, of course, Doctor. I understand. I'm glad we've found out why she's been unwell.'

'Well that's not quite the whole picture. Bella should get better with the iron, but because of her recent infections she's going to need a kidney scan. We need to make sure we're not missing anything.'

Dominic watches as the cat bounds down off the wall. The bird takes flight.

'Oh, really? When will that happen?'

'The ultrasound should be sometime in the next four to six weeks. Then there's another scan she'll need within the next six months.'

Undeterred the cat crouches low, its head static, frozen, camouflaged in the brown flecked bushes.

'I wasn't expecting this, Dr. Crofton. Thank you for being so thorough.'

The cat waits patiently, in the shadows. It stands still, totally focussed.

'No problem. Is there anything else I can help with?'

A bull finch alights on the feeder.

'Mr. Peterson?'

Dominic wonders whether he should tap on the

window but the cat launches itself, its supple spine straight as an arrow, and catches the bird mid-air. Not a drop of blood spilt, just feathered carnage.

'Oh, sorry, no, I don't think so... except, well, yes, there is one thing that's been worrying me.'

'Yes?'

'Well. I worry about family history. My wife had multiple sclerosis and she had lots of problems with her kidneys. Is that hereditary? Could there be a connection? Sorry if I sound like a hypochondriac, but I've been so worried about her.'

'Well, don't worry. I really don't think there's a connection. Let's see how things progress once we have the results from the tests. How is she, by the way?'

'She hasn't got much of an appetite. Complains of tummy aches and feeling tired, but I think we're managing okay, for the time being.'

Dominic stands up and peers outside. No sign of the cat. Just a bird feeder swinging in the breeze.

'Okay, well do get back in touch if you have any further concerns.'

'Thanks again, Doctor. I will.'

You bet I will, he thinks, as he puts down the phone.

12

RUTH

MAY 2005

Wednesday. Her half day. But the morning's workload always bullies the afternoon's respite into submission. At lunchtime it's the weekly practice meeting. Her mind flashes back to the agenda. Margaret's case tops the list. It's vital she puts forward her defence. Trepidation lassoes her like a choke lead.

As she enters her consulting room, there's an envelope propped up on her computer keyboard. Her heart lurches wondering if it's from Dom. The spidery handwriting isn't instantly recognisable. She slides a flowery card out of its envelope.

'Dear Dr. Cooper,
Just a wee note to say thank you very much
for looking after Dad in his final days. Mum
and I appreciate your care and support. It
means a lot to us as a family.
Thank you and God Bless,
Anna Jones.'

She casts her mind back to the end-of-terrace house
on Bramwell Estate. They had brought Cyril's bed
down to the front room, where he was the centre of
attention to the constant stream of visitors: grandchildren, district nurses, former colleagues from the Post
Office. Whenever Ruth visited, the house was always
full, but everyone melted away when she appeared,
save for the constant presence of Mabel and Anna
at his bedside. Cyril always had a story to tell, and
a great sense of humour. 'Promise me, doc,' he said,
transfixing her with his watery grey eyes, 'promise me,
that you won't send me into hospital. I'm comfortable here. I don't want no body pumping me chest or
trying to keep me going with those jump leads.' She
would draw her chair up to the cot sides of the bed
and take his waxy hand in hers. They both laughed
at his jokes, but their mutual expressions and locked
handshake were an acknowledgement that they were
both on the same wavelength. Ruth smiles to herself.

He achieved his final wish of dying at home, surrounded by his family. She'll miss him.

She logs on to the computer and notes that she's supervising the trainee doctor this morning. Hastening along the corridor, she pops her head round Emma's door.

'Morning, Emma. How are you this morning?'

A young girl, exuding calm efficiency looks up. A smile dimples her cheeks.

'Hi, Ruth,' she says. 'I'm okay now, thanks. Although I had a panic earlier this morning. Jessica was grisly all night. Thought she might have a fever but she was all right when I dropped her off at nursery. Probably teething. Doesn't stop you feeling guilty though, does it?'

Ruth bites her lip and lets that remark pass. 'Better let you crack on. We can catch up over coffee at the end of surgery. I'm in Room 10 if you need me.'

The morning passes quickly. Just time for a mini tutorial afterwards, though sometimes she struggles to teach Emma things she doesn't already know. Today it's the new European guidelines on urinary tract infections in children. Ruth makes a mental note to add it to her educational log as she makes her way to the coffee room.

She lifts the post out of her pigeon hole and sifts through it. The usual pieces of medical junk mail, pharmaceutical advertising, course invitations. Her fingers linger over the last envelope. It's franked with three words that cast fear through her whole being. General Medical Board. General. Medical. Board. She knows it can't be a subscription reminder. The coffee room is empty. She sits down and, as her fingers slide open the envelope, her stomach reels as if she's in a lift that's ascending too quickly.

Dear Dr. Cooper,
We write with regard to two recent referrals to the General Medical Board, namely:
Case 2651 Filed 17/2/2005 by Mr. A Tremayne.
Case 2652 Filed 26/3/2005 by Abbey Pharmacy.

These cases have been considered by our Board. In the first instance referral will be made back to your local Professional Standards Committee, who will be in contact with you shortly.

On completion of their investigations the Committee will make one of three recommendations to the GMB:

- Closure of the cases
- The issue of a warning
- Referral back to the GMB for consideration of possible negligence proceedings.

Please note that it may take up to eighteen months for the Professional Standards

Committee to report on their findings. We recommend that you inform your medical defence organisation.

We are aware that referrals to the GMB can cause stress for medical practitioners and offer a free confidential helpline (see below) should you wish further support. The enclosed booklet provides more details on the GMB investigation process.

Please acknowledge receipt of this letter.

Yours faithfully,

Her fingers trace over the words, the brushstrokes getting harder in the vain hope it might erase them. *Eighteen months?* Surely it shouldn't take that long. They should be able to tell, unequivocally, that it was genuine human error. Shouldn't they? Nobody died. It could have been worse. Much worse. Why that length of time? Swallowing hard she tries to suppress the lump in her throat. She tries stuffing the letter back in the envelope but her hands are shaking too much.

She'll ring Dom. He would put things into perspective for her. She hesitates. Would he? It might expose her as incompetent. She's frightened. Ashamed. Embarrassed. And this isn't going to go away in a hurry.

What would her parents have thought? About the complaints. About Dom. Her mother would have enveloped her in a cocoon of floral scent, wool and hairspray and would have told her that everything was going to be okay, as she squeezed her tight. Eleven years since her death from breast cancer and she still thinks of her every day. Would she approve of Dominic? Good looking, educated, well mannered. She probably would. Much older, widowed, with a young child. Why torment herself with hypothetical questions? Her father would have been less sympathetic. *Stress?* The word 'stress' didn't exist in his dictionary. Even when he accompanied her to the clinic all those years ago he wasn't convinced it was stress. No, as far as he was concerned you met life's obstacles head on and just got on with it. He didn't understand that minds could fracture as easily as bones. Ironic that the pressures of redundancy and unemployment may have forced him into an early grave when he died of a stroke, aged sixty.

She pushes the letter down the side of her bulging equipment bag, forces the zips and picks up the printed computer summaries for her two allocated home visits. As she makes her way out to the car park, one of the receptionists stops her in her tracks.

'Ruth, I'm glad I've caught you,' she says.

Foreboding envelopes her.

'The duty doctor has gone out to an emergency and there's another visit request come through. Orchards Care Home. Expected death. Do you think you could do it, please?'

'Of course, no problem.'

Taking the print-out from the receptionist, the bundle of notes slips from Ruth's hand and it falls to the floor, like her mood.

★

Ruth places her thumb over the old man's eyelids and gently strokes them closed. His skin is cold now, and yellow as tallow. She takes a step back and bows her head for a second, then looks up at Matron.

'Are the family still here? Shall I have a word with them?'

'No, they left about half an hour ago, but if you come into my office we can complete the paperwork.'

Ruth nods and unclips the stethoscope from around her neck. Collecting her ophthalmoscope case from the dressing table, her eyes are drawn to the cards which clutter its surface. A vintage car proclaims 'Happy Birthday, Dad', and another, 'To Grandad', is handmade in crayon. On the wall is a black and white photo of a smiling couple on their wedding day, the bride, with crimped hair and a buttoned crepe suit, next to her groom in Army uniform. Adjacent is a framed certificate recognising thirty years' service with the Electricity Board. A life well-lived has been condensed into the microcosm of a care home bedroom.

Back in the car she switches on the radio just as the one o'clock news is finishing. She wonders what Dom is doing. Thoughts of him constantly distract her. That day by the boating lake. His touch as he pulled her out of the way of the cyclist. No, she must remain focussed. Sifting through her papers she looks at her remaining requests. A review following hospital discharge after a stroke, and a note from the district nurse to look at a wound. They'll have to wait until after the practice meeting, she thinks, as she turns back towards Parkside Surgery.

★

One forty five. Ruth rushes into the meeting room, breathless and apologetic. Priya is there, plus Tony and Lesley, two of the doctors.

'Don't worry, you're not late,' says Lesley, pouring orange juice into a plastic cup and handing it to Ruth. 'We can't start till the others get here. Must be finishing their visits. Help yourself to a sandwich. Plenty to choose from.' She glances at Tony and leans over towards Ruth. 'Tony and I were just talking about the Tremayne case. That could have been any one of us. Sorry I've not had a chance to come and talk to you about it but we're here to support you anyway we can.'

'Absolutely,' agrees Tony, nodding his head vigorously.

'Thanks.'

It's a wonder they can't hear the pulsing in her ears, thinks Ruth, as she sinks into the seat. She takes a few long breaths, then takes a sip of orange juice. The hammering in her chest subsides and she reaches over the table for a paper plate and sandwich. Soon Emma enters, followed by Paul and Sally, and the meeting starts.

'Just three case reviews today,' announces Sally, the Practice Manager. 'Who'd like to kick off first?'

Ruth locks eyes with Sally. She can't be last today. She needs to get this over as quickly as possible.

'Do you mind if we discuss Mrs. Tremayne first?' She coughs, attempting to clear her throat.

'Fire away,' says Paul.

Ruth takes a deep breath and launches into a well-rehearsed script about the day she was on emergency duty and was inundated with requests for urgent advice, emergency appointments, immediate visits. It's a scene she's played out countless times in her mind. A scenario which makes her feel nervous every time she thinks about it, whether at three in the morning, or now after reading this morning's letter from the General Medical Board. At times her voice wavers and cracks. At one stage tears well, but she blinks them away. She stops and, for what seems like minutes, there is silence round the room, punctuated solely by the crinkling of crisp packets.

'Thanks, Ruth,' interjects Paul. 'Any learning points you'd like to highlight?'

Her sandwich lies untouched on its paper plate.

'Just that I've only got myself to blame,' replies Ruth. Her nails dig white crescents into the palms of her hands, but she's not allowed to go any further.

'Whoa, hold on' interrupts Paul. 'I think it's important to state something to everyone in this room. This is not a blame game. We're only human, sometimes we all do things that, maybe with hindsight, we would have done differently.' No-one speaks, but heads nod.

Ruth stares at her sandwich.

'So,' he continues, 'with that in mind, are there any points that you'd like to share with the team?'

Ruth gives a weak smile and looks at her plate. A dry cough causes her to look up. Five pairs of eyes are looking at her. Paul's words about learning points echo in her head. 'Yes,' she continues, 'It's impossible to diagnose the cause of pain over the phone, even when you think you know the patient well. When giving telephone advice always think about red flag signs. Sudden onset of worsening upper abdominal pain may mean a heart attack. Mrs. Tremayne was known by me to have gallstones and, with hindsight, that threw me off track.' Her voice wobbles. It hurts to admit this. 'Always offer safety-netting advice-that is, advise the patient to ring back or call an ambulance if the symptoms get much worse.' She hesitates. 'Oh and make sure you document carefully in the notes what has been said to the patient.' She bites her lip.

'Thank you, Ruth,' says Sally. 'If you could write up a case review and circulate it by e mail that would be great. Now, moving on, Case Number Two.'

There's a shuffling of notes, as everyone turns to the next case on the list. A tear rolls down Ruth's cheek. She feels a soft kick under the table and looks across the table to see Lesley nodding gently, her mouth upturned in a gesture of solidarity.

★

At the end of the meeting everyone, apart from Paul, files out of the room but Ruth holds back. She doesn't want to be accosted in the corridor again. Her morning's work isn't yet complete. The table is strewn with used plastic cups and crumbed paper plates. Paul opens a packet, studies its contents and turns out a coronation chicken sandwich onto a napkin.

'Uncertainty,' he says, without looking up. 'It's what we deal with all the time.' The lines round his eyes soften. 'Don't you think that's enough for one day, Ruth? Isn't this supposed to be your half day? You better get going while there's still some of it left.'

'I will.' She pushes the chair back. 'Thanks for your support.'

'That's okay. We're a team, remember? If ever there's anything worrying you, you can come to me and have a chat about it, okay?'

She sways a little. Should she tell him about the letter from the GMB? Maybe he already knows about it. 'Well, I was wondering how to proceed with Margaret,' she says. 'I'd like to visit her when the time is right.'

'Plenty of time for that, once the complaint is resolved. Trust me.'

'Thanks, Paul.' She slinks out of the room.

The waiting room is eerily quiet as Ruth walks past reception.

'Still here?'

Ruth gives the receptionist a weary smile.

'The meeting's just finished. Oh, do me a favour please, Ginny. I've still got two visits. I'm not going to have time to come back and print out the prescriptions. Would you pass me a prescription pad for my bag, so I can handwrite them?'

'Sure.'

Ginny slides open a drawer and passes over a pad of green paper. 'See you tomorrow. Don't work too hard.'

'Ta. You too.'

13
RUTH

Val must have seen her walking up the path because she's at the front door before Ruth rings the doorbell. Val puts a finger to her lips. 'Sshh,' she warns, 'I've just got him off to sleep.' She gives her friend a hug. 'Hey, good to see you.' They retreat indoors and Val runs her eyes over the linen suit, the smart sandals. 'Just come from work? I thought Wednesday was your half day?'

'Well, it's supposed to be. Been another bummer of a day, actually. Six extras on top of morning surgery, three visits and a practice meeting. I'm shattered.'

'God, I've got all this to look forward to when I go back in September,' Val says, wiping her hands on her T shirt. 'Don't know how I'm going to manage.' She feels in her pockets, then pats the top of her head and looks satisfied when she locates her spectacles. 'Sounds like you could do with a glass of wine. I know I could.' She laughs. 'But four thirty's probably a bit too early. Tea?'

They walk through to the back of the house. Ruth loves Val's kitchen. It's open plan with a large pine table on one side and a sofa and play area on the other. Large patio doors lead out to the garden. Today the low afternoon sun casts its warm rays over a rug where two little girls are playing. They've set out a miniature tea set, and each is absorbed in her own individual chatter.

'Hello, Alice,' Ruth says, to the dark-haired toddler who is stacking cups. Both little girls look up. Ruth finds herself drawn to her blonde-haired companion. The sharp angles of her shoulder blades and the pinched cheekbones are instantly recognisable.

'Bella! Hello, you! What a lovely surprise.'

The fair-haired girl looks up through her fringe. She gets up and runs over to Ruth, knocking her legs.

'Look what I've got,' says Bella, holding up a pink plastic cup.

As Ruth bends down to grasp the toy she can't help noticing Bella's pallid cheeks, the purplish semicircles under her eyes and how skinny she looks compared with her three-year-old playmate.

'Are you having a tea party?' Ruth laughs. 'That looks fun.'

Bella runs back to the table and carries on with her task.

Ruth turns to Val. 'How come?' she whispers.

'Mike arranged a meeting with Dom this afternoon,' says Val, filling the kettle. She lowers her voice a fraction. 'He said I should offer to look after Bella.' She turns so that her back is to Bella. 'I'm a bit nervous to be honest. He's very protective of his daughter.' Her forehead appears creased in curiosity. 'Anyway, how's it going?'

Ruth smiles. She edges in closer to Val, and angles an eyebrow. 'That's a loaded question if ever I heard one.'

'Is it now? You always were a dark horse, Dr. Cooper.'

Val walks over to the patio doors and opens them outwards. The air smells fresh and Ruth detects the faint fragrance of honeysuckle.

'Girls,' Val says, addressing the playmates, 'as it's such a nice sunny day Ruth and I are going to sit outside in the garden.' Neither of the little girls look up. She loads up a tray and hands it to Ruth, who follows her friend out into the bright sunlight.

Val opens out the parasol above the glass-topped rattan table. The teapot and mugs are placed on the table and both women slide onto the plump cushions.

'You and I have a lot of catching up to do' says Val, before Ruth can get a word in. 'You need to bring me up to date with events since the Ball.' She pushes a mug in Ruth's direction.

Ruth sits back in her chair and takes a long gulp of her drink. She takes stock of her friend, who leans forward on the edge of her seat. It amuses Ruth to see her interest.

'Actually, there's not very much to say.'

Val's shoulders drop. She looks disappointed. 'Oh, come on. I know that's not true. How many times have you seen him?'

Ruth lowers her voice. 'I've been pre-occupied with work, and I guess he's been busy dealing with his own situation.' She kicks off her shoes and tucks her legs under her on the cushion. 'You don't mind, do you?' she asks, pointing to her feet. Val shakes her head and gestures to her to continue. Her frustration is palpable, and Ruth intends to spin this out for as long as possible. 'We agreed to meet up one evening,' Ruth continues, 'but that fell through at the last minute. I was really looking forward to a nice leisurely evening but he couldn't get a babysitter, and I had an emergency at work. My last patient came in at six thirty and needed a referral to the Crisis Team.'

Val inches forward with every sentence. 'And?'

'You know what it's like.'

'I'm not interested in work. What happened with Dominic?'

'I didn't get home till gone eight. So that date was a disaster.' A robin hops on the bird bath and Ruth watches it bob its head in the water before flying away.

'Go on. And then what?'

'Well, after the Ball we went out for lunch. That's when I met Bella.'

'And?'

'And what?' Ruth's cheeks colour.

'Oh, give me a break. There's got to be more to it than that.' Val picks up a chocolate wafer and snaps it in two.

Ruth regards her with shy amusement. 'He's really nice. I kind of feel sorry for him, all the stuff he's had to deal with. He needs time. And she's a sweet little girl.' She sweeps her hair back off her face, twists it into a knot and pushes it under her collar. 'Anyway, it's me that should be asking you. You probably know him a lot better than I do.'

Val is about to take a bite of her second biscuit but pauses and returns it to the plate. She looks thoughtful. 'Ha,' she says, 'where do I begin? Well I first met Dominic through Mike's work then found out that his wife was a doctor. I guess, as couples, that meant we both had a lot in common. You must have been off doing your GP rotation, at the time.' She stops, and stares ahead for a few seconds, as if weighing up what she is going to say next. 'Actually I've been feeling very guilty.' She fiddles with the back of her earring.

'Guilty? Why?'

Val doesn't reply but untucks her legs from under

her, stretches them, then pats the cushions on either side.

Ruth tries to dampen the trill of anxiety unleashing in her stomach.

Val studies her closely and her words seem measured. 'Madeleine and I used to be good friends. We fell out over … over a disagreement about six years ago. It was petty, but you know how these things can fester. Then she became ill and Dominic and Madeleine kept us at arm's length. I always got the impression they preferred it that way.' She pauses and readjusts the cushions for the second time. 'When Alice and Ollie came along I guess our priorities changed,' Val continues, 'and Mike and I kind of lost contact with them. Which, of course, I regret.' She waves away a wasp. 'Mike went to Madeleine's funeral, but I couldn't go at the last minute because Ollie was ill. I feel guilty about that too.' She sighs. 'Anyway that's all water under the bridge now.'

'What do you mean?

'Christ knows, we all do things we regret.'

'I don't understand.'

Val closes her eyes and taps the fingers of each hand together as if she's meditating. After what feels like many seconds she opens her eyes and turns to Ruth. 'I mean I could have been a better friend to Madeleine but it's too late now. Maybe I can make amends by helping Dominic out with Bella.'

The tension in Ruth's shoulders lifts and she rests back. They sit in companionable silence for a few seconds. The sound of a strimmer strikes up from a neighbouring garden. 'But d'you know, I was wrong about Dominic.'

'Wrong about what?'

'Well Mike was keen for you to meet him but I warned him off. Said he was too much of a control freak. But with Bella he's a changed person. It's re-markable.' A wasp hovers near her wrist and she waves it away. 'From what I can gather she's been quite a sickly child. Poor little soul. He left me a bag of medi-cines: Calpol, Piriton, Trimethoprim. Complete with instructions, bless him. He forgets I'm a doctor. He's so attentive and caring. It breaks my heart to see them together, especially when I think of Alice having a mummy and a daddy.'

The bumblebees move in and out of the laven-der bushes, as Ruth considers this information. It was true Dominic appeared arrogant at times but if you knew how to handle him he was a softie.

'Don't get me wrong,' Val continues, 'I really like him. I have a lot of sympathy for him.' She leans for-ward and says in a whisper, 'and he's very good looking.'

They both laugh.

'Here,' says Val, lifting the teapot, 'would you like a top-up before this gets cold?' She refills Ruth's mug, then leans back. Suddenly her posture stiffens. She looks at her watch. 'That didn't last long,' she says, as a baby's cry becomes audible from the window above their head. 'Probably all that noise coming from next door. Make yourself at home while I go and fetch Ollie.'

While she's gone Ruth glances round the garden, then looks up at the windows of the neighbouring houses. Satisfied she is sheltered from prying eyes, she lifts up her skirt, then rolls her sweaty tights down her legs. She sculpts them into a little ball and stretches her legs. The low afternoon sun warms her face. Should she tell Val about the replies she's had on likeminds. com? What would Val say? Probably that men are like buses. You wait ages then three come along at once. The smell of freshly mown grass drifts over the fence. Ruth readjusts the cushions at her back then closes her eyes again. The company director looked hot, not so the university lecturer. But why is she even thinking this, now that she's met Dominic? Although did she really want to rush into a relationship with someone who has a child and was so recently bereaved? Maybe that additional responsibility was why he came across as controlling. She could understand that. And now she understands why Bella looks so pallid.

A gurgling sounds brings her out of her daydream and she opens her eyes to find Val standing over her, cradling a fractious baby. She plonks a bottle of milk on the garden table and hands over the mewling bundle to Ruth.

'Here we are, Ollie,' she says, depositing the baby in Ruth's lap, 'Auntie Ruth can give you your bottle, whilst Mummy gets the girls' tea ready.' She gives Ruth a broad smile, accompanied by a shrug of the shoulders. 'You don't mind, do you? I won't be long. Give me a shout if you need to. Besides, it's a lovely day for sitting in the garden.'

★

She must have been sitting in the garden for about twenty minutes. There's still not a cloud in the sky and the strimming from next door has stopped. Adjusting her seat under the parasol, so that Ollie is out of direct sunlight, she cradles him in her lap, breathing in his yeasty smell. His chubby fingers grasp the sides of his bottle and his face is a picture of dreamy contentment. He hasn't a care in the world and she feels envious. A butterfly alights on the table and for a second its tortoiseshell wings glint in the sunshine before it flies away. Bliss. But in her mind there is an alternative narrative, and it runs through her like sandpaper over splintered wood. Loss is an indeterminate emotion which stabs you when you're least prepared. She dandles Ollie on her knee and he obliges her with a one tooth smile which dints his face.

14
RUTH

Mike strides across the lawn, smartly-suited, a bottle of wine and some glasses in his hands. He beams at her. 'What a lovely surprise!' She readjusts her hold on the baby and wriggles to the edge of the seat. 'It's okay,' says Mike, 'don't get up. You're doing a great job there,' and he leans forward to plant a kiss on her cheek and stroke the top of the baby's downy head. Ollie babbles in delight.

'Ollie's been keeping me company in the sunshine,' says Ruth. 'How are you? Busy day?'

'Productive day, thanks.'

Ruth feels a bristle of panic. She knows she doesn't look her best. Is Dominic about to emerge into the hazy sunshine? She smooths her hair and brushes crumbs off her blouse.

'Yes, Val said you've been with Dominic. Is he still here? Shall I go in and say hello?'

'Oh, I'd leave them to it if I were you,' says Mike, as he twists the cap on the bottle of wine. 'They're sorting the kids out. Plenty of time to say hello later. Val's persuaded him to stay for supper, and we're hoping you will too.'

Their eyes meet, as she considers her plans for the evening. She's got nothing to lose, has she? She wonders if Dominic has said anything about her to Mike.

'Save you having to cook tonight,' he adds, in case she needs any encouragement.

Ruth shrugs her shoulders and smiles. 'Why not?' she says. 'Sounds like a good plan.'

'Excellent,' he says. 'Now let me pour you a glass of wine.'

★

'Will you two quit taking about motor-racing,' Val remonstrates. 'Not all of us are interested in Formula One.'

'Maybe you should be, darling,' says Mike. 'One of these days you might be grateful.' Dominic reciprocates with a smirk and continues twisting noodles round his fork.

Val shrugs her shoulders. 'Meaning what, exactly?'

'You know Lucky Pagoda, the mobile phone company?' continues Mike. 'It looks like they're going to buy and manage one of the teams. We had an interesting conversation about it this afternoon.'

Val looks up and feigns a yawn. 'Tell me more. If you must.'

'We met Gary Sharp, today,' says Mike. 'Remember him?'

Val seems to be smothering a laugh. 'Not "Steel Bollocks Sharp?" What the hell was he doing there?'

Ruth bites her lip, trying her best to keep a straight face.

'He moved over from LIFFE too. He's an independent broker now. Reckons Lucky Pagoda's one to watch.'

Val frowns. 'I'd be a bit wary of him to be honest. All mouth and no trousers. Which reminds me, you both scrubbed up well for your meeting today, if you don't mind me saying.' She blows Mike a kiss across the table.

It occurs to Ruth that she is still in her work clothes too. The waist band of her skirt feels rather tight and her feet ache. She rubs one heel over the other till her sandals loosen off her feet. Almost immediately she is conscious of other toes on hers, but then they are retracted. For a split second she is unsure what to do.

'I think we all scrubbed up well today,' adds Dominic, smiling at her. Any reservations Ruth had about him earlier have now disappeared.

'I reckon McLaren Mercedes have the best chance this weekend,' says Dominic. He hovers the wine bottle over Ruth's glass, but she covers it with one hand and shakes her head. Half of his face is in shadow, the other illuminated by the low ceiling pendants.

'Depends on the qualifying session on Saturday,' says Mike. 'Whoever gets pole at Monaco virtually has it in the bag. It's impossible to overtake on that street circuit.'

Val pushes her chair back. 'I'm glad the girls went off okay. Alice didn't even want a story tonight. I think they were both exhausted.' She stands up. 'I'm going to make some coffee. Or tea? Any takers?'

She gathers some plates together and carries them over to the dishwasher. 'Bella?' she is heard to say, and everyone looks round.

Bella is standing in the doorway, trailing a blanket and sobbing. Dominic scrapes his chair back and rushes over. 'It's okay, Bella, Daddy's here. What's the matter, sweetie? Did you wake up and wonder where you were?'

'Sick. Been sick.' Her words emerge in tearful gulps.

Dominic lifts up the blanket, which is covered in yellow stains. 'Poor darling,' he says. 'It's soaking wet.'

He turns to Val. 'Sorry, Val. You wouldn't happen to have a spare T shirt I could borrow, would you?'

'Sure,' says Val 'I'll go and get one and I can check on Alice.' She turns and bounds up the stairs.

'Let me help,' says Ruth, jumping to her feet and hurrying over. A smell, like rotten eggs, makes her gag. 'Poor Bella, are you not feeling well?' she asks, as she crouches down. 'Here, let me have a look at you.'

'It's okay, Ruth,' says Dominic, edging between them, and almost knocking her sideways. 'We'll manage, thanks.' As he bends down his dark hair flops over his brow and he squints up at Ruth, the colour drained from his face. 'She'll be fine. Let's get you cleaned up, darling, then we ought to go home.'

Val appears with a T shirt, towel and fleecy blanket. He takes Bella by the hand and leads her to the downstairs cloakroom, followed by Val. Soon the sound of running water can be heard.

Ruth turns to Mike. 'I was only offering to help,' she says, smarting at the unexpected barb.

'Oh, don't take it personally, Ruth, he's under a lot of stress at the moment. He's had quite an intense afternoon, you know. I'm helping him sort out Madeleine's estate and it's anything but straightforward.' Mike shakes his head, then upends a wine bottle into his glass. The last few drops bleed into the crystal.

'I've put Alice in our bed,' says Val, appearing a few minutes later. 'She didn't stir. Maybe if I change the sheets, you could go in her bed tonight, darling, then I can keep an eye on her? Poor Bella, I hope she's okay. She seemed fine this afternoon.'

Now it's Mike's turn to shrug.

'Well, let me clear up here,' says Ruth, 'then I'd better get going too.'

'That's okay, Ruth, honestly, there's not much to do.' Val moves towards her to give her a hug. 'Plus I've got all day tomorrow to tidy up, whereas you've probably got an early start, remember?'

'Okay,' replies Ruth, in what feels like a weak surrender, but she's tired. 'I'll just go and say good-bye to Dominic.'

'Dominic? He's gone. He was anxious to get home.'

'Gone?' Ruth looks from Val to Mike, in case she's missed something. 'But he didn't even say goodbye.'

'I think he's worried about Bella. He just bundled her up and told me to say his goodbyes for him. Poor guy.'

15

RUTH

Smarting. Humiliated. Confused. Three days since the evening at Val's that turned sour and Ruth can't stop thinking about him. Her mind drifted to him this morning, with every length of the pool she swam. She's constantly distracted by thoughts of him while driving.

Why had Dominic behaved that way? Why had he cut her off? Why should he feel so protective towards Bella?

Her car tyres spit pebbles as she veers into her driveway and she switches off the ignition.

Loss, thinks Ruth. Loss, that's why. Loss and the fear of losing again. It made sense. As his wife's health declined, Madeleine would have become more and more dependent on him, while, at the same time, he was taking on full responsibility for bringing up his child. Poor Dominic. Poor Bella.

Still, it would be good for her to have a break. To create some space for herself, while she considered her options. There was certainly no harm in going on a date tonight.

Emerging from the car, into the spring sunshine, a breeze ruffles her hair and tightens her complexion. As she opens the tailgate of her car, billowy white clouds move across her vision, reflected in the glass. Saturday. If she'd been in Melbourne she might have been heading down the Mornington Peninsula for the day. Hitting the beach at Sorrento, with Mark, for a spot of surfing and a picnic, then taking the ferry over to Queenscliff and coming back as the sun set over Port Philip Bay. Happy, sun-kissed days. Before it all went wrong.

No, she can't afford another mistake with men.

Her neighbour, opposite, is already out in his garden, clipping his hedge. Two photinia flank his gravel path, their pink and red foliage shaped into globes, which poke authoritatively above the laurel hedge, like traffic wardens' lollipops guarding his gate. He looks up when her car door clashes and gives a cheery wave. As she returns the gesture she notices a small green van crawling along the road. The driver must have spotted her because suddenly he accelerates. He pulls up outside her drive and winds the window down.

'Excuse me, Miss. I'm looking for number twenty seven? Dr. Cooper?'

'Yeah, that's me,' she nods, but the affirmation is couched in curiosity.

'Glad I caught you. Delivery for you.' He jumps out the van, then his head and shoulders disappear into the back of his vehicle as he pulls out a package wreathed in Cellophane and ribbon. He hands it over, his smile framed in blooms.

'Gosh, thank you,' says Ruth, her arms outstretched. 'I wasn't expecting a delivery.'

'Nice surprise for you then, Doc,' he says. 'Have a good day.' He's back in the van and disappears up the road before she has a chance to say anything else. She looks across the road. Her neighbour has set down his clipping shears and is grinning broadly at her.

Back in the house she sets the flower arrangement down on the kitchen table and carefully peels away the layers of Cellophane with scissors. There's a small white envelope stapled to the front and her hands tremble a little as she opens it.

'To brighten your day. D x'

Signed with a kiss. She swallows hard. It's a perfect arrangement of delicate white rose buds and pink lisianthus, encased in a swathe of purple and white honesty. Honesty. Her favourite. She closes her eyes and imagines herself back in the Banqueting Room of the Town Hall, the night of the Ball. She turns the card over and notices a message on the back.

'I may not be perfect, but when I say sorry I mean it.'

'Ha,' Ruth exclaims. 'Dominic Peterson, you charmer. But you're going to have to try harder than that,' she says, popping the card into her handbag.

★

She arrives at the Rose and Crown fifteen minutes early, and reverse parks into a spot just past the entrance. There's no sign of the white Corsa yet, but from this vantage point she can see every movement in and out the car park. Better to introduce herself in the parking lot. Less anxiety-provoking than scanning a crowded bar for a blonde-haired guy in his thirties whom she's never met before. She wonders if he'll be anything like his photo.

There's a comedy news quiz on the car radio, but her attention drifts. Why should she feel guilty for thinking about other men? Dom's arrogance piques her, but sometimes she finds it enticing. What was it Val said? 'He keeps everyone at arm's length, but he's a changed person since Bella came along.' A latter day Mr. Rochester, perhaps? Ha, but she's no Jane Eyre. And Rochester had something to hide, so that analogy doesn't really work.

Anyway it won't hurt to go on a date with Ralph. At least that's what he calls himself on his profile page, but she suspects that's not his real name, any more than hers is Vicky. A thirty year old 'Company Director.' That could mean anything. Into rugby and rowing. So hopefully fit.

Pulling down the sun visor at the top of her windscreen she checks her appearance in the mirror. As she pokes around in her handbag she sees Dominic's card, pulls it out and turns it over and over in her hand. 'Dominic Peterson,' she says to herself. 'This could be your "get out of jail free" card.' Selecting a mascara wand and tube of lipstick, very carefully she edges towards the mirror and flicks the nylon brush over her top lashes. She checks her appearance again. The brush is poised over the lower lashes, just as she feels a sneeze erupting. Must be the dust in the car. Too late. A sudden involuntary quivering of her nose causes her to poke the tip of the mascara brush into the corner of her eye. It stings and she can feel her eye watering. She curses and looks at her reflection. A black line, like a tyre mark, has skidded across the side of her nose and her teary eye looks red. On the news quiz someone has just told a joke and the radio crackles with sound of canned laughter. She moistens the corner of a tissue with her tongue and dabs it on her face, erasing the extraneous make-up.

There's the sound of tyres on gravel. A blur of white and chrome scuds across her vision. Six thirty eight. He's late. Thank God she didn't go in early. She checks her appearance for the final time, gets out of the car and smooths the creases in her linen Capri pants. Hovering in the shadows she peers over her wing mirror until she gets a better view of him. It's obvious he hasn't seen her because he has his sun visor down and is rubbing his teeth with his finger. She hangs back until he gets out of the car. Broad-browed, blonde hair, clipped on the sides, tousled on top. Sun-streaked skin to match. Yes, it's him, he looks like his picture. Makes a change. She steps forward.

'Ralph?' She smiles in his direction. He looks up, and his features freeze, then soften, when he recognises her.

'Vicky?' His face breaks into a broad smile and he walks towards her. Blue and white striped polo shirt. Thick gold box chain visible through the open-neck collar. Gold stud in his ear. She's not sure if lots of gold jewellery on a man is that attractive. She offers her hand but he steps closer and kisses her on both cheeks.

'That was good timing,' she says, 'both of us arriving together,' as he steps to one side and ushers her through the entrance to the bar.

★

From her seat in the alcove, Ruth watches Ralph return from the bar with a glass of white wine and a pint of bitter. His wide smile is beguiling.

'Here we go,' he says, placing the drinks on the table. 'Cheers.'

'Cheers.'

'Are you okay? Your eye looks very red.' Ruth wishes he hadn't drawn attention to it.

'Oh, I'm fine. Just a bit of hay fever, I think.'

They sit and look at each other for a few awkward seconds then laugh simultaneously. Ruth casts a quick glance around her to see who is in earshot. 'So, what have you been up to today?' It's a bland question, but what else is there to say? Her companion leans forward, his elbows nudging his pint, and tells her how he's been to an auction this morning and sealed a deal on another property for modernising. That's what he does. Buys properties that have been repossessed, renovates them and flogs them on for a massive profit.

'Yeah, I've been doing it for a good few years now. Got lots of experience as a builder and built up a network of mates I can rely on to get the work done. Course it helps if you're a cash buyer.' He takes a sip of his pint, then creases his lips over the foam. 'What about you?'

'Oh, I've had a busy day, went for a swim, caught up on a few domestic things, the usual.' There's the sound of laughter coming from the direction of the bar and, as she turns her head in that direction, she catches sight of a man throwing his head back at a nearby table. The irregular profile of his nose is instantly recognisable. Suddenly she feels a dart of panic. The last thing she wants is to bump into Mike here.

'No, I mean what do you do?'

Ruth slinks down in her seat and leans sideways to get a better look at Mike and the company he's with. Alarm pricks her with the realisation that it could be Dominic. Mike gets up and walks towards the door and she shrinks back behind a pillar. From this vantage point she can't see, but at least she's obscured from view until she can decide what to do.

'Your profile says you work in healthcare.'

Ruth turns back to the stranger sitting opposite her. She wishes Ralph would keep his voice down. There might be patients in the pub. Worse still it could attract the wrong sort of attention.

'Oh, I work in the NHS. In admin. Bit of a boring job really.' She bites her lip. He's a sweet guy and it's a night out but, as he curls his hand round his pint glass, she can't help noticing the stripe of white, unblemished skin at the base of his left fourth finger. Enough. They haven't the slightest thing in common. Even when she asks him about the rugby and rowing it turns out he's an armchair spectator, although he did go to Twickenham once.

Ruth angles her seat. Mike's table is visible in the triangle formed between Ralph's left ear and his shoulder. There's still no sign of him reappearing but the man he was with stands up. It's definitely not Dominic. Time to make a move. She finishes her drink.

'Ralph, it's been nice meeting you but I really need to get going.'

'Really nice to meet you too, Vicky,' he says, standing up. He looks disappointed but gives her a kiss on the cheek. Then he lowers his voice and whispers, 'I feel really guilty. I should have told you something earlier.' Ruth braces herself. It's not going to come as a surprise for her to hear that he's going through a divorce, or some other complicated domestic arrangement. She widens her eyes and waits for him to say something.

'My name's not really Ralph. It's Mark.'

She feigns a laugh. 'Well it's been really nice meeting you, Mark.'

'You, too, let's do it again soon!'

'Yes,' she says, but she's turned her back on him, so doubts whether he can hear.

Looking directly ahead, her pace quickens, eager to create distance between her and her failed encounter, and she heads for the door. A sudden pain knots round her ankle and as she falls forward she instinctively puts out her right hand and braces herself for more discomfort. Instead she comes into contact with the wiry pelt of a lurcher and finds herself at eye level with its snout.

'Ow,' she exclaims, 'damn dog.'

'Ooh, careful dear,' says a woman's voice. As she tries to stand up Ruth feels the tug of a dog lead twisting tighter round her feet and an explosion of heat in her ankle.

'Here, let me help you,' says a disembodied voice, as she feels a pressure under her arms and is hoisted up to stand.

'I ... I didn't see the dog under the table,' says Ruth turning to vent her anger at the dog's owner. Instead she comes face to face with the man at Mike's table. Piercing green eyes. Receding hair. Collarless black shirt. Firm grip. No sign of Ralph, or Mark, who has disappeared into the shadows. The man hooks his foot under a chair, slides it towards her and helps her sit down. Her ankle burns.

'Here,' he says, 'don't put any weight on it till we have a look.'

Ruth glances down. Already a lump the size of a golf ball has erupted on the side of her ankle.

'Well, would you credit that,' says another voice, all too familiar to Ruth. 'I leave my mate for five minutes while I go to the loo,' says Mike, 'and when I come back he's hooked up with some company.'

Ruth looks at Mike, then at his friend who looks as confused as she feels.

'Mike. Fancy that. Didn't expect to see you here,' says Ruth. 'I tripped over the dog lying beside the table. Your friend very kindly helped me.' She moves her foot and winces. 'Aren't you going to introduce me?'

'Gary Sharp,' says the stranger, holding his hand out to Ruth and speaking before Mike has a chance to say anything. 'I'm a colleague of Mike's.'

'I'm Ruth. Nice to meet you,' she says, wondering where she's heard that name before, 'although maybe not in these-

'Is Dominic here?' Mike interjects, quickly scanning the room.

'Er, no,' says Ruth, wishing that he was. 'I was about to ask you the same question.' If she'd rung him this morning when she received the flowers she might not be in this mess now.

Mike visibly relaxes. 'Well, that ankle looks sore. Hopefully just a sprain, but we can help you home,' says Mike. 'If you give me your keys I can drive you in your car and Gary can follow in his.'

Ruth hesitates. She just wants to go home and put this evening behind her. She can rest with an ice pack and hopefully the ankle swelling will recede. Mike's offer, however, makes sense.

'Thanks. That would be a great help,' she says, delving in her pocket and bringing out her keys.

They help her to her feet and she hobbles out of the pub, linking arms with Mike.

A sudden thought alarms her.

'Mike?' she says, squeezing his arm gently.

'Yes?'

'You won't say anything to Dominic about seeing me in the pub, will you?'

Mike appears to consider this carefully then a smile spreads across his face. 'Of course not. Let's just say this evening never happened, shall we?'

She relaxes her grip. 'Good plan.'

As far as she's concerned Dominic Peterson is forgiven.

16

BELLA

'Time for bed,' says Courtney, as soon as Daddy goes out. 'Remember the drill. Pyjamas, teeth, bed.' It's not even dark. Courtney collects Bella from school. And babysits. She's very bossy.

She moves all the papers around on Daddy's desk and tells Bella to tidy her toys. Then she follows her upstairs.

'Ooh, I'd like to see that,' Courtney says, picking up the book by Bella's bed. The one with lots of photos of her Mummy and Daddy. Bella wants to snatch it off her. To say no.

'I'll bring it back later,' says Courtney. She better. Courtney puts those dangly strings in her ears then pretends she can't hear.

Bella sits on her bed with her box of stickers. There's a goldfish. And a dinosaur. The dinosaur's her favourite. The stickers say, 'I've been brave.' That's what the nurse says when she goes to the doctors.

'This won't hurt,' says the nurse when she takes off the bandage where Daddy put the cream. Then she jabs her arm. 'See? What did I tell you? Not even a little sting. My goodness, Bella, you're the bravest girl I've seen this morning. I think you should have a sticker.'

Bella's not scared of nothing. She counts her stickers. 'One, two, three, four.' She gets up to twenty but can't remember which number comes next.

Daddy says she has to go to hospital soon. He says the doctors want to take her picture and she must be brave. Maybe she'll get more stickers. But she's nearly run out of pages in her book.

Courtney is talking loudly downstairs. Bella tiptoes to her door. Presses her ear to the crack. Courtney is on the phone.

'No, no, no,' she says, 'I've told you before. It's not fair.'

Maybe her boyfriend's been naughty again. Grown-ups can't be naughty though, can they?

Footsteps. Bella climbs into bed and switches on her light. The holes in it make freckles, which move around the wall. She opens her drawer and takes out her crayons.

Maybe Mummy would like a picture. But Mummy's not coming back. Daddy says she's gone to heaven. That's where the angels sing.

Courtney sticks her head round the door.

'What are you up to, little monkey?' she says. She comes in, puts Bella's crayons back in the drawer and pulls the curtains shut. 'Lights out now, Bella.' She tucks her in. 'Night, night.' She smells of mints and cigarettes.

It's dark now, except for a stick of light coming through the bedroom door.

17

RUTH

Ruth needn't have worried. He'd understood. She'd phoned him on the pretext of thanking him for the flowers, of course, but he must have noticed the hint of anxiety in her voice. Part nervousness, part lack of self-confidence. After last night's disastrous evening in the pub she just wanted to hear his voice.

'Why don't I come over?' he said, 'I'm sure Courtney won't mind babysitting. Can't have you driving if you're trying to rest your ankle.'

She'd tripped over the uneven flagstones in her back garden, she'd told him, while carrying a heavy watering can to refill the bird bath.

As they sat downstairs drinking coffee it had been

so liberating to off-load her worries to him. The panic she felt on missing Margaret's diagnosis, the tremulous anxiety that engulfed her when the pharmacist told her she'd prescribed ten times the usual dose of morphine for a dying patient. He seemed to get it. To understand. As he listened, he nodded, and squeezed her hand. Inevitably their discussion soon moved upstairs.

Dusk filters through the half-opened curtains now, casting spindles of shadow across the room. There's the soughing of trees outside, their dark green profiles bristling against a silver sky. Inside the bedroom the air is warm and viscous. The duvet has been kicked into a rumpled ball. As she stretches her legs, her toe catches on the corner of the sheet, pulling it down to expose her breasts. Her nipples prickle, and she exhales slowly.

Dominic lies facing her, one side of his head buried in the pillow. She gazes at the exposed contours of his face and there's a smoothness to them which is more apparent when he's asleep. The tension lines round his eyes have softened, and the angle of his mouth has lifted. She watches the rise and fall of his chest, and her eyes followed the band of dark hairs down to the crescent-shaped scar under the left side of his rib cage. Very gently she traces it with her finger, his skin squirming at the tickle of sensitive nerve endings round its puckered edge. He opens his eyes.

'You're ticklish,' she says.

'Maybe,' he replies in a throaty voice. 'My splenectomy scar. I'll tell you about it later.'

He shifts across the bed. 'But first,' he says, pulling her into a kiss.

They make love, and afterwards he rolls onto his side, avoiding pressure on his arm.

As the shadows in the room lengthen, the projected slats of her stickleback chair throw lines across the bed that cover them both, like the bars of a cell. It's an odd image, so she rises and moves over to the window to pull the curtains. Outside, rain puddles on a garden bench, and the roses trailing the sill are beaded with moisture.

She turns around and switches on the bedside light, and he's staring at her. And now she's conscious of her nakedness. He blinks, then his face breaks into a broad smile. Little wisps of his hair float with static, as he lifts his head from the pillow. Propping himself up, his eyes move across her body. He holds out his hand and pulls her on to the bed.

'I was dreaming about you earlier,' he says, pinning her arms beneath her. 'But it's not a dream.' Then he presses his body close and she can feel his warm breath in her hair. He tangles his legs around her again, as they roll over damp patches of mattress, and, once again, her anxieties are pushed to the perimeter of her consciousness.

Later they lie back, with the duvet pulled up over their shoulders. Ruth studies the uneven emulsion on the ceiling. He's the first to speak.

'Do you ever think about dying?' He turns to look at her.

She raises her head slightly, pondering the weight of the question.

'From time to time. Why?'

'I don't know. I've thought about it a lot recently. Obviously.'

There's an inflection in his voice she hasn't heard before.

'You see,' he continues, looking away, 'if I had a choice I'd much prefer it to be quick, rather than lingering. And I don't think anyone dies peacefully, no matter what the announcements in the death columns say.'

'Maybe.'

'I mean, take that patient of yours, for instance. If the pharmacist hadn't noticed your mistake, and the patient had died, it might have been a blessing.'

'You can't be serious.' Ruth makes no attempt to mask the horror in her voice. 'I know you're trying to make me feel better, but that's not the point. It was a genuine mistake. I don't want to be struck off.'

'It's okay,' says Dom, poking her in the ribs, 'lighten up. I don't always mean what I say. Still, don't you think it's odd that we all know we're going to die, but we don't have any say in how or when?'

Ruth tries to find the right words.

'I'm glad of that. But you could say the same about life. We don't have any say in how, when, or even where, we're born.'

The silence between them is measured by the barely discernible rise and fall of the bedclothes that comes with their breathing.

He turns to face her. 'My scars. I promised I'd tell you about them.'

'You did.' Ruth nestles against Dominic's shoulder wondering what's coming next.

'Difficult to know where to start. It was an accident. A horrific accident.'

Ruth feels Dominic's muscles tense. 'I understand if you'd rather not tell me, Dom.' Her words are ignored.

'My father was a pilot. Born and brought up in the UK, although his father and grandmother fled Armenia during the First World War. He met my mother when she was working as an air stewardess. By all accounts they were a glamorous couple. Things started to go wrong when they got married and I came on the scene.' The resentment in his voice becomes apparent. 'My mother gave up work to look after me, while my father was often away for days at a time in far-flung destinations. The cracks set in when he started to have a series of affairs. I don't know how old I was when that started. It's not the kind of thing you notice when you're a child, but my mother tolerated it for several years apparently.'

Ruth studies a silvery cobweb hanging from the lampshade above them.

'What I remember most is the fights they would have when he came home. Shouting long after I had gone to bed. Clanging doors. Shattered crockery.'

'Poor darling.'

'He got into debt. Started drinking heavily.' His voice wavers.

'Dom, you don't have to go on if you don't want to.'

As if he hasn't heard Dominic continues, his voice like a fine veneer which could crack at any time. 'One night, in the middle of summer, I had gone to bed but couldn't sleep in the stuffy heat. I could hear muffled voices downstairs which gradually got louder. My father was shouting and swearing. Then I heard the clatter of footsteps on the wooden staircase outside my room. My mother screaming, "Get away from me."'

He pauses and swallows. 'I heard my father shriek, "this time I'm going to kill you, you stupid bitch" and her pleading for mercy. I got out of bed and looked around my room for something to defend my mother with. I lifted my cricket bat and went into their bedroom.'

Ruth feels the sweat pooling at the back of her neck and unsticks her body from Dom's skin.

'When I entered their room all I could see was the hulk of my father's frame hunched over my mother. He had her up against the window and his hands round her neck. She was making horrible noises like she was snoring.'

'Oh my God, how aw–'

'I didn't think twice. I took a swing at his head. He was taken by surprise, let go of my mother and lashed out at me. I lost my balance and fell through the plated glass. I was eight years old.'

Ruth sits up and brings her hand to her mouth. She feels sick. Dominic lies impassive, staring at the ceiling. 'I ruptured my spleen and smashed my forearm in three places.'

Ruth brings her hand down gently to rest on Dominic's thigh. She looks at the atrophied musculature and can only feel pity, not revulsion. Volkmann's ischaemic contracture. That's what she remembers from her final exams, though she'd never seen it until now. The wasted muscles deprived of their normal blood supply, in the aftermath of a nasty fracture. The scarred tissues pulling his hand into a claw deformity as the tissues healed. The chronic pain he continued to endure against the background of a splintered family. He turns to look at her and a muscle twitches in his cheek. 'Ruth, I owe you an apology. I've been such a shit recently. Things haven't been easy for me.'

'Darling, don't be silly. I'm the one who should be apologising. What you've just told me…I had no idea. That's awful.'

'My father's dead now. Cirrhosis of the liver.' He grinds his teeth. 'Poor bastard. My parents split up when I had my accident. Went their separate ways. My mother brought me up on her own, then many years later, long after I'd left home, she re-married and moved to the States. She came back once, when Bella was born. But I don't kid myself that that was to see me. It was to see her new granddaughter. Haven't heard from her since.'

Ruth nods, her words inadequate.

'Of course Bella's my main concern now. I'm so worried about her,' Dominic continues.

'I know, I know. I understand.'

'I haven't told you, but she's got to go for a scan tomorrow.'

'A scan? What scan?'

'The doctors think she may have scarring on her kidneys.'

Ruth's shoulders drop. 'Because of her urine infections?'

'I think so.'

'That's par for the course, Dom. Routine. It shouldn't be serious,' she says, trying to reassure him.

She lifts his hand up to her lips and kisses it, and is caught by a sudden draught, as the duvet is lifted. Dominic arches his back. The moment is gone.

'What time is it?' he says, peering over her shoulder, towards the bedside clock.

'Ten past ten,' she says, rolling back and screwing her eyes tight to focus on the illuminated display.

'I said I would be back around eleven.' His head lolls back on the pillow.

'Ruth?'

'Yeah?'

'I hope you understand that it's easier if we meet here for the time being. For Bella's sake. I mean, it's early days.'

'Of course.'

Her words curl away from her in disappointment. Of course she understands. But she wants to prolong this moment. Now. Here. In her bed.

The expression in his eyes changes. 'I'm going to have a shower, then I better get going.'

Alone in her bed that night she mulls over the details of his accident. His words about death had unsettled her but now she understands. That's his way of coping. He's been dealt more than his fair share of death, after all. Pulling the duvet around her, she falls asleep to the sound of a solitary owl, calling from the cemetery at the bottom of her road.

18

BELLA

Daddy is happy today. As they set off for her picture test, his head bobs up and down, as he sings.

'Miss Polly had a dolly that was sick, sick, sick, So she called for the doctor to come quick, quick, quick… join in Bella,' he says. 'Come on, you know the words.'

She doesn't want to join in. She cuddles Roo and looks out the window. Cars go past. They stop at a zebra thing and a lady crosses the road holding hands with three children. The little girl on the end is skipping. She has bright yellow shoes. When the car starts again Bella turns her head and watches the yellow shoes disappear.

When they get to where they are going, Daddy gets cross.

'Would you look at that idiot,' he says. 'I was going to go in that space.' They drive round and round in an upwards circle. 'Here we go,' he says, and stops. 'Come on, Bella. We better hurry up, we're going to be late.' He goes over to a door and presses a button then says, 'This is taking too long, let's go down the stairs.' By the time they get to the bottom of the stairs Bella can feel her chest going, 'BOOM, BOOM, BOOM.'

'Now remember,' Daddy says, as they find the right room 'you need to keep still when you are having your picture taken. It won't take long then we can go home.'

There's a lady with glasses standing behind a desk.

'Mr. Peterson?' she says, then she looks down at Bella and smiles. She has a big hairy spot on her chin. 'And this must be Isabella? Excellent. Take a seat, please. Won't be long.'

The room has that funny smell. There's a little table in the corner with comics on it. Bella sits next to her daddy. She has a funny feeling in her tummy and doesn't want to look at the comics. A lady with lots of teeth appears.

'Isabella Peterson?'

Suddenly she's frightened. She sits back on the chair as far as she can go. Hangs on to her daddy's arm. But Daddy peels her fingers off his sleeve. Slides her forward.

'Yes,' he says to Big Teeth Lady. 'Here we are.'

'Lovely,' she says, as she holds out her hand. The boom in Bella's T shirt is getting bigger. 'You can come in with us too, Mr. Peterson. It shouldn't take long.'

Bella sinks to the floor, clinging to Daddy's trousers. She starts to cry. Her tears sting. She's not going anywhere.

'Sshh', says Daddy. He calls her a silly billy. If she lets go of his trousers he'll come in with her. And if she promises to keep still she can have some Smarties when they get home.

Big Teeth Lady is waiting.

They follow her into another room with lots of cartoons on the ceiling. A lady with frizzy hair is there. Frizzy Hair Lady lifts Bella onto the bed and tells her to lie down. The boom boom gets bigger and quicker, as if it's going to run away. Bella thinks the lady puts some bags of flour by her legs so she can't move. From here she can see the pictures on the ceiling. It's Alice in Wonderland and the White Rabbit and a whiskery man with a funny hat. Frizzy Hair Lady squeezes her hand, while Big Teeth Lady says, 'Now my little princess, I want you to look up at the ceiling and tell me what you can see.' But Bella looks down and sees that Big Teeth Lady has a tube in her hand. The jelly on her tummy is cold and she tries to wriggle. Frizzy Hair Lady is holding her so tight she can't move. She starts to cry.

'Oh, it's okay, Isabella,' says Big Teeth Lady. 'Let's sing a song. Old MacDonald had a farm Ee-I-Ee-I-O.' She makes moo noises, then oink noises, then quack noises. Bella's nose is full of snot. She buttons her eyes shut.

Big Teeth Lady is making miaow, miaow noises when Bella opens them again. 'All finished!' she says. 'Over to you, Daddy.'

Daddy lifts her up, carries her outside and puts her down.

'What a good girl you've been, Bella.' He has his pretend smile.

Bella wipes away a drool of snot and tears with the back of her hand.

'It's okay, darling,' says Daddy, but she yanks her arm away from him.

'I hate you,' she screams, stamping her feet. Hot tears run down her cheeks, snot gurgles at the back of her throat. 'You never say what you mean!' Her shoulders shake up and down, then the sick comes spilling out all over the floor. Her legs feel very wobbly, then suddenly she is lying on the floor and kicking her feet in the air.

'I – want- my - mummy!' she sobs, as smelly wet strands of hair cling to her dress.

19

RUTH

MAY 2005

D r. Alison Winterbourne sits at the computer table in Ruth's office and pushes her spectacles through her hair. 'I just need to run the confidentiality procedure past you again, given your involvement with the Professional Standards Committee.' She smiles benignly, accentuating the latticed wrinkles round her eyes.

Ruth nods. She grasps Alison's agenda. Getting ready for her appraisal has been a bit like gathering information for her tax return. She's been so pre-occupied thinking about Dominic and Bella that procrastination has intervened until the last minute. She's not sure she's fully prepared. A sudden movement under the desk alerts her to a carrier bag, which is twitching like a motorised toy. She delves inside it and extracts her phone. Now is not the time for interruptions. Just as she presses the phone's 'off' switch she can see a text from Dom, but her colleague's eyes are boring into her. Bad timing. The screen goes black.

'Right,' says Alison, visibly relaxing as she takes a sip of her coffee. 'Let's get started then.' She settles her spectacles on her nose again and leans forward towards the computer screen, near enough for Ruth to observe the grey roots raked across her scalp, like wood ash in a blackened grate.

Over the next couple of hours Ruth painstakingly goes through all the audits she's completed, the tutorials she's supervised with the trainee, the meetings she's attended, the on-line modules she's completed. The discussion is intense, punctuated solely by Ruth getting up to switch off the radiator and open the window when the air feels so dense with dialogue that it's suffocating. The pineapple smell of the air freshener is making her nauseous. Briefly she thinks about her phone. She's itching to check what Dominic has said. Can she excuse herself to go to the loo or offer her colleague another coffee? Her colleague continues unabashed. She pushes her spectacles back and forth on her head at frequent intervals and the conversation is supportive, her demeanour sympathetic.

'I have to say,' says Alison, as she shuffles sheets of paper on the desk, 'despite all the stress you have been under over recent months, you've been very thorough in demonstrating your ability to keep up to date. It's not often we get the chance, as doctors, to take stock of what we've done and applaud it but there's a lot here to be commended. Well done.'

Ruth quickly shifts her focus to the photograph above the examination couch. She knows that if she looks directly at her colleague she may burst into tears. She can't help it when people are being sympathetic towards her. The picture is a panorama of mountains and lakes, peaks with the lustre of icing sugar reflected in the blue lagoons like candied almonds. It reminds her of her childhood holidays in the Lake District.

She composes herself and mirrors the amiable smile.

'Thank you.'

'I can see you've completed a proposed learning log for next year. I have just one more recommendation to add. Child safeguarding. Am I right in saying that your last update would have been when you were in Australia?'

Ruth nods.

'Fair enough. Not a bad idea to complete another module. Familiarise yourself with local protocols and current procedures.'

'Yes, of course. I'm sure that can easily be arranged.'

'Great. Well, just to round up, I'm aware that the investigation into Alan Tremayne's complaint about his mother is still ongoing. However it's very good news that the Professional Standards Committee is satisfied with your learning from the Prescribing complaint.' She pauses briefly to extract a tissue from her sleeve and blow her nose.

Ruth's pulse quickens. She braces herself for what might come next.

'I understand that the Medicines Management Team has issued a reminder to all practices urging care when prescribing oral morphine solution. They've removed the concentrated solution from its formulary. So, as far as your involvement goes, that case is now closed.'

For Ruth, the relief is too much. Closed? Resolved? Concluded? She has kept her emotions in check until now but can't hold back the tears any longer. She reaches under the computer screen for the box of tissues and sits in silence dabbing her eyes. It seems like an uncomfortably long interval before she looks up again, but when she does Alison is smiling.

'It's okay, Ruth,' she says, propelling her chair, on its castors, to within an arm's length. 'I'm here to support you. It's been a stressful time. Everything's okay.'

Ruth has to look away again. She pinches the skin on her fingers until her flesh turns white.

Alison's spectacles are back on, as she scrutinises her watch. 'Ten past one,' she says. 'Okay now, is there anything else we haven't discussed that you would like covered?'

Ruth is about to ask her if she would like another cup of coffee, but there's a knock at the door. She looks at Alison and shrugs her shoulders, as if to say 'I'm sorry, I told the staff I didn't want any interruptions,' but before she can continue the door opens and a receptionist has her head round the door.

'Dr. Cooper, I'm sorry to interrupt. I know today's your half day but all the doctors are out on their visits. There's a lady who's turned up saying her baby's not very well. I've told her that the surgery is closed for lunch but she insists on being seen. I wouldn't normally do this, but the child doesn't look well. I'm worried it might be an emergency. Could you come and look, please?'

Ruth looks at her doctor colleague who nods. Alison stands up and gathers her papers, which she arranges in her briefcase. 'Please. Go ahead. We're finished here.'

Ruth turns to the receptionist. 'Okay, Julie,' she says. 'Can you take her into the Treatment Room, please, and I'll come along in a sec.' She turns to Alison. 'Thanks again. Actually it's been a huge relief to talk through some of my issues.'

'You're welcome. I hope it was helpful. I can hang around a bit, if you like, in case you need a hand.'

'Thanks,' says Ruth, her features softening into a magnanimous smile. 'Well if you're not in a hurry and don't mind?'

Ruth picks up her ID card to lock her computer and, gathering a few pieces of equipment, leads Alison out of the room. They walk along the corridor towards the open door of the Treatment Room but Ruth quickens her pace when she hears the desperate pleas for help coming from within. Both doctors race into the room. A woman, Ruth guesses to be in her twenties, is pacing up and down with a blanketed bundle in her arms. Ruth peels back the crocheted cover to reveal a baby, probably between six and twelve months old. Its fragile frame is pale and mottled, it has a tense, bulging soft spot on top of its skull and a speck of froth at the corner of its mouth.

'Hi,' she says to the young woman, whom she doesn't recognise. 'I'm Dr. Cooper. This is Dr. Winterbourne. We're here to help,' she says immediately taking hold of the child and placing it on the examining couch. Its little body feels as rigid as a board and it's making so much effort to breathe that it grunts. Ruth feels a momentary flash of panic but reaches over to the resuscitation trolley, slides open the top drawer and pulls out some equipment to assist the baby's breathing.

'How old is this little one?' she asks the woman. 'What's happened today?'

The woman says her little boy Elliot is seven months old, has had a temperature for twenty four hours, been off his food and she was getting him out of the car in the surgery car park when his eyes rolled back and he started jerking. Ruth's hands are a blur of movement, as she listens to the mother, whose name she learns is Bryony. Ruth looks up at the receptionist, who is hovering on the periphery.

'Julie, can you ring 999 for me,' she says. It surprises her to hear her own voice sounding so unruffled and authoritative. With a nod of her head she indicates towards the mother and continues, 'And please take Bryony with you and get all the patient details off the computer. Tell ambulance control that an immediate response is required.' She looks at Alison, as Julie hastens out of the room. 'No point in wasting time.' She has placed a mask over the baby's face and Alison assists by attaching the connecting plastic tubing to an oxygen cylinder.

'There's a pulse oximeter on the counter there,' says Ruth, gesturing in the direction of the sink. Alison picks up the plastic clip, with its winking red display, and peels back the covers on the baby to expose his legs. A blotchy rash is encroaching the creases of his chubby thighs. Purple and red blooms on a torpid landscape. The doctors lock eyes with one another. They are both thinking exactly the same thing. Meningococcal septicaemia.

'The emergency drugs cupboard is over there,' says Ruth, signalling in the direction of the far wall, as she secures the oxygen mask over the baby's face. 'Actually, could you take over here and I can get the antibiotic ready?'

Alison moves forward. As they swap roles Ruth can see that the baby's lips have pinked up a little. She senses her own pulse bounding. She steels herself to take slow, deep breaths.

Ruth swings open the cupboard door and picks up a vial of white powder, checking the label. 'Benzyl penicillin. For intramuscular or intravenous use.' She looks down at the tiny child on the bed. Her hands are shaking and she's not sure she trusts her clinical acumen to administer that much drug into a tiny vein. Especially now that his circulation has virtually collapsed. It'll have to be intramuscular. Swiftly she makes up the injection, just as a paramedic enters the room. Thank God. It's okay. She's not on her own. She can do this. She focusses on the task in hand, as the paramedic watches in silence. She draws the syringe back, as white liquid fills its chamber, and looks across at Alison. 'Three hundred milligrams benzyl penicillin for intramuscular use. Check.'

Alison checks the vial and nods in agreement. 'Yes. Three hundred milligrams benzyl penicillin.

Correct.' Ruth slides the needle into the baby's thigh just as another paramedic appears, wheeling in a stretcher trolley. The female paramedic nods at her male counterpart.

'All ready for you, Doc. What've you got here, then?' Ruth glances up just in time to see the male paramedic flashing a look of consternation towards his female counterpart. Alarm spirals in Ruth's stomach. These guys know an emergency when they see one. The paramedics both step forward, their gloved hands moving briskly over equipment. In a reflex action Ruth steps back. There's a tacit understanding that they need to act swiftly.

'Seven month old boy. Pyrexial illness for twenty four hours. On arrival possible convulsion in the car park. Temp thirty nine five. Capillary refill time more than two seconds. Sats ninety two in air. Heart rate a hundred and sixty. Tachypnoea of sixty.' Ruth pauses for breath herself, her mind is racing, her face feels hot, but she feels in control, 'Non-blanching purpuric rash on limbs. Suspected meningococcal septicaemia. Given oxygen. Sats now ninety seven. Three hundred milligrams benzyl pencillin administered left thigh.' She checks her watch, 'One twenty seven pm'

'Thanks, Doc,' says the green-suited healthcare professional, moving towards the baby's head and observing the rise and fall of its tiny chest. 'Sats are fluctuating,' he says, looking at the pulse oximeter, and turning to his colleague. 'Better keep the mask on, and this little fella's going to need a drip. He turns to Ruth. 'Have you rung the hospital?' he asks, as he scoops the baby in his arms and gently transfers him to the trolley.

'Not yet,' replies Ruth. 'Just about to.'

'Is that mother in reception?' the second paramedic asks. 'She'll be coming with us I take it?' Ruth nods. Perspiration trickles down her back. She feels as if she's just run a race.

'I'll follow you out to the ambulance,' says Ruth, 'then I can explain to Mum what's going on, while you're loading up. Thanks, guys, you were here really quickly.'

'Luckily we were just round the corner at The Orchards when we got the call,' says the man, flicking up the stabilising struts on the trolley with his foot. He looks at Ruth. 'Better get a move on, then,' he says and he disappears out of the room.

Ruth looks across at Alison, who is leaning back on the sink. She looks flushed but she smiles.

'I'll leave you to it then, Ruth.' She picks up her bag. 'I've only ever come across that twice in my career. Well done. You'll be needing that second cup of coffee now.'

Ruth walks over to her and gives her a hug. 'I'm glad you were here.'

'Never forget, Ruth, you're a good doctor.'

Ruth gives a half-hearted smile. 'Well, that's enough excitement for one day. I hope he's going to be okay. I'll let you know what happens. Thanks for the opportunity to talk today. I really appreciate it.'

Ruth's legs have a gelatinous fluidity, as she leaves the room. She follows the ambulance personnel down the corridor, past the reception desk where the baby's mother is standing. Bryony is on her phone but she immediately puts it down, and a look of panic darts across her face. She rushes over to the trolley and clutches at the little boy's blanket.

'He's going to be okay, isn't he?' she says to Ruth.

'He's very poorly,' says Ruth softly, 'but he's in good hands. I'm just going to ring the children's specialist at the hospital, to let them know you're on your way. You can travel with Elliot in the ambulance, but it's really important that you go now. It's urgent.'

Bryony tugs at Ruth's sleeve. 'But he is going to be okay, isn't he?' The colour has drained from her face. 'I need to speak to my partner.' She lifts her phone back up. 'I'm just trying to get hold of him. He's at work. I need to see if he can meet me at the hospital.'

Ruth nodes encouragingly. 'Phone him from the ambulance.' She looks up at Julie who comes round the other side of the reception desk and puts a hand on Bryony's shoulder.

There's a clash of the front door and the female

paramedic appears again. 'We need to get going,' she says and Ruth can hear the tension in her voice.

Quickly Ruth ushers Bryony to the front door and into the ambulance. As she moves away she can hear the young woman's tremulous voice, 'Yes, I need to speak to him now. Please tell him it's an emergency. A desperate emergency. Yes. Please. Now. His name is Alan Tremayne.'

20
RUTH

A stillness descends in Ruth's consulting room. The phone lines are silent. She slumps forward, her elbows on the desk, her head in her hands. It's as if a high centrifugal force has been spinning her thoughts out of control, but now it's stopped and her mind is in a state of collapse. The baby might die. The thought was unbearable. She'd done everything she could and acted quickly, but what if that wasn't enough?

Elliot Tremayne, Elliot Tremayne. She hadn't made the connection, until she heard Bryony utter her partner's name down the phone. Alan Tremayne. Margaret's son. Her complainant. Fear grips her. What if Elliot doesn't survive? A double blow for the Tremayne family.

She switches on the computer and checks the Tremayne household details:

Bryony Marsh age 28
Alan Tremayne age 31
Morgan Tremayne age 3
Elliot Tremayne age 7 months

She needs to share this with somebody. But who? She needs more time to think. A rumbling in her gut reminds her she's not had anything to eat since six this morning. She lifts up the carrier bag from under the desk and heads upstairs.

The staffroom is deserted. The slatted blinds are half drawn, the infringing afternoon sun kept at bay, but the room feels airless and humid. She walks over to the window and releases the catch. The radiator is on high and the sudden intake of fresh air causes her to sway a little, as she wedges the casement open. Steadying herself she walks over to the sink, and fills the kettle, which churns with flakes of disturbed lime scale.

She flops down on a low sofa. The coffee table is scattered with the scree of hasty tea breaks. Back copies of *Woman's Own,* their pages jagged where recipes have been tugged out, litter the table top next to copies of the *British Medical Journal*. She picks up a magazine and flicks through the pages absentmindedly, her thoughts drifting to the turmoil the Tremayne family will be going through. First Margaret, now Elliot. Why is life so unfair sometimes? Take Bella, for instance. To grow up never knowing how it feels to be clutched to her mother's bosom, to never experience her mother's laughter, her pride, her tears. Instead she must vie for the attention of a father who is contending with his own grief and his demons from the past. Dominic's revelation about his accident had come as a shock to her. But sympathy for him had soon given way to anger at his father, and revulsion at the injustice that had been caused. At least Dominic felt he could take her into his confidence. As they had got to know each other more intimately over the past few weeks she felt the feeling was mutual. They trusted each other. With time she hoped Bella would trust her too. Hopefully it wouldn't be long before Dominic relented to letting her stay overnight at his house.

Dominic. *Dominic.* She'd forgotten about the text message. She scrabbles for her phone in the depths of the plastic carrier bag, extracting two satsumas and a soggy tomato sandwich as the door opens. Paul Franklin walks in and jerks his head back in surprise.

'Ruth. I thought it was your half day?'

'It is. I'm just having a quick breather but I'm finished for the day.'

'How nice. I've got half an hour before my Minor Ops Clinic starts. Mind if I join you?'

'Please do. Kettle's just boiled.' She shuffles along to the end of the couch, moving papers.

There's a rumble and a click and Paul's head is clouded in steam. He flicks the lid of the pedal bin with his foot, as he discards a tea bag, comes over to the sofa and sits down.

'So, how has your morning been?'

Ruth utters a polite laugh. 'Mm, well now,' she says, adjusting her cushion, 'how long have you got? This could take a while.' She's not sure if she detects a flicker of concern dart across his face, but it soon disappears when she smiles at him.

'I had my appraisal this morning.'

'How did it go?'

'Better than expected, to be honest. The Professional Standards Committee has closed my case on the morphine prescribing incident.'

Paul nods. 'That is good news. Actually I saw the e mail from Medicines Management. The concentrated morphine solution has been removed from the formulary. Makes sense.' He reaches over the table, helps himself to a biscuit from a tin, and appears to scrutinise it in closer detail before biting off the end. 'I'm pleased for you, Ruth. Nobody deserves to go through all that stress. Things have to go through official channels, I get that. It's just a shame that it has to take so long.' There's a genuine warmth in his expression.

She clears her throat. 'But that wasn't the main drama of the morning.'

He narrows his eyes a fraction. 'What do you mean?'

'D'you know Bryony Marsh? Twenty-eight-year old mother of two kids. Lives on the Bramwell Estate?'

Paul looks puzzled. 'Tell me more.'

'She brought in her seven-month-old baby over lunchtime. We were closed but Julie heard her battering on the door. Turns out the baby was in extremis. Meningococcal septicaemia, I'm sure of it. Purpuric rash, bulging fontanelle, grunting, rigid, had the full complement.'

'Dear God. What happened?'

'We resuscitated the baby in the Treatment Room. Alison, my appraiser, gave me a hand.'

'Thank goodness you were here.'

'Mm, I just hope he survives.' Ruth's voice starts to waver. 'But there's something else you should know.'

'There is?'

'The child. It's Alan Tremayne's son. Margaret Tremayne's grandchild.'

Paul leans forward and rests his elbows on his knees, his chin cupped in his hands. Ruth can sense his thought processes at work.

'Ah, of course. Yes, I know the family well. I just didn't make the connection when you told me the mum's name. She's got another child who's about three. I referred the kid to the cardiologists for a persistent cardiac murmur. Turns out it was innocent.'

Ruth's eyes widen. 'Really? I wasn't aware of that. That might explain why he feels so strongly about his mother's case.'

'Maybe.' He stands up and smooths his trousers. 'Goodness, you could have done without that excitement this morning. Well done.' He starts to walk away then thinks better of it and turns round. 'Do you want me to follow up the case this afternoon?'

'I'm going to ring the hospital later. Thanks for offering but I can handle it.'

'Well, keep me posted, won't you?' he says, and he hurries out of the room.

★

Ruth glances at her watch. Just after two o'clock. It's so tempting to kick off her shoes and stretch out on the sofa but she knows she'd fall asleep and that's such a waste of her afternoon off. After this morning's drama she hasn't the energy to do much else. She decides to check her messages. Fuck. Her phone. She'd been meaning to check. She removes her phone from the carrier bag and switches it on. Four missed calls from Dom. Four? One voicemail. But it's not from Dom. Just her local garage advising that her MOT is due. She rings Dom. It goes straight through to voicemail. She hesitates, then leaves a message.

'Darling, it's Ruth. Sorry I missed your calls. I had to switch my phone off for my appraisal. Hope everything's okay. I'll try again later.'

She looks at the call history. Four calls sent over the space of two hours. Her plan for her afternoon off is now very clear.

21
RUTH

Ruth reaches the roundabout onto the by-pass and turns left, instead of right. Flicking her attention between the clock and the speedometer she accelerates so she can reach Byefield before Dominic leaves to pick Bella up from school.

There's an afternoon drama on the radio about domestic violence. Ruth tightens her hands round the steering wheel, only loosening her grip when she comes to a standstill at a red traffic light.

Ten minutes later she turns down the High Street, past the Rose and Crown, along the perimeter of the park and into Tindall St.

Cars are parked on either side of the street of Victorian townhouses, leaving room for only one line of traffic. She sighs in frustration when she sees a bin lorry sibilating along the road, like a bronchitic pausing for breath every few minutes. Squeezing her car into a gap on the roadside, she walks the last few hundred yards.

As she circumvents the wheelie bins obstructing the pavement it's obvious that it isn't just the rubbish truck that is holding up the traffic. An ambulance is stationary further up the street, its back doors open and blue light flashing. Ruth quickens her step then breaks into a trot when she realises it's parked outside number twenty three and Dominic's front door is wide open.

The pounding of her heart seems to fill her entire chest cavity, squeezing the breath out of her. She swings back the wrought iron gate and bounds up the stone steps to the front door, catching hold of the balustrade, as she stumbles in her haste.

'Dominic? Dominic!' she shouts.

A woman in a spotty raincoat emerges from the front door. She stops when she sees Ruth, her eyes flashing.

'The ambulance,' gasps Ruth. 'What happened?'

The woman looks her up and down. Her mouth moves like a guppy coming up for air but no words emerge.

'I'm a doctor,' says Ruth, clutching the woman's arm. 'Maybe I can help?'

The woman's features harden. 'Are you Ruth?'

Ruth nods.

'Thank goodness you're here. I'm Courtney. Babysitter. I dropped in on my way home from school. Dominic had already called the ambulance. They're with Bella now. I better get going now that I'm no longer needed.'

'Oh my God,' says Ruth, pushing past Courtney.

Shuffling backwards, whilst holding the steel rim of a chair, is a figure in a green uniform. A second paramedic holds the opposite edge of the frame and gives directions, as they navigate a route outside. They halt as Ruth enters. A head appears, filling the gap at the top of the basement stairs. Dominic's face is ashen, his eyes flash with alarm. Ruth looks down at the ambulance personnel's precious cargo and sees a small figure, like a mannequin, her face covered with an oxygen mask, her chest inflated like the stretched skin of a new football. Bella.

Ruth stands to one side and lets the paramedics pass.

Dominic tugs at Ruth's arm. 'Asthma,' he says. 'Her cold had got worse over the last twenty four hours. I kept her off school this morning…but…this afternoon…she couldn't breathe' His words escape in a brittle staccato. She takes his arm and follows Bella outside to the ambulance.

'How is she?' she asks the paramedic, as he lifts the chair into the back of the ambulance and secures it. The ambulance man looks across at Dominic.

'It's okay. She's a doctor.' Dominic says. 'You can explain.'

'Acute bronchospasm,' replies the paramedic, 'Sats have improved with a nebuliser and she's had steroids but we're taking her in so the Paeds can cast an eye on her.'

Ruth clambers into the back of the ambulance, kneels down beside Bella and squeezes her hand. It feels clammy and limp. 'It's okay, darling. You're going to be all right. Daddy is coming with you.' Bella looks at her. Her pupils widen like spreading ink blots, her breath barely audible over the soft draught of the oxygen tank. Ruth strokes the top of her head then jumps down onto the road. 'You must go with her, Dominic,' she says grasping his sleeve and pushing him forward.

'I'll follow later in my car.' His voice sounds feeble, afraid.

'Go now, Dom,' urges Ruth, 'She needs her Dad.'

His vacillation fills the space between them.

She extends her arm. 'Here give me the keys and I'll lock up for you. Give me a ring when you get to the hospital. Let me know if there's anything you need and I can bring it down for you.'

'All ready,' pipes up the ambulance driver. He is standing in the middle of the road and has his right palm upturned against the stationary traffic.

'Go on, Dom,' repeats Ruth softly.

He reaches into his pocket and hands over the keys.

'Okay,' he says. He looks defeated. 'I'll call you as soon as I get there.'

He climbs into the back of the vehicle and the door slams shut.

22

RUTH

Ruth follows the sound of voices downstairs to the kitchen. The radio crackles with static as voices come and go. She switches it off and, as silence descends, she surveys the scene. The kitchen table is littered with papers. Some are piled high in one corner and her eye-line is drawn to the top of the stack. It's a list and she can just decipher the words:

1. Script.
2. Lucky Pagoda deadline.
3. Arch.Dis.Child.
4. Pride of Britain Awards.

Odd. She lifts her fingers off the sticky tablecloth. In

the corner a pedal bin overflows with foil trays, smattered with rice and yellow stains. Particles of food litter the gas rings on the cooker. Above it is a framed photo of a young woman, looking directly at her. Her shoulder-length blonde hair flies away from her freckled face, as if whipped by the wind. She looks happy, confident, sexy. Madeleine reminds Ruth of when she was a student.

The clock on the cooker reads three twenty. It will take the ambulance about twenty minutes to get to the hospital then at least another hour, maybe more, before Dominic will have any news. She feels an overwhelming temptation to roll up her sleeves and tidy up, but worries that might be interpreted as interfering. So what? It's the least she can do to be helpful.

She looks under the sink and pulls out a roll of black bin liners. Shreds of plastic wrapping, dotted with mouse droppings dust the shelf. A container of mouse bait has been breached and, as she tugs at it, she knocks a few bottles to the floor. To her dismay an insidious stain, the colour of tinned rice pudding, starts to spread across the lino, and the smell of polish assaults her nostrils.

'Damn,' she says out loud. Rinsing a cloth in the sink she mops up the spill, then reaches into the dark recesses under the sink and extracts all the bottles, lining them up on the floor tiles. Her eyes alight on a tall aquamarine bottle. Gin? Why? Why would Dominic keep gin under the sink when he's teetotal? Carefully she replaces the bottle as far back in the cupboard as possible. Next she presses her foot on the stainless steel pedal bin and lifts up the ends of a black bin liner, as some of its contents vomit onto the floor. She crouches down to pick up a couple of silvery blister packs and looks more closely at the labels: ibuprofen and gabapentin. She rocks on her heels taking this in. Both painkillers. She knows Dominic takes ibuprofen for his headaches. But gabapentin? Why would he take that? She chews on her thumb nail. Poor guy, he must be suffering more than he admits. The burden of chronic pain must be unbearable. She ties the ends of the bin liner together, lifts it, and lugs it up to the front door.

Assorted mail has spewed through the letterbox and, as she picks it up, an air mail envelope catches her eye. It bears the distinctive U.S stamp of a bald eagle and has a postmark from Miami Beach. The address is handwritten and, as she turns it over she reads the sender's name: V. Zuckerman. Didn't Dominic mention that his mother lives in America? She picks it up again and, inexplicably, sniffs it for any trace of scent. Then she ascends the next flight of stairs.

Bella's bedroom door is closed, but the door next to it is partially ajar. Curiosity gets the better of her. She pushes it open a few inches. Sparsely furnished, there's an old dressing table with a liver–spotted mirror, some cardboard boxes on a pale lino floor, and a smell which Ruth can't quite place, like a secret held close between the pages of a musty old book. She retreats and pulls the door close towards her. There's another room, next to the bathroom, its door open sufficiently wide for Ruth to see moving crystals of light reflected on the French grey walls. She walks in and the double bed dips as she lies down. She closes her eyes and enjoys the tranquillity for a few minutes, feeling like a latter–day Goldilocks. A furtive excitement teases her. Dominic's bed. How long before he relents and agrees to her sharing this bed, as well as her own?

She sits up and brushes her hair free of her collar, knocking her earring which falls to the floor.

'Oh, God,' she mutters, as she dives down and pats the wool pile around her. There's no sign of the gold twist anywhere. Tentatively she lifts the lamp from the bedside table, switches it on and directs its beam under the bed. She cocks her head to the side so that it's parallel to the floor and scans the area carefully. Soon she spots the tiny golden seed, but not before her eyes have alighted on a plastic bag over spilling with medicines. She flattens her body on the floor and reaches under the bed to pull it nearer. Gabapentin, diazepam, codeine, tizanidine –

A loud chime of the doorbell makes her freeze. It comes again. This time the ring is longer and more insistent. Shit. It's probably Dominic. He doesn't have a key. She shoves the bag under the bed and flees downstairs.

A woman stands on the front doorstep. Probably in her forties. Straw-coloured hair, scraped into a doughnut. Mismatched glass beads dangle from her earlobes, others twist round her neck on leather laces. Cheesecloth dress. Crumpled cardigan. She lifts up the lanyard round her neck and flashes an ID card.

'Afternoon. Brenda Madingley, Byefield Social Services,' she says, and before Ruth can reply she holds out a toy kangaroo. 'I found this on the step.' Ruth takes it and turns to put it on the hall table. Turning back she is met with a hint of cheap scent and body odour, as the woman crosses the threshold.

'Took me ages to find somewhere to park,' she says, adjusting the shoulder strap of her bag, which is bulging with plastic folders. 'Is it always this busy?'

Ruth shrugs her shoulders and feels almost apologetic. 'Excuse me if I look a little confused,' she says. 'Are you sure you've come to the right place?'

'Mr. Peterson, Twenty Three Tindall St?' she says, pulling out one of the folders and reading an address label. 'He should be expecting me.' Her features soften. 'He is here, isn't he?'

'I'm afraid not,' says Ruth. 'We've had a bit of a crisis this afternoon. Oh and I'm Ruth, by the way. Dr. Ruth Cooper. I'm a family friend.' She pauses. It puzzles her that a social worker has come knocking on Dominic's door. She's sure there's a rational explanation. And she recognises that look on the social worker's face. She's got a busy caseload of visits to get through. She's wasted precious time finding a parking space. And now she's got to go back to the office and say she's had a fruitless trip. Only to come back and repeat the experience another day. Ruth knows exactly how that feels. 'Would you like a cup of tea?' she says, sensing the woman's defeat.

They go downstairs and, as Brenda sits at the kitchen table, Ruth lifts some magazines from the coffee table and places them discreetly on top of the pile of bills by Brenda's elbow.

'You've just missed Mr. Peterson,' says Ruth, opening and closing cupboard doors in the search for teabags and hoping that Brenda doesn't notice how unfamiliar she is in these surroundings. 'His daughter, Bella, has been taken into hospital.' She notices how Brenda's posture stiffens at this.

'Oh dear, I hope it's not serious.'

'I think she'll be okay. Asthma attack.' Ruth stops suddenly, wondering if she's gone too far by breaching confidentiality, but Brenda is nodding as if Ruth's telling her nothing new. 'Is tea okay, by the way?'

'Thanks, just with milk, please.'

Ruth douses a teabag in a mug, adds a slug of milk and slides it over the table to Brenda.

'I hope you don't mind me asking,' says Brenda, taking a pen out of her bag, and opening her folder, 'but you said you were a family friend. Know the family very well, do you?'

Ruth feels her cheeks colour. 'I've got to know Dominic and Bella quite well in recent months.' The social worker studies her closely. 'Only since his wife, Madeleine, died actually,' Ruth adds, feeling a flicker of guilt. 'I don't think it's been easy for Dominic, being widowed with a young child.'

Brenda says nothing.

'But it's not routine to have Social Services pay you a visit, is it, after a bereavement?'

Brenda leans forward. 'Did Mr. Peterson not mention to you that we had an appointment?'

'He may have done. I haven't seen him for a few days. Bella's been off school with a cold and that's probably what caused her asthma attack. She's not a well child. Recurrent infections, problems with allergies. Bit of a relentless cycle. I've seen it all before.'

'You have?'

'Yes. Oh, I should have explained. I'm a GP at Parkside Medical Centre.'

'With Paul Franklin and Lesley Fellowes?'

'Yes. That practice.'

'And you know Bella quite well?'

'I do. Very well. Lovely little girl. But she's not been well. One infection after another, on top of her allergies. Dominic has been coping so well, all things considered.'

'She's had quite a bit of time off school, though, hasn't she?'

Ruth wonders how she's got into this conversation. The social worker is making her feel quite defensive. She's a fellow professional though. Ruth needs to trust her to keep relevant medical information confidential. 'I know she's had to have various appointments for tests, if that's what you mean,' Ruth continues. 'I think there's been some genuine concern, because her mother had multiple sclerosis. There's a need to see if there's any immunological link with Bella's illnesses. But then, that should all be on her medical records.' She hesitates then continues, 'Obviously she's not my patient but, if she was, I would say that there are legitimate medical reasons for her poor school attendance.'

Brenda nods. She stops scribbling in her notebook and instead picks up her tea.

'That's very helpful, Dr. Cooper. Thank you. Or may I call you Ruth? It's been a while since I popped into Parkside. I used to come to the multi-disciplinary meetings every quarter.' She smiles. 'Work is far too busy these days.' She leans forward clandestinely. 'But as a GP you'll know exactly what I mean.'

She drains her cup then packs her notebook and folder into her bag. 'That was just what I needed,' she says, smiling benignly. 'Thank you very much.' The chair legs grate on the floor as she stands up. 'Now I better get going. I'll look out for you at Parkside next time I pop in.'

23

RUTH

It must be four years since Ruth's last visit to the children's hospital but, as she walks down the main corridor with its toothpaste blue walls and carbolic smell, ambivalent recollections are stirred. As a junior doctor she would walk these deserted corridors at night, the sound of her theatre clogs rebounding off the cold stone floors. She recalls the fatigue she felt on weekends on-call. Often she was beyond sleep as she inserted cannulae through papery thin skin into the tiny veins of little babies. She smiles at the memory of a successful resuscitation or a positive intervention in a seriously ill child.

This evening visitors shuffle along the passages, some engaged in conversation, others with flat expressions, their thoughts internalised. Personnel wearing lanyards hurry past, dodging human obstacles, as if on a busy moving walkway at an airport.

She reaches the lift to Jubilee Ward but sidesteps it and bounds up the stairs clutching a toy kangaroo plus the comics, colouring books and crayons she had bought on the hospital concourse. As she approaches the ward for the under-twelves, the stark clinical ambience of the main corridor changes to one of bright cheerfulness. A mural of giraffes, elephants, lions and cheetahs leads visitors on a colourful safari to the ward entrance.

Ruth lifts her hand to press the intercom just as the door swings open. A woman emerges whom Ruth recognises but can't quite place. Dark hair swept back into a ponytail. Collagen-filled lips. Leggings and an oversized sweatshirt. They exchange glances, then the young woman back-tracks and tugs at Ruth's sleeve.

'Dr. Cooper. It's Bryony. Bryony Marsh. Elliot's mum.'

Ruth stares at the young woman and is transported back to the turbulent scene of the Resuscitation room hours earlier.

'Bryony. Yes. Of course.' She scrutinises her face trying to gauge what she should say next. 'How's Elliot?'

The grip on Ruth's arm gets tighter. 'He's had his lumbar puncture. You were right, Dr. Cooper.' Her voice wavers. 'They reckon that injection you gave him probably saved his life.'

Ruth squeezes Bryony's arm. 'That's good news.'

Bryony releases the grasp and stands back a little.

'I can't thank you enough. The doctors say he's not out of the woods yet but hopefully he's on the mend.'

'I'm glad.'

'Are you going onto the Ward? I can open the door for you.'

Ruth nods and Bryony turns to the keypad on the wall.

'The code is K 259XZ. Save you waiting an age before someone answers.'

'Thanks,' says Ruth, 'keep me posted, won't you?' She leans her shoulder against the heavy ward door, which swings open.

The soft light and muted noise of the ward exudes calm and Ruth looks round for the nurses' station. There's an office door open, and beyond it a young woman is hunched over a computer screen, but she looks up and smiles when Ruth taps gingerly on the wooden frame.

'Excuse me,' Ruth says, 'I'm sorry to bother you but I'm looking for Isabella Peterson.'

The woman swings her chair round ninety degrees and appears to study Ruth's face intently. A widening smile creases her face.

'Ruth? Ruth Cooper! My God, it's been ages.' Her hands curl round the armrests of her chair as she levers herself up. 'The last time I saw you was in the Union Bar. What the hell have you been up to since then?'

The woman's eyes flash with a certain roguishness even though there's a weariness about them. The shoulder-length brown hair has been replaced by a shorter bob, streaked with gold tints. Put her in 'mufti', in the greasy spoon cafe of the Students' Union and her mate from Med School is instantly recognisable.

'Sheena Walker,' Ruth exclaims.

'Henderson, now actually,' her friend interjects.

'How bloody good to see you!'

They hug and Sheena pulls up another chair.

'So, what brings you here?' asks Sheena. She leans back, looking her friend up and down.

'I'm visiting Bella Peterson. Daughter of a friend of mine.'

'Ah, yes, Bella' nods Sheena, 'the little girl in Cubicle 4. I admitted her this afternoon. She's settled now. So you must spare me a few minutes for a catch up. I'm trying to remember the last time our paths crossed. Not since graduation probably?'

Ruth smiles. 'The good old days, eh? Nine years. I can't quite believe it.'

'I know. What have you been up to since then?'

'Oh God, where do I start? Did my GP rotation, including twelve months here in Sick Kids, then went off to Australia. Lasted about eighteen months in Melbourne then decided I missed the UK too much. I've been working as a salaried GP at Parkside for the past nine months. What about you?'

'Specialist paediatric registrar. Decided to do Paeds after my elective at McGill in Montreal. The job here suits me perfectly. It's half General Paeds and half on the Renal Unit. Got married last year too. Steve's a specialist surgical registrar. So we've just got to hope that we can get consultant jobs not too far apart from each other when we're ready to apply.'

Ruth nods, but feels a slight sinking sensation in her stomach at hearing about another contemporary's wedded bliss. 'Sounds good,' she says. 'And that reminds me. Remember Val Escott? I've linked up with her again, since coming back from Oz. Married. Just had her second baby. She works at Mulberry Lane Practice.'

'Really? We must go out for a-'

Their conversation is interrupted by a loud double knock on the door and the soft timbre of a male voice. 'Excuse me, I'm leaving now but I just wanted to say thank you for all your care this afternoon.'

Ruth wheels round at the sound of Dominic's voice and their eyes lock.

They both mouth each other's names but no words

come out. Ruth looks at Sheena and gathers her belongings. 'I better get going. See you again soon.'

'For sure.'

Dominic edges back from the door, but catches Ruth's hand as she brushes past him.

'Ruth,' he says, 'I was going outside to ring you. I can't get a damn signal on this phone.'

She squeezes his fingers. 'That would explain why you haven't returned any of my calls. How's Bella?'

'What were you doing in the office?'

Ruth feels flushed. 'You're not going to believe this,' she says, smiling in an attempt to deflect the accusatory tone. 'I came up here to find you, and it turns out that the paediatric registrar is a girl I trained with.'

'Really?' His eyes flash with menace.

Bewilderment pricks her conscience. 'Yes. I just had a quick catch up with her. Haven't seen her for about nine years. How cool is that? But more to the point, tell me about Bella.'

'She's asleep now. She seems settled.' His tone is flat.

'I've brought some things for her,' says Ruth, lifting up the toy kangaroo. 'I figured she might be missing this.'

Dominic's features soften. 'Come with me, you can see her,' he says, leading her by the hand. 'You can leave it by her bed, then why don't we go for a coffee?'

The door to Bella's cubicle is wide open and

they tip-toe inside. The curtain rail is drawn right back behind the head of the bed. Ruth gazes down at the small bundle engulfed under the large expanse of white, cellular blanket. Bella has her mouth open and is breathing in regular, quiet rasps. Damp tendrils of hair cling to either side of her face and her hand rests on a small teddy bear, her fingers curled loosely round its leg. Carefully Ruth places Roo beside Bella's left shoulder, and deposits the books and crayons on the bedside cabinet. She looks at Dominic with a smile and they both retreat out of the room.

★

It feels odd to be sitting in the hospital canteen as a visitor, rather than a member of staff. Ruth listens to Dominic's update as they sit at a table separated from other diners by a wooden trellis trailing fake vines.

'The doctors have said Bella's asthma is unstable. They're going to keep her in for another forty eight hours or so.'

'Have they said why she's in a cubicle by herself?'

'Yeah, I think it's to keep her in isolation from infection.'

'Really. Seems odd. Especially if they need to keep an eye on her.' Ruth's spoon chinks against the enamel of the coffee mug.

'They've done some more blood tests. Still has a low white count, they told me. Doesn't that make her more susceptible to infections?'

'I guess so. Poor Bella. Listen, Dom. Do you want me to have a word with Sheena and get some more information?'

Dominic seems distracted. His expression has darkened, like a cloudy day, and the space between them feels weighted, like a shifting barometer before a storm. He buries his face in his hands for a few seconds. She leans over the table and strokes his hair but he jerks his head back. When he looks up, Ruth can see that his eyes are glistening.

'No. There's no need. She explained everything to me earlier.' His voice trails away. 'I'm sorry, Ruth. I've not been feeling my usual self recently.'

His usual self? What's that? Polite? Charming? Caring? He's all these things to her. But his mood has appeared volatile lately. She can't recall the last time he laughed or shared a joke. He must be depressed. What about the alcohol she found in the house, the pills? Now's not the time for confrontation. All she feels is an overwhelming sympathy. This is going to take patience and plenty of understanding.

'It seems like you're having to cope with an awful lot of things on your own, Dom.'

'Maybe.'

'You don't have to. You can share things with me.'

'Thanks.'

'I mean it. Are you going to stay with Bella again tonight?'

'The ward staff have said I can but I'm going home. I won't sleep a wink in the recliner chair they've given me. Plus I have some urgent business to conduct in the morning. I'll be back tomorrow. What are your plans for tomorrow?'

'Work. As usual. But I can take time off, if it would help?'

Dominic gives a half-hearted smile. 'Thanks. No need. As long as I can get hold of you on your phone.'

Guilt jabs her like the twist of a corkscrew. 'I'll make sure,' she says, 'and before I forget here are your keys.' She pulls them out of her pocket and pushes them across the table. 'That could have been awkward.'

'Yeah. Except Courtney has a spare key. I suppose I could have rung her as a backup.'

'Courtney? Your babysitter?'

'Yes.'

'I met her coming out your house earlier. She looked so worried, poor girl.'

Dominic shoots her a look. 'Yeah. It's more complicated than you think.'

'What do you mean?'

'She called round to see me because she'd had another row with her boyfriend. She thought maybe I could have a word with him. Intervene somehow.'

He clicks his tongue against his teeth. 'Not sure that I have any influence there. Anyway, events soon overtook us, with Bella.'

Ruth flinches. This doesn't exactly chime with what Courtney had told her. But then she was hardly likely to confide in her on their first meeting, was she? 'That reminds me,' she says. 'You had a visitor after you left.'

'I did?'

'Yeah. A social worker. Said you should have been expecting her.'

Dominic averts his eyes for a second. 'First I've heard of it. Why would I be needing a social worker?'

Ruth shrugs her shoulders. 'I was hoping you'd be able to tell me.'

A young girl in a cap and apron approaches their table and they both lean back as she takes their cups away, lifts up a spider plant on the table and wipes the vinyl top clean.

Dominic clears his throat. 'Bella's been off school a lot recently. I wonder if that's anything to do with it.' He strokes his chin. 'The trouble with the bloody authorities,' he continues, 'is that nobody really understands. They're just a bunch of jobsworths.' His posture stiffens. 'Anyway, I'm just going to call back in on the ward before I go home. I'll speak to you tomorrow.'

'Keep me posted, Dom. Ring me in the morning,' urges Ruth, as they both stand up and manoeuvre their chairs under the table. 'I'm here for you.' She comes round the table to his side and reaches up to kiss him on the cheek. 'Sleep well, my darling. Hope Bella's better in the morning.'

24
DOMINIC

There are three people before Dominic in the queue for the front desk. They form a chain, keeping a respectful distance behind one another, although the roped chrome posts offer no acoustic barrier. The man at the front of the line has his arm outstretched and is jabbing his finger forward, as his voice rises in indignation. Dominic cranes his neck as the receptionist shakes her head.

'I'm sorry,' she says, 'but unless it's an absolute emergency the first appointment is next Monday morning.' Now it's the man's turn to shake his head. He buttons his coat, turns up his collar and skulks away. An elderly woman shuffles forward and Dom follows suit. Raindrops from his upturned umbrella puddle on the floor as he waits his turn. Eventually the way is clear and he steps up to the desk.

'Morning, Sharon,' he says. 'Busy at the coalface, as usual, I see. Thank you very much for finding me an appointment at short notice. Sorry I had to cancel yesterday.' He lowers his voice. 'My daughter was rushed into hospital.' He waits until the flicker of concern passes over the receptionist's face like a shifting cloud. 'She's out of the woods though. All being well she should be home tomorrow.' He glances over his shoulder. The queue behind him is mounting. 'Anyway, thought you and the girls might be in need of some sustenance on your coffee break.' He lifts up a wet carrier bag and deposits it on the counter.

The receptionist's features soften as she glimpses the foil wrappers of chocolate biscuits. 'Mr. Peterson, you know that's not necessary,' she says, standing up and taking ownership of the carrier bag, 'but thank you, it's much appreciated.' Her cheeks colour slightly. 'If you'd like to take a seat, I'll let the doctor know you're here.'

Dominic follows a trail of muddy footprints into the stuffy waiting room. It's packed, and several people shuffle their chairs sideways so that he has enough space to sit down. He squeezes in between an elderly gentleman, who leans forward with both his knotted hands resting on the crook of his walking stick, and an obese woman, whose brassy hair is scraped back off her face and piled into a tight doughnut on the top of her head. The air has a muggy quality, a damp animal smell. A snotty-nosed toddler brushes against his knee.

'Careful, Tyler,' says the woman on his right. 'Watch what you're doing.'

A hush descends again until Dominic becomes aware of a soft rasping wheeze from the old man, punctuated every few minutes with a rattling expectoration, like the sound of a bin lorry being emptied. Dominic turns away from him and looks down at the blue-speckled carpet. He thinks about the letter that arrived yesterday. His mother. Why now? She'd been absent while Madeleine was ill and didn't show up for the funeral. *A change of heart,* she had said, *let's make a fresh start.* The spidery scrawl also indicated that she was coming over to the UK next month. *I miss my granddaughter,* she said. *I want to be part of her life.* The hair on the back of his neck prickles. That wouldn't be the real reason, of course. Oh no. She must be in debt again. This could be tricky. He'll have to engineer it so that she doesn't meet Ruth. Such bad timing. Just as he was getting to know Ruth better. He sighs. It feels so good to be back in a physical relationship again. The heat of another body nuzzling his. Warm breath in his ear. The yield of her soft skin. So comforting. The fact that she was a doctor was an added bonus. A walking medical compendium.

The buzzer goes. Doughnut-hair woman stands up and weaves across the waiting room, instructing Tyler to come with her.

Dominic looks at the illuminated display, then at his watch. Dr. Baranska is running ten minutes late. He takes out his phone and taps the screen for the Financial Times. He turns to the Lex column but his eyes are drawn to the headline about Lucky Pagoda. The Formula 1 merger looks to be going ahead. Gary Sharp was right. Hadn't Mike predicted this? He's going to have to move quickly to make his investment. He spends the next ten minutes checking his stocks and shares then sends Gary a text just as the buzzer goes and his name lights up on the LED display: Dominic Peterson to Room 6.

As he enters the consulting room the doctor swivels round in her chair. She's much younger than expected. Shoulder-length hair, crisp jacket, co-ordinated jewellery. Not the demeanour of someone who's running twenty minutes late. No apology. She stands up and offers her hand.

'Mr. Peterson? My name is Dr. Baranska, I'm the locum doctor standing in for Dr. Crofton.' They sit. Dominic wonders if he should speak first. Her body language suggests he should.

'Thank you for seeing me. I was due to see Dr. Crofton yesterday - he knows me very well - but my daughter was taken into hospital.' The doctor momentarily glances at the computer screen then at Dominic. 'But that's not why I've come. I've been getting a lot of migraines recently.'

The doctor sits back in her chair, her back to the computer, and her hands in her lap. She looks at him intently. She listens as Dominic recounts the nausea, the flashing lights, and the throbbing temples. He pauses to draw breath then mentions the sleepless nights, the heaviness in his chest. A weight he feels that sometimes makes it difficult for him to breathe. He stops. He looks at the floor. The wastepaper basket under the desk is full. He looks up. There's a grey-rimmed cup of tea on the desk. He looks at the doctor. Tiny pearl earrings. He wonders if they're cultured or fake. She sits, smiling, but says nothing, so he continues. He shares his worries about his little girl, her asthma, her allergies, her infections, his concerns that the hospital doctors aren't taking him seriously. He wonders if he can have some more codeine for his migraines. It's the only medicine that seems to work.

The doctor waits until he's finished.

'Mr Peterson,' she says, 'do you mind if I do an examination? Check your eyes, your blood pressure, listen to your heart and so on?'

Dominic yields to the checks, then he is talking again before the doctor has had time to take her stethoscope out of her ears.

'There's something else that's been worrying me, Doctor,' he says. 'Have you heard of Tatotsubo cardiomyopathy?' He looks closely for a reaction. If anything there is a slightly raised eyebrow as her eyes flick upwards to the clock on the wall.

'Broken heart syndrome?' She inhales slowly. 'Mr. Peterson, you've been through a lot recently'. Castors wheel across lino so that their knees are almost touching. She lowers her head to make eye contact with him. 'It's a really tough time for you at the moment but it's going to get better. Trust me. You know, it's quite common for patients to research their symptoms on the internet. There's a lot of information out there but not all of it is helpful. I have your full medical record here in front of me and I have examined you thoroughly. I want to reassure you that there is no evidence that you have Tatotsubo cardiomyopathy.' She propels her chair back and reaches over to the printer. 'As for the codeine tablets I'm not sure they're the best choice for you. Dependence can be a problem. And rebound headaches too, when you come off them. I can give you an alternative which will be much better.'

Dominic looks at the unlined face of the doctor sitting opposite him. She has youth on her side but not experience.

'Now,' she says, as she leans forward and hands him his prescription, 'have you thought about seeing a counsellor?' She hands him a booklet which is covered in butterflies and the title 'Bereavement- Key Facts.'

He takes this as his cue and stands up. Not the outcome he'd hoped. He grasps the slip of paper. 'I'll give it some thought, doctor. Thanks for your time,' he says, and leaves.

On his way out he stops by the front desk. The receptionist looks up and smiles.

'Sharon, I'd like to book a follow-up appointment with Dr. Crofton, please,' says Dominic. 'The next available one, if possible. Oh, and can I borrow your pen a minute? I need to fill in a repeat prescription request for some more codeine.'

25

BELLA

Bella feels better today. Brenda says she can go to the playroom. 'There are lots of toys in here, Bella,' she says. 'You can play with whichever ones you want.'

Bella decides to explore. There's a sand pit. A dolls' house. A kitchen. Even a doctor's set. She opens the lid of the doctor's case. Empties it on the floor.

'Can I give you a check-up, Brenda?' she asks.

'A check-up? Okay, sure.'

Bella taps on Brenda's knees with a hammer. She tells her to open her mouth and say 'Aah.' She wraps the blood pressure machine round Brenda's wrist and pumps it up, then sticks the dangly tubes in her ears and shakes her head.

'Dear, dear,' she says. 'You need some sweeties to make you better.'

She looks in the kitchen. In the cupboards. On the shelf. In the jars. No sweeties. She'll just have to pretend.

'Which ones would you like?' she says, holding out the tin. 'Dolly mixtures or Smarties?'

'Mm, thank you, Bella. I'll have a Smartie.'

'You can have a pink one with some fizzy pop. Only one, though. We need to save the rest for later.'

She looks around. The dolls' house has a lot of furniture in a jumble. There's a funny little toilet with a lid, which she puts in the bathroom. The washing machine and the buckets go downstairs. She stuffs little squares in the washing machine and tuts.

'Dear, dear,' she says to the doll, 'only naughty girls wet beds.'

She picks up the bedroom set. 'Now look what you made me do.' She unpicks the tangle of furniture. 'The little girl can go in this bed. And the daddy in this one. Ssh, Ssh, daddy, don't cry. Daddies don't cry. Let's go to the park. That will make you feel better.'

There's the sound of a bell and Brenda stands up. 'Lunch is ready, Bella. Are you hungry?'

Bella isn't hungry.

When they get back to her room her Daddy is there. He opens his arms and gives her a big hug.

'Good news, darling,' he says. 'You can come home.'

Bella doesn't want to go home. She likes it in hospital.

26
RUTH

MAY 2005

'Help yourself to coffee,' says Dominic, his arms encircling an overflowing laundry basket. 'I'll be in the utility room.'

Something has irked him. She's barely been in his house two minutes and he seems offhand. Distracted. Gruff.

She adjusts her eyes to the shaded gloom of the basement kitchen and places a cooler bag and wicker hamper on the granite worktop.

'Hello, you,' Ruth says to Bella, who is kneeling by the sofa, brushing the mane of a plastic pony.

Bella looks up, scowling. 'What you doing?'

'I thought we could go out today. Would you like that? Maybe have a picnic. Depends what Daddy says.'

'Don't want to.'

Knots of intransigence seem to bind Dominic and Bella this morning. Ruth wants to comb them out, free the tangles.

As she fills the kettle, a mobile phone vibrates on the kitchen worktop. She can't resist a look. Mike's name flashes on the screen.

LP shares up 9%! Suggest another 500. Call me

Whatever that means it's none of her business. She selects a mug from the dresser and scans the cupboards for instant powder. Lifting a jar of Arabica granules from the shelf, several packets of pills fall onto the counter: sumatriptan, penicillin, paracetamol and codeine. Intuitively she runs the diagnoses through her head. Migraine treatment. Preventative antibiotics. A reflex action and she admonishes herself for it.

'Right that's the last lot in,' says Dominic, entering the kitchen. He hesitates when he sees Ruth fingering the packets, his eyebrows angled for an inquisition.

'Sorry, I accidentally knocked these off the shelf.'

Dominic reaches over to the hand sanitiser by the sink and says nothing.

She goes over to the sofa and sinks into the squashy cushions. Dominic continues his tasks unabashed, looking under the sink, sliding drawers, banging cupboard doors. She pretends not to notice, picking up a magazine and feigning interest in a fashion article. The distracting sequence of noises in the background seem to get more insistent the more she ignores them.

'I'm going upstairs,' says Dominic, 'to sort out some sheets for Bella's bedroom.' He paces towards Bella, who shrinks into the shadow of Ruth's legs. 'Because Isabella has been a naughty girl today, hasn't she?'

Ruth feels the imprint of Bella's shoulder against her knee.

'I'll be back down in a minute,' he says, then he disappears.

She looks at the red rims of the little girl's eyes. Her lower eyelashes are matted. She looks like she's been crying. The corner of her mouth is pinpricked with tiny ulcers. She's wearing a faded T shirt with a picture of a blue kitten and a grey pair of knickers. Her toes, dotted with tiny chilblains, have a purplish pink tinge to them and when Ruth places her hand on top of Bella's it feels milk-bottle cool. They sit in companionable calm for a while, Ruth listening to Bella's conversation with her toys.

'They look pretty,' says Ruth, picking up one of the ponies.

'This one is Twinkle,' says Bella, holding up a purple piece of plastic, 'and yours is Marigold.'

'Marigold has shiny hair, just like you, Bella. Can

I brush it?' Ruth lifts up a toy brush, but then spots a pack of playing cards. 'Ooh, great, my favourite,' she says, reaching over to the stack of assorted jungle animals. 'Do you know how to play Snap, Bella? I can show you. It's great fun.' She slides off the sofa and on to her knees, and begins to shuffle cards. Bella watches with interest.

There's a movement at the periphery of Ruth's vision.

'You two having fun?' says a brittle voice. Dominic, in loose fitting T shirt and jeans, is standing barefoot next to them. In one hand he clutches some clothes, which he has draped over his opposite arm. 'If we're going out later you better get dressed, Bella.'

Ruth stands up and takes the clothes out of Dominic's hands. 'Bella, why don't you show me where your bedroom is? I can help you, while Daddy has a cup of coffee.'

She widens her eyes at Dominic. He reciprocates with a weak smile.

'Good idea,' he says, then hesitates. 'Ruth, before you go upstairs could you do me a favour?' He lifts up a wad of papers, which have spewed over the kitchen table. 'I've got so many forms to fill in, now that the probate for Madeleine has come through. You wouldn't mind witnessing my signature on this one, would you?'

'Sure.'

'This one's to close her e mail account. You wouldn't believe how difficult it's been to wade through all this bloody red tape.'

He scrawls his signature on the paper and Ruth adds hers underneath.

'By the way,' says Ruth, 'I think you had a missed call on your phone while you were upstairs. See you in a minute.' She bundles the clothes under one arm. 'Come on, Bella, time to get dressed.'

★

Bella's bedroom is a confection of ice cream colours. Yellow and pink dots sprinkle the pleats of her curtains, complementing the minty green walls. Ruth perches on Bella's duvet and lays out Bella's clothes: a yellow T shirt with appliqued hearts and stripy cropped leggings.

'These are pretty,' says Ruth. 'I guess you're a big girl now, you don't need me to help you. Can I look at one of your books while you get dressed?'

Bella stands, watching her, and bites her lip.

'Do you know my mummy?'

It's question which disarms Ruth for a second.

'She died-ed.'

'I never met your mummy, Bella, but I know she was a special lady.'

Ruth reaches down to the side of the bed to

pull up a book but instead hooks the tail of a soft toy. 'Oh, Roo,' she says. 'I remember meeting you.' She pulls the toy kangaroo into her lap and smooths its fur.

'No,' says Bella. She snatches it off Ruth, her face a twist of anguish. 'You'll hurt his leg!'

Ruth retracts her hand. 'Oh, poor Roo, what's the matter with his leg?'

'Daddy shut the door on him.'

'Oh dear.' Ruth gets off the bed and kneels on the floor so that her face is level with Bella's. 'I can have a look at him, if you want. Try to make him better. I'm sure it was an accident.'

Cautiously Bella loosens her grip on the animal and casts her eyes downward, as it slides through her fingers. As Ruth leans closer a familiar smell irritates her nostrils. Ammonia. Dried urine. The smell of care homes. She takes Bella by the hand.

'Let's have a little wash before you get dressed,' she says, 'then I can tell you all about kangaroos.' They walk across the landing to the bathroom. 'D'you know, I've seen a real kangaroo, Bella. They live in Australia.'

'Uncle David lives in Stralia.'

'Oh, that's nice.'

'He gave me Roo when lots of people came to the house.'

Ruth inserts a plug in the basin, turns on the tap and whisks her hand in the water until it heats up.

'Australia is a really faraway place.'

'Is it farer away than heaven?'

'Mm, I think heaven is a bit further.' She swishes her hand in the soapy water. 'Right,' she says. 'All ready.' She plunges a face-cloth under the warm water then wrings it out, as Bella stands patiently, her face upturned towards her.

'This is the way we wash our face, wash our face, wash our face,' sings Ruth, as she wipes Bella's nose and cheeks. 'Do you know this song, Bella?' As Ruth continues to sing, Bella screws up her nose and twists away, as the flannel moves over her face.

'Right,' says Ruth, after she has patted Bella's face dry. 'Arms up.'

Bella obliges by raising up her arms, as Ruth pulls her T shirt over her head. She sponges Bella down, back and front, then wraps her in a towel.

'Good girl,' says Ruth crouching down beside her. 'Teeth next, then you can get dressed.'

Ruth takes in Bella's unflinching stare.

'Ruth?'

'Yes?'

'Are you Daddy's friend?'

Ruth smiles. 'Yes. But I can be your friend too. Would you like that?'

Bella takes a moment to consider the question, her eyes unblinking.

'Yes. Can we play Snap when I've got dressed?'

27

DOMINIC

Dominic looks at the car dashboard. Twenty five degrees. They nudge along the poplar-flanked gravel road into Windridge car park. He flicks on the air conditioning. A slice of cool air ruffles the hair on his forearms.

'The first warm day in ages and the masses come out in their droves.'

Ahead of them a line of cars alternate between making abrupt stops, then skittering forward, like lizards seeking shade in a desert. He counts the roofs. There's at least twelve cars in front of them in the queue.

Ruth drums her fingers on the armrest. 'I'd forgotten it's a Bank Holiday weekend.'

'Sod it. Well, we've come this far, may as well stick

with it. Besides, I'm starving.' His frustration is metered out by the gnawing sensation in his gut. The morning had not started well. Just after six o'clock he had woken with a start when he detected a tugging at the edge of his dreams. He opened his eyes to find Bella's face inches from his, her pupils like smudged charcoal. She pulled at his T shirt and told him she couldn't sleep. She didn't tell him she had wet her bed for the third night in a row. He discovered that later. This was becoming a tedious habit and he chastised her for it. He looks at her now in the driver's mirror. She's nodded off to sleep in the heat. Her mouth is half open, exposing her gappy teeth. From time to time she gives little gasps.

There's a short tap on the horn, from the car behind. He switches his concentration to the windscreen and can see that a large gap has opened up between his car and the one in front.

'Okay, okay, keep your shirt on,' he says out loud, venting his frustration.

After a protracted delay they pull into the car park.

He pulls down his window visor and checks his appearance in the mirror. Not bad, considering he's had very little sleep. Moistening the tips of his fingers with his tongue, he slicks back some stray hairs behind his ears. He gets out of the car, stretching his arms into a stiff arc above his head, then places his hands on his hips and arches his back. Far-away voices are dulled by a thick curtain of warm air, which feels over-blown with pollen. There's no hint of a breeze. Dominic tries to remember if he's packed some anti-histamines. He turns to open the back door of the car for ventilation and Bella stirs in her seat. A line of drool has dried in a silvery line down her T shirt. She blinks several times.

'I'm thirsty,' she says, unclipping her seat belt and clambering over the booster cushion.

'Stay there, Bella, just a second, while Daddy unloads the car,' says Dominic. 'Then we can go for our picnic.'

Ruth swings her legs out of the front seat and stands up. She tugs the creases out of her trousers and straightens her top, then picks up a rolled tartan rug, which she slings over her shoulder.

'Follow me, Bella,' says Dominic, weighed down by a cool bag and hamper. Ruth takes her hand, as they make their way towards the picnic area by the lake. The long grass whips against his ankles. The dry heat edges into his nostrils and the back of his throat. He stops to switch loads round when his right arm starts to ache and his fingers blanch from the pressure of the handles. He scans the perimeter of the park. Family groups bunch up on benches, their paraphernalia spilling onto groundsheets and rugs. A dog is shooed away, as he tries to invade a picnic. A gaggle of teenagers playing Frisbee, others enjoying makeshift rounders, using plastic bottles for stumps.

There are no tables free, so they lay down their rug on a flat patch of ground, in the shade of a tree.

Dominic feels a tugging on his sleeve and twists sideways to see Bella.

'Daddy, I need a wee.'

Dominic looks at Ruth, who is unpacking the contents of the hamper and doesn't appear to have heard. His jaw muscles stiffen.

'Daddy, I need a wee. Wee.' The voice is louder and more insistent.

'Bella, I wish you'd thought of that before we walked all the way over from the car park.'

Ruth looks round and is on her feet.

'It's okay, Dom. Bella and I can go over to the washrooms. Our hands are sticky anyway, aren't they, Bella?'

Dominic watches them trail back over the park, hand in hand. He takes a bottle of ginger beer out of the cool box, then sits down, resting his back against the knotted trunk of a lime tree. A breeze ruffles through the branches above his head, causing the little red leaf buds to bob like miniature boxing gloves.

He takes out his phone and re-reads Mike's message, then dials his number.

'Dominic?' Mike's voice is distinct, clear.

'Hi, mate. Thanks for the message.'

'No worries. Lucky Pagoda. You bought in last week at three fifty. It's had a good run to three eighty already.'

'I know. I checked. That was a good call of Gary's.'

'I've just been speaking to him. Their balance sheet is solid. It's ripe for the F1 takeover. Think you need to take another punt.'

'What do you mean?'

'Transfer another five hundred thousand. Madeleine's assets have been paid into Bella's trust fund now. They're secure. You've got spare to take a gamble. Lucky Pagoda's got a low price-earnings ratio. Little debt.'

Dominic whistles through his teeth. 'You sure?'

'It's a win-win situation, mate. Speculate to accumulate and all that.'

Dominic's mind is working overtime. It's a lot of money.

'Dom? You still there?'

'Yes.'

'Good. Think about it. But you'll need to move fast before every muppet starts buying in.'

Dominic sits up straight. 'I've thought about it. First thing tomorrow morning. I'll have it organised. Thanks for the tip-off.'

'Good man. You know it makes sense. Speak soon.' The line goes dead.

Dominic lifts the bottle of ginger beer to his mouth and takes a long, cool drink.

He leans back against the tree and closes his eyes. His luck is about to change for the better.

28
RUTH

P redictable. The morning after a Bank Holiday weekend and already Ruth's appointment screen looks like a screenshot from a busy day at air traffic control.

She lifts her hair free of her collar, closes her eyes and takes some deep breaths. At least the weekend had ended on a relaxed note. Despite Dominic's initial intransigence the day out at Windridge had lightened his mood. He'd even agreed to her having a birthday dinner party next week. And to letting Bella stay overnight. Bella. Ruth had watched her chasing bubbles round the park yesterday. Her health remained an enigma. The vague symptoms: the tiredness, the tummy aches, the poor appetite. Dominic's lament that he never felt listened to by health professionals. All this continues to puzzle Ruth. Could she be missing something? Hardly. She knows Dominic pretty well by now. This was simply a family adjusting to life after bereavement.

She places her hands across her chest and feels it rise and fall as she takes deep breaths. In through her nose. Out through her mouth. Slowly she counts to ten, allowing her thoughts from the weekend to drift away. Calmness descends. Control.

She opens her eyes and notices that four more telephone consultations have been added to the screen. Time to move on.

Her first patient is a woman in her sixties, her thinning hair scraped back into a bun, like a cottage loaf. Her papery skin is stretched tightly over her face, a rough rash scales her cheeks. Normally she looks stooped, but today she seems taller. She eases herself onto the chair. 'Have you had the letter from the hospital yet?' she asks Ruth.

'I have indeed, Mrs. Tomlinson. It's starting to add up.'

'Yes. The specialist sounded very encouraging. Said you'd put me on some new tablets.'

Ruth looks at the hospital letter, then back again at the woman's face. Of course, the red cheeks were classic. A butterfly rash. The joint pains, the kidney infections, the cough. It all made sense. Systemic lupus erythematosus.

'Well I'm pleased we've made progress with the diagnosis. Once these tablets take effect you're bound to feel better.'

'Thanks, Dr. Cooper. I was beginning to feel I was making a fuss over nothing, being tired all the time and what not.'

'Not at all,' says Ruth, clicking on the laboratory results, her patient's words echoing in her head. Making a fuss over nothing. Tired all the time. An itching realisation creeps over her. Sure enough she had a low white count, low platelets, anaemia and an abnormal immunological profile.

Ruth prints out the prescription and hands it over.

'I'm booking you in for another blood test with the nurse,' she says, 'then I'll see you again in a month.'

As soon as the patient leaves she clicks on her medical database.

'Systemic Lupus Erythematosus: a chronic, multisystem, inflammatory connective tissue disease of auto-immune origin.'

The words jump out of the screen at her. It's going to take some time to research this in more detail, but she'll come back to it later. The vague, non-specific symptoms like tiredness and no appetite. Bella's symptoms. The results of the blood tests. Bella's blood picture. Dominic being told he was making a fuss over nothing. Why the hell hadn't she thought of this before? She can't wait to tell him.

With a hint of satisfaction, she presses the call button to summon her next patient, and swivels in her chair to greet him.

★

A blue rectangle from the computer screen is the sole illumination in the kitchen. Everything is quiet, save for the sound of traffic stirring up puddles on the road outside. Ruth opens her electronic log book but instead of clicking on her appraisal folder she reopens her file on 'Systemic lupus erythematosus.'

'A connective tissue disorder of auto-immune origin.'

She scrolls down the list of symptoms: fatigue, weight loss, cold hands and feet, mouth ulcers, respiratory problems, kidney injury, blood disorders, heart disease, seizures.

As she gets further down the screen she can feel her heart beat quickening.

'SLE in childhood can be very difficult to diagnose, due to similarities with other auto-immune conditions such as multiple sclerosis, and a lack of diagnostic criteria.'

She retraces the words on the screen. Multiple sclerosis? She continues. 'Children present with more acute illness and have more frequent renal, haematological and neurological involvement at the time of diagnosis.'

She stands up, and switches on the main light. The room takes on a shifting phosphorescent quality, like a search beam. Mentally she thanks Mrs. Tomlinson, her SLE patient, for the prompt. The kidney problems, the asthma, the low white count, the anaemia. Bella's symptoms seemed to fit the picture. And there's even the possibility of a genetic link, given Madeleine's multiple sclerosis. Suddenly it's as if Ruth has been tapping away at a coal seam and has unexpectedly struck gold.

She squints in the harsh light. Taking a glass from the shelf, she fills it with wine from the fridge. As it rolls over her tongue, the gooseberry flavour sours her mouth, leaving a bitter after-taste when she swallows. She returns to the computer and sits in contemplation. She wonders if Bella has had auto-immune profiling carried out. Difficult to suggest when she's not her doctor. And frustrating when she wants to help, but doesn't want to alienate her colleagues. She decides on a compromise and scans eight pages of medical notes, which she sends by e mail to Dominic. They can discuss it tomorrow.

29
RUTH

'What time are we expecting Val and Mike?' Dominic runs his fingers through his tousled hair, which is still damp from the shower.

'Not till seven,' says Ruth taking a casserole out of the oven and giving it a stir. 'But this is already prepared. Chicken, sweet peppers, chorizo and tomatoes. I can do the rice once they arrive.'

'I've had a letter from my mother,' says Dominic, leaning against the kitchen counter. 'She's planning a visit next month.'

'Gosh. How long since you've seen her? Four years?'

'When Bella was born. She didn't come over to Madeleine's funeral, so there's got to be a pressing reason why she's coming over now. Probably needs more money.' He looks distant. 'My father left her in a lot of debt. Then she remarried and her money troubles seemed to be over. Except I hadn't banked on her profligate spending.'

Ruth takes a lettuce out of the fridge and begins separating the leaves in a colander.

'It'll be nice for Bella to meet her though, won't it? She won't remember her from the last time.'

'Yeah, poor Bella. My mother is her only grand-parent. She has an uncle, Madeleine's brother, but he lives in Australia. Madeleine's parents died before Bella was born.'

'Did you ever meet them?'

'Edna and Norman? Oh, God, yes. I don't think they ever approved of me. They were plain-speaking, take–as–you–find northerners. Edna always looked like she was in the presence of a bad smell whenever she met me, and Norman, who was a hearse driver with the Co-op, kept quiet and did as he was told.'

Ruth laughs, but inwardly she thinks how sad that is. Her own parents are both dead. She understands what loss is. It's a factor which draws her even closer to Dom.

'That's a bit harsh. When's your mother coming over? I'd like to meet her.'

A flicker of concern appears to cross Dominic's face.

'It'll have to be another time, I'm afraid. She'll be

staying in London, so I'll take Bella there at half term to see her.'

Ruth shakes the lettuce under the cold water tap, then pats it dry with some kitchen towel. So that's what the letter from America was about.

'You must show me some photos of her. What's her name?'

'Mm, I'm not sure I have any photos, I'll have a look. And it's Viviane. Viviane Zuckerman now.'

'Mrs. Zuckerman, of Miami Beach. Wow, sounds very glamorous.'

Dominic rounds on her. 'How do you know she lives in Miami Beach?'

In her mind Ruth is halfway to telling him she picked up his mail the day he left for the hospital.

'You told me, remember? The night after Bella was admitted to hospital.'

Dominic ponders this for a second. 'I did?'

'Yep.' She feels herself swaying a little and holds onto the worktop to steady herself. It's the second dizzy spell she's had today. Maybe it's because she hasn't eaten today, but she's got no appetite. Even the smell of reheated chorizo is making her nauseous.

'Oh, before I forget,' says Dominic, his tone lightening, 'thank you for the notes on SLE. Really interesting. I've got Bella an appointment at Whitehall Clinic next week, so we could be making progress.'

'Whitehall Clinic?'

Dominic takes a business card out of his pocket and turns it over in his hands. 'Whitehall Clinic. Private Primary Care Consultants. We pride ourselves on holistic care,' he reads.

'Must be new,' Ruth replies.

'Well, there's no harm in getting a second opinion, is there?' he says, as he catches her sleeve and pulls her towards him. He plants a kiss on her forehead, then another on her lips. 'Who's a clever doctor,' he says. 'Thanks for letting me bring Bella here tonight.'

'You know I've wanted that for a long time.'

'Well I don't think I can rely on Courtney to babysit anymore. That's the third time in a row that she's let me down.'

'Every cloud has a silver lining, as they say,' says Ruth, her smile widening.

'Bella loved helping you with the cake.'

'You know how fond I am of her. And you know what? If we can persuade Mike and Val not to outstay their welcome, you and I can have an early night.'

Dominic strokes the pearls round Ruth's neck. 'I'm glad you like your present, darling. Happy Birthday. You look beautiful.'

★

'You're not dieting again, are you?' asks Val, following Ruth through to the kitchen. 'You don't need to. You hardly ate any supper.'

Ruth notices Val's eyes taking in her figure, scrutinizing her up and down, lingering on her belly.

'I haven't had much of an appetite recently, especially for the booze. Had the odd dizzy spell too.' She peels back the waxed cover from a chunk of Stinking Bishop and wants to retch. 'Here,' she says, passing it to Val. 'Can you do this for me, it reeks.'

'Well, you know what I'm going to say, don't you?' Their eyes meet and Val gives her a look, the look that spells p-r-e-g-n-a-n-t.

Ruth glances through to the conservatory where Dominic and Mike are deep in conversation. She lowers her voice. 'I did a test yesterday. Negative. Mind you, it's probably too early to tell. I'm only two days overdue.' She goes over to the sink and fills a glass with water, then takes a sip. 'And can you stop staring at me. I'd be as surprised as you if it was positive. Although I did forget the odd pill last month.'

Val muses for a few seconds. She opens a box of crackers and arranges them on a plate. 'What can I say?' She hesitates, as if weighing up whether to say any more, then goes ahead regardless. 'You haven't exactly wasted much time, have you? Right. Shall we take these through?'

30

DOMINIC

It's gone eleven o'clock. Dominic wishes Val and Mike would go home.

'Oh my goodness, look at this photo,' says Val, picking up a silver frame from the windowsill. 'How old were you then, Ruth? I'm guessing from your mother's flares and her Sindy doll hairstyle you must have been eight or nine.'

Ruth takes the picture from Val's hands and laughs. 'Yeah, probably about eight. That was taken on our caravan holiday in Scotland. Probably why I'm rocking the tartan trousers, ha, ha.'

'Aw, your Mum and Dad were such lovely people. I'm so glad I got the chance to meet them when we were at Med School.'

Dominic listens to this idle chit chat, feigning interest from time to time. He wants to wind up this conversation.

'It's so cool that you have all these childhood photos dotted around the house,' continues Val. 'What about you, Dom? I don't think I've ever seen a photo of you as a little boy. I bet you were a real charmer.'

Dominic is conscious that all eyes are on him.

'Oh. There's bound to be some photos tucked away somewhere,' he says, shifting in his seat.

'Dominic's mother's coming over next month,' announces Ruth.

Dominic recoils at the unwelcome proclamation. His nostrils fan with discontent.

'Oh, wonderful,' says Val. 'I'd love to meet her. Didn't she move to the States, just after your father died? Your poor dad. Cancer's a bastard.'

Dominic feels the invasion of cool night air and stands up to slide the conservatory doors shut. Ruth is staring at him, but he ignores Val's question and looks back at Ruth, trying to convey his irritation. They've overstayed their welcome now, and he wants to go to bed.

'Actually, the other day, I came across some great photos of you and me at Med School,' Ruth says to Val, lifting up the cafetiere and offering her another cup of coffee. 'There're upstairs. I must show you before you go.'

Dominic coughs. He needs his sleep, or his migraine will punish him. His eyes meet Ruth's and he raises his eyebrows, but she seems intent on pursuing this line of conversation. A moth throws itself repeatedly against the lamp above their heads.

'Remember after the May Ball when we went down the slides in our evening dresses at five in the morning? I've got a photo of that. Do you remember going to the all-night bakery afterwards? I've got one of that too.' She stands up, dropping her napkin to the floor. 'In fact I'm going upstairs to get them. Wait till you see our ball gowns. You'll die laughing.'

'Ruth,' Dominic protests, but it's too late, as she disappears out of the room.

He yawns loudly and makes no attempt to cover it up.

'It's okay, Dom,' says Mike. 'We'll get going as soon as Ruth comes back. Give me a shout on Monday and we can get a date in the diary for our next meeting.'

'Yeah, will do.'

They sit in companionable silence for a few minutes. Val helps herself to a large glass of water. Mike edges bits of cheese round his plate.

After ten minutes, or so, Val looks up at Dom. 'She's either fallen asleep up there or she's going through the whole box of photographs.'

He laughs politely, then stands up and starts clearing plates away.

Suddenly, a shrill yell comes from upstairs. It scuds down the stairs and into the hall, and whips round corners into the kitchen, seeking them out with urgency. A clattering on the stairs. Ruth shouting for help.

Within the space of two heartbeats Val and Mike are on their feet, the stain from an upended bottle of Rioja haemorrhaging over the white tablecloth. Breathlessly they follow Dominic into the hall where Ruth is standing, the colour drained from her face.

'Quick. Call an ambulance. Now. It's Bella.'

31
RUTH

Ruth accompanies Dominic to the hospital, following the ambulance through the neon-lit, rain-sodden streets. It speeds through the town centre, adeptly dodging revellers who spill out of pubs into the queues for nightclubs, until it draws up outside the illuminated entrance to the Accident and Emergency Department.

Left alone to her thoughts, while Dominic is in the Resuscitation room with his daughter, the main waiting area reminds her, bizarrely, of an all-night ferry crossing she had once taken. The hemmed-in petrol blue walls. The smell of cleaning fluid. Semi-somnolent people shifting on uncomfortable chairs. Relatives trudging up and down to vending machines.

Someone throwing up into a cardboard container in the corner.

Eventually a young doctor ushers her into a curtained-off cubicle, where Dominic sits. The doctor tells her that Bella has had a lumbar puncture but is now sleeping peacefully and has been transferred up to the Children's Ward. He wants to hear Ruth's firsthand account of what happened.

Looking at the young man who sits opposite her, earnestly taking notes as she speaks, she's reminded of her life as a junior doctor. He's probably been on duty since yesterday morning and, no doubt, isn't clocking off till Monday. She can't help but feel sorry for him. All the same, despite the hour and the queue of patients waiting, he insists on going through the history in meticulous detail.

Bella seemed well during the day, she explains, and had settled for the evening on the sofa bed in Ruth's study. She's unsure how much detail to give, but explains that she had gone upstairs, looking for some photos to show her friends. When she reached the top of the stairs she could hear a noise, which sounded like Bella snoring, so she decided to check on her. Instinctively she knew things weren't right as soon as she entered the room. A wedge of light from the landing outlined a thrashing of bedclothes. Flicking on the light she saw Bella, foaming at the mouth and in the throes of a grand mal convulsion.

Her eyes had rolled back in her head, and her arms and legs exhibited jerky movements, like a rag doll being tossed on a trampoline.

'Why didn't you call for help straight away?' the doctor asks, his eyes never leaving her face.

Why? She has asked herself the same question several times while sitting in the waiting room. She thinks carefully before formulating an answer.

'Probably because I went into automatic professional mode,' she replies. 'You know what I mean? Checking Bella's airway was protected until she stopped convulsing. I couldn't leave her on her own till then.' Ruth looks at the doctor for a reaction but he remains silent and impassive, so she continues. 'As soon as she stopped shaking I placed her in the recovery position then quickly scanned her arms and legs for any sign of a rash.'

The doctor listens, prompting her at regular intervals to add more precise detail, causing Dominic to interrupt, 'No she hasn't had a fever today,' 'yes, she had a recent admission with asthma', 'unfortunately she's been beset with several urinary tract infections recently.' Eventually he thanks them both and advises that Bella will be having more tests tomorrow.

Back in the corridor Dominic guides Ruth by the arm.

'I'll take you home, then I'll pick up a few things and get a taxi back to the hospital. I'm staying here tonight.'

Ruth can sense his agitation, can feel his distress. She squeezes his arm. In her head three letters keep repeating themselves. 'SLE, SLE, SLE.'

'Dominic, I never mentioned my theory. I should have said something to the doctor about SLE. I need to go back.'

With his arm round her shoulder he navigates round the puddle-pocked car park until they find their car.

'Plenty of time for that tomorrow, darling. Let's see how Bella is in the morning.'

★

Ruth taps K259XZ onto the keypad and enters the ward.

The familiar silhouette of Sheena, bending over a trolley, can be seen in the office, her fingers walking over the spines of notes. Ruth taps lightly on the door and walks in.

'Morning, Sheena.'

The doctor looks up, and registers recognition, but there is something about her countenance which, to Ruth, suggests her being caught unawares.

'Ah, Ruth. The very person. I've just been talking about you with my consultant.'

'You have?'

Sheena puts down her file and moves towards her.

'We wondered if we could have a chat with you about Bella? The little girl who came in last night with a convulsion? Her father has given us your details as an emergency contact. You're a family friend, aren't you?'

Ruth feels her cheeks colouring. 'I know Bella's father very well.'

Sheena smiles, and there's an unspoken understanding in her eyes.

'Well, have you got a minute? I'm just going to bleep my consultant.'

'Sure.'

As she is talking Ruth's eye-line is drawn to the monitor over Sheena's left shoulder. An image comes into view over the television screen, grainy but instantly recognisable. A tall, broad-shouldered man with dark hair, which flops over his face as he bends forward. It's Dominic. He's leaning over a little figure in the bed, which must be Bella.

Sheena has turned her back to Ruth now and is on the phone asking for Dr. Elmahdy. Ruth concentrates on the monitor, waiting to see if it changes to a different angle of the ward. It doesn't.

'Right,' says Sheena, wheeling round. Their eyes meet and it's obvious that Sheena has noticed Ruth looking at the screen. 'She's just on her way.'

'Fine. I'll just pop out onto the ward and let Dominic know I'm here.'

Sheena edges closer and touches Ruth's arm.

'I wouldn't if I were you, she'll be here any minute now. And it's probably best if we have a chat in private first.'

★

Ruth feels sick as she taps on the door and walks into Bella's cubicle. She can't decide if it's anxiety or a justifiable disruption of her physiology. Her period is now three days late. However the knot of unease in her stomach tightens further when she is greeted with a smile from Bella. Her conversation with Shaba Elmahdy has unsettled her. It makes her question her convictions as a doctor. Surely she had proved her competency by managing Elliott Tremayne appropriately? Why did the paediatricians doubt Ruth's theory of systemic lupus erythematosus with Bella?

'Ruthie!' exclaims Bella.

Dominic looks up from his newspaper. His face folds into a smile.

'Ruth. Good timing.' He stands up and pecks her on the cheek. 'Mike has been trying to get hold of me urgently. I need to go out and make some phone calls.'

'Hey, Bella,' says Ruth, her arms outstretched. 'Give me a hug.' She squeezes the little girl and turns to Dominic. 'So, how's it all going?'

Dominic pulls up a chair for her. 'Here have a seat and I can give you a quick update.'

Ruth unzips her shoulder bag and brings out a brightly-coloured booklet which she hands over to Bella. 'Look what I brought for you,' she says.

Bella clambers over the bedclothes, her cheeks shiny and pink. 'A sticker book,' she exclaims and takes it from Ruth's hands.

'Someone's much brighter today,' says Ruth, and she sits down and twists sideways to give Dominic her full attention.

'The lumbar puncture last night was normal,' begins Dominic, 'as were the blood cultures. So hopefully it was a one-off. The consultant, Shaba Elmahdy, has been round this morning and she wants to keep Bella in for a few more days, though, because she needs an EEG and a brain scan.' His voice exudes control. 'I asked her if Bella has had auto-immune profiling done,' he continues. 'She said she had, but when I pushed her to clarify that, it turns out she's been tested for anti-nuclear factor, but not anti-phospholipid antibodies.'

'Gosh,' says Ruth. 'Good for you. I wish I'd been there. I'd liked to have seen her face.' Ruth is impressed at Dominic's grasp of terminology. She's glad she's been able to help.

'The things is,' says Dominic, his eyes narrowing a fraction, 'I have this theory. I think the steroid treatment that Bella had for her asthma has masked the progression of her disease.' He sits back and pauses, as if deliberating over his words. 'That's why it's proving difficult to make a diagnosis. I think SLE is a real possibility. You've been so helpful, darling.'

Ruth nods. 'You're welcome.' She smiles. 'I take my hat off to you, Dr. Dominic.' She turns to Bella. 'Okay, so you're not quite ready to come home yet, sweetie pie, but I'm pleased you're better. How about I spend some time with you now, whilst Daddy does his phone calls?'

'Can we play a game?' The liquid blue eyes seek out her agreement.

'Of course we can. What would you like to play?' She scans the room, as if looking for ideas, but her eyes drift up to corners of the ceiling, to the smoke detector, to the monitors above Bella's bed. She wonders where the camera is located.

'Snap?' says Bella.

'Good idea,' replies Ruth. 'I love playing games.'

32
RUTH

Ruth turns over in bed. She feels Dominic shift until his hand comes to rest on her thigh. A few minutes later a soft nasal rhythm occupies the space between them again. She lies in the darkness, her worries internalised. The nausea, the sickness, the dizzy spells. Yesterday she'd pulled into a layby on one of her home visits when her vision temporarily blurred. It can't be an infection. No raised temperature. No diarrhoea. In fact she'd been constipated for a few days instead. What was her body trying to tell her? If her period doesn't come by the weekend she'll do another pregnancy test. When is she going to tell Dominic? What would it achieve? Besides he's got more than enough to worry about with Bella.

She thinks about her conversation with the pae-diatricians today. The repartee had been friendly and light-hearted to begin with, as Shaba Elmahdy entreated her to pull up a chair, then spoke to her in her 'I've heard it all before, you can tell me anything' sort of voice. As her questions became more intrusive-'What *exactly* is the nature of your relationship with Bella's father?' Ruth found herself becoming increasingly defensive. It's a question she has asked herself repeatedly since. Sometimes the closer she gets to Dominic, the more conflicted she feels. It's as if there's something else going on, but she can't quite put her finger on it.

Her theory about SLE seemed to hold little weight with her paediatric colleagues. All Bella's tests had been clear. 'Surely it's not such a clear cut picture in children,' she argued. Shaba conceded a little by agreeing that an EEG and brain scan would be more conclusive, but Ruth still felt piqued. That's when she decided to challenge them about the possibility that Dominic was being monitored. It didn't escape her notice that, at this point, Sheena and Shaba exchanged quick glances. She wanted to say, 'I'm a professional too, please treat me like one,' but she hadn't. 'Safety is our paramount concern,' Shaba countered, fixing her with hooded eyes, 'and we have CCTV throughout the hospital, not just on the children's ward.'

But why keep Bella in hospital? EEGs and brain

scans can be done as an outpatient. She's overthinking things again. Time to practice her mindfulness. Feeling the weight of her body she lets go of her thoughts. She adjusts her position until she can feel Dominic's warm breath in her hair. He murmurs something into the pillow and she lifts his hand and brings it up, so that it cups her breast. Then they lie, like spoons, until the trill of a blackbird breaks the silence.

★

The chime of the alarm sears through their slumber. Ruth rolls over, with a frayed sense of wakefulness. She groans.

'So much for setting the alarm early so I could go for a run before work. I'm exhausted.'

Dominic's arm reaches over her shoulder.

'You didn't sleep well. You were fidgeting all night.'

'I know, Dom. So were you. I've been mulling things over in my mind.'

'About what?'

'So many things. About me. About you. But mostly about Bella.' She props herself up on her elbow. 'Dominic, have the medics asked you anything about me?'

'What do you mean?'

'About our relationship.'

'No.' His hand seeks out hers in the darkness. 'Why?'

Ruth hesitates, weighing up whether what she's about to say is a good idea. 'I'm just a bit wary, that's all. I have a feeling they might be monitoring us.'

Suddenly Dominic sits up in bed and snaps on the bedside light. His eyes flash with indignation. 'What the hell do you mean by that?'

'They seem intent on keeping Bella in hospital for a long time, that's all.'

'I'll ask to speak to the consultant when I go in today. I'm not standing for any of this nonsense.'

'Oh, I wouldn't do that,' says Ruth, immediately regretting disclosing her concerns. 'Maybe it would be better to be patient. A few more days won't do any harm, and it gives you and me a chance to spend more time together.' She lifts up her hand and gently strokes his hair. His features visibly relax.

Leaning over him she switches off the light and sinks back down in the bed. She bites her lip. She was going to ask him about his father's death too, about the fact that he'd told her his father died of cirrhosis but Val mentioned it was cancer. Now is not the time.

They lie side by side. A filmy light filters through the curtains, shifting the shadows on the walls.

'But, seeing as you've mentioned it, this might be as good a time as any to ask you something,' he says.

'Go on.'

Dominic's hand squeezes tighter. 'I've been worrying about what might happen to Bella, if anything happened to me.'

'That's only natural, Dom. But nothing's going to happen to you.'

'Maybe. But she's got no near relatives. Apart from my mother. And I wouldn't exactly call her near.'

'Okay.' Ruth wonders where this conversation is going.

'Darling, would it be okay if I named you as Bella's next of kin?'

Ruth stifles a gasp. This was not what she'd expected. She loves Bella. But she's only known her for a few months. Would she really be prepared to take on that responsibility? But she's prepared to get pregnant, isn't she? Her throat constricts with emotion. She swallows but can't prevent the tide of emotion swelling in her chest. Turning her face into the pillow, she lies motionless, until she sniffs away her tears.

'Talk to me, darling.' Dominic is stroking her head, twisting strands of hair round his finger.

She can't keep it to herself anymore. She decides to tell him. That more than anything she wants a child. That she had a miscarriage when she was in Australia. And the fact that she couldn't tell anyone about it at the time. 'I even told work I had flu,' she says, 'because it was taboo.' He hears about Mark, and the pain she felt on uncovering his deceit. 'You never think it's going to happen to you,' she says, burying her head in the pillow.

'Everything's going to be all right,' he says. 'You've got me. And you've got Bella.'

She turns round to face him.

'We've got each other,' she says, through her watery smile. 'Of course I'll be Bella's guardian.'

She pulls him close, guiding him into her, with a wordless urgency. She can feel the dip in his stomach, as he presses against her abdomen, then her arms move up and her fingers thread through his hair. As they move against each other, skin to skin, it is as if their anxieties are being pushed into another space. He groans softly, and they fall apart, in a tangle of limbs.

33

DOMINIC

JUNE 2005

The workshop reception area is deserted. Dominic strikes the bell on the counter. Through the glass behind the till he can see his car. It's above head height, on a ramp. Not a good sign. He tries the bell again. A spotty youth appears, clutching an oily rag.

'Ah, Mr. Peterson,' he says, wiping his hands on his overall. 'Not quite ready for you yet. Maybe another ten, fifteen minutes. Just need to check the wheel alignment, then I'm done. Help yourself to a coffee. I'll be as quick as I can.' He disappears before Dominic has a chance to reply.

Ten to three. He'd hoped to be home by three. At least Courtney had agreed to collect Bella from school, although he'd tried to be at the school gates every day since Bella was discharged from hospital. He needed to keep up appearances. Show them he was a devoted dad.

Courtney seemed to have forgiven him too. Hadn't she moved on and found herself a new boyfriend?

He glances round the waiting area with its teal blue walls and shabby chequered linoleum. By the window there's a coffee machine and, adjoining this, a row of vinyl chairs. A television is mounted high on the opposite wall, its volume muted, headlines scrolling across the lower part of the screen about London's bid for the Olympic Games.

He walks over to the window. From here he has a good view of the High Street. Maybe he should go to a coffee shop over the road. There's a woman coming out of the one opposite and her raincoat is strikingly familiar. Navy with white polka dots. He squints for a better look at her. Courtney. Surely she can't have forgotten about collecting Bella? She's with a man who clutches her arm as they walk down the street but he's partially obscured by a black and white golf umbrella. Curious. Is this the boyfriend she's always talking about? The one who is quick to start arguments?

Dominic pours himself a coffee and sends a text:

Just checking you're still ok to collect Bella? Car having MOT. Back shortly

The reply is instant:

On my way. See you later.

He settles back in his seat, his eyes drifting up to the television monitor. There's a Formula One car on the screen now, against the back drop of a race-track. It looks like Silverstone. He wishes his could turn up the volume, but it's the headlines that attract his attention. Lucky Pagoda has been banned from Formula One. Dominic stands up and walks over to the screen. The words are on a continuous loop. Scandal. Banned. Dropped by the International Automobile Federation. Links with the China State Tobacco Enterprise.

Dominic raps on the counter, just as the mechanic reappears.

'All ready for you now, sir,' says the fresh-faced youth. 'Your car's passed its MOT. Just a couple of advis…

'Can you unmute the television,' says Dominic impatiently.

'Sorry, sir?'

'The television. I want to hear the news. It's important.'

'Em. I'll need to find the..'

'Now. Please. It's important.'

Dominic stares at the screen. It changes to

233

another item. The moment is gone. He needs to get home. He turns back to the mechanic. 'Too late. Can I have my keys?'

'Of course,' says the youth, passing a sheaf of papers, and his keys, over the counter. 'If I could just have your card details, please and I can go through what I've done.'

Dominic inserts his card into the machine and hurriedly taps in his PIN number.

'Not much on the advisories,' the mechanic continues, 'the offside front and rear tyres are reaching their limit. Best get them replaced in due course, although the tracking is okay. And your brake pads could do with a renewal next time.'

Dominic hasn't got time for this. He retrieves his card, picks up his keys and without a word of thanks he's gone.

★

Opening the front door Dominic flings his coat and papers to one side. He clatters downstairs to the kitchen and sifts the bundles of paper on the table, looking for the TV remote control. His pulse accelerates. Sweat pools in his armpits. He hears the clash of the door upstairs.

'Daddy?' Bella's voice percolates through the floorboards.

'Downstairs, darling,' he replies.

Courtney appears in the doorway. Behind her the frame of the tall man from the coffee shop. With the black and white umbrella. Gary Sharp.

'Gary?' Dominic looks at Courtney, then back to his colleague. 'Well, this is a surprise. I hadn't realised you two knew each other.'

Courtney looks embarrassed. 'Oh, come on, Dom, I'm sure you did,' she says, 'I told you. Gary and I have been going out for …' she turns to her boyfriend as if trying to read his lips, '…for at least a couple of months.'

Gary Sharp steps forward and taps Dominic's upper arm. 'All right, mate?'

'Bella and I are going upstairs,' says Courtney breezily. 'She wants to show me something in her bedroom.' She follows Bella out of the room.

Gary shifts his weight from one foot to the other. 'Have you heard the news?'

'I… I,' Dominic hesitates. 'I saw the headlines. About Lucky Pagoda. Is that what you mean? I haven't had a chance to hear the full story.'

Gary Sharp looks downcast. He pulls out a chair. 'It's not good news, I'm afraid. Do you mind if I sit down?'

Dominic feels sick.

'The FT ran a story this morning on the China State Tobacco Enterprise. They own the Lucky Pagoda Formula One team. They also have the monopoly in Chinese tobacco sales.' He sucks air in through his teeth. 'The International Automobile Federation has issued a joint statement with the World Health Organisation stating that tobacco advertising in F1 and any links with the tobacco industry are to be banned from the end of this season.'

'This doesn't affect me, though, does it?' Dominic's pulse quickens.

'Your shares…Oh, Christ, I don't know how to say this.'

'What about my shares?'

Gary's expression clouds over. 'I'm sorry, Dominic. This isn't easy. They've crashed.'

'What do you mean?' Dominic can hear his voice getting louder. He approaches Gary who pushes his chair back and pulls himself up to full height, so that his chin comes level with Dominic's brow.

'They've plummeted on the back of this news. Worthless. God, this isn't easy.'

'Too fucking right,' retorts Dominic. He pushes Gary back. 'I fucking trusted you.'

'I know. I know. I didn't see this coming.'

'Well you didn't see this coming either,' says Dominic, raising his right hand to swing a punch. He winces at the pain in his shoulder. His fingers go into spasm as he tries to clench his fist.

Gary grasps his forearm. 'Steady on, mate. We can work something out.'

'Get out. Get out now.'

Gary retreats, as Courtney reappears.

'Bella's in the bathroom,' says Courtney, 'she'll be…'

Gary swings her round, with his hand on her shoulder, and hustles her out of the door.

They leave without a further word and Dominic watches them going up the basement steps, hand in hand.

The shame. The humiliation. Being taken in by a fraudster. And his own pitiful lack of strength. He needs to retaliate somehow but he doesn't know how. Rushing upstairs to the first floor landing he looks out the window to see if he can identify Gary's car. There's no sign of the couple. They are not going to hear the end of this.

Back in the kitchen he switches on the twenty-four-hour news. The headlines continue to taunt him. He flicks to the FTSE column on his phone. He feels numb. Paralysed. Laced into a straightjacket. Unable to breathe.

Why hadn't he seen this coming? His brain does some quick-fire arithmetic. Christ, he might lose his house. He switches off the TV, replacing the remote control on the pile of papers on the table. And that's when he sees the letter with its characteristic blue and red franking. His mother. The last thing he needs. But there is a way out of this mess. Potentially. He could ask Ruth for a loan. For his mother. Of course.

34

RUTH

Above Ruth's desk at work, tacked to the cork board, between a poster on hand-washing and another of a talking condom, is a hand-drawn picture of a cat in multi-coloured crayon.

'Look what I made for you,' Bella said, her eyes shining as she pressed the paper into Ruth's hand, the day she came home again from hospital. 'I drew a picture of Tilly, sitting under a rainbow. Brenda helped me make it.'

'Brenda?' Ruth asked. The name sounded familiar, and then she remembered seeing her coming out of the ward. Brenda, the social worker, the same woman who had turned up on Dominic's doorstep the day the ambulance was called.

'That's lovely, darling,' Ruth said. 'I'll put it on the wall in my office so I can see it every day.'

Ruth has watched Bella closely, in the days since the picture went up, and her cheeks have filled out more, her hair seems glossier. She's back to her usual innocent banter. Yesterday, when Ruth asked her to go and wash her hands she stood, with her hand on her hip, and said she'd do it 'in a minute.' Bella was on the mend.

By contrast, Ruth isn't feeling any better. Her period has come late. Her morning surgery drags. By eleven o'clock the thought of coffee makes Ruth feel sick. She settles, instead, for water. Maybe she's dehydrated. The nausea and headaches are still there, even though she knows she's not pregnant. She opens the window but there's hardly any movement of air. The atmosphere has a muggy heat, like a swimming costume which has been rolled into a suitcase still wet.

She'd agreed with Dominic that she'd go home tonight. She needs to pick up a few things, plus finish her accounts. It had been his idea for her to move in permanently and, the more she thinks about it, the more it makes sense. Making an appointment with the lettings agency had been much more straightforward than she'd anticipated. She drags her thoughts back to the present and reaches for the call button.

Her last patient is eighty years old, brought in by her daughter because she's having dizzy spells. As she listens to the younger woman recounting the story, she looks at the old lady's expressionless face and observes how she rolls her thumb repeatedly over the tips of her fingers. Ruth looks at her prescription chart. She's on sixteen different medications, many vital to managing her Parkinson's disease, but half her drugs have been prescribed to counteract the side effects of the other half.

'I think I know the reason for your dizzy spells, Mrs. Wright,' Ruth says, laying her hand on top of the elderly lady's, and feeling it tremble under her fingers. 'And I think that, by stopping one of your tablets, we can sort out the problem.' Satisfied that there's no-one else waiting to see her, Ruth spends the next half hour going through her patient's drug chart, cancelling two drugs which work to lower blood pressure, but which, together, exaggerate this to dangerous effect. She concludes by asking her to come back for review in a couple of weeks. The daughter expresses her gratitude and morning surgery finishes satisfactorily.

'Dizzy spells,' Ruth writes in Mrs. Wright's notes. 'Iatrogenic cause. Diuretic discontinued. Beta blocker reduced.'

Drugs. They should always be the first thing to consider. Always. Just one of the many causes of dizziness. She congratulates herself on another correct diagnosis.

★

Fingers of light point through a leaden sky, as Ruth departs on her afternoon visits. The clammy heat sucks at her energy, like a leech. Fronds of warm breath mist the car windows. She pulls into the drive of the first house, stirring up loose chippings which crunch under her tyres. Switching off her engine she checks her phone, which has vibrated at regular intervals during her journey.

Three new messages. All from Dom. The air conditioning has cut out and now the atmosphere feels oppressive.

Bella has temp this morning. Given Calpol but no better. Ideas?

Have rung GP for appt as no reply from you.

Ring me when you get this message as may be home late.

She sighs. How did he manage before? She wonders if this will change when she moves in permanently. Maybe she should ignore the messages until later. Maybe if she disregards them things will sort themselves out. But instead her mind drifts to Bella, and she taps Dominic's number on her phone.

'Dom? How's Bella?'

'Oh, at last. Thank God you've rung. Miserable. Sick. Complaining of earache. She's had Calpol. I've got a doctor's appointment this evening.'

'But she was fine this morning, wasn't she? Do you want me to come round later?'

She holds her breath momentarily, hoping he'll

say no. She needs to have this evening to herself. Her paperwork has been pushed down the list of her priorities, until she can ignore it no longer.

'No need. That's why I was ringing you. Don't know what time we'll be back. I'll ring you later.'

'Okay, but if you change your mind just let me know.'

'I will. Maybe come over tomorrow? I want to ask you a favour. Nothing urgent. Oh, and Ruth?' He hesitates and his voice sounds distant.

'Yes?'

'I love you.'

Ruth hears the clash of a front door and looks up to see her patient's husband striding towards her car.

'Listen, I've got to go. Love you too. Speak to you later.'

★

An eerie light percolates through the glass-roofed atrium. The waiting area is empty. Ruth walks through to reception to deposit some pathology specimens in the courier's bag. The office is quiet. Both receptionists, who are manning the phones, are chatting over their cups of tea.

'Can't believe how quiet it is,' says Ruth.

Julie looks up. 'There's been a few cancellations. Did you hear the thunder earlier? There's more on the way too, according to the forecast. Typical British summer.'

Ruth walks over to a filing cabinet. She slides open the drawer and takes out a notepad.

'Just taking a prescription pad for my visits, ladies.' It had puzzled her earlier when she went to write a prescription and couldn't locate her pad in her bag. So unlike her to go on a visit unprepared. The receptionists don't look up.

She wanders back to her room. Time to complete some medical insurance forms. There's also a letter from Social Services requesting more information on a child protection case. Ruth clicks open the little boy's electronic records. She can see that he's been a frequent attender with episodes of minor illness and has had lots of time off school. His mother, a former drug addict, has another child who's in foster care and she's pregnant again with a new partner, residing at the same address. Ruth adds an alert on his notes, and completes the form.

She leaves work at six thirty and runs across the car park in the pelting rain, as if dodging bullets. She flings herself into the car seat, her tights clinging to her legs in wet streaks. With dismay she realises she needs milk so, stopping at the twenty-four hour grocers, she repeats the performance, being blunted by the wind, as she exits the car. Once through the front door her clothes are peeled off and dropped on the floor in a sodden trail which soon reaches the shower.

For the first time in ages it feels good to have the place to herself. She has a shower then goes downstairs in her dressing gown to make a tray to take to her study. Two slices of toast, a plate of salami and cheese, plus a bowl of olives and another of nuts. She's tempted to pour herself a large glass of wine but, instead, settles for a large cafetiere of coffee.

The low-wattage bulb from the desk lamp casts a cone of light over her credit card statements, as she scans down them, highlighting the petrol bills. Her fingers hover over the monthly fee for Likeminds.com. She casts her mind back over the hopeful, failed encounters. Another image supersedes this now. It's Bella, her hand outstretched, presenting her with a handmade card. Ruth reaches for a highlighter pen and strikes through the line with surgical precision. A reminder to cancel her subscription. With a pang of regret she realises she's been a bit selfish this evening. Picking up the phone she rings Dominic's number, but it goes through to voicemail.

'Hi, it's Ruth. Just checking you're both okay. Hope Bella is feeling better. Ring me when you get this message. I love you.'

Within a couple of hours she has filed the mountain of post-it notes, receipts and bills into some kind of order. As a reward she pours herself a large vodka, tops it up with cranberry and climbs into bed. She wonders whether she should try the phone again. Five past ten. It goes straight through to voicemail as before. She'd expected a call by now. She wonders what time Bella's appointment was. He could be putting her to bed. Or maybe they've both fallen asleep. It wouldn't achieve anything to drive round to the house now. She'll just have to be patient. As she settles down in bed she can hear the wind battering the garden furniture outside. Metal chairs slide across the patio and clash against the fence. She should have brought them inside but it's too late and too inclement to go outside. The volume on the TV is adjusted up slightly and she slides down under the duvet.

When she wakes, the credits of the late night horror movie are rolling across the screen. Percolating through the haunting music, however, is the sound of the front doorbell. Although she hears it, with its persistent, intrusive monotone, it takes her a while to dissociate it from the screen and realise that someone is at the front door. It can't be Dominic. He has a key. Besides, it's quarter past midnight now and surely he would have rung first.

She clambers out of bed and walks over the landing to the rain-splattered window of the guest bedroom, lifting the curtain. She can't make out the figures standing by the front door, but under the sepia spotlight of the streetlamp is the ghostly outline of a police car.

35

RUTH

She stands at the front door, silently screaming. The street is ink black, but the high visibility jackets lend a garish hue to the police
constables' faces. One of them is talking. Looking at
his pimpled brow and pock-marked cheeks, Ruth
suspects he's several years younger than her. Her dressing gown flaps around her legs, so she pulls it in tight.

1242 reads the number on his epaulette. She stares
at it. A thread has come loose from the stitching. It
curls under the numbers, like a cedilla, and she wonders whether, if she pulls it, everything will unravel
and go away.

She must have invited them in, because now she's
sitting in her front room and the policewoman is

asking her if she takes sugar in her tea. She opens her mouth to speak but no words come out. She's in a time warp, and the only sensation she feels is a dull pain in her chest.

PC 1242 is apologising that it's taken so long to notify her.

'It happened around seven fifteen this evening,' he says, 'and although the gentleman had ID on him there was no one else at that address. It was the hospital that gave us your details as next of kin. I believe there are no other relatives?' He puts his hand on her knee, then retracts it as an afterthought when the policewoman returns with a tray. Instead he crouches forward, bringing his head close, and says, 'The little girl, she's in ITU, but she's going to be okay.'

Ruth tries to process his words. She can hear voices upstairs. She must have left the television on. The policewoman's radio crackles, and spits out random words, 'Lima Charlie, Lima Charlie.'

A sour taste bubbles in her mouth. Noises and imagery crowd in her brain. Excel spreadsheets swim across her vision. Collar numbers and petrol receipts merge. PC 1242 is pulling her into a different life and she tries to resist. He's saying something about a need to identify the body. Just a few hours ago she'd been sitting in her study doing a menial task, which she'd deferred repeatedly. She would give anything to go back to that moment.

Both sets of eyes are on her. The expressions behind them are those of professional objectivity, but their mouths downturn in an arc of sympathy.

'I'm sorry, would you mind saying that again, please?' She's shocked at how diminished her voice sounds.

'When you're ready we can take you to the hospital.'

She stands up, but her legs give way, and she feels a steadying hand on her back, as she sinks down onto the sofa.

'I'm very sorry,' says the young man, lightly tapping the back of her hand. 'I'm so very sorry.'

★

It happened on the road coming off the dual carriageway, towards the town centre. Just after the Dog and Duck pub and the farm shop there's a series of bends and dips before the road straightens out past the rugby club and into the new estate. There'd been a flash flood earlier in the afternoon. Seems the car had taken a corner at speed but, instead of following the camber, had ploughed straight on into a tree. There were no other vehicles involved. The police are reluctant to give her any further details at this stage. Instead they tell her, en route to the hospital, that there will be an inquest, when all these factors will be taken into account. By way of comfort, however, they assure her that there was no prolonged suffering. He was killed instantly.

The words sound hollow. This is no comfort to her at all. Reality has taken on a twisted dimension now.

She asks them if she can see Bella first. If she can touch her, feel the heat from her body, listen to the noise of her breathing, there is still hope. He could be just resting in another room, out of view, soon to come round and tell her not to worry.

'You're the one overthinking things this time,' he would say, with a smile. He would guide her by the arm, and they would go home, reassured that Bella was in good hands.

Instead, a nurse in blue scrubs leads her down a white corridor until they come to a four-bedded bay. A beeping cadence resonates round the ward, a constant reminder of the lives that hang in the balance, their physiological equilibria being artificially maintained. They come to a halt, by an oversized bed next to the nursing station, and the nurse lifts up a chart. She looks at Ruth and nods towards the mass of wires and tubes centred on the bed.

Ruth doesn't recognise Bella at first. The pale contours of her skin and the whiteness of the crisp cotton which surrounds her has melded into one. Her chest swells in regular gasps, like the gills of a fish out of water. Her hair, like skeins of bleached wool, has been combed back off her face. Her closed eyelids have a pearly translucency.

A thin blanket covers the lower part of her body, but multiple crimson pinpricks stipple her abdomen and chest. Her left arm is swathed in bandages. The only clue that it's Bella comes from the strawberry birthmark in the hairline of her right temple.

The sight of her tugs at Ruth's emotions. She reaches over and lifts Bella's hand. As she strokes the underside of her fingers they feel warm and elastic. They spring back together when she lets go. She wants to wrap her in her arms. Protect her.

She's conscious of a presence at her right-hand side and turns to see a young man, also kitted in scrubs. He holds out his hand.

'David Long,' he says. 'Specialist registrar. And you are Dr. Cooper?'

'Ruth. Yes.'

'She's stable now. Concussion, multiple abdominal and chest contusions, but thankfully no major bleeding. The pattern of bruising is consistent with wearing a lap belt. The good news is that her scan shows no evidence of brain or spinal injury. Right-sided Colles fracture too,' he continues, pointing to her arm, 'but that, of course, is secondary.' He stops and stares at the floor, allowing her to digest the information, then looks up at her, as if anticipating questions. The air feels stifling. She wants to say, 'Please look after her. She's fragile. You don't know the full story,' but instead she says nothing.

'I need to explain something else to you,' he says, drawing up two chairs and indicating for her to take a seat. 'We need to make Bella subject to an Interim Care Order.'

'I don't understand.'

'It's so the hospital can make decisions regarding her treatment. Decisions that will be in her best interests.'

Ruth notices how his words seem measured.

'It's necessary because both her parents are deceased.'

'But why can't I be nominated to do that? It's what her father would have wanted.'

'It may be that you'll be able to take on that responsibility in the future. It's just that, legally, at the moment you can't. Bella's needs will be considered by Social Services and the social workers will take your views, and your status as a potential guardian, into account.'

'Is it really necessary to go through all this legal red tape? I'm medically qualified. I can liaise with you regarding immediate necessary treatment.' She can feel her neck getting hot, her voice is a crescendo of anxiety.

David Long brings his head in close.

'I fully appreciate that and I'm sure all this will be

taken into account. As a doctor yourself you'll understand that we need to follow lawful procedure.' He straightens his back. 'We'll need to keep a close eye on her over the next few days,' he says. 'Please feel free to ring the Unit at any time of day or night.' He smiles, then rises and retreats.

PC 1242 is hovering on her periphery. Ruth remains rooted to the spot, wanting to stay there and delay the inevitable.

She looks again at the figure, lying like a porcelain doll, in the bed. And suddenly she feels calm. She breathes in the scent of purity and hope. She must summon every last ounce of energy she has. For Bella's sake. So many challenges lie ahead, not least the first daunting task. Breaking the news to Bella of her father's death. She shudders. Dominic. The police are waiting. She's ready. She nods at PC 1242 and walks out of the ward.

36

RUTH

After a short drive the patrol car passes through an automated barrier into the car park at the back of the General. It's a stark contrast to the Children's Hospital which, from the exterior, resembles a wedding cake, with its tall sandstone pillars. Here the wards are all on one level, reflecting its past as a TB sanatorium. A single corridor, with heavy-duty flapping plastic doors at either end, bisects the length of the hospital. At this late hour it's deserted, save for a couple of housemen who glide past them avoiding eye contact, either totally absorbed in their thoughts, or not wanting to be delayed on their way back to snatching a few minutes' precious sleep.

Halfway down the corridor PC Rob Collins, for that is PC1242's name, unlocks a door, which opens onto a small courtyard. The rain slants across their shoulders as they walk briskly to the building on the far side. The policeman rings a bell and a few moments later a man, wearing a pigeon grey lab coat, opens the door and ushers them in.

It's much colder in the mortuary. Ruth can feel the prickle of goose bumps on her arms. A wash of grey surrounds her, from the smoke-coloured walls, to the filing cabinets at the far corner of the room, to the nameless individual gesturing for her to take a seat. She draws up a plastic chair and turns to look at the man who's addressing her. He looks to be in his fifties, with wires of grey hair clasping his egg-shell skull, and a goatee beard trimmed short to resemble a pan scourer. Metal-rimmed spectacles perch on the end of his nose. He flicks through a foolscap folder and extracts a form.

'I just need to take a few details, before you go through to identify the body.'

Ruth flinches, but he doesn't look up. Instead, he presses a Biro down on a scrap of paper and scores across the sheet a few times until the ink bleeds through. He then asks her a series of questions: what's her relationship to the deceased, what's the deceased's ethnicity and religion, did the deceased have any distinguishing features, tattoos, for example? She answers in robotic fashion until the last question, then deliberates over her words as she describes Dominic's previous injuries. The mortician meticulously completes the form, without once making eye contact, or passing comment.

He puts down his pen and sits back.

'Obviously, the body can't be released to the funeral directors until the Coroner's Officer is satisfied. As there'll be an inquest this may take some time. We'll know more on Monday.'

A strained cough can be heard behind Ruth. The mortuary assistant looks over Ruth's shoulder, then addresses her directly. 'Ah, yes. I'm very sorry for your loss.'

There's the scraping of chairs, and Ruth feels a light touch on her shoulder. Her eyes meet those of PC Collins.

'Ready?'

She nods and drags her feet as the policeman leads the way, with the policewoman following closely behind.

A single strip light illuminates the adjoining room. Against the far wall is a tall bed, on top of which lies a discernible mound, covered in a white sheet. Ruth's legs feel spongy and she looks away. There's a sink by the opposite wall and beside it, in front of a frosted glass window, is a vase of flowers, their bent, plastic petals shrouded in dust.

A chair is pulled up alongside the bed and Ruth

sinks on to it, but then realises that, soon, she will have to stand up. The wrapped bundle is now above her eye level and the plastic sheeting under the body has come adrift, revealing wooden rollers within a metal frame.

She grasps hold of the chair to steady herself and pulls herself up. Taking her nod as his cue, PC Collins slowly peels back the corner of the sheet.

She reaches into her bag for her stethoscope, actions propelling her faster than thoughts, but her equipment isn't there. Why should it be? They haven't asked her here to verify death. Of course not. Her eyes come to rest on the shiny toecaps of the police constable.

'Please take your time,' he says, shifting his weight from one foot to the other.

As she lifts her head their eyes meet. She mirrors his professional smile and turns to look at the body. The slight parting of his mouth and depression of his jaw is evidence that the leathery muscles of his neck have contracted. Rigor mortis has already set in. His hair has been parted to the left of centre, and trained in either direction. It's so uncharacteristic of him that she reaches over and brushes it forward with her fingers. It feels lank. Matted. It dawns on her, in slow motion, the reason why his hair has been fashioned this way. She gags. The rim of a dark, oily crater is visible over his right parietal bone. The boggy depression proof, if she needed it, that death had come instantly.

She bites her lip until she can taste metal in her mouth. Her fingers are greased with congealed blood, and bile bubbles in her throat. She feels a steadying hand on her back, but resists the temptation to sit down. She swallows hard and turns to look at the policeman.

'Just one more thing, please. Just so I can be sure.'

The constable is studying her face intently, as if searching for clues.

Leaning against the cold metal of the trolley she edges the white sheet further down. He's dressed in a short-sleeved hospital gown. She swallows her revulsion when she spots the label attached to his wrist, but it's the withered right arm that draws her attention. Her eyes follow its contours across his abdomen, where his hand rests like a stiffened claw. If there'd been any thread of doubt, it is now dispelled. She bends down, her kiss on the back of his hand a warm imprint on a cold waxwork.

'Yes,' she says, her breath curling away from her in the icy night air. 'This is Dominic Peterson.'

As she turns, she stumbles over the chair, and pushes past the policeman, just making it to the sink in time before she throws up. The back of her throat burns and her stomach feels as if it has been wrung out. Speckled circles of light appear before her eyes.

She sinks to her knees. And now she feels as if she's hovering over the scene, a mere observer, watching a disaster movie, as the credits roll and the screen goes black.

37
RUTH

Val is on Ruth's front doorstep. Eyes red-rimmed. No words. Ruth hugs her and stands back.

'Where are the kids?' asks Ruth.

'My next door neighbour said she would have them for the afternoon.' Val steps over the threshold. Mike is hovering not far behind. He clasps Ruth's arm but avoids conversation.

In the kitchen Val fills the kettle, smells the milk.

'Help yourselves,' says Ruth, 'but not for me. I've had enough tea for now.' She lifts a pile of papers and couple of carrier bags off the table to make room for their cups. 'They gave me these last night,' she says, picking up a set of keys and twisting the keyring round her finger. 'As well as his watch.' Her voice breaks. 'I went round to his house this morning.'

'Darling, we would have come with you. You don't need to do that kind of thing on your own.' Val's forehead creases with worry.

'I just wanted to pick up a few things for Bella. You know, for when...' Her voice trails away.

'How is she?' asks Val. 'What's the latest?'

Ruth runs her fingers through her hair. 'Still on a ventilator. Going to be on ITU for a few days, then transferred to the Children's Ward. The main thing is she's stable. I'm not going in tonight. I'll ring them instead and go in tomorrow.'

'I can come with you, if you like,' says Val, coming over towards Ruth and laying her arm on her shoulder.

'Thanks, but I'll be okay.' She shrugs away from Val's grasp and looks at them both. 'You know it was only a few days ago that Dominic asked me to be Bella's guardian.' Her words are stilted, her voice not her own. 'It was if he had some ghastly premonition.'

Val and Mike exchange anxious glances.

'What?' says Ruth, trying to read their expressions. 'What are you thinking?'

'How did he sound when you last spoke to him?' asks Mike, his eyes glistening.

Ruth thinks back to their conversation the previous night. Guilt and sorrow envelop her, like unwelcome friends. 'He was worried about Bella and I brushed him off by telling him to go and see his GP.' She hesitates, parking her thoughts. She had told Dominic she was too busy. She interlocks her fingers and closes her eyes. 'For fuck's sake, how could I be so selfish?'

'Please, Ruth, don't beat yourself up about it. I'm feeling guilty too.' Mike searches her face. 'Did he mention my phone call on Wednesday?'

Ruth opens her eyes. 'What do you mean?'

'He had a bit of bad news.'

'I …I don't understand.'

'Dominic and I have been working together on his investment portfolio. I think you probably knew that?' He waits until Ruth nods, then continues. 'When the Grant of Representation came through for Madeleine's estate I helped him put together a trust fund for Bella. But instead of putting *his* investments into it he wanted to speculate a bit. He was convinced he could make a killing on a deal with the Lucky Pagoda telecoms business.'

Ruth's heard all this before. How can this have any relevance?

'Anyway, he went ahead, and sunk a large amount of money into shares, which took off when Lucky Pagoda announced their F1 takeover bid.' Mike's voice begins to waver. 'And then last week it all went wrong. The Chinese State Tobacco Enterprise, or

CSTE, which holds the monopoly of all tobacco trading in China, announced that it had subcontracted twenty percent of its business to Lucky Pagoda.'

'Mike, darling,' interjects Val, 'I don't think this is relevant.'

'Except that the Formula One Association withdrew its contract and Lucky Pagoda has gone bust, taking Dominic's money with it.' His breath escapes in a low whistle. 'Do you know what he said to me last week? "Risk is a great aphrodisiac, Mike." Jeez. Where the hell did he get that idea from? He lost more than five hun-'

'Darling,' interjects Val. She fires him a reproachful look.

Ruth sits in silence. She thought she knew Dominic so well. She'd hoped they had a future together. But he hadn't told her anything about this. What else did he keep from her? So many questions. She must focus on Bella now, but it's hard not to reflect that sympathy and resentment make poor companions.

'I'm sorry, Ruth,' says Mike. 'That was tactless of me.'

They sit, with their heads bowed, as the kitchen clock ticks away the silence between them.

'As I was leaving the house this morning I met one of the neighbours,' says Ruth. 'Felt like I'd been ambushed, you know, the way she suddenly appeared, as I was coming down the steps. Said she'd heard the awful news and wanted to know how Bella was.' An image tugs at the corner of Ruth's memory. It's of Bella, running around in circles, chasing bubbles, the day they went to Windridge. She wants to allow this picture space to breathe, to relive the sound of the little girl's squeals when she caught a gloopy sphere on her wand and it burst, sprinkling her with soap suds. The scuffed knees, the gappy smile, the hair pulled back into a French plait in different shades of barley. Instead the sketch is being drawn over by another scene. A little girl lying in a hospital bed, blending into the pillows, transfixed by bleeping monitors and pulsing tubes.

'Yeah, it was on local radio this morning. Apparently the road wasn't reopened until around noon.' Mike looks as though he could go on, but has thought better of it. He stands up and paces up and down the room. He pushes his hands deep down into his pockets causing his jeans to ruffle down his legs.

The air in the kitchen feels weighted with predicaments.

Ruth's head pounds. The pain around her temples is exaggerated with every movement. As she lifts her hands to rub her forehead she can still smell the formalin under her fingernails. The smell of the mortuary is still on her, despite having scrubbed her hands in a manner which would put Lady Macbeth to shame. The cloying odour makes her gag. As she rubs her eyes, a gritty sensation scours the inside of her eyelids.

'Listen, guys. Would you mind if I went upstairs for a lie-down? You're very welcome to stay, but I feel exhausted.'

Val and Mike look at each other. 'Of course not. Do you want us to stay?'

'No, the kids need you. I'll be okay, honestly.'

'Maybe we better get going then,' says Val, standing up and gathering her things. 'But will you ring me tonight? After you've spoken to the hospital?'

'Yeah. I will' Ruth nods and she walks ahead of them to open the front door.

There's a man walking up the path. Medium build. Close-cropped hair. The crisp contours of a suit poking out from under a waxed jacket. As he approaches her, he holds out his hand.

'Dr. Cooper? Afternoon. My name is Detective Sergeant James Macmillan. I'm your Family Liaison Officer.' He takes her hand. 'I'm very sorry for your loss.' He stands aside, allowing Val and Mike to pass, then bends down and picks up a bunch of flowers, which has been left on the doorstep.

'May I come in?'

38

RUTH

James Macmillan has trustworthy eyes. The colour and shape of almonds, they remind Ruth of Winston, the chocolate Labrador she had as a child. She can hear the smile in his soft Scottish accent.

'Do you mind if I take off my jacket?' he asks and, without waiting for a reply, he peels off his Barbour and places it on the back of a chair. A tin rattles to the floor and, as he bends down to retrieve the box of mints, Ruth notices the fingertips of a blue latex glove poking out from one of his jacket pockets.

'Excuse the state of the kitchen,' says Ruth, 'and me, for that matter,' looking down at her grubby sweatshirt and the detergent-stained jogging pants she's used as a towel, every time she dries her hands. 'I've probably had about four hours sleep in the last twenty four.'

He shoots her a look which says he's seen it all before.

'Rob Collins mentioned you,' she says. 'But is it usual to have a FLO, when I'm not "family"?'

His smile widens slightly, just enough to reveal an asymmetry of his upper teeth. He places his phone and a leather organiser on the table.

'The hospital had your details. You were named as an emergency contact in Mr. Peterson's personal effects. Plus, his last recorded phone call was with you.' He clears his throat and averts his eyes, leaving Ruth to wonder if his last sentence was intended.

Her cheeks feel hot. His phone. Why hadn't they given her that?

'As you know,' he continues, 'there'll be an inquest because of the road traffic collision.' He pauses, and looks at her intently. 'Dr. Cooper, I want you to know that I'm here to help you, while that investigation is underway.'

She nods. It's not often she gets called Dr. Cooper, when out of the surgery, but at least he's treating her as a fellow professional. They're on the same wavelength. They talk the same language.

'You'll probably see quite a bit of me in the next

few weeks,' he continues gently, 'so if you have any questions or worries please make me your first point of contact.' He extracts a card from the inside pocket of his suit, and slides it over the table. 'My phone number.'

'Thanks.'

'I expect you have lots of questions.'

'I'm curious as to how the system works, when there's an inquest.'

'Of course. Perhaps if you'd care to tell me a little bit about Mr. Peterson, I can-'

'Dominic.'

'Sorry?'

'His name is Dominic.'

She has tried so hard to stay calm and in control, but now she can feel the tears welling, and her voice wavering.

'Of course,' says James Macmillan, softly. 'Dominic.'

They sit in silence and the air feels swollen with hurt. Outside, the spiny branches of a pyrocantha bob in the breeze, scratching the corner of the kitchen window, like an unwelcome visitor. In the corner of her vision a blue tit taps on the window, then flies away. Her eyes sting and her mouth feels dry. Ruth stands up and walks over to the kitchen counter. She tears off a large piece of kitchen roll and blows her nose vehemently. She needs to stay calm, focussed.

'Would you like a cup of tea?' she asks, lifting the kettle and wheeling round to face James Macmillan.

'Sure, that would be great. Thanks.'

She gives him a half-hearted smile. 'If I start at the very beginning, this account could take a long time. Oh, and please call me Ruth.'

'Whenever you're ready, Ruth. And I'm James, although most people know me as Mac.'

Mac. He reminds her of Jimmy McBride, one of her University lecturers. Empathetic with his patients, popular with his students. She hands Mac a cup of tea and pulls up a chair opposite. After half an hour Ruth realises she has given him lots of information but, to Mac's credit, it has felt like a friendly, informal chat. He puts down his pen, and moves his chair back.

'Thanks, Ruth. I better get going. I expect you'll be tired. Is there anything I've forgotten, that you'd like to ask me?'

'No, I don't think so.' Her mind feels cluttered.

'In that case, there's just something else before I go. Firstly may I have the keys to Dominic's house, please? I need to go round and make an inspection, maybe remove his computer etc. It'll only be temporary and it's part of our evidence gathering for the Coroner. I'm sure you understand. All his personal effects, such as his wallet and phone will be returned to you in due course.'

Ruth lifts a weighty key-ring from the work-top and hands it over. 'Of course. Here you go.'

'And secondly…um… your phone. Would you mind if I took it to run some checks? It won't take long. I can drop it round to you later today or you can come with me to the police station and wait while it's done.'

'*My* phone? Why do you need that?'

'Just routine checks. We've established that Mr. Peterson's last phone call was with you. It just helps build up a timeline for the Coroner.'

Ruth looks at the clock on the cooker. Two forty. She can't face a trip to the police station. 'What time could I have it back?'

'In a couple of hours I reckon.'

Ruth feels weary. 'Always happy to help the police with their enquiries,' she says, handing over the phone. 'Put it through the letter box later. I'm going to bed.'

He stands up, lifts his coat from the chair and slips the phone into his pocket. 'Thanks. Remember, call me if you have any queries.'

Ruth sees him out. As she watches his white BMW disappear she wonders if she's done the right thing. Dominic's keys? Is it usual to ask for the keys to the victim's property? And to ask for her phone? Regret stings her. She should have gone with him. Still, what harm can it do?

She goes back into the kitchen and straightens the kitchen chairs, but there's something caught under a chair leg. Bending down, she extracts a small aerosol can which must have rolled under the table, when Mac dropped his mints. She scrutinises the label. Pepper spray. She reminds herself that she's dealing with a professional. Although he feels like a friend.

39

RUTH

The silver Honda comes out of nowhere, cutting across the right side of her vision, as she pulls out of the parking space. She slams on the brakes. The driver swerves, clipping her wing mirror. The single, continuous blast of his horn reverberates in her head, as her engine splutters and stalls. She restarts the car, her sweaty fingers clamped round the steering wheel, then pulls away into the busy line of traffic. Her headaches have got worse over the last few days. Her scalp feels as if it's shrinking into a tight cap over her skull. Fortunately the nausea and dizziness have disappeared. She just needs to remain focussed.

At the surgery a jam-jar of yellow, pink and orange

gerbera has been placed on her desk, its neck decorated with pink gingham ribbon. Its unsophisticated simplicity is touching, adding a welcome vitality to the otherwise drab surroundings.

'They're from my garden,' says Ginny, as she places a mug of coffee on Ruth's desk, then stoops to give her a hug. 'Lesley has swapped her Baby Clinic for your Emergency Duty this afternoon, by the way.' Ruth notices how she stops short of saying 'We thought it would be easier for you' and she's grateful. She should be finished by four, and she can drop into the Children's Hospital on her way home.

She'd received a mixed response when she turned up at work on Monday morning. Some of the receptionists had greeted her with smiles, then busied themselves with jobs. Others avoided eye contact. Paul Franklin phoned her over the weekend saying he wasn't expecting her at work, but how could she let her colleagues down? Besides, what else was she to do if she didn't go in? Bella was in hospital. And Dominic was... Dominic was...yes, she needed to keep busy. It focused her on tasks that she could achieve, rather than allowing her to dwell on events that couldn't be changed.

Monday evening had been the hardest of all. Bella had been taken off the ventilator, and moved to the children's ward over the weekend. Shaba Elmahdy was waiting for Ruth. Bella needed to be told about her father, she stressed, before she started to ask, 'Where's Daddy? When's he coming back?'

'Breaking bad news,' thought Ruth, the tutorial we had as final year medical students, during our General Practice placement. But it hadn't prepared her for this. Both women went into the cubicle where Bella was lying. Bella opened her eyes, as her curtains swished back, and gave a lopsided smile on recognising Ruth. There was no skirting round the truth. Bella needed to know the facts. But the sight of her jerked Ruth's emotions to the extent that she mouthed to Shaba, 'I can't do this,' and her eyes filled with tears. Instead she took off her shoes and jacket and climbed into bed with Bella, placing an arm round her shoulder. She could feel the heat from Bella's head, as Bella leant back into Ruth's chest.

'Bella,' said Shaba, resting her hand on Bella's blanket. 'I have to tell you some very sad news.' Ruth could feel Bella's muscles tensing, as she clutched her toy kangaroo. 'I'm afraid Daddy has been in an accident, and he died.' Ruth stifled a breath, as Shaba stroked Bella's hand. The paediatrician waited for a reaction but there was none. 'I'm very sorry to tell you this sad news, Bella,' Shaba repeated slowly, 'but your Daddy has died.'

In the silence that followed Ruth tightened her grip on Bella, as her own vision blurred with tears. She twisted round to face Bella.

'I'm sorry, darling,' said Ruth, fighting back the tears. Bella stared at her, unblinking.

'It's okay to cry, Ruth,' Bella said, lifting strands of hair off Ruth's face. 'It's okay to cry.'

The words chimed like the sound of broken crockery. Then Bella burst into tears and they held each other tight.

Thinking about it now causes the tears to well again. She looks down at her phone. A voicemail earlier, from Mac, and now a text.

Please advise good time to call, or arrange visit.

What could he possibly want? She doesn't need any more sympathy at the moment.

She dials the number for the Children's Hospital and asks to be put through to Bella's ward. The clerk is non-committal when Ruth asks how Bella is, so she asks to speak to a nurse. Bella is going for an X ray later in the afternoon, she's told, so Ruth decides to defer her visit until the evening. A draught from the door catches her, and a movement at the corner of her eye-line.

'Your door was open,' says Paul Franklin, his white-haired countenance appearing round the door frame, 'although I did knock.'

She smiles. 'Morning, Paul. Come in, have a seat.'

'I won't, thanks,' he says, leaning back against the examination couch, so that he's almost perched on the edge of it. 'I just came in to see how you are. The words may seem inadequate at a time like this, but I just want you to know we're all thinking of you and we're behind you all the way.'

Paul always knows exactly what to say. She remembers the party that was organised for the practice staff and their families last Christmas. He arrived with two little boys in tow, who looked to be about five and seven. She'd been about to ask him if they were his grandchildren but she heard the younger one addressing him as 'Daddy.' Later, Ginny told her that Paul's first wife died of cancer sixteen years ago, leaving him as a single parent to three teenagers. Nine years ago he found happiness again and remarried. She looks again at the benevolent demeanour, the empathetic eyes, and has so much respect for this family doctor. He's experienced the rawness of life, over the past forty years, both professionally and personally.

'I appreciate it, Paul. I'm doing okay, thanks.'

'And the other thing to tell you,' Paul continues, 'is that I've organised a locum for you. Starting on Monday.'

The gratitude she felt a few moments ago now recedes, like water vanishing down a plughole.

'It's not necessary. I can manage, really.'

'I know you can,' he says softly, 'but that's not the point. You've got more than enough to contend with at the moment.' He walks over to her and squeezes her arm. 'There's no pressure on you to undertake any of your surgery commitments. We can play it by ear, but I want you to take as long as you need.' Then he taps her arm and is gone.

She sits in stunned solitude. Is she not trusted to do a good job? People used to call her capable. Her parents. Her friends. 'If you want something done, ask Ruth,' they would say. 'She can always be relied upon.'

She feels utterly wretched. And alone. Shit happens. Yes. But she's had it in shovel loads in the last six months. It's time to be selfish. She picks up the phone to return Mac's call.

40
RUTH

The café across the road from the hospital is quiet. While she waits for Mac she lifts up a newspaper on the adjoining table. She flicks through the pages then returns to the headline on the front page. *Tragic tot survives crash* it reads, but she stares at it for several minutes before it sinks in. Underneath is a picture of the mangled wreckage of a black BMW; in another shot, a bouquet of flowers tied to a tree, just visible above the blue and white police tape. She wonders who left them. Sadness cloaks her. There's a photo of Dominic on page two, but she has to read the caption several times to realise that it's him. It must have been taken over ten years ago when he was working in London, because the text describes how he previously escaped an IRA bomb blast at the Stock Exchange in 1990. She stares at a younger version of the Dominic she knows, and curses him. Why had he kept so many things from her? And why does he have the audacity to look back at her, with the confidence of someone in the prime of life?

She checks her watch. From her window seat she spots Mac paying the taxi driver, then skirting round traffic as he crosses the road. He looks pre-occupied when he enters, patting the pockets of his blazer, then bringing out his phone, checking it, then placing it in his inside pocket. She waves and he acknowledges her with a smile.

'Hey, Ruth. Good to see you. I'm sorry I'm late.'

Ruth wonders if his excuses for being late might mirror hers: a case conference that went on longer than expected, an urgent phone call from a relative, an unexpected death, but, other than an apology, no explanation is given for his delay. He takes his phone out of his jacket again, then places it on the table in front of them. He doesn't look like a policeman today. He's wearing jeans with a white shirt and stone coloured blazer. He could be an estate agent, or an insurance broker, or someone on a blind date. Only the close-cropped hair, and the eyes that continually scan the café, give him away.

'Would you like another one?' he says, gesturing towards her coffee cup.

'Sure. Decaf cappuccino, thanks.'

He returns with two cups of coffee and sits down. 'What's the latest on Bella? How is she?'

He says this, Ruth is convinced, by way of polite conversation. She feels sure he will be keeping tabs on her improvement.

'She's making progress, but I'm not going in till later. She's having an X ray this afternoon. She knows about Dominic, poor little girl.' Her fingers drum out her anxiety on the table top. 'Will anyone be speaking to her about the accident?'

'Yes, for sure, but only when the time is right. And you can rest assured that it'll be handled sensitively. Just to keep you up to date on the Social Services front I've spoken to Brenda Madingley. She says she knows you.'

'Brenda? Yes. I've come across her at work, but she came out to visit Dominic a few weeks ago.'

'She's been assigned to Bella's case, as part of the Duty Assessment Team. I'll text you her number. She wants to arrange a meeting with you as part of her initial viability assessments. She wondered if you could give her a ring.'

'Her *what,* sorry?'

'It's a formality. She needs to make initial inquiries and carry out assessments to determine what will happen when Bella leaves hospital. Anyway, it's early days. There'll be plenty of time to revisit this in the days and weeks ahead.' He sits back and studies her. 'What about you? How have you been doing?'

'Signed off work.'

'Really? Probably a good thing, yeah?'

'I'm not sure. I prefer to keep busy. The practice has organised a locum to cover my work indefinitely. It seems I don't have much say in the matter.'

'Why? How long have you been there?'

'About nine months. It makes me feel a bit insecure, to be honest. I did my GP training here then went to Melbourne for a couple of years. Took this job when I came back.'

Mac's face folds into a smile. 'Small world. I was in Melbourne ten years ago. Had a career break when I came out of the Red Caps.'

'Red Caps?'

'Royal Military Police. Might have been deployed to a war zone if I'd stayed. Instead I went off to Australia and worked as a fitness instructor. Met my wife there. Four years later I was back here in the Police Force.'

'Your wife is Australian?' The sinking feeling in Ruth's chest is instantaneous. She doesn't give him a chance to reply, but stirs her coffee with an intensity that could make the pattern on the porcelain disappear. 'I lived in Malvern for eighteen months. You probably know it.'

'I do indeed. And ex-wife. It didn't work out. And she stayed in Oz.'

The swirling stops and she drops the teaspoon. 'Oh, I'm sorry.'

'No matter.' His mouth tenses. 'And anyway I shouldn't be talking about myself.' He hesitates. 'Ruth, I don't want to upset you, but I need to know a little bit more about Dominic. Did he have many friends? It seems like you're the one person who knew him best.'

Ruth gives a small snort, bridling at the irony of this. She's not sure she knew him that well at all. She twists a strand of hair round her finger. 'Mike and Val Armitage are good friends. Mike's a former colleague of Dom's from the Stock Exchange.'

'Were they the couple leaving the house the day I met you?'

'Yes, that's right. They were.' Ruth is startled by his clear recall.

Mac makes a note on his phone. 'Do you have their number? I'd like to contact them.' He taps the numbers in, as Ruth recites them.

'You know Dominic is a ....' She stops mid-sentence, and inspects her nails. 'Dominic was a very doting father. I was always struck by how caring he was with Bella. He was a bit of a worrier, though. But I could understand that.' She lifts her cup, then immediately replaces it on the saucer, conscious that her hands are shaking. 'I think it was because of Madeleine's medical history, plus the fact that he thought he had to cope on his own.' She bites her lip to stop it trembling.

'What about his own health?'

'Oh, he had more than his fair share of problems. Migraine, asthma, eczema. And chronic pain from a childhood accident.' She stops and looks at him. 'Why do you need to know all this?'

'I'm just trying to build up a picture, that's all. For Bella's sake, really. You don't have to tell me, if you don't want to.' His voice is gentle, not abrasive like some of the duty officers she's come across at work.

'No, that's okay.'

'Sounds like he had a lot to deal with. I guess he must have been taking quite a bit of medication too, to get him through the day.'

Ruth thinks hard about this. About the foil blisters of ibuprofen, codeine and gabapentin. About the drugs under his bed.

'I don't know,' she says, dabbing at the milk foam which has settled above her upper lip. 'That's not something we ever discussed.' She leans back, working her shoulder blades against the chair. 'I should get going,' she says. 'I want to go and see Bella on the way home, although I'm actually quite tired now.'

He raises a quizzical brow. 'Where's your car?'

'Across the road in the hospital car park.'

'Well I want you to ring this number when you're finished on the ward. Call a taxi to take you home.

Give them my name and it'll go on my account.' He slides a card across the table.

Ruth's sure she's okay to drive home, but she's not going to argue with a policeman. She nods and takes the card.

'There's something else I want to ask you, Ruth.'

Her eyelids feel heavy. Maybe she should have settled for a double espresso to keep her awake, despite the risk of worsening her headache.

'Yes?'

'This may sound odd, but do you know of anyone who might have a grudge against you?'

She sits up abruptly, knocking her napkin to the floor.

'A grudge? Why do you say that?'

'Nothing major. There's been a few anonymous abusive messages posted on-line about you on your surgery website. The police are trying to trace the user account.'

'My God. When was this?' she says, the inflection in her voice rising. 'Why didn't I know about this earlier?'

'It's okay. The website is moderated so they were deleted immediately. That's probably why you didn't know about them. It's highly unlikely that anyone else noticed them either, so don't worry. I mention it just in case you can help us.'

Ruth stands up, her pride needled. 'Well, thanks

for giving me something else to worry about.' She gathers her things. 'On that note, I must be off.' Her voice wobbles. 'Let me know if you get any more information, Detective Sergeant, won't you?'

'Ruth. I'm sorry. Perhaps I shouldn't have mentioned it.'

She brushes past him, her shoulder bag almost clipping his phone off the table. 'Maybe you shouldn't have.' She turns away from him so he can't see the glittering of her eyes. 'But it's too late now.'

41

RUTH

Ruth pulls on the metal banister, hoisting herself up the twisting stone staircase to the ward. She is still stinging at Mac's words. A grudge, he said. A grudge? Why had she been singled out by someone who has grievance against the health service? Or was it a direct attack on her? Someone connected to Margaret Tremayne, maybe? An individual who knew about her prescribing error? Surely not connected to her history with Mark? My God, everyone makes mistakes. Doctors are only human. She doesn't know which is worse: being targeted by a bitter individual, or the fact that Mac knows about it.

The corridor is quiet, and the tall paned windows magnify the stark lighting, giving the place a ghostly green sheen. She arrives at Jubilee Ward and taps K259XZ on the key pad. The door opens and, silently, she slips on to the ward. The door to the office is closed. There's a nurse, wearing a red tabard, halfway down the ward. She's standing next to a drug trolley and is measuring liquid into a dispenser. She doesn't look up.

In the side room on the right Bella is propped up on pillows. She has her eyes turned towards another person in the cubicle. It's a woman, who sits, with her back to Ruth, her oiled black hair twisted like a rope, at the nape of her neck. She turns round as Ruth enters, and she has an air of faded elegance about her. From the lines which fan out from her espresso coloured eyes, and the plum coloured lipstick which has seeped into the tiny fissures round her lips Ruth reckons she is in her seventies. There's something about her face which feels familiar and it comes to Ruth when the woman smiles and there is the faint curl of her lip.

'Ruth, Ruth,' says Bella, her hands outstretched.

The woman stands up and the magazine, which was balanced on her knee, falls to the floor.

'Ah,' she says offering her hand, 'Bella has been telling me about you.' Her grip is firm and she seems reluctant to let go. Her eyes wander across Ruth's face, then take in her dress and seem to linger on the pearl necklace round Ruth's throat. They lock eyes again.

'I'm Bella's grandmother. Viviane Zuckerman.'

42
RUTH

A lady wearing a WRVS tabard clears tables and collects trays. She gives the women a wide berth. To her this must be a familiar scene: two strangers forced into a difficult conversation over their instant coffees.

'Please call me Viviane,' says the woman sitting opposite Ruth. 'Let's not be formal.' She roots in her handbag and pulls out a pack of Marlboro Lights, offering one to Ruth, who shakes her head and smiles.

'Viviane, I'm sorry, I don't think you're allowed to smoke in here,' says Ruth, lowering her voice. 'But we can go outside if you like.' The thought strikes Ruth as quite appealing at this precise moment.

Viviane purses her lips, and replaces the packet in

her bag. 'I forgot. They've changed the rules since the last time I was in the UK. Never mind.'

They sit in silence for a while, looking round the café, exchanging polite glances with each other, stirring their coffee.

'This must be very difficult for you, Viviane. I'm really sorry.'

'Yes, sure is.'

'How did you find out?'

'I wrote to Dominic a few weeks ago. Told him I was coming over. He didn't reply so I rang him last week.' Her words sound choked. 'I never dreamt it would be the last time I spoke to him.' She clears her throat and her chest rattles.

The hospital radio streams from a speaker in the corner. Ruth leans forward to hear what Viviane has to say.

'Arrived a few days ago. Got a taxi to the house,' Viviane continues. 'One of the neighbours spotted me walking up the path. She brought me into her house and told me about the accident. It was such a bolt out of the blue that I kinda went hysterical.' She pauses to catch her breath. 'An emergency doctor was called to give me some tranquilisers and then the police arrived and told me the details.'

She stops here and takes a strip of pills out of her bag. She presses one out of its foil and into her palm, then swallows it with a swig of coffee. 'They sorted out my accommodation in a local hotel and gave me the contact details of a local cop. Macmillan, I think his name is, but I haven't spoken to him yet.'

Ruth's posture stiffens. Odd that Mac hadn't mentioned this. Maybe he was bound by rules of confidentiality. Maybe he'd forgotten. 'I've met Mac,' Ruth replies. 'I guess he's the best person to co-ordinate the investigations.'

Viviane makes no response. 'So utterly tragic. Such a waste,' she continues. 'You know Dominic and I never had an easy relationship. He was a very bright child but he was always getting into trouble. He was headstrong. Liked to be the centre of attention …but I guess I could have been a better parent.'

Ruth looks across Viviane's shoulder, to a poster on the wall behind her. It's advertising Mindfulness classes. 'Be Calm. Be Happy. Be Mindful,' it reads. She takes a slow deep breath. 'You mustn't be hard on yourself, Viviane.'

'The last time I visited the UK,' says Viviane, 'was just after Isabella was born. Dominic made it quite clear he didn't want me there. I wish I'd been more assertive. I should have been there for Madeleine, and I wasn't.' She lifts her cup with a liver-spotted hand and sips her coffee. Her eyes narrow a fraction, as she looks at Ruth. 'How long have you known my son?'

Ruth silently counts the months on the fingers of one hand. It's no time at all. How can she convince this woman that she has some claim on him? On Bella? And without sounding too insensitive? Madeleine's only been dead seven months.

'I got to know him through the hospice,' she says. 'I'm a doctor at a local practice.' Technically that was correct, even if the facts were a little skewed. Heat suffuses her cheeks. She digs her hands into the chair cushion to stop her tremor.

'Ah, a doctor,' says Viviane, transferring her lipstick to her napkin.

Ruth is grateful she leaves it at that. They smile at each other through the background noise of the hospital radio, the clanking of plates and the whirring of the coffee machine.

'So what happens next?' says Viviane eventually.

'You mean…with Dominic?'

Viviane's fingers graze her chin. 'Yes.'

'At the moment it's up to the police to finish their investigations. Then the Coroner delivers a verdict on the cause of death.'

'Surely there's nothing to investigate. It was obviously an accident.'

'It's a formality, I guess, but it's out of our hands.'

'You know I've nursed and buried two husbands through cancer,' says Viviane, stroking her brow. 'But I never expected to bury my son.' She extracts a tissue from her bag and dabs her eyes.

Ruth wants to know more about Dom's father

but bites her lip. She's only just met this woman. No doubt there'll be plenty of time to get to know her better over the next week or two. She has so many questions for her. 'I'm so sorry,' she says. 'My mother died of cancer. It's a cruel disease.' She twists her earring. Deep breath. One thing at a time. 'Was Dominic close to his father?'

'Not really, and that's something I regret dearly. When Dominic was a toddler his father was absent a lot, through work. Ironically, when his father became ill and was at home all the time, Dominic became a bit of a rebel. With hindsight I realise this was his way of getting attention.' She sits back. 'You know, Rose, there's lots of things about my life that I regret.'

'Ruth,' says Ruth softly. 'My name is Ruth, not Rose.'

'Oh, yes, I'm real sorry' replies Viviane. 'You must excuse me, I get muddled.'

Close up Ruth can see the grey rings of old age round Viviane's pupils.

'You remind me very much of a nurse, who became a close family friend after Dominic's accident,' Viviane counters. 'Her name was Rose. Dear Rose, I wonder what became of her.'

Ruth is conscious of the pervasive smell of boiled cabbage coming from the kitchen. She takes a sip of her drink, trying to suppress her nausea. It puzzles her why she's had vomiting spells recently. Another manifestation of stress, no doubt. 'Ah yes,' she says. 'His accident. Poor Dominic.'

Viviane twists her fingers. She looks exhausted. The music has stopped and a soft wheeze can be heard. 'Indeed,' she nods. 'He spent weeks in hospital, then years of out-patient visits. His father was absent through ill health of his own, then I was left coping as a widow. Something I did badly.'

She pauses and Ruth sits in silence, threading her thoughts. Sounds like his mother is being economical with the truth, but who can blame her? She's not going to reveal a history of domestic violence to a stranger. 'It's so hard,' says Ruth, 'So hard.' She pauses, before adding, 'I don't know how to say this, without sounding trite, but it's never too late to mend bridges. Bella is a darling little girl.'

'You're right. You know Madeleine's death made me realise that I want to have more of a role in my grand-daughter's life. That's why I wrote to Dominic. And now this...It's Bella who needs me now.' She breaks off, as her voice falters.

Ruth looks at the older woman and feels conflicted. She hadn't expected Bella's grandmother to become part of the equation in Bella's care. And she's not sure she welcomes it. Her life has been turned on its head in a matter of months. She feels confused, upset. She needs space and time to process what Viviane has told her.

'Ruth, I wonder if you'll excuse me,' says Viviane, as if mirroring her thoughts. 'It's been a long day and I'm very tired. I expect you're feeling the same way too. I must get a taxi back to the hotel.'

'I can give you a lift.'

'It's okay, my dear. Listen, I don't have a cell phone, but you can contact me at the hotel if you need to get hold of me.'

'Yes, of course.'

Both women get to their feet, and Ruth is unsure of whether to kiss Viviane or not. Instead she leans forward, catching a whiff of nicotine and hairspray. She clutches Viviane's arm. 'Make sure you get some rest and I'll see you soon.'

Viviane turns, and there's the rasp of nylon as she negotiates her frame around the closely packed tables and out of the café.

43

RUTH

JULY 2005

Ruth can't help but lament the dispersal of June's squally showers, and the emergence of cloudless blue days. Patients want to stop her in the supermarket for a chat. She has to hurry in from her driveway, so that she's not waylaid by another well-meaning neighbour. The house has become her retreat. She looks outside from the pleat of her upstairs curtains, rocking on her heels and tilting her head back when someone rings the doorbell. Every morning she scans the post anxiously. No date yet from the Professional Standards Committee about the Tremayne complaint. It sucks that being signed off work has deferred the hearing even further. No more word from Mac either, but what should she expect? The inquest may take weeks. This morning the free newspaper landed through the letterbox. Thankfully it's full of adverts. Already the crash is old news.

She has a routine now, whiling away her day in front of the computer, marking time by the sound of the number twenty eight bus, which passes her window at precisely ten and three o'clock. In the late afternoon she waits till the clatter of schoolchildren abates, before slipping out to the hospital for an hour. At night she welcomes the crush of darkness and lies awake, listening to the scratch of twigs on the window or the mewling of a cat fight which resonates like a baby's cry.

★

There's a noticeable change in the ward atmosphere on Ruth's visits. The office door, just past the ward entrance, is always closed now. There'd been no sign of Sheena Henderson, the registrar, recently. According to Shaba, Sheena was now working on the Renal Unit. Still, it was odd she hadn't been in touch. Maybe she was too busy.

It irritates Ruth that there's always someone else present in Bella's room when she visits. Whether it's a nurse dropping in to check Bella's dressing, or the play therapist reading stories, or even the cleaner moving jugs of water round and wiping surfaces. There's no privacy. Today it's Brenda who's waiting for her.

'Afternoon, Ruth. How are you today?'

'Fine, thanks,' she replies, flatly. Brenda's cheeriness is not going to faze her.

'Bella and I have had a nice afternoon, haven't we?' says Brenda.

Bella has her head down and is studiously scribbling over a piece of paper, her fist clamped round a stubby crayon. Her opposite arm lies encased in plaster.

'Sounds good,' says Ruth, making her way over to the far side of Bella's bed. 'You've collected a few more names and pictures on your plaster too.' She tickles the side of Bella's face. 'There's hardly any room left.'

Bella skews her head towards her shoulder, as she giggles. 'Do another one, do another one,' she urges.

'Okay, let's see,' says Ruth, picking up a pink felt pen and scratching a cartoon face on the cast.

Brenda spreads some papers over the bed. 'Bella and I have been doing some drawings.' She points to one of them on a large piece of lining paper, which curls at the edges. 'This one is a tree.' Ruth can see that it has several names on it, encircled by green and brown squiggles.

A nurse enters the room. 'Time for tea, Bella,' she says.

Ruth clenches her jaw. Another annoying interruption.

'Great' says Brenda, rolling up the sheet. 'Whilst you have your macaroni cheese, Bella, I'm going out with Ruth for a little while, to see if she can add any more branches to this tree. See you soon, sweet pea.' She stands up and ushers Ruth out of the room.

★

The visitors' room is small and plainly furnished, with a high window. There's a couch and water dispenser against one wall, and a Formica table and four chairs opposite. Brenda indicates towards the table and they both pull up a chair.

'I thought this would be a good opportunity to update you on the local authority procedures,' she says. She unravels the paper. 'There is, of course, a more meaningful narrative behind this picture.'

'Of course,' says Ruth. 'It's a genogram.' She wants to say, 'I'm not stupid, you don't have to patronise me, I know a family tree when I see one,' but resists. She needs the social worker to be on her side. Instead she folds her hands between her knees. Brenda's wearing different earrings today, but she still has the same hand-crafted look about her, and this extends to her squiggly drawings. 'I'm afraid this genogram is going to look like a tree in winter,' Ruth adds, deliberating on her words. 'Sparse with a few twigs.'

Brenda smiles, but has her pen poised over the sheet. 'I've spoken to Mrs. Zuckerman, and I understand that she's the sole surviving relative on Mr. Peterson's side. But there's an uncle in Australia?

'Yes. Madeleine's brother David. He lives near Brisbane. As far as I'm aware there's no-one else.' Ruth pauses. 'I should add that Dominic – Mr. Peterson– and I had talked about guardianship for Bella before. I know it was his firm wish, that if anything happened to him...' She hesitates. 'Not that he had a premonition of anything, you understand, he was just very thoughtful... yes, that if anything happened to him, he wanted me to be Bella's guardian.'

Their conversation is interrupted by a knock on the door. It opens a fraction and a nurse squints round the side. 'Sorry to interrupt, Mrs. Madingley. I wonder if I could have a word with you, please.'

Brenda frowns. 'Only if it's urgent.'

The nurse gives a silent nod.

'Would you excuse me for a moment,' says Brenda, rising to her feet.

With the room to herself Ruth picks up a magazine. It's full of celebrities she doesn't recognise and, as she looks at their designer kitchens, and designer babies, she feels nothing but contempt and disappointment. She sits chewing her nails and flicking pages for a few minutes, and is about to get up and go back to Bella's room, when the door opens again.

It's Mac. He's accompanied, not by Brenda, but by a man in a navy suit. His face remains impassive in response to her look of surprise. Her throat constricts. This can only be bad news. Before she has time to stand up, he speaks.

'Ruth, I want you to meet Detective Inspector Peter Miller.'

Ruth stumbles to her feet and shakes hands with the man. His grip is firm, but clammy. She hopes he doesn't notice when she wipes her hand down her skirt afterwards. He has a heavy monobrow, which brings his eyes too close together. He's wearing what appears to be a regimental tie, and his suit looks grubby at the edges. 'Please, do take a seat, Dr. Cooper,' he says.

The sound of distant sirens serves only to heighten Ruth's anxiety, as DI Miller opens his leather-bound file and sifts through some papers. Ruth has an expectancy now that there's been some progress made. But on what? Dominic's accident? Bella's Care Order? Her heart thumps more forcibly and her breath quickens. She looks at Mac but he's avoiding eye contact. The air in the room is oppressive and she can feel her collar sticking to the back of her neck. There's another knock at the door, and it opens before a reply is given. A staff nurse enters, nods in acknowledgement to both men, then walks over to the water dispenser. She fills a paper cup with cold water and places it in front of Ruth, before smiling at her and taking a seat on the sofa. No explanation is given for her presence but to Ruth, it's obvious. It's a non-verbal cue to prepare for bad news.

Potential explanations jumble in her mind. Maybe they've found something on Bella's scan? But a detective wouldn't be tasked to deliver that news. Maybe an unusual discovery at the scene of the accident, or a fault found with the car? Perhaps the coroner needs to clarify some information about Dominic?

Ruth looks down in her lap. *Long, slow, deep breaths, in through her nose, out through her mouth, 1 and 2 and 3…* Whatever's coming next, she can handle it.

The sound of a chair scraping makes her look sideways. Mac has stood up and moves away, so that he is behind her. She twists around, but he's standing at an angle that obscures his face. Detective Inspector Miller clears his throat, and Ruth turns back. His eyes have a cold neutrality.

'Dr. Ruth Cooper, I am arresting you on suspicion of the attempted grievous bodily harm of Bella Peterson, due to events leading up to her hospital admission on the twenty first of May two thousand and five.'

Ruth takes a sharp intake of breath. A cold wave

of fear passes through her. She brings her fist down on the table, surprising herself at her vehemence.

'No, no, this is wrong.' Her voice is a trembling crescendo. 'You've made a terrible mistake.'

DI Miller holds up his hand and continues, as Ruth feels the prickling onset of hyperventilation. 'You do not have to say anything, but it may harm your defence if you do not mention, when questioned, something you later rely on in court. Anything you say may be given in evidence. You will now accompany us to the police station, where you will be provided with a full explanation of the grounds for your arrest.'

He nods at his colleague and, as Mac moves forward, Ruth catches the glint of handcuffs in his right hand. His face is denuded of expression.

'This isn't true, Mac, you've got to believe me,' she protests, clutching at his arm. 'I need to see Bella.' She tightens her grip, forcing him to look at her. 'I trusted you.' She holds his gaze for several seconds, determined to imprint her innocence on his vision.

He studies her face and swallows several times, as if drowning his words. She digs her nails into his arm.

'DS Macmillan?' prompts DI Miller.

If there was any glimmer of doubt in Mac's face a few seconds ago, his expression reverts to one of professional impartiality, as he lifts Ruth's wrist.

'Please, Mac, no handcuffs,' implores Ruth, 'at least not until we're outside the hospital.'

44

RUTH

The custody suite is airless. The smell of Jeyes Fluid wrestles with the whiff of dried urine. Ruth follows Varsha Dhasmana, duty solicitor, into a windowless room, where DI Miller sits at a table with a female colleague. He points at two chairs with stained upholstery and indicates for them to sit down. In the harsh fluorescent light Ruth squints at the woman who sits diagonally opposite.

'Detective Sergeant Sandra Bailey,' says the woman with streaked coppery hair. 'I'm your Family Liaison Officer now.' She fixes her with a narrow gaze. 'DS Macmillan is no longer assigned to your case.' Folds of skin at the corners of her mouth appear to have dragged the smile from her eyes.

Ruth stings with regret at hearing this news. She had felt she could trust Mac, that he believed in her innocence. Was he conflicted in his professional duty? How will she ever know? And how the hell can she prove this miscarriage of justice? Despair constricts her like a leaden weight on her chest.

The last she saw of Mac was the back of his head as they drove to the police station. Thankfully they'd agreed to her request for no handcuffs in the hospital. In the back of the car, they were redundant. She was locked in, and looking towards the windscreen she'd spotted the camera above the driver's mirror. Not that she would try anything stupid. Once he'd handed her over to the custody sergeant he disappeared, without even making eye contact for a final time. Her cheeks smarted with humiliation when the sergeant explained her right to free and independent legal advice, and the opportunity to inform someone of her whereabouts. How can she convince them of their incredible mistake?

She gnaws at her thumb. Little blebs of blood prick the base of her nail. Hopefully it won't take long for Val to arrive.

'You need to be aware that, henceforth, all our conversations are subject to audio and video recording. Do you understand?' DI Miller's cough causes Ruth to look up. A metallic taste in her mouth and the strip lighting, which casts a sallow mask over the detectives' faces, bring her surroundings back into focus.

'I understand.'

'Good.' He presses the button on a black device on his desk. 'DI Miller. Interview with Dr. Ruth Cooper. Thursday twenty first of July, two thousand and five. Commenced nineteen ten hours. Dr. Cooper, could you please confirm for me how long you have known Dominic Peterson?'

'Since March.'

'This year?'

'Yes.'

'Can you be more specific? When exactly in March?'

'We met at the Sycamore Hospice Ball on March the twenty fifth.'

'And I understand Isabella Peterson's illness started around that time. Is that correct?'

Ruth feels light-headed. A confusing collage of dates and images jumbles in her mind. 'I'm afraid I have no knowledge of Bella's previous medical history.'

'Very well. When did you first meet Isabella Peterson?'

'It was the day after the Ball. So that would be March the twenty sixth.'

'And did you discuss her health with her father at that time?'

Ruth thinks back to that afternoon in the Cardamom Café. She remembers it with the clarity of an autoclaved optical instrument. Dominic wore an olive green polo shirt and brown tweed jacket. Bella was pre-occupied with her drawing. He asked her if multiple sclerosis was hereditary and if urinary tract infections in children were common. They brushed hands under the table when she knocked over the water jug. She felt sorry for him. He was grieving.

'Dr. Cooper?'

'I'm sorry, please could you repeat the question?'

'Did Dominic Peterson discuss his daughter Isabella's health with you in March?

'Possibly. I can't recall exactly.'

'Very well.' DI Miller turns over a sheet of paper. 'Tell me, is the name Brenda Madingley familiar to you?'

'Yes. Of course. Brenda. The social worker. She was on the ward today when you…she was on the ward today.'

'Is it correct that you met her at Dominic Peterson's house on Wednesday the eleventh of May?'

Ruth thinks back to the time they first met. It was the day of her appraisal so that date must be correct. 'Yes.'

'And would it be correct to say that you persuaded her to close a safeguarding case on Isabella Peterson?'

'I wasn't-'

'Objection,' interjects Varsha Dhasmana, placing her hand on the table, in front of DI Miller. 'My client doesn't have to answer that question.' She turns to Ruth and gives her a tight-lipped smile.

DI Miller lifts up a transparent plastic envelope and a smaller clear packet. 'I have here Exhibits A and B,' says DI Miller, leaning towards the microphone. 'Exhibit A: Eight sheets of A4 paper on the aetiology and presentation of Sys– Systemic Lupus Ery-thematosus from Dr Ruth Cooper's computer. Exhibit B: a solid gold stud earring. Dr. Cooper could you tell me why both these items were found in a carton of drugs at Dominic Peterson's house?'

Ruth looks away. Her earring. She'd forgotten about it. But surely that doesn't prove anything? She gives a half-hearted shrug. 'You'd have to ask…' She stops when she realises what she is about to say is both ridiculous and redundant. She looks at Varsha, who is scribbling notes. She wills her to make eye contact, but the solicitor has her head down and seems focused on documentation. This is ridiculous. Ruth wonders at what stage, if at all, she can halt the conversation and demand to speak to Varsha in private. 'I don't know.'

'Does the earring belong to you?'

'It's similar to one I lost some time ago.'

DI Miller is handed another packet by DS Bailey. The black leather looks familiar.

'I have here Mr. Peterson's wallet,' says DI Miller. 'I want to ask you about some of the contents.' He hands over a folded piece of green paper. 'Could you have a look at this, please, Dr. Cooper, and tell me what it is.'

From the print, Ruth can see that it's a prescription. She unfolds it carefully and scrutinises it. It's a prescription for one hundred codeine tablets, made out to Dominic Peterson. The handwriting and signature are hers. She turns it over in her right hand. This is completely at odds with anything she remembers. Her elbow rests on the arm of the chair, her head buried in her left hand. This can't be possible. When did she write it? She looks at the date but the numbers become blurry and she looks away. 'May I have a glass of water, please?' she says, her voice wobbling.

Varsha puts down her pen and looks up. 'I'd like to request a break for my client,' she says, gathering her things.

The detectives exchange glances. DI Miller sits back in his chair and emits a low whistle of exasperation. 'Very well. Interview terminated nineteen twenty three hours, July twenty first two thousand and five.' Miller and Bailey stand up. 'Come with us, please. We'll resume our questioning later.'

45

RUTH

Val's face is the epitome of anxiety, as she scans the cell.

'D'you think we're being recorded here?'

'Who gives a fig?' says Ruth, squinting at her friend. 'This is a complete travesty of justice.' She paces up and down. 'D'you know, Val, I feel sick all the time. The slightest movement of my head sends shooting pains over my scalp.'

Val lightly touches her shoulder. Guiding her to the bench they sit, side by side. 'We're going to get through this, promise you,' she says, taking Ruth's hand in hers and squeezing it.

Ruth twists her feet and studies the scuff marks on her shoes. 'I'm so tired,' she says, her voice disappearing between her knees. 'They showed me a prescription they'd found in Dominic's wallet. It's in my handwriting but I don't remember writing it. And why would I write it for Dominic anyway? Varsha tells me it's one of many. It must be forged.' She thinks back to the times she couldn't locate her prescription pad amongst her equipment. When Varsha asked her whether Dominic could have stolen it from her bag Ruth hadn't been able to countenance it at first, but hadn't this prompted her to remember the stashed alcohol and other drugs she'd found in Dominic's house? 'They say Bella's illnesses started when I first got to know Dominic. That, as a doctor, I've been pulling the wool over their eyes. That I was fabricating the symptoms. That I knew exactly what I was doing, trying to pretend it was an obscure disease.' She pulls her hand away from Val's to grip the underside of the bench, as her chest heaves and the sound of retching percolates the cell. Acid burns her throat. Her brow pricks with moisture. Her head feels as heavy as a wrecking ball as she raises it towards Val. 'He was an addict, Val. And I just didn't see it. How could I be so bloody stupid? He suffered years of chronic pain, and one disastrous life event after another. Is it any wonder that he tried to find an escape?'

Val jerks back against the wall and groans. 'I don't believe I'm hearing this.'

'What do you mean?' She focuses on Val's face hoping to find answers in the knotted countenance.

'He was a liar, Ruth, for Christ's sake. This hurts, I know, but be realistic. You've been wrongfully arrested and yet still you're trying to defend him. You need to wake up to the fact that things were going on, undetected, before your eyes. Unless…' Her eyes widen as she scrutinises Ruth's face.

'Unless, what?'

'Unless, you're not telling the whole truth. Unless you've got something to hide.'

Ruth rests her elbows on her knees and lowers her head. 'I'm innocent. I promise you.' Words bubble in her throat and she doesn't know whether to suppress them or free them. 'Val, I'm worried sick. You don't know the whole story.'

'Go on.'

Ruth's fingers thread through her matted hair. She's navigating unchartered territory now and needs to iron out her thoughts. She blots her brow with her sleeve and looks up. 'I promise you, I'm innocent,' she says, her voice taking faltering steps. 'You've got to believe me.'

Val nods, studying Ruth's face. 'I do believe you.'

'But I'm petrified.' Ruth clears her throat. 'You and I understand mental illness, as doctors, but I'm worried they're going to take one look at my psychiatric history and think they're dealing with a mad woman, and that's going to totally prejudice the case against me. I still feel the stigma and shame, even though it's unjustified.'

They sit with their heads bowed, the silence punctuated by the sound of shouts in the corridor.

'What do you mean?' Val's voice sounds hesitant.

The scuffle of feet. The sound of profanities. The clash of a door in the corridor.

Ruth unstrings the words in her head. 'Oh God, I thought I was getting over this. When I was a teenager I suffered from low self-esteem, lack of confidence. Nothing unusual in that, you might think.' Her voice escapes in strangled gulps. She can feel the acid rising in her throat again, but she has to keep going. 'My parents really pushed me to get into medical school and I didn't think I was up to it. Then when I did get accepted there was always the pressure to do well in my exams. It started a spiral of anxiety. Then depression.' She turns her head sideways. 'Do you remember the electives we did in fourth year?'

Val considers this for a moment. 'Sure. I went to a missionary hospital in India. And you had a research attachment in Scotland.'

'A research attachment? Is that what I told you?' She squints at her friend. 'Well I suppose that's one way of describing a private psychiatric clinic at the foothills of Ben Nevis,' she says, 'but it's also where I was admitted with severe depression following a suicide attempt.' She feels Val's grip tighten. They sit in silence until the tension in Val's grip lessens.

'Ruth, I'm sorry. It must have been so hard for you.' Val hesitates. 'But, you know, you don't have to tell me this if you don't want to,' she continues.

'Oh, but I have to, it's important. And I have to prove my innocence.' She lifts her head, twisting her hair round her fingers as she looks at Val. 'I had a rocky time to start with. I can still recall every tiny detail of the ward where I was admitted.' Suddenly she laughs. A look of concern flashes across Val's face. 'Ha, it's bloody ironic. I was banged up in a place just like this.' She gets up and walks over to the wall, giving it a resounding kick. 'My room was like a cell and I had a bed with a rubber mattress. I had to sleep with my door open so that someone could keep an eye on me, and the glaring light from the corridor kept me awake every night.' She clicks her tongue against her teeth. 'Well, what do you know, life has come full circle.'

She turns and looks at Val, who appears to have shrunk against the wall.

'I was really, really low, Val. But gradually with medication and Cognitive Behavioural Therapy I improved.' She rolls up her sleeves and extends her forearms in Val's direction. The pale white and lavender lines which criss-cross her arms are barely discernible now. 'And slowly I healed. On the outside, at least.'

Val stays silent, but her eyes flick between Ruth's arms and her face.

'I really thought I was over this, Val. I continued my studies and I passed my exams. But then I was admitted to hospital in Australia. Investigation of chest pain, palpitations, spells of breathlessness. At one point they thought it was my thyroid. Turns out it was recurrent anxiety. Panic attacks. I was put back on the tranquilisers and had another course of CBT.' She walks over to the bench and sits down, pushing her hands underneath her thighs, to stop them from shaking. 'I'm not on medication now,' she adds as an after-thought.

There's a calming hand on her shoulder. 'It's okay, Ruth. It's okay. You've been ill. There's no shame in that. Honesty is always the best policy. You need to be up front with Varsha and tell her everything.' She lowers her voice, so that it's barely a whisper. 'Listen. You know the symptoms you told me about: the nausea and dizzy spells you were getting when you thought you were pregnant?'

'I wasn't though. I had my period.'

'I know, but the nausea and dizziness carried on, didn't it? Until recently?'

Ruth tries to think back but her timescales are too muddled. 'Yes, I think so.'

'Exactly. The sickness and giddy spells stopped. But your headaches have got worse.'

'Hardly surprising, all the fucking stress I've been under.'
'No, you don't get it. Look at me, Ruth.' Gently Val takes Ruth's chin in her hand and turns her face towards her. She takes a long look at her face. Then she takes her phone out of her pocket, switches it on to torch mode and shines a beam in Ruth's eyes.

'Fuck,' she says, switching it off and returning it to her pocket. 'I need you to be honest with me, Ruth. Have you been self-medicating: opioids – codeine, whatever?'

'No. Definitely not.' She can't stop her body from shaking. She makes fists with her sweaty fingers.

'You've been getting rebound headaches from codeine withdrawal.' She grasps Ruth's shoulders. 'Look at me, Ruth.'

Ruth studies Val's face. Concern is mapped across her brow but sympathy reflects in her eyes. 'And you're telling me the truth?'

'I swear.'

'I believe you. Have they taken DNA samples yet?'

'Just fingerprints and buccal swabs.'

'Okay we need to speak to Varsha, and you need to request hair samples.'

Ruth's eyes feel gritty. 'I don't understand. And I'm tired.'

'You don't get it, do you? You need toxicology tests on your hair. Nausea, dizziness, rebound headaches, slow reacting pupils. Opiate withdrawal.'

She cups Ruth's face in her hands. 'Dominic was trying to poison you.'

46

BELLA

JULY 2005

Bella sits on her bed. She opens her notebook at a white page, picks up her red pen and chews it. What can she draw? Having a notebook is much better than talking to someone because YOU CAN'T TRUST NO-ONE.

Yesterday she told Jenny she was upset. Jenny is the nurse with the cartoon apron.

'Promise you won't tell anyone,' said Bella.

'Promise,' said Jenny.

Then the next minute Brenda comes in and sits down on Bella's bed.

'It's okay to be sad, Bella. Everyone feels sad sometimes. Do you want to talk about it?'

See? Her daddy always told her that secrets are meant to be kept. She's not telling nobody nothing. Instead she takes big gulps, because the lump in her throat keeps bobbing up and she needs to squash it.

She misses her daddy. And Ruth. It was her birthday and only Granny came to see her.

'Now I'm five,' Bella told her.

'Five? Well, look what I've brought you,' said Granny Zuckerman, giving her a present. It had eyes like shiny orange marbles. A nose like a chocolate button. A red bow round its neck. 'I thought he could be friends with Roo.'

His name is Little Ted.

Brenda and Jenny brought a cake. Everybody sang 'Happy Birthday.' She asked if she could have fizzy pop but Brenda said no.

'Only squash, Bella,' she said.

Her mouth felt wobbly when she heard this. She told Brenda that Daddy always gave her fizzy pop as a treat. Can't she have a treat on her birthday? When she was good she got special sweets too. The pink Smarties and the white ones that make the pop go fizzier.

'I hope you cleaned your teeth afterwards,' was all Brenda said, giving her a tickle.

She looks down at the white paper and draws a big circle. But then she has a better idea. If she dots the pen over her hands she can pretend she's ill. She feels a smile unzipping across the cracks in her lips.

Dot, dot, dot, she goes, over her fingers. Measly spots.

This is fun.

Roo and Little Ted lean back on the pillow and watch her.

Slash, slash, slash, up her arm. Just like Horrid Henry.

She looks up when Jenny comes in and wonders if she'll notice.

'Lunch is ready,' says Jenny. 'Oh my goodness, Bella, what have you done to your mouth? You're bleeding.' Jenny looks worried. She presses a buzzer and two nurses run into the room.

Bella drops her pen. She's frightened. Why is her mouth bleeding?

She puts her hand up to her mouth, then Jenny starts laughing.

Jenny lifts up Bella's arm. 'Oh dearie me,' she says. 'You silly billy. Just look at the mess you've made with that pen.'

47

RUTH

The slow, excruciating onset of cramp moves up Ruth's right calf. She jumps up, trying to evade the paroxysm of pain, but it's too late, and she hobbles around in the darkness. Her dreams have been splintered with drunken arguments but, as she sits down on the wooden plank bed and orientates herself, she realises that the disruptive nocturnal clashes were authentic.

As if on cue the fluorescent lights flicker into action, bringing the blue plastic mattress and white toilet bowl into sharp focus. Despondency envelopes her. A police cell. It's beyond belief that this has happened.

Lifting her hand to her head, she sieves strands of greasy hair through her fingers. The nylon track suit clings in patches to her back and the odour of stale sweat lingers. Her throat fissures with thirst. She's desperate for a pee but she's pretty sure that's a camera, not a smoke detector, on the ceiling. Instead she stares at the plastic strap of her flip flops and counts the ridges on her toenails.

She thinks about Bella, sitting on the ward, surrounded by toys, but not by a loving family. She wants to wrap her arms around her. Tell her everything is going to be all right. But is it? What the hell is going to become of her? Is there a future for both of them in each other's lives? At home there's a toy pony sitting on her kitchen table ready to be wrapped for Bella's birthday, waiting to be added to her collection. Bella's birthday. Has she missed it? She doesn't know. She's at a loss to work out what day of the week it is.

There's the tinny sound of a window panel being scraped. The door opens. She glimpses the black and white cravat of the female custody sergeant, then the smartly clad figure of Varsha Dhasmana, who enters the cell.

'Morning, Ruth,' she says, hovering, her phone in one hand, the other hand clinging to the shoulder strap of a bag bulging with files. 'What sort of night did you have? Hope you managed to get some sleep.'

'Crap, if you must know,' she says, forcing a pinched smile. 'What time is it?'

Varsha looks down at her phone. 'Eight fifteen.'

She pushes it into her pocket and extracts a card, which she extends to Ruth. 'The good news is that you're being released on bail. I want you to take this and call me if you need anything. Go home and get some rest.'

Ruth stretches her legs. Fatigue has suppressed any relief she might feel. What she wants more than anything right now is a pee, a shower and her own bed. 'So what happens next?'

'Your case will be referred to the Family Courts.' She pauses. 'Because ultimately this is about Bella and what happens to her.' Ruth tries to digest this information but is distracted by her ballooning bladder. 'Then, if the Crown Prosecution Service think there's a case for pursuing criminal charges there will be further proceedings in the Crown Court.'

Ruth slides her feet into her flip flops, stands up and takes a few paces. A stale yeasty smell follows her round the cell.

'I'm hoping it won't get that far,' continues Varsha, resting her bag on the floor and straightening up. 'I'm sorry, Ruth. This is a protracted business but I'll do everything I can for you.' She hesitates. 'As things stand you're innocent… unless proven otherwise.'

The bitch, thinks Ruth. *She's supposed to be on my side. Was she about to say 'until proven guilty?'*

'This means you can apply for Bella's custody,' Varsha continues, 'but the Local Authority will want a psychiatric report. The toxicology reports will take several weeks.' She lifts her bag, then swivels on a stilettoed heel and adds, 'And I can tell you the date of the inquest. August the fifteenth. Only I wouldn't worry about that now. I'll call you over the next day or two and we can have a recap.' She hesitates, then turns back. 'Are you going to be okay on your own?'

What kind of question is that, Ruth wonders. She doesn't really have any choice.

*

Val's car stutters to a halt outside number twenty seven. She turns to look at Ruth.

'I'll come in with you. I'm not in a rush to get back.'

Her neighbour across the street is putting out his bin. Ruth slinks down in her seat until he has retreated out of view, then sits up.

'Thanks.'

Ruth picks her way carefully up the drive, which is chequered in shadow by the sloping sunlight. Dewdrops glisten on the laurel bushes, like brimming tears. It feels soothing to be out in the open air. She takes her keys, and is about to place them in the front door when she hears someone calling her name. Wheeling round she is confronted with a ricochet of shutter clicks.

'Could I have a word, Dr. Cooper?' barks a man in a bulky gilet, from over the hedge. He lowers his camera. 'For the Tadwick Gazette?' The intrusive words cast a net of confusion over her. But her front door is open now and, as she pushes against the mail which has crested behind it, Val looms in her wake to block his view.

The door snaps shut behind them and, as Ruth bends down to pick up the letters she can feel her heartbeat galloping away from her.

'Christ, I wasn't expecting that,' says Val, her voice wavering. Her face is milk-bottle white. 'Don't go answering the door, unless you know who it is.'

'No chance of that', says Ruth, her eyes drawn to the envelope with the conspicuous frank mark, GMB. 'Listen, Val, you wouldn't mind hanging on for a bit, would you?' She clasps the mail tightly, but can't stop her hands from shaking.

'Sure. I'm going to make you some breakfast, for a start. Better to wait till the coast is clear any…Ruth, what's the matter? Are you all right?'

Ruth feels her legs buckle and she staggers over to the stairs. She sits hunched over her knees, her head in her hands. The envelope slides from her sweaty palms onto the carpet. 'It's this. It's from the General Medical Board. This is just the last straw. I don't know if I can take much more.' She looks up. 'Can you break the, I mean can I open the … oh, I don't know what I mean. Just take it, Val. Give me the bad news.'

She tries to swallow but the roof of her mouth feels shrivelled. Then the pounding in her head starts again, and within seconds her heart is hammering like a horse kicking its way out of a stable. She knows what to do. Slow, deep breaths. In through the nose, out through the mouth. In through the ... nose...out...through... she closes her eyes and tries to think of something pleasant: of lowering her aching muscles into a steamy, luxuriant foam bath, listening to her favourite music, of inhaling the rose bouquet of scented candles.

When she opens her eyes Val is watching her. Empathy. Patience. Both are mapped over her face. She waits, until Ruth is prompted to occupy the silence between them.

'Well?'

'Well it's here in black and white and it's good news.' She holds the piece of paper out towards her. 'The Professional Standards Committee held a meeting last week. Given recent circumstances they decided your presence wasn't necessary, although you can request the minutes if you want.'

'Go on,' says Ruth impatiently, her heartbeat quickening.

'They've considered your response, and that from several others, including your appraiser, and the case has been closed.'

'Closed? The Tremayne case? Closed?'

'Closed. Completed. Finished. Resolved.'

Ruth holds her hand out to see for herself, but Val grasps it and pulls her to her feet and into a tight hug. She can feel the breath being squeezed out of her. Eventually the tension in her arms is released and Val takes a step back to look at her.

'Onwards and upwards, my pal.'

★

Hunched at the kitchen table, Ruth watches the timer on the cooker, as it meters out the beats. Twenty four minutes since Val left, and she hasn't moved from the spot, twirling the paper in her hands.

A minestrone of words stir in her subconscious, and sporadically a phrase bobs to the surface, like a pasta alphabet.

...Satisfied that you have provided adequate reflection ... Serious Untoward Events that were brought to the Professional Standards Committee...taken steps to ensure your medical knowledge and skills are up to date...considered the testimonials to your conduct and behaviour for the period of time in question... satisfactory conclusion...now closed.

Satisfactory. Closed. She repeats the words out loud. She should be pleased. Elated even. But all she feels is numb. She rewinds events to remind herself what started this angst. Margaret Tremayne and her heart attack. The duplicitous gang of blood cells that had clotted Margaret's arteries and mimicked the pain of gall stones. Will Margaret be able to forgive her? She picks up a pen and starts doodling on the envelope. She starts off with small circles but then the swirls get bigger. Then she writes her name, as if signing an autograph. She repeats it, until it looks like a schoolgirl's detention homework. Line after line of her name. Her signature never looked that neat when she was signing prescriptions. She was usually in a hurry, leaving a hasty scrawl. The only time she was careful was when she was witnessing official papers. Like probate documents. Her breath quickens. Of course, Dominic had her signature from Madeleine's probate documents. The signature on the prescriptions was an exact copy of the one on the probate document. He'd copied it. But it was too neat. Too careful. Not her usual prescription signature.

Shadows move across the wall and she glances out across the back garden. The newspaper reporter who doorstepped her has unsettled her. She looks in the direction of the perimeter of the garden and across the wooden panelled fence. There's no access into the property from the back, but she feels nervous, so she gets up and pulls the blinds in the conservatory. A clicking noise by the back door makes her jump and she becomes aware of a movement, at floor-line. The familiar warmth of Tilly, brushing against her legs, makes her smile.

'Tilly, my darling girl, I've missed you,' she says, bending down to stroke the grey and white fur. The cat leans into her legs and gives a throaty purr. Ruth picks her up, finding comfort in the pulsating heart-beat, palpable through the warm pelt. The cat unfurls her body from Ruth's embrace as Ruth walks over to the counter and picks out a pouch of cat food. She presses the meaty chunks into a bowl, places it on the floor and straightens up.

As she turns she spots the toy pony on the kitchen chair, still in its clear plastic box. She sighs, then goes upstairs for a shower.

★

Ribbons of steam curl round the gap in the shower door. Stepping over her discarded tracksuit, Ruth stands before the mirror. She smears her finger over it, creating a little spyglass. Runnels of condensation trickle downwards, mirroring the salty tears reaching her lips. She fumbles in her make-up bag. Prises her razor out of its plastic compartment. Slides open the shower door.

A daddy long-legs scurries up the tiles, trying to make its escape in the sultry heat. Ruth unclips the shower head and points it towards the insect, sluicing it downwards.

'Itsy bitsy spider,
Climbed up the water spout
Down came the rain
And washed the spider out.'
The words stream out of her mouth as the dismembered interloper swirls down the plughole.

She's in control now. She knows what to do, and lifts the blade.

And as the water flows, like liquid cochineal, the relief is instant.

48

RUTH

'Flexor carpi radialis, palmaris longis, flexor carpi ulnaris,' Ruth traces a line over the lumpy gauze which covers her forearm, mapping out her musculature. As she lies on her bed she remembers her Anatomy lessons as a student. Carefully dissected nerves that looked like tapeworms. Exsanguinated pearly blood vessels like small-bore cables. Embalmed tissues. She would smell the form- aldehyde on her clothes when she went home in the evenings, could feel the gristle under her fingernails the next day. She stares up at the ceiling. Ironic, when all these years later she uses her expert knowledge to self-harm with meticulous precision. Maybe the old cliché is true. Ignorance really is bliss. She slides under the duvet, welcoming its embrace.

An invasive sound makes her jump. Peeling back the cover she strains to hear. It goes again. A tinny noise from downstairs. The doorbell.

She shrinks back inside her fleecy cocoon but the harsh noise is penetrating and repetitive.

Bloody reporters. How dare they? Whoever it is, their persistence emboldens her. She flings back her bedcovers, grabs a dressing gown and stalks over the landing to a vantage point behind the curtains.

Apart from her car, her driveway is empty. She scans the street for activity but, other than a young woman pushing a pram weighted with carrier bags, there's no-one else to be seen.

A sudden movement at the corner of her vision startles her, and she shrinks back against the wall as the familiar sight of Paul Franklin's head comes into view. He walks away from the house, down her drive and she flattens herself against the wall and waits until the crunch of shoes on gravel diminishes.

Dragging herself back over the landing and into the bathroom, she flops onto the toilet seat. A sideways glance into the mirror reveals a hollow-eyed, gaunt frame she hardly recognises. It's an effort to complete her ablutions, but she empties her bladder, then hauls herself up by holding on to the washbasin. Her brush snags through her hair, making her wince.

Fastening the cord of her dressing gown tightly round her waist she goes downstairs. A scrap of paper lies on the doormat.

As she bends down to pick it up a dark shadow looms through the frosted glass. A slit of light appears through the letterbox and, as she looks up, her eyes partner those of Paul Franklin's.

'I don't make a habit of peering through people's letterboxes,' he says, 'so I wonder if, on this occasion, I can come in?'

★

Paul Franklin leans back, his hands curled round his coffee mug. 'There's no doubt the Professional Standards Committee reached the right decision. It's just unfortunate that official channels take such a damn long time to reach their conclusions.' He looks directly at Ruth and his features soften. 'Conclusions that are all too obvious to people like you and me.'

Ruth shakes her head, unable to find the words. Her hand rests down the side of the chair and alights on Tilly's back. Her cat has remarkable intuition and she loves her for it. She lifts the animal onto her knee and strokes her. 'You realise I've had to be referred back to the GMB again, now that I'm involved in legal proceedings with Bella's case, don't you?'

Paul nods. 'Poor little Bella.' His eyes skirt the

perimeter of the room before resting on Ruth. 'Are you going to fight for her?'

As the words soak in she can feel the heat spreading over her cheeks. 'So you believe I'm innocent?'

'Of course I do.'

Ruth chews her bottom lip. 'I don't know what to do, Paul. I guess my priority is to prove my innocence. Then who knows. It's so hard trying to compute what has happened to me in the last five months. I was only just getting to know Bella when all this happened.'

He fixes her with his powder-blue eyes. 'Alan Tremayne came to see me yesterday.'

'Alan Tremayne?'

'Yeah, Margaret's son. Booked a double appointment. Came in with a thick sheaf of notes he'd downloaded from the internet.' Paul rubs his chin. 'It was a bit of a heart-sink moment, to be honest.' He puts down his mug and leans forward. 'But it transpires that all he wanted to do was ask how he could help you.'

'Bit late for that, isn't it?' She feels herself bristling with contempt.

'He's very grateful that you saved his son's life. Took me through the events of the day you admitted the baby to hospital and said how he'd always remember your kindness and sheer professionalism.'

Ruth studies the carpet. She remembers that day

all too well. She had felt the surge of adrenaline coursing through her own veins, as she took control of a life-threatening situation. It was a perfect reminder that anxiety can be channelled in a positive way, if you put your mind to it. 'I was just doing my job. And glad I could help.' With her foot she smooths the pile on the carpet. 'How's Elliott doing now?'

'Very well. Been discharged from hospital. The Plastics team are pleased with his skin grafts. And he passed his audiology test, so it's all good news.'

'Good. I'm pleased.'

'But, that wasn't the main purpose of his visit. He wanted to drop the complaint he made against you for your treatment of his mother.'

'Pah! Too late. And now irrelevant.'

'Ruth, please hear me out.' A myriad of fine lines fan out from his eyes. 'I thanked him, but had to explain that the complaint was already being processed through official channels. That it was impossible to reverse. I think he felt genuinely sorry when he heard that. So he offered to write a testimonial in support of you. Think about it. It could be worth having on file.'

He pauses and Ruth follows his eye-line which rests on her arm. She flinches and stretches her sleeve over her wrist. When she looks up again he's watching her.

'My turn to be grateful, then,' she says, with a weak smile. 'Oh, and in case you're wondering, I scraped my arm on a door at the police station. An accident.'

'None of my business.' He shrugs his shoulders. 'You know, something, Ruth,' he says, after an age, 'I've been practising for nearly forty years and I still have nights when I lie awake, unable to sleep.' He shifts in his seat and looks directly at her. 'Many's the time I've worried that I've missed a diagnosis. In fact, on occasions, I have. But often our patients have empathy, in the same way that we do. We're only human.'

The words burrow into Ruth's insecurities. She lifts her coffee mug and can't bring herself to look at him. The phone rings in the hall. She glances at Paul, feeling embarrassed at the untimely interruption. The phone continues to ring.

'Go ahead. Answer it,' he urges. He stands up to leave.

'It's fine. It's on voicemail. And it's probably just another reporter wanting to nose.' But as Ruth sits down she can hear the voice of Varsha Dhasmana talking in the hall.

Paul's words sound muted and distant, as he bids her goodbye, as if she is listening underwater, but a calmness returns, along with a deep sense of sadness.

49

RUTH

AUGUST 2005

Standing by the public entrance to the Coroner's Court, DS Bailey is instantly recognisable by her stance, the streaked coppery hair and the black suit. She scans the car park, checking every angle.

'Well done. You decided to come after all,' she says, as Ruth approaches, flanked by Val and Mike. 'I'm sure it's the best thing in the circumstances.'

Ruth hopes she's right. The events of the past week have drained every ounce of energy from her limbs, but for the third day in succession she'd dragged herself out of bed, pulled on her smart trouser suit and brushed her hair into a semblance of respectability. She could understand why Viviane Zuckerman had elected not to come. Far too upsetting. Instead she'd decided to stay on the ward with her grand-daughter.

PC Collins's statement yesterday had shaken Ruth. He'd described how he'd been first on the scene, followed by the paramedics and fire service crew who had extricated Bella. In her grief she was transported back to that night when she'd been unable to contact Dominic, and had been buffeted by the wind and needled by the rain as she went about her visits. The hardest part was listening to him describe how Dominic had suffered a massive head injury, as the car chassis crumpled round the tree and how, as the policeman reached over the twisted metal to switch off the ignition, he'd had to ignore the sound of a mobile phone ringing in the deceased's pocket. She's returned many times to this scenario over the last twenty four hours. This was a new hypothesis to her. There were no witnesses to the accident. Had she contributed to it by trying to contact Dom while he was driving? But then there were other factors that were being taken into consideration. Tyres reaching their limit on tread. A worn brake pad. Dominic's hand contracture that may have affected his grip. She's not consoled by these facts.

Their small group huddles into the building. At least there's expectation of a conclusion this afternoon.

She digs her hands into her pockets. As soon as it's finished she can go home to bed.

DS Bailey guides the group past the court usher and into the Family Room. Ruth knows the routine now. She takes a seat next to the water dispenser, and adjusts the creases in her trousers. Mike hovers in the corner of the room, runs his fingers through his hair and smiles every time she catches his eye.

'Coffee anyone?' asks Val, placing a plastic cup under the drinks machine.

'No thanks,' Ruth replies. 'Think I'll avoid the caffeine. Maybe just a glass of water.' Her mouth feels dry and she grips the side of the chair to stop her hands from shaking.

The door opens a fraction and the usher mouths something to the detective.

'Should be ready in about ten minutes,' says DS Bailey. She takes a tissue from her pocket, lifts it to her mouth, and extracts a piece of chewing gum. 'Coroner's just summing up, then our case is next.' The lid of the pedal bin snaps shut.

Ruth takes a sip of water, trying not to spill any. The air in the room smells stale, heavy with the recycled breaths of many tense conversations. The Coroner's words from yesterday run in a continuous loop in her head, 'the purpose of this inquest is to ascertain facts, not apportion blame ...ascertain facts, not apportion blame.'

No witnesses. Slippery road surface. Increased stopping distance. Strong crosswinds. Poor visibility. Worn tyres. Shoddy brake pads. Deficient steering. She holds onto these facts from yesterday with a determined tenacity. Hopefully today will provide answers.

After several minutes there's the sound of muffled footsteps and muted voices from the corridor outside. Their assembled group in the Family Room fidgets, and prepares to move, and for the third and final time Ruth checks that her phone is switched off.

★

Ruth studies the diamond edging on the crimson carpet, which leads the way to her seat. She'd spotted the press earlier, given away by their scruffy jackets and customised lanyards. The same crew as yesterday, and the day before. They're probably looking at her now, as they sit in a gaggle, powering up their laptops, but she denies them the satisfaction of an acknowledgement.

'All rise for the Court,' booms the clerk and the sound of chair springs resonate round Ruth, as seats flip up.

The Coroner, neat shoulder-length hair, crisp dark suit, slash of damson lipstick, acknowledges her with a seemingly benign smile. Ruth sits back down, nudging knees with Val.

As the formal preambles are read out and the

Coroner reminds the assembled gathering of the questions she is required to ask: 'Who, where, when, why?' Ruth allows her attention to drift. She glances over at the wall clock beneath the Royal Coat of Arms. One minute past two. It's only when Ruth registers the words 'post-mortem' and 'medical reports' that her thoughts are jerked back into focus.

The Coroner passes a thick ring-bound file over to the Coroner's Officer. He casts his eyes downward, through the spectacles perched on the end of his nose, clears his throat and begins to read.

'Post mortem findings: cranial blunt force and penetrating trauma, depressed fracture of right parietal bone.'

Ruth tries to compute the words. The impassive neutrality of the Coroner's Officer's voice disconcerts her. To the uninitiated he sounds as if he could be reading the shipping forecast.

'Intimal and medial tear of thoracic aorta, secondary to fracture of the sternum.'

Poor, wretched Dominic. He didn't stand a chance.

'Pulmonary contusion and haemothorax.'

She feels the bony edge of Val's knee pressing into hers and she reciprocates by taking Val's hand and squeezing it.

'Toxicology results,' the Officer continues, 'showed a plasma codeine level of zero point three four milligrams per litre, consistent with therapeutic amounts, a gabapentin level of four point four milligrams per litre, and no evidence of recreational drugs, such as cocaine or heroin.'

Ruth loosens the buttons on her jacket and shifts in her seat. Codeine and gabapentin. No surprises there. Chronic pain from his old injuries.

'Plasma ethanol concentration was seventy five milligrams per decilitre.'

There's a pause and Ruth looks up. Dominic didn't drink alcohol.

'Thank you,' says the Coroner. The gold nib of her pen glints in the natural light filtering through the domed roof. 'A report from Mr. Peterson's GP was requested, to provide details of medical history. This is of particular relevance given the toxicology results, which show evidence of borderline ethanol intoxication and the presence of an opioid and gabapentin.' She nods at the Officer. 'Thank you. Please continue.'

Ruth casts a sideways glance at the press corps. A middle-aged man with straw-coloured hair is studying her, as he chews the end of his pencil. Her eyes run over the beige gilet, then back to his face. His eyes haven't moved, and she's not sure if she can detect the flicker of a smile. Sweat pools under her arms. The Tadwick Gazette. Of course. She darts a look back at the Coroner's Officer, who is opening another file.

'Report from Dr. Crofton, GP at Mulberry Lane Practice. "I knew Mr. Peterson for approximately four years. During that time his repeat medication consisted of ibuprofen and sumatriptan for migraine, prophylactic penicillin, salbutamol inhalers for asthma and emulsifying ointments for eczema. Nil else.'"

Ruth's head jerks a fraction. Nil else? What about the codeine? The gabapentin?

"'In January two thousand and five,'" the Officer continues, "'Mr. Peterson's wife died, after a long illness. In the weeks after her death he became a frequent attender at the surgery. Bereavement counselling was suggested to him. He exhibited signs of anxiety regarding the health of his four-year-old daughter. His daughter was admitted to hospital on a number of occasions and on twenty fifth April two thousand and five she was referred to Social Services regarding safeguarding concerns. Three weeks before his death Mr. Peterson consulted me with stress-related symptoms. He expressed worry about his daughter. He also described financial concerns. He was not prescribed any medication at that time but instead was referred for Cognitive Behavioural Therapy. When he attended for review one week later he disclosed acute anxiety due to losing a significant amount of money in a business deal. He was referred to the Crisis Team. Two days before he died he was referred back to me by the psychiatrist as he was deemed to be at low risk of self-harm, with no evidence of suicidal ideation.'"

Val's grip on her hand gets tighter. Ruth shuffles her feet and sits up straight. She tries to unknot the significance of these emerging facts. No mention of codeine or gabapentin from the GP. Where the hell did he get these from? Madeleine's drugs? The forged prescriptions?

The air in the courtroom feels very stale and warm. She leans down and extracts a notepad from her handbag and fans herself with it. Where does this leave her? She can't speak to Varsha till later. Anyway Varsha will want to read the court papers first.

Val leans in. 'Are you okay?' she whispers and her hand seeks hers for a second time. Ruth nods and sits in stunned silence, the Coroner's mantra of 'fact finding and not apportioning blame' lapping over her.

A member of the press, who was yawning just a minute ago, has now straightened his back. The usher has moved to within a few feet of where Ruth sits. The atmosphere in the courtroom changes as the Coroner begins her summing up. Her calm, clear voice percolates through the still air.

'Having considered all the facts presented to me over the past three days I am now in a position to answer the questions I am required to ask. I conclude a verdict of accidental death. I offer my condolences to the family and friends of the deceased.'

She rises, and everyone stands. Then she picks up

her notes, smiles at Ruth, and with a bow of her head, turns and disappears. The court usher holds an arm out towards Ruth.

Ruth's legs feel hollow and, as she stands, she can feel herself swaying. As soon as they are out of sight of the public, and back within the confines of the Family Room, Val gives her a hug.

'Accidental death?' stutters Ruth. She has so many questions still. Forged prescriptions. His acute anxiety. His financial dealings. Her eyes prickle with tears.

'Look at it this way,' says Val, 'it's another hurdle completed.' Her words recede as Ruth sinks into a soft chair.

The door opens and the usher appears again, radiating calm and benevolence. She hands Ruth a leaflet. 'If you have any further questions, my dear, this leaflet may help.' Ruth takes this as her cue. They need to leave. The Family Room is needed for relatives connected to the next case.

'Listen, you guys,' says Val, as she presses the car keys into Mike's hand. 'I'm desperate for a wee. You go without me and I'll see you back at the car.' She disappears.

The colour has drained from his Mike's face. 'Accidental death,' he echoes. He looks at Ruth, his eyebrows knotted. 'I suppose that's the only verdict she could reach, given all the facts. You know, the bad weather conditions, the state of the car, the fact the shrinks had said he wasn't suicidal.' He moves closer to Ruth and hugs her tightly. As she brushes his cheek it feels sweaty, sticky. 'I'm sorry, Ruth. I'm really sorry.'

Ruth's emotions jumble, like odd socks tossed around in a tumble drier. It's not like Mike to get so upset. But Val's right. This is one more step towards closure.

'Thanks, Mike. Give me two minutes. I just need to sit and compose myself before we go outside.' She leans forward, and closes her eyes. Her turn to be self-centred now. Dominic's dead. Poor selfish bastard. She looks up and nods. 'Okay, I'm ready.'

Mike offers his arm and she links with it as they make their way out into the bright sunshine and across the car park. The man in the beige gilet is there, hiding behind a camera. There's a hail of shutter clicks, then he disappears, camouflaged against rows of glinting wing mirrors. The configuration of the car park seems to have completely changed. Mike looks at her with questioning eyes. 'I can't remember where we parked, can you?'

Ruth shrugs her shoulders and casts a look around. At the far side of the car park she sees Val, shaking hands with a man who has his back to her. Val spots her and quickly moves away. How odd. Ruth focusses on the shoulders and head of the tall individual who moves swiftly under the shadow of the aspen trees, which tremble in the wind. She's not sure why, but the cropped hair and suit look strangely familiar.

50

RUTH

Other than a solitary dog-walker the tow
path is deserted. Ruth digs her hands in her
pockets, content to appreciate the space and
calm of the day. For the most part she and Val walk in
silence, the only sounds being the chirrup of a chiff-
chaff from the branches overhanging the river, or the
distant chug of a narrowboat.

'Good idea of yours to come out here,' she says
to Val, after they pass the sign indicating half a kilo-
metre to the lock-keeper's cottage. 'I'd forgotten how
peaceful it is.'

'Mike and I would sometimes come up here on
a Sunday afternoon. In the days before kids. By the
time we finished the loop from Tadwick Mill to the

boathouse we had put the world to right.' Val laughs, as she sidesteps a barbed bramble.

'I had a phone call from Varsha yesterday,' says Ruth. 'Bella's interim care order is up for review this week.'

Val carries on walking, stumbling over a hidden dip in the path.

'She's been discharged from hospital,' Ruth continues, 'and is in temporary foster care, but Social Services won't say where she is.'

'I guess that's to be expected, isn't it?'

'Poor Bella. I love that little girl.' She waves a buzzing insect away from her face. 'Varsha gave me a date for the court hearing too. Twenty sixth of September. She says I can apply to join the proceedings, to hear what's being discussed.'

'I thought that would be automatic, given you're seeking custody.'

'Apparently not. I need permission from the Judge. And that's not all. I have to consent to a psychiatric report at the request of the Local Authority.' She stops in her tracks. 'That's worrying me. Not only that, but the police are conducting their own investigations in parallel for the Crown Prosecution service.'

Val whistles through her teeth. 'Jeez. Anything but straightforward, eh, but I suppose a protracted business is to be expected.'

'Surely it's in my favour that Dominic was taking

drugs that weren't prescribed for him? He'd have to be taking them of his own volition. They couldn't try and pin that on me.' She searches Val's face. 'Could they? Even with those prescriptions that were clearly forged?' She thinks back to the carefully executed signature on the green notepad, too meticulous in its precision to be genuine. 'The trouble is…' Her voice trails off.

Val stops walking and turns towards Ruth. 'What?'

'Bella. I'm not sure that I'm the right person to commit my life to looking after her now.' She sniffs. 'Assuming that the court finds in my favour, of course.' She searches Val's face for a reaction. 'And I feel so guilty for thinking that.'

'You know what I think?' says Val, screwing her nose up in the sunlight. 'I think that, first and foremost, you need to look after yourself. This has all happened in such a relatively short space of time. Hard as it is, you've got to look to the long term and not put yourself through more anguish and pain.'

'But that's just selfish, surely?'

'But don't you see? You've always put others first, whether it's your patients, or those close to you. Your own wellbeing has got to be a priority if you want to carry on doing that. Ruth? Ruth?'

She knows Val is right. Hadn't she convinced herself already that she needed to be selfish if she was going to get through this? She reaches into her pocket and pulls out a tissue. When she finishes dabbing her eyes Val is smiling. 'Another five minutes or so up this path should bring us to the Tadwick Lock Café. C'mon, I could do with a coffee,' she says and leads on.

★

The café is decked out in primary colours with decorative toleware adorning every shelf and counter. Even the outside tables have little enamel ashtrays painted with peonies and oxeye daisies. They draw up two chairs and Val checks her phone. 'No news is good news,' she says. 'Either that or Mike has fallen asleep in front of the telly whilst Alice is running riot.' She places the phone on the table. 'I'll give him a ring in a minute. What are you having?'

'A filter decaf thanks.'

Val nods and disappears inside. The sound of laughter prompts Ruth to look to her right. The lock gate is about one hundred metres away and a red and blue narrowboat approaches. It's going so slowly that a man in a striped sweatshirt steps off it onto the towpath, whilst shouting instructions to a young girl who stands on the prow, her little body bulked out by the cumbersome floats of a lifejacket. She looks to be about six or seven years old. Ruth watches their body language as the man, presumably her father, bends down to pick up a thick rope. She tries to imagine herself as a parent. At one time it was the single most important aspiration in her life. But at what cost?

A jarring noise distracts her. Val's phone vibrates on the tinny table-top, and rattles towards her. Val spoke too soon. They had told Mike they would be a few hours. Surely it could wait. She wonders if she should answer it and looks down to see a name pop up which startles her. Mac. Mac? The same Mac who escorted her through the hospital and into a waiting police car? An image flashes through her mind of the mysterious figure talking to Val in the car park of the Coroner's Court. Mac. Yes, the very same. She feels panicked. If she ignores it, it will go through to voicemail and Val could deny it ever existed. It's on its third ring and she needs to make an instant decision. She presses the 'answer' icon and waits.

'Hey, Val. Some more good news.' The Scottish burr is instantly recognisable. It speaks again, filling the space between heartbeats. 'Val? Val, can you hear me?'

'Here we are,' says Val, appearing with a tray, 'I succumbed to some almond polenta cake as well. I couldn't resist.' Her face constricts with concern as Ruth scrapes her chair back and holds the phone out towards her.

'For you,' says Ruth, her voice rising in indignation. 'A mutual acquaintance.' Her cheeks smart with humiliation as she stomps back down the towpath, her head down to avoid making eye contact with the young man, who is instructing his daughter not to lean over the side of the boat. She can hear her name being called but she quickens her step. Eventually there is a tug on her sleeve.

'Ruth, I can explain everything,' says Val, in short staccato breaths.

'I trusted you!'

'Please, let me explain. We're doing our best to help you. You've got to believe me.'

Ruth grabs Val's wrist as their eyes connect. 'We? What the hell is going on, Val?' I deserve to know the truth.' Val doesn't flinch.

'Okay. But first let me make a phone call to Mac. Then I'll explain.'

Ruth lets go of her wrist and walks back up the path to the café, where the coffee and cake are untouched. She slides into a seat and drains her cup. Mac? Why is he involved in some kind of subterfuge with Val?

She jumps as she feels a pressure against her legs, then the wet muzzle of a dog snuffling her hand.

'Sorry, love,' says a middle-aged woman who is scurrying up the towpath in the down-draught of her Labrador. 'He has a nose for a piece of cake.' She smiles, clips his lead to his collar and drags him away. Paranoia lurks everywhere. Further down the path Val is pacing, still mumbling on her phone. After a few minutes she re-joins Ruth. She's pale. A pinched smile. No words.

'Well?'

Silence.

'What's going on, Val? Why are you in cahoots with Mac? Don't forget he's the one who fucking arrested me! Answer me!'

They both look around. The woman with the Labrador is far down the towpath, out of earshot. The outside tables are deserted.

'I need to come clean with you, Ruth. This is not easy.'

'Too fucking right it's not easy.'

'Please hear me out. I want to tell you everything.'

A deep sense of unease crawls over Ruth's skin.

'It's probably best if I start at the beginning.'

'I'm all ears.'

'Some weeks ago I remember having a conversation with you in our back garden.'

Ruth shifts in her seat.

'I mentioned that Madeleine and I had a disagreement six years ago.' Val's face twists, as if in pain.

'And?'

'It was about Dominic. It was before Bella was born.'

'I don't understand.'

'Dominic and I had an affair.'

'What?' says Ruth, her voice rising an octave.

'I know, I know. It was wrong. How could I have been so stupid as to fall for his charm?'

'Oh my God. You bitch!' Ruth swipes her hand upwards but Val grasps it before it strikes her face.

'Ruth, don't. Please!'

'How long did this go on for? What about Mike?'

'It was brief. I know that doesn't excuse it. It was when Mike and Dom were working in London. I was a junior doctor. We all worked crazy unsocial hours. Dominic was charming, good looking, persuasive. It was a fucking huge mistake.'

Ruth can't quite believe what she's hearing. How the fuck was she so naïve? She'd told Val all her secrets. And now Val was scheming behind her back.

'I was so bloody stupid,' Val continues, 'but it was the risk-taking that was so intoxicating. At first, that is. Until Dominic became threatening.'

Ruth resists the temptation to walk away. She needs to hear more. 'Go on.'

'He was very controlling. Demanding. Used to getting his own way. Then at other times he was as docile as a kitten. Kind. Gentle. Deserving of sympathy for the tough upbringing he'd had. I saw the error of my ways and it came to an end. I tried to blank it from my mind. But not before I told Mike.'

Ruth sits in stunned silence.

'We went through a very rocky patch, Mike and I, but, thank God, we stuck together. Dominic never found out that Mike knew and we decided it was better that way.'

She jumps to her feet and rounds on Val. 'Honesty is the best policy,' she says in a mocking tone.' That's what you told me in the police cell, after I'd been banged up on suspicion of harming Bella. You fucking cheat.'

She turns her head into the breeze, hoping it will stop the smart of tears. She'd been so gullible. She's so messed up. Events had happened so quickly over the past few months that her actions had outrun her emotions. Did she love Dominic? She thought she did but now she's not so sure. He hadn't loved her. She walks further down the path, her back to Val. Love hurts. It fucking does. She quickens her pace, anxious to put some distance between her and her friend. She needs space to think this through.

Under a riverbank willow, a fissured wooden bench comes into view. She flops down on it, her elbows on her knees. Why did Val keep this from her until now? If Dominic was so controlling why had she encouraged her in their relationship? And where does Mac come into all of this?

She's conscious of movement to her right. Val takes a few steps towards the water's edge and sits on the ground a few feet in front of her, her back turned.

They sit in silence, Ruth considering her next action.

Minutes pass. A dragonfly hovers on the water's edge, its diaphanous wings a cerulean blue. Ruth knows she should swallow her pride and say something but it's Val who speaks first.

'Ruth, I've been a damn fool. When we were at Med School it was always me who took risks after late night parties. Always me who needed cover for failing to show at early morning workshops. And you were always there for me, whether it was holding my head above the toilet bowl after a late night blinder or lending me your lecture notes so I could blag my way through vivas.'

Ruth thinks back to the tiny terraced house they used to share as third year students. Eking out their student grants to feed the meter and using their coats as bedspreads in winter, it was so darn cold.

'They say the older you get the wiser you become,' Val continues, 'but it wasn't until I became a mother that everything changed.'

Does she realise what she's saying, thinks Ruth, the dart of pain catching her between her shoulders. She can't bring herself to look Val in the eye.

'What I mean,' says Val, 'is that Bella is at the centre of all this. I try not to forget that.'

Ruth can feel the indignation rising within her.

'And I don't? Is that what you're saying?'

'Oh, Christ, I'm not explaining myself very well, Ruth. What I mean is that everything changed for me when I became a parent. And I thought it had for Dominic too. He was a changed man. Or so I thought. That's why I didn't warn you off.' Swatting flies away from her face she twists round to face Ruth. 'I made a terrible mistake. I'm sorry.'

'How can I trust you anymore? I confided in you. You let me down. And why the fuck are you colluding with Mac?'

'I've made some terrible mistakes in the past and I want to make it up to you. Mac contacted me when he was still assigned to you as your Liaison Officer. He really believes in your innocence, Ruth. He's rooting for you. So am I.'

'But he was replaced by Sandra Bailey.'

'Only once the police started to conduct a criminal investigation. He believed in your innocence from the beginning. He was taken off your case due to a perceived conflict of interest. Don't you see?'

Ruth reaches in her pocket for a tissue and blows her nose. The pressure in her head is oppressive.

'For fuck's sake, Ruth, he was the one who helped me arrange your bail,' says Val, her eyes flashing, 'as long as-'

'As long as what?'

'As long as I promised not to tell you.'

Ruth feels sick. Bail? She'd been so pre-occupied with thinking about Bella, the process of how she'd been released from custody hadn't even occurred to her.

'Look,' Val says, standing up. 'We're just aware that there's enough going on without upsetting you further, that's all. Especially when it's not necessary.'

Ruth gives a derisory snort. 'Oh, believe me, you couldn't possibly upset me any more than I already am.'

'That phone call,' says Val. 'From Mac. Just now.'

'What about it?'

'Do you remember the time when Mac told you about the anonymous derogatory posts that were deleted from the NHS website?'

Ruth had forgotten about this in the aftermath of recent traumatic events, but her conversation with Mac in the café across the road from the hospital is now brought into sharp focus.

'Yes. So?'

'Have you heard of Tor browser?'

'Tor what?'

'Tor browser. It's computer software that prevents the sites you visit from learning your physical location. In other words, Tor browser protects your privacy and anonymity when you're browsing the web.'

Ruth's pulse quickens. She holds her breath for a few seconds, fearing more bad news.

'When the police examined Dominic's computer they found Tor Browser. However the NHS site had been bookmarked as a favourite so the posts could be traced. Unbelievable some of the content: "This Dr is under investigation for fitness to practice", "reacts badly to stress", "has her own emotional problems."'

Ruth feels her stomach clench.

'So he was trying to discredit me? Is that what you're saying?'

'It wasn't him that was trying to discredit you. The posts didn't come from Dominic.'

'I don't understand.'

'Someone else had access to his computer, and used a different password.'

'That's ridiculous. Who?'

'Does the name Courtney Weaver mean anything to you?'

'Courtney Weaver?' Courtney? *Courtney?* 'I feel sick,' says Ruth. 'Courtney Weaver is Bella's babysitter.'

51

RUTH

SEPTEMBER 2005

'On the questionnaire you've ticked that sometimes you think you'd be better off dead?' The inflection in the young man's voice makes it sound like a question but Ruth says nothing. She closes her eyes and tries to process his words. She has no image to distract her. Only black nothingness. A white noise in the background, probably the air conditioning. Perspiration trickles down her back. Can he detect her anxiety, through the scent of fresh linen which wafts across the consulting room?

A disembodied voice talks again. 'Is that something that has ever crossed your mind? Have you ever thought about killing yourself?'

She shifts awkwardly in her seat, trying to unstick

the seat of her trousers from the upholstered leather. Opening her eyes a pair of polished shoes, Church's by the look of them, comes into view. Not a single scuff on the toecaps, the brown leather so shiny that the burnished brass lamps are reflected in them. She lifts her head and meets his gaze. His dress sense belies his age. The glint of a gold cuff-link, the cavalry twill. He's probably no more than three or four years older than her, but he's no stranger to a trouser press.

'What do you think? Of course I fucking have.'

He presses his lips into a thin line, and she follows his eyes as they drop downwards to her arms. She pulls at the cuffs of her sleeves, tucking in a stray corner of gauze.

'I didn't do any of the things I'm accused of, you know.'

'I'm not accusing you of anything Miss Coop- Dr. Cooper. I think you know why you're here. The Local Authority has asked for a psychiatric report as part of your assessment to be Bella's guardian.'

Bella's guardian. It feels strange to hear that. 'Well that's easy then,' says Ruth, eyeing him with some suspicion. 'All I have to do is tell the truth and it will be obvious that this is all a complete waste of time.'

'Hopefully not a waste of time.' The young man smiles. 'Of course I expect you to be honest with me, Dr. Cooper.' He leans forward. 'That way we can work together to secure the best possible outcome.'

'Oh, for goodness sake, call me Ruth, please. We're fellow professionals after all.'

There's a pause and Ruth hears the beeping of a pedestrian crossing from the street below.

'Very well then, Ruth. Do you mind if we go back to my question? You say that you have thought about killing yourself. What methods have you considered?'

The question makes her snort. 'Look if I'd been serious don't you think I'd have done it by now?'

'What about others? Have you thought about or harmed other people?'

'Primum non nocere. Recognise that? You should. Do no harm. It's part of the Hippocratic Oath. I'm a doctor. I help people, I don't harm them.' It's tempting to add a profanity it's such a stupid question but she refrains. He's supposed to be on her side, after all. She takes a deep breath and her eyes partner his for a second.

'Except I could quite cheerfully throttle an ex-boyfriend if I met him now.'

'Dominic?'

His response catches her off-guard. She had meant Mark. Strange how she still can't let go of his image.

'No. Mark. I met him in Australia. We were serious for nearly a year until I found out he'd been lying to me. Thought we had a future together but it turned out he had other plans. With his wife and children.'

'Is that why you came back to the UK?'

'I guess so. Perhaps if I'd stayed there I wouldn't have been in the mess I find myself in now.'

The young man rocks back in his chair. 'What about Dominic? How do you feel about him?'

Ruth looks beyond her questioner to the name card on his desk. Niall Freeman, Consultant Psychiatrist. That is the only information she has about him. No photos gracing the desk, no sporting trophies on the shelves, an absence of framed certificates on the walls. No clues. He's not giving anything away. Everything about this room looks temporary. Yet his face is familiar. She closes her eyes and tries to compute why. A cough interrupts her train of thought and she studies the face of the man sitting opposite her. Where has she seen him before?

'Ruth?'

'How do I feel about Dominic?'

He nods.

'Sad. Mostly sad. I feel sorry for him and for poor little Bella.' She bites her lip and looks at her feet. 'But conflicted. I thought I loved him. He didn't love me.'

Niall remains impassive.

'All my friends say that I always see the best in everyone but no-one is born evil. I strongly believe that. Dominic was dealt a very bad card. He told me about his troubled upbringing, his horrific childhood accident. It left him in chronic pain for the rest of his life.' She looks up and gives a weak smile. 'Maybe I'm just gullible. Naïve. It transpires he was probably trying to poison me.' She wants to add that she thinks he was harming both Bella and her. And there's the abusive posts from Courtney too. Should she tell him about them? What would that achieve? It would make her seem paranoid. No, she mustn't prejudice her case. After all, hadn't Niall said he was acting in her own best interests?

Niall doesn't say anything but reaches inside his tweed jacket to extract a white handkerchief. In the process she catches a glimpse of his red braces with their owl motif. And then it happens again. That feeling. Why does he seem familiar?

He dabs at his nose then puts the handkerchief away. 'What about your childhood? Was it happy?'

She adjusts her pose, grateful to change the subject.

'I'm an only child. Born in Lincolnshire. Went to a convent school. The nuns were quite strict.'

'Did you do well at school?'

'Depends what you mean by well. I was Head Girl. Probably because I was in the right place at the right time. Got good grades in my exams, but it didn't come naturally to me. I had to put in the hours.'

'And your parents?'

'Less strict but they wanted the best for me, and were keen for me to pursue an academic career. They were so proud when I got a place to study Medicine.

I was the first member of our wider family to go to University, and I went to Leeds. Looking back, going to University probably meant more to them than it did to me. My mother died of breast cancer eleven years ago, then four years later my father died of a stroke. If they were alive today I'd feel I'd let them down.'

'What do you mean?'

'You're not serious, are you? Arrested for attempted grievous bodily harm. Unable to cope at work. A major complaint against me. A near miss at work. How much more do you want? I'm a failure. Always have been.'

'How about a high achiever instead? A perfectionist, maybe?'

Ruth shrugs.

Niall Freeman rests his hands in his lap and twiddles his thumbs. 'Let me tell you something, Ruth. You've heard of Imposter Syndrome haven't you?'

Ruth wonders where this conversation is going.

'It's okay, there's no need to look alarmed. Strictly speaking it isn't a syndrome. I prefer to call it "Imposter experience." It reflects a belief that you are inadequate, incompetent or a failure, when all the evidence suggests that you are highly skilled and successful.' His face softens. 'I was giving a lecture to a group of medics a few weeks ago and I asked for a show of hands as to how many had ever felt like an imposter. I'd say more than seventy percent of those in the room put their hands up, and most of them were women.' He leans forward. 'What I'm trying to say to you, Ruth, is that you are not alone. The complaint, the near miss, it goes with your job. You mustn't be too hard on yourself.'

She knows he's right. How many people have said this to her before? Val and Mike for a start. Her appraiser. She turns her head towards the window, not wanting to make eye contact. A group of gulls is clustered on the window-sill of the flats opposite, jostling for position on the narrow ledge, and waiting to swoop down on the street for any scraps spilled from the waste bins. Ruth's eyelids feel heavy again. Last night was another of broken sleep. She longs to go home and lie on her bed. In the far recesses of her mind Niall drones on, and she nods her head at regular intervals just to satisfy him that she's listening.

Niall's voice intrudes once more. 'Quis custodiet ipsos custodies.'

'I'm sorry?'

'I saw you looking at the plaque by the window.'

Ruth adjusts her eyeline to the framed quote adjoining the casement. She hadn't noticed it before.

'It means "who guards the guards?" A reminder that, as doctors, we need to look after ourselves.' He glances at the open file on his desk. 'I want to take you back to Bella, again. How do you feel about parenthood?'

The question disarms her like a punch in the solar plexus. She tries to form words but her tongue is dry. 'Do you mind if I have a glass of water?'

Niall nods, stands up and walks over to the water dispenser in the corner of the room. He hands her a brimming waxed cup and she tips the ice-cold liquid down her throat. She tosses the empty container into the bin by his desk. 'I know I would make a good mother, if that's what you're asking.'

Niall says nothing.

'I was pregnant once,' she says, digging her nails into her palms. She must remain calm, stay in control. 'In Australia. Got to ten weeks then I had a miscarriage. I couldn't tell anyone about it, not even at work.' She can feel her voice wavering but she must press on. 'As far as work was concerned… I was… I was off for a few days with a tummy upset.' Her throat constricts as she forces the words out. 'It's something I think about a lot,' she says, unable to stop the well of tears which roll silently down her cheek. She pinches her skin, annoyed that she's allowed Niall to see her at her most vulnerable.

There's a clatter of metal and broken glass from the street below, followed by the raucous cries of gulls as a vehicle trundles away. Ruth studies her shoes until a hand bearing a tissue crosses her line of vision.

'I understand this is not easy for you, Ruth,' says Niall, offering her a handkerchief.

Blobs of mascara transfer to it like ink spots on blotting paper. How could she be so stupid, breaking down in front of him? She sits in silence, twisting the paper tissue round her fingers.

'I think we've discussed enough for today,' says Niall, after a protracted pause. 'There's been a lot to take in, especially our conversation earlier about your diagnosis of Borderline Personality Disorder.' His words make her reel again. Why hadn't anyone else suggested this diagnosis to her? All those weeks she had spent in the clinic in Scotland. The hospital admission in Australia. No one had ever discussed Borderline Personality Disorder with her before. In a way it had come as some relief to have an explanation for her anxiety, her emotional instability, her episodes of self- harm. It was starting to add up. It also made sense to hear Niall say that her symptoms had been triggered in the wake of recent events. What did he call it? Abandonment sensitivity? But nobody had ever mentioned Borderline Personality Disorder. Nobody. Why?

'You may think it odd that you've been given a name, at this late stage, for your collective symptoms,' says Niall, as if reading her mind, 'but I think it will help you. It means we can target your treatment effectively. I'm going to recommend something called MBT. Not CBT.' He deliberates over his abbreviations, seemingly apportioning capital letters to them to give them greater importance. 'Mentalisation–based therapy,' he continues. 'It will give you greater insight into relationship difficulties. Help you trust again.' He reaches across his desk and hands her a slim booklet. 'I'm going to give you this to read at your leisure. It explains some of the mood patterns and symptoms we've been talking about.' He hesitates. 'And one more thing.' He slides open a drawer full of little brown bottles. 'I suggest you start taking these antidepressants. One at night to start with. Should improve your sleep, if nothing more.'

'Can I ask you something, Dr. Freeman? And may I call you Niall?'

'Sure.'

'You believe I'm innocent, don't you? I need to know whose side you are on. Dominic's inquest revealed he was taking prescription-only medication that wasn't his. Gabapentin. Codeine. Those prescriptions for codeine were forged. Looking back I think I may have unwittingly given him medical information that he used to bluff his way with the authorities.'

Niall smiles. The kind of smile that indicates that time is up. That the meter has run out.

'Ruth, as I said earlier I'm not accusing you of anything. I am your advocate. I have your best interests at heart. You must trust me. Please.'

Trust? *Trust?* How can she be sure? She's heard that too many times before.

'I still have so many questions.'

'We can have another chat next week, you know.'

'The Coroner recorded Dominic's death as accidental. A post mortem report was read out at the inquest. But surely there was something missing?'

'What do you mean?'

'A psychological autopsy. It's not for me to tell you your job but, as well as providing the Family Court with a psychiatric report on me, shouldn't Dominic's psychiatric history be looked into?'

Niall stands up. 'The Family Court will be taking all relevant evidence into account.'

Reluctantly Ruth extends her hand, taking the little plastic bottle from him. She looks at the label, then back at Niall.

'There's only seven tablets here. That's not going to be enough.'

'Same time, same place next week,' he says, proffering his hand. 'I want to monitor your progress.'

However, as she gets to her feet and looks into his eyes, there's an unspoken understanding between them that's not the only reason for the paucity of pills.

'See you then,' she says, and without a backward glance she opens the door onto the corridor, descends the wide, marble staircase and walks out onto the street.

52

RUTH

Ruth unravels the wire paper clip until it resembles a spindly question mark. She gouges the end of it into the base of her thumb, twisting it until shiny beads of blood bubble to the surface. Her hand hovers over the paper, the words blurring through her tears.

Why?

Why did you do that?

Why did you leave me?

Hadn't Niall told her to write down her thoughts?

'It can be cathartic,' he said, as he handed her the

booklet. 'Articulating the written word. Instead of the spoken. A form of release perhaps.'

He was right. She smears blood over the page, obliterating the questions. Tilly watches her with unblinking eyes, her tail wrapped round the chair leg.

'What's your secret, Tilly? Whenever I walk out that door you never know when I'm coming back. Yet still you love me unconditionally.'

Ruth reaches down to lift the cat who dodges her grasp, startled by the sound of the phone. Ruth glances at the screen. Varsha. She hesitates. Two options.

'Ruth?'

'Hi, Varsha.' She lifts her thumb to her mouth and presses on the puncture site.

'How are you?

'Fine.' A pause. Is Varsha waiting for her to qualify that single word with more mundane pleasantries? A robin alights on the windowsill, then flies off as Ruth turns her head.

'Good. I need to give you an update. Her Honour Judge Howe has given her permission for you to be present at the hearing next Wednesday. This is progress. Thought we might pencil in an appointment for you to see me on Monday. We can go through the formalities of court procedure.'

A trill of anxiety catches Ruth's breath. Recognition from the authorities that she's a key player. That's got to be a good sign. 'Okay. Yes.' Her voice wavers. 'I'd be grateful. I need to know what to expect.'

'Well, I can't predict an outcome you know that.' The words are clipped, direct, incisive.

Ruth's tongue moves over her lips, which taste of rust.

'Ruth?'

'Yes, I'm here.' She switches to loudspeaker and props the phone against a sauce bottle.

'Okay, good. How about next Monday three thirty, in my office?'

'Sure.'

'Cafcass has almost finished its information gathering. In-'

'Cafcass?' The acronym swirls in Ruth's head. She tries to process it but it doesn't make sense.

'Yes, remember? The Children and Family Court Advisory and Support Service. You recall the interview you did with my colleague last time? She explained it to you. It's all part of the fact-finding exercise, as instructed by the Judge.' There's a hint of impatience in the terse voice.

'Yeah, yeah, sorry. You'll have to excuse me, I'm feeling a bit tired.'

'Well, in addition to your report they've got accounts from Mrs. Zuckerman, Bella's grandmother, and the consultant paediatrician Shaba Elmahdy. Plus there's a new development.'

'Go on.'

'David Morgan. Madeleine's brother. He's arrived in the UK from Brisbane. He wants to make an application for custody of Bella.'

Ruth digs the metal into her thumb turning it round and round like a screw. She holds her breath. There will be time to scream later.

'I thought it important you know now,' Varsha continues. 'Just so there are no surprises.'

Australia. 'Is it further away than heaven?' Bella once asked her. She can picture Bella sitting on her bed clutching Roo, her only constant comfort. She's let her down. She's deserted her. Guilt knots her every time she sees a child in the supermarket, in the street, from her window. How will Bella ever forgive her?

'I'm sorry to burden you with more information, Ruth, but progress has been made in another important area too.'

Ruth leans in to the phone, anxious not to miss a word over the loud pulsing in her ears.

'The toxicology results are back. Your hair samples are positive for codeine.'

So it was true. He was trying to poison her. The paper clip sinks deeper. What was his motive? Control? Manipulation? But why?

'I guess…I … I'm not… I don't know what to say. Surely that's got to act in my favour?'

Varsha's voice has a tinny edge. 'All that says to the Court is that you were taking it. There's no presumption as to how it was administered.'

'What?' Ruth wants to protest but is unable to form the words. Isn't Varsha supposed to be on her side? She bites her lip as her anger swells, the distant voice of her solicitor reaching out to her.

'Ruth, are you okay? Ruth can you hear me?'

Ruth isn't listening any more. The missing prescriptions. The nausea and dizziness. The rebound headaches. The hollow disappointment at not being pregnant. And now the rage. The humiliation. The poisoning. The more she discovers about Dominic the nearer she is to understanding the bigger picture.

The disembodied voice tapers to a halt. Ruth swallows her bloodied saliva, disconnects the phone and goes upstairs.

★

Ruth tugs at the sleeping bag in the bottom of the airing cupboard and places it on the bed next to a canvass holdall. She puts her trainers in the bottom of the bag, then a scrunched-up pair of pyjamas. Her sweat shirt and jogging bottoms next. What else will she need? Surely not that much. A jumper, a waterproof, her phone charger and toiletries. Underwear. She'll need a change of underwear. She pulls open the top drawer of the oak chest and sifts through the gossamer knickers, the lacy bras. The curled edge of an envelope pokes through a jumble of tights. Ruth extracts it from the drawer and sits on the edge of the bed. She holds the envelope to her face and closes her eyes. The faint hint of musk makes her nauseous again. Why, Dominic, why? What possessed him to poison her? And why was he poisoning himself?

Her thoughts drift back to the Coroner's report. Alcohol, codeine and gabapentin. He never drank alcohol. Not when he was with her. What was he trying to achieve with that toxic cocktail? Mask the ischaemic pain of a wilted forearm? Blot out the memory of a violent father? Or assuage the grief of losing his wife? She opens her eyes and slides out the card.

Darling Ruth,
Happy Birthday,
All my love,
Dominic x

Hot tears well as she pores over the words. The unmistakeable brittle strokes, the imperfect 'R', the incomplete 'D'. As she traces the letters with her finger, realisation creeps over her like cracks spreading over ice. The perfectly executed signature on the green script pad. Perfect, except for the tiny anomaly of someone who was left-handed by accident. She winces as she sinks her teeth into her lower lip. Here is the evidence. Varsha must be alerted. There's still time before next Wednesday. She rushes downstairs and rummages through her desk. Her chest feels tight, her breaths an effort. She takes a picture of the handwriting with her phone, then stuffs the card in a large manila envelope and scribbles a hasty note to her solicitor to go with it:

Forensics need to compare this handwriting with the prescriptions.

Madeleine Peterson was prescribed gabapentin and codeine.

Dominic was harming me.

Her hand hovers over the word 'me' as a cold wave of fear slices through her. She guides her hand over the page, her grip accentuating the tremor in her hand. Striking out the last word she tries again.

Dominic was harming Bella, and me.

53

RUTH

The motorway service station café is quiet at this early hour. No families, no laughter, just a few single men hunched over their breakfast baps and tabloids.

She'd had no particular plan last night but, on reaching the end of the dual carriageway, she turned left onto the motorway and soon she was heading north, with each depression on the accelerator creating more distance between her and the imbroglio she was leaving behind. After three hours the traffic thinned, the commuter vehicles had long since disappeared and she found herself weaving between articulated lorries, straining her eyes to see through the fog. Her head felt heavy, her limbs ached. When a juggernaut came bearing down on her, the continuous blast of its horn rocking her attention, she pulled off the road at the next Travel Lodge.

Sleep had been a welcome respite, free of intrusive thoughts. Whether it was sheer exhaustion from the drive, or the hotel room which consumed her in beige anonymity, she couldn't be sure, but now, as she sits stirring her coffee, she feels refreshed and buoyed by her decision. She pulls open the concertina folds of the map, smoothing out the wrinkles over the UK's northernmost region. Scotland. It makes sense. DS Bailey and Varsha Dhasmana can go to hell. Dr. Ruth Cooper is now in control. She could be in Morayshire by lunchtime. Would Elinor Mc Bride remember her from all those years ago? She drains her cup, scrapes back her chair and heads for the car park, swinging her keys.

★

The straight contours of the A9 draw her into the horizon. The sun glints off passing wing mirrors, the air freshly-ironed beneath a cloudless sky. Elinor was always the epitome of discretion. Maybe she'll put her up for a few days, no questions asked. Every year they would exchange Christmas cards until Ruth went to Australia. Ruth really should have made more effort to keep in touch, especially after all the kindness the

retired nurse had showed her. Instinctively Ruth puts
her foot down, guilt spurring her forward.

She switches on the radio. Two women are debat-
ing paternity leave. A dart of pain catches her between
the shoulder blades. She pictures them, smug in the
studio, dressed in their mumsy catalogue clothes. The
noise of a horn jolts her, a car almost blindsiding her
as she drifts across the carriageway. Her attention is
dragged back to the present, as she switches off the
radio and checks her mirrors.

Ten years since she last made this journey north.
Her father came with her then, both of them side-
stepping memories of her mother for fear of upsetting
each other. It's never occurred to her till now but it
must have been hard for him making that expedition
to the clinic, supporting a daughter who disproved
his theory that a 'stiff upper lip' was the best response
to splintered circumstances. Her throat constricts. She
leans forward and presses the CD player into action.
The road ahead opens up against the backdrop of
Enya's melodic refrains.

The cottage should be relatively easy to find.
She can remember the cemetery at the foothills of
Drumnabreich, about five miles along the coast road
east of Inverness. That was always the landmark for
turning off onto the single-track road which wound
along the densely-wooded hillside of Scots pine and
Douglas firs, until the track petered out into a narrow

path. Many was the time she made that journey in the depths of winter, looking out for the reflective tops of snow poles which marked the side of the road. The landscape is sure to look very different now, with the bracken and heather melding into a rich tweed of russet and magenta, but she's bound to recognise the terrain as she gets nearer. Much easier to recall are the flickering coals and steaming mugs of tea as they sat by the fire eating homemade shortbread, while Elinor recounted memories from her early days as a nurse. She had a genial face, the sort that would dimple with kindness when Ruth arrived for a weekend's respite from the clinic. So different from the hawk-eyed countenance of Sister Immaculata in the convent. The memories galvanise her forward. She's guessing Elinor must be in her late seventies now. Maybe she'd be glad of the company.

By mid-morning the hues of the panorama change. Watercolour greys, blues and neutrals mutate into vibrant acrylics of purple, yellow and green. Cheered by the sight of the heather in full bloom, Ruth feels lighter, more energised. When the road crests a hill, bringing the Kessock Bridge and glittering Beauly Firth into view she can feel her shoulders lifting.

She heads east just before the turn-off for Inverness town centre and soon the road runs in parallel to the shores of the inlet. She parks her car in the market square of the first village she encounters. The single-storey grey stone and whitewashed houses that line either side of the main street are instantly recognisable. She spots the butcher's shop with its chequerboard displays of Scotch pies and Lorne sausage, the newsagent with its billboard for 'The Press and Journal.' Even the Post Office is still there, although it looks to have been incorporated into a Spar supermarket behind the market cross.

She steps inside the bakery, where the yeasty smell of freshly-baked bread combines with the hint of almonds and coffee. Ordering a takeaway cappuccino from the man in the floury white jacket she casts her eye through the glass display. She spots a tier of rowies, the lardy pastries only found in this part of the world. How she used to crave them on frost-ferned mornings, after she had run a lap of the clinic grounds.

'Anything else, Miss?' The man is holding out a Styrofoam cup, smiling.

She picks up a cellophane-wrapped packet of tablet. Elinor always had a sweet tooth.

'I'll take this, please, and a couple of rowies.' She hesitates, glancing along the counter. 'Do you have sandwiches?'

'We do indeed,' says the man, indicating towards a blackboard with an infinitesimal list of bread varieties and fillings. 'What would you like?' He waits patiently as she scans the list. 'On holiday are you?'

Caught off guard Ruth darts him a look but he has his head down, as he separates the edges of a waxed paper bag.

'Kind of. Revisiting some old haunts. Actually, perhaps you can give me directions?'

'I'll do ma best.'

'Alt–na–Beinn. It's the first turn-off past Dunbeg cemetery, isn't it? Am I on the right road?'

The baker twists the ends of the paper bag and places it on the counter. 'After a wee holiday place, are you?'

She must look perplexed because, after a few seconds silence, he continues. 'Alt-na- Beinn? The cottage that's for sale, up the Dunbeg track?'

Ruth feels her cheeks colour. She's aware of a small queue shuffling behind her back.

'For sale? No, I hadn't realised. I … I used to… I used go there on holiday … when I was a child.'

'All boarded up now. Been on the market these past eighteen months. Now then, which sandwich filling d'you fancy?'

Ruth feels confused. She orders a tuna and salad sandwich, pays for her purchases and takes them outside where she sits on a low stone wall. She hadn't been expecting this. What of Elinor? Where had she moved? The cottage must have become too much for her. If only she'd contacted her when she came back from Australia. She takes a bite out of her sandwich then stuffs it back into the paper bag. The last of the coffee tastes bitter. The shop has emptied of customers, so she goes back in.

The man is chopping tomatoes on a wooden board and looks up, his eyebrows arched.

'Hi. I hope you don't mind,' says Ruth, 'but I've been thinking about what you said. About Alt-na-Beinn.'

He rests his knife on the workbench and turns to face her. 'Aye?'

'The lady who lived there. Elinor Mc Bride. I used to know from years back. Do you know where she's gone? I'd like to trace her.'

The man's features soften. 'I guess it must be a wee while since you were last here. Nellie Mc Bride died two years ago. I'm sorry if that's come as a surprise to you.'

54
RUTH

She spots the 'For Sale' sign on the main road, past the Free Church hall and by the far corner of the cemetery. As she negotiates the bend to follow the road uphill, she can see that its wooden post has rotted and the tin sign has erupted in rust, like a spreading pox. She switches the car heater on full blast, conscious that the darkening sky has created a distinct chill. The dried-out track is rutted with pot holes and canopied by branches weighted with elderberries. Ruth presses on and after five or six minutes comes to the clearing. Weeds sprout up through the paved surface, a stone urn lies smashed on its side. She reverses her car onto a level piece of ground with the hillside at her back and switches off the ignition. She sits with her head against the steering wheel and closes her eyes. She feels drained. Poor Elinor. She'd been a spinster but were there any other family members? If only Ruth had known, she hates to think of her being on her own at the end. Regardless of what the baker said, she still needs to see the cottage for herself. She lifts the bag of tablet from the front passenger seat, pulls on the ribbon and the cellophane springs open. Popping the buttery candy into her mouth, the sugar dissolves on her tongue. She reaches into the back of the car for her jacket, pulls it on and goes outside.

Despite the tree cover on her right the wind whips her hair as she strides up the path, and the fir trees which slope down on her left bristle like an excited audience. She rounds the bend and there it is. The white-washed cottage. The gabled bedroom windows under the slate roof. The front porch where she used to leave her wellies for fear of trailing mud across Elinor's Persian rugs. Now it carries an air of neglect. The porch door is locked but peering through the glass she can see a stack of junk mail on the floor next to a rusty milk-bottle holder. She presses her nose to a window but the reflected light from the low afternoon sun makes it impossible to see inside. Brushing flecks of green paint off her jacket she wanders round to the back of the house. The ground beneath her feet squelches as she moves into the shade. The kitchen door is padlocked, but the shadows afford a better view into the downstairs sitting room, now denuded of curtains. She leans against the sill and lurches forward as it disintegrates in rotting clumps exposing a hole between the glass pane and the frame. Intuitively she looks over her shoulder, then laughs. No-one's watching her. How could she be so stupid? The thudding in her chest becomes more forceful as she pulls her jacket sleeve down over her hand, reaches through the gap and lifts the window latch.

55

RUTH

Sunbeams filter through the front window, casting the room in a butterscotch glow. Gone is the green Dralon settee with its Antimacassar of embroidered flowers. The recess where the chenille-covered table used to be is bare, and the Monarch of the Glen no longer presides above the fireplace, casting its marbled eye on Ruth from its lacquered frame. Instead, peeling wallpaper and rust-tacked floorboards enclose a hollow space, which echoes with the sound of her squeaky boots. Despite the scent of old newspaper, which combines with a hint of leaf mould, the cottage is warm and dry. The terrain may have changed but it clothes Ruth in welcome memories. She pushes open the door at the far end of the room and makes her way upstairs. The window under the gable is knitted with cobwebs but through them she can see the slope of pine woods and the distant sparkle of the Firth. The room on the right is where she used to stay. She would lie in bed under a sloping roof, listening to the hoo hoo of the tawny owl at night, and she would feel safe, whilst Elinor slumbered in the room opposite.

Thoughts of Elinor prick her with guilt. 'Nellie' the man in the bakery had called her, a term of endearment. Elinor always showed her such kindness. It pains her to think that Ruth never enquired about Elinor's own family or her friends. She taps open the opposite bedroom door and her eyes rest on the lavender-sprigged wallpaper, and the brass rings which dangle from a bare curtain pole. Strange how Elinor's absence can leave large holes in the surroundings, like a moth-eaten cashmere shawl which is still comforting but never as warm. She hopes Elinor wasn't on her own when the end came.

Glancing at her watch she sees it is just after two o'clock. She'll need to get going if she's to sort out her accommodation for the night. Heading back into Inverness is probably the best option but anonymity is something she craves. That's probably lacking in all but the big hotels, which are bound to be expensive. As she turns on her heels to make her way downstairs her eyes catch a glint of something on the floor. Bending down and scraping away the dust she lifts up a tiny tarnished pin brooch. How long had it lain there undisturbed between the cracks in the floorboards? She rubs it against her sleeve and examines it more closely. A Celtic knot with a central amber cabochon. A symbol of loyalty and friendship. Ruth smiles. She never used to believe in fate but she knows now that her decision to leave Tadwick had been the right one. She need look no further for a roof over her head tonight.

★

The hardware store on the Nairn road has everything she needs in its end-of-season sale: an inflatable air-bed, a folding chair, a camping stove and aluminium cook set and a torch. The lime-scaled tap at the cottage had streamed rust-coloured water so she buys eight litres of bottled Highland Spring and some food supplies when she stops at the supermarket.

As soon as she comes down to the main road her phone doesn't stop buzzing. She glances at it in the car park: three missed calls from Val and one from DS Bailey. She contemplates listening to voicemail then decides against it. Having no signal at the cottage is a blessing.

Back at Alt-na-Beinn she climbs the path beyond the cottage and watches the sunset from the wooden bench situated on the crest of the hill. The midges have long gone but it's still warm enough to sit here without her jacket, enveloping herself in peace and tranquillity, secure in the knowledge that her car and the cottage is not visible from the road. As she watches the winking lights of aeroplanes arcing towards the airport she wonders where Bella is now. Having a bedtime story from a foster carer? Asking if her daddy is now with her mummy? Remembering that Ruth had promised to take her to the adventure playground once her plaster cast was off?

A career, marriage, motherhood. When Ruth was a little girl that trajectory felt assured. Adoption was never on the master plan. And now she is effectively on the run. If she's going to take on this incomprehensible responsibility she needs to draw deep on her energy reserves. 'Take care of yourself first,' her therapist said, 'or you will have nothing left to give others.'

She shivers as the temperature drops and, picking up her mug she retreats down the hill to the cottage, walks round the back and passes her belongings through the gap in the window frame before clambering indoors.

56

RUTH

Ruth walks past the window of the estate agent on Argyle St for the second time. The first time she had lingered over the display, scanning the photos for Alt-na-Beinn but, amongst the grey stone houses, the executive apartments and the picturesque crofts there's no sign of the white-washed cottage. Of course it's not going to be on view. Didn't the man in the bakery say it had been on the market for eighteen months? It will have been consigned to the drawers of the back office by now. She decides against entering the shop and enquiring after it. Too risky. Especially now that she is a sought-after person. Four days she's been gone. That's all. But it hasn't stopped Val ringing her every day. Each time she travels to within a phone signal there are fresh messages on her voicemail.

'Ruth, I'm worried about you. We're all worried about you. Please let us know you're all right.'

We? Who's we? The police? The lawyers? Social services? In the end she had texted her back.

Don't worry about me. I'm safe. Just need some space. I'll call you when I'm ready.

She turns left at the end of the street, then meanders past the Castle before heading along the banks of the Ness, until she comes to a bench on the opposite side of the river to the theatre. She sits down, content to watch the promenaders. Two women pushing buggies are chatting to each other, their lilting accents carrying on the breeze. They stop every few paces and turn round, to check on the progress of a little girl who trails behind. The youngster looks to be about Bella's age. Shoulder-length blonde hair. A blue pinafore dress and cardigan with the buttons wrongly aligned. Dragging her feet.

The hearing is in two days. Ruth should have been meeting Varsha today. She feels sick when she thinks about it. She still can't decide if she can face the journey south for the hearing, but she knows that if she doesn't make the effort it will scupper her chances of being awarded custody. She can't help staring at the little girl who is clutching an ice cream, the cone pitched forward at an angle of forty five degrees. The child is momentarily distracted when one of the women calls out to her to hurry up and the chocolate scoop slides onto the pavement and puddles like a slushy snowball. The little girl's eyes widen and a few seconds elapse before she bursts into tears. Ruth wants to run up to her and tell her it's okay, she'll buy her another one, but instead she watches silently as the woman grabs her sleeve and scolds her for being so careless. Ruth looks away, an embarrassed witness. But there is something that bothers her, like a persistent toothache, as she watches the group recede into the distance. Dominic would rarely tell Bella off. He always knew how to make things better. There was always the promise of a treat, to make up for the absence of a mother. Unsettled, she gathers her belongings and heads for the nearest coffee shop.

Taking her cappuccino to the far recesses of the café Ruth sits down, pulls out a notebook and pen, which she places on the table and connects her phone to wi-fi. There's a couple a few tables away, sitting side by side, both scrolling down their phone screens and ignoring each other.

Tentatively Ruth taps EMF into the search engine. A blue icon winks from the screen as gradually the pages of the Electronic Medical Formulary load. She takes her notebook and draws a chart on the paper, then scribbles a list in the first column: codeine, gabapentin, ibuprofen, tizanidine. What else did she find in the box under Dominic's bed? She turns her head and gazes absentmindedly at the wall maps of Costa Rica and East Africa, while trying to picture the scene in Dominic's house that day. Oxybutynin? Dantrolene? Diazepam? Baclofen? She can't be sure but she writes them all down. She lifts her cup and a swig of hot coffee hits the back of her throat. Meticulously she works her way down the list, writing the drug name in the electronic search box and reading the adverse reactions. Her fingers hover over the results for gabapentin: urinary tract infections, leucopenia, convulsions. She double checks the search box. Gabapentin. No mistake. Her hand is shaking and she accidentally taps the back button and loses her place.

'Excuse me, miss, but are you okay?'

Her eyes adjust to the young man in the long apron who is looming over the table.

'Yeah, fine. I'm fine, thank you.'

He leans in a bit closer and lowers his voice but the café is empty, save for the couple on their phones. 'Only you sounded like you were in pain and you look a bit pale. Can I get you anything?'

Ruth digs her nails into her palms. 'Maybe a glass of water, thanks. But I'm fine, honestly.' She smooths her hair, placing a loose strand behind her ear.

Gabapentin. White capsule. Adverse reactions: Urinary tract infections. Leucopenia. Convulsions.

Taking a packet of wet wipes out of her bag she runs one across her face, and uses another to rub across her hands. Her T shirt sticks to her back and, as she unpeels from her skin she's conscious of the stale smell of sweat. She reloads the screen.

I-b-u-p-r-o-f-e-n. A pink convex tablet.

The guy with the apron returns and places a plastic cup of water on the table. He's about to go but Ruth taps his arm. 'Actually, could I have another cappuccino, please?' He nods and disappears.

She scrolls down to section 4.8 Undesirable effects. Skin rashes. Risk of bleeding. Bronchial asthma. Asthma? She sighs. Why does she have to check this? She knows it. But she's not quite finished. She writes on her pad, returns to the website, then stops and leans back.

Ibuprofen, a pink convex tablet. Gabapentin, a white capsule.

A Smartie that is given as a treat. A white capsule that goes fizz in pop.

The waiter returns with a coffee and she takes a gulp, burning the roof of her mouth.

The hearing is in forty eight hours. She's going to have to act fast. This time she taps a number into her phone. It's answered on the second ring.

'Val?'

'Ruth? Ruth! Is that you?'

'Listen, Val, I'm fine. Please don't ask me any questions. I needed some space.'

'We've been worried sick about you. We've even ...' There's a hesitation then a cough.

'Sorry? You've what?'

'Never mind. Where are you?'

'I'm safe. Listen you've got to help me. I've been doing some research. I don't know why this didn't occur to me sooner. I guess my thought processes have been a bit clouded.'

'I'm listening.'

'Side effects of gabapentin and ibuprofen. UTIs, low white count, convulsions, asthma. Not to be confused with Systemic Lupus Erythematosus.'

'What are you talking about, Ruth?''

'I'm saying that they weren't Smarties that Dominic was giving to Bella. I want you to promise me something.'

'Go on.'

'I'm about to e mail Varsha a statement and I'll copy you in. I want you to make sure that it's produced for the hearing on Wednesday.'

'Will you not be there?'

'I don't know yet. But promise me. Will you?'

'Yes. I promise.'

'Are you sure? You promise?'

'Yes, of course, now just...'

Ruth disconnects the phone. The back of her neck feels hot as she composes her statement. She had been so convinced that Bella's symptoms were suggestive of SLE. Maybe the authorities were already on to this. But how can she convince them that it was Dominic, not her, poisoning Bella?

57

RUTH

The humidity in the foyer feels oppressive. The attendant hands her the locker key and pushes a rolled towel across the counter. Muttering her thanks Ruth grasps it and crosses the tiled floor towards the changing rooms. Tinkling laughter echoes through the glass panel on her right. The pool looks busy. A red swimming cap and a blue one move in opposite directions, slicing through the water like traffic on two sides of a motorway. Two young boys at the far side chop the swell with their hands as they throw a ball. A third one takes a running jump at them from the poolside, disappearing in feathered spume. She's glad she's only here for a shower. Four days of sleeping rough have taken their toll.

The changing room is empty and much cooler. She unwinds the stained crepe bandage from her wrist and stuffs it in her pocket. Discarding her clothes she wraps herself in the off-white towel, steps over the pile of garments on the cubicle floor, into the shower and turns on the taps. Soon the steam starts to rise. She submerges herself under the rapid-fire spray and lets her imagination drift.

Never a deep sleeper, last night's dream had been particularly unsettling. She was in the courtroom. Before the judge's summing up Ruth was asked if she would like to add anything to her statement.

Yes, please, Your Honour, she said, standing up. And then her words came tumbling out, in a continuous loop, crackling through the courtroom audio system, *the truth is my best defence, the truth is my best defence...* From the public gallery a figure had shouted *'Truth above all'* and she'd looked up to see a man in a check shirt and red braces. Niall Freeman. It disturbed her.

When she woke in a cold sweat the crackling noise from her dream continued and she realised it was coming from the adjoining room. She'd tried to ignore it, sliding as far down as possible in her sleeping bag and pulling the quilted material closely round her ears. But sleep was ineffectual. In the end she'd grabbed her torch and kicked open the door of the neighbouring bedroom. Scanning the room quickly the beam had landed on a scrunch of newspaper, which had been stuffed into a gap in the windowsill and was now pulsing in the breeze. It was hard to get back to sleep after that, as she tried to orientate herself in terms of time scales. Tuesday. Twenty four hours until the decision on Bella's future. That had been the deciding factor for Ruth. The reason she had packed up her things and resolved to go home. But not yet.

The changing room door clashes, then a whistling tune stops abruptly.

'Oh, hello,' a voice calls through the fug, 'it's just the cleaner. No worries, I'll come back later.' Another resonant clang.

Ruth reaches round the curtain for her towel and pats her legs and arms dry. The scars on her wrist are pink and tingly, criss-crossing like a skewed chequerboard.

She dries her hair, and looks up at her reflection in the mirror. Still dark circles under her eyes but a definite improvement on the dishevelled creature she feared she was becoming.

'Too busy for you in the pool today?' says the young man in reception, taking back her key and handing her a clipboard.

Ruth nods. 'Another time, I think.' Satisfied that her signature is a squiggle that only her postman could decipher she slides the pen and chart over the counter and walks towards the cafeteria.

Within seconds her phone comes alive, like a wasp

trapped in a jam jar. She pulls it out of her pocket and glances at the screen. Seven missed calls from Varsha.

Seven?

Surely that'll have been over the course of the last few days? But why have they all come through now? Must be the absence of phone signal at the cottage.

She orders a coffee and takes it to a table near the window, then dials voicemail.

'Ruth, Varsha Dhasmana here. I hope you're okay. You must call me when you get this message. There've been some important developments.'

The clock on the far wall reads nine thirty. Will Varsha will be in her office? She tries the number. No answer. Maybe she's in court. Or even the police station. What good would it do to leave a message? No, she'll try again later. She sips her coffee then turns her attention back to her phone, tapping 'Niall Freeman' into the search engine.

Several pages load with a consistent theme. High profile cases of criminality, child abuse, wrongful accusations and his role as a forensic psychiatrist. She clicks on a link from a tabloid newspaper. There he is, in his trademark red braces, standing outside the Old Bailey. The headline reads: 'Accused mum's relief after baby drug drama.' Intrigued, she reads on.

The story involved a twenty-four-year-old single mother, Bridget Weaver, accused of harming her nine-week-old baby who had suffered recurrent breathing difficulties and abnormal heart rhythms. Niall Freeman, who had been giving evidence in the case, as an expert on Munchausen's Syndrome by Proxy, had stunned the jury by stating he believed that Bridget had not induced illness in her baby son. Instead he thought that the symptoms exhibited were due to a drug the baby had been prescribed for reflux. Freeman produced data on the number of adverse reactions caused by this drug, Absorbix, and it had been withdrawn from the market. Bridget was acquitted and her baby was returned to her care.

Ruth remembers the case well. It was widely publicised. She had discussed it with her colleagues because this was a drug that they prescribed frequently, before it was banned. She remembers the slightly eccentric dress sense of the psychiatrist issuing his press statements on TV but she hadn't paid much attention to the accused, or her family. Until now. She magnifies the image on her phone. There's Niall standing outside the Old Bailey with Bridget Weaver and her sister. Ruth's heartbeat accelerates. She looks more closely at the features of the sister: dark shoulder-length hair, drawn up in a clip on one side. Narrow eyes. Eyebrows like slugs. Courtney Weaver. Bella's babysitter.

Ruth's stomach clenches. Thoughts whirr in her brain, like a helicopter's rotor blades before take-off. She needs to stay focussed. Remain calm. This is significant but she needs to determine why. Courtney's sister had been accused of fabricating illness in her baby. She was found innocent and the cause attributed to the side effect of a drug, but not before her baby had been taken away from her. Niall Freeman had helped secure her acquittal.

Ruth thinks back to Bella. The urinary tract infections. The asthma attacks. The convulsion. The side effects of ibuprofen and gabapentin which mimicked those exact same symptoms. Surely Courtney couldn't have been involved in inducing Bella's illness? What would be her motive? On the other hand, hadn't she been found as the source of those abusive on-line messages about Ruth? Why had she felt the need to do that?

Ruth taps more words into the search engine on her phone and tries to digest the result:

Fabricating or inducing illness, formerly known as Munchausen's Syndrome by Proxy- a rare form of child abuse…occurs when a carer exaggerates or deliberately causes symptoms of illness in the child… usually in children under the age of five…most cases caused by the mother but can be a father, foster parent or childcare professional at fault…a large number of perpetrators have borderline personality disorders and a history of self-harm…

Ruth gasps as she traces over the words of the last

sentence again. The cards are stacking up against her. She pushes the table as she jerks back her chair. Her coffee cup rattles on its saucer and her phone smashes to the floor. She needs to speak to Niall before it's too late. Scooping up her phone she rushes out of the café, her shoulder bag smacking her thigh. The rush of cold air pinches her face. Hurriedly she dials his number…and listens:

'Thank you for calling Dr. Niall Freeman. I am sorry I am unavailable at the moment but if you would like to leave a message I'll return your call as soon as possible.'

'Niall,' she howls, 'I'm innocent. You've got to believe me. I need to speak to you, Niall.' But her words, whipped by the biting wind, disappear as vapour trails.

58

RUTH

It will take at least six hours to drive home, but Ruth doesn't need to leave just yet. Much better to arrive home when it's dark. There'll be time to contact Niall Freeman in the morning, before the hearing.

Punctuating the journey back to the cottage she stops at the garden centre on the Nairn Road, and by ten thirty she is reversing her car into the parking space at Alt-Na-Beinn.

She loads up the car with her belongings and takes a last look round the cottage interior. It's freckled in sunlight, a warm valediction. One day she hopes she'll be back.

Long strides take her up the hill, following the public footpath, and past the wooden bench. She continues climbing until she reaches the glade, where the sound of trickling water mixes with the rustle of leaves. Looking up, crystals of light shimmer through the tree canopy, mirrored by the droplets that trickle from the spring. The clootie well. A place of healing.

Ruth takes the small crepe bandage out of her pocket and unravels it. As she dips it in the water it deepens in colour from eggshell to deep oatmeal, and the wrinkles of congealed blood ingrained in its fibres mutate from red to brown. She pulls it from the water, wrings it out and walks over to the conifer. Its branches resemble bottle brushes and, as she pulls on one, several pine cones tumble to the ground. Lassoing the crepe strip over the branch she fastens it into a knot. She'd seen clootie rags on a visit to Culloden. Lengths of cloth left tied to branches by the well, as part of a healing ritual. Strange, yet fitting, that she had come to this place seeking healing. This place was her refuge. Her sanctuary. Here she had found strength. The time was right to say goodbye and head home to defend herself.

Her footsteps downhill feel weighted with emotion until she reaches the bench and sits down. A trilling sound overhead draws her gaze upwards to a fan of reddish-brown and white feathers. Two red kites wheel high above the valley, swooping and rising with the thermals. Extracting the brown envelope from her pocket Ruth reads its contents: campion, buttercup, borage, forget-me-not, ox-eye daisy, corn-flower. Elinor would have loved them.

Below the bench is a gentle slope which flattens out to an area roughly the size of four car widths. She clambers down onto the plateau and mapping out the perimeter with her feet, she scatters the wildflower seeds in her wake. From the far side of the meadow she can see the fluttering of graveside flowers in the burial ground and, below that, the twists and turns of the road as it snakes in and out of the tree canopy.

The glint of chrome makes her start. There's a car coming up the track. A black 4x4. She crouches down, trying to make herself inconspicuous, and she watches its progress as she rocks back and forth on her heels. The thumping in her chest gets more forceful. This is a no-through road. Whoever it is will see her car parked alongside the cottage.

She waits for it to disappear, then gets up and runs back to the wood for cover. A car door slams and there's the beep of an alarm. Ruth finds a vantage point in the shade. A man with a crew-cut, beige slacks and a blue fleece is inspecting her car. He walks round it, his hands shielding the reflection as he peers through its windows.

Suddenly he looks up and scans the area forcing Ruth to dart back to avoid being spotted. And that's when she recognises him. But it's not his car. He retreats. Maybe he's checking out the cottage? A snap decision needs to be made. She's going to be discovered but it needs to be on her terms.

★

Clinging to the shade of the treeline, Ruth edges towards the cottage. The chassis of the black Discovery eclipses her car. Both the vehicle and its registration plate are unfamiliar. Her breathing becomes shallower as she verges nearer. He must have gone round the back of the cottage. Stepping out into the sunlight her shadow stretches out before her on the sandy coloured earth. But there's a much taller silhouette which overshadows hers. Its long legs and head and shoulders elongate into a willowy apparition and a chill permeates the air. Ruth wheels round to face her stalker.

'Mac!'

'I'm sorry, Ruth. I didn't mean to scare you.'

Ruth feels her shoulders slump as she confronts her pursuer. So many questions. But, for now, no words.

He makes no movement. 'I've…we've all been worried about you.'

'But…how did…?'

Mac's face creases into a smile. 'You'd never pass

muster as a professional fugitive. Your phone call to Val the other day.' His features soften and delicate lines fan round his eyes. 'We traced the signal to Inverness. Your car's been picked up several times on CCTV in the town. It didn't take long to spot your movements and follow you.'

Ruth bites her lip. The relief she feels that someone cares about her gives way to fear. If she's been followed then surely she could be prosecuted for breaking and entering a property.

It's starting again: the quickening heartbeat, the rapid breathing. The panic that she'd worked so hard to control. She brushes past Mac and walks back up the path, anxious to create some space between them. Heading towards the bench she's conscious that he's following her but she craves the open space.

They sit at opposite ends of the bench. The only sound is the clucking of a pheasant in the long grass. In the distance a fishing vessel breaches an azure surface. Sunlight breaks through the shifting cumulus to warm Ruth's face. There is no denying it. She has to go home and face her challenges head on. She knew this would happen. She has a renewed determination to do this. But she wanted it to be on her terms.

She turns to look at Mac.

'Listen to that,' she says. 'Listen to the sound of silence. It's so peaceful up here. It's something I've craved, Mac. I needed to get away. Find some space.

Away from phones. Interruptions. Demands. I needed time out.'

He studies her face but does nothing to fill the silence.

'I'm not perfect,' she continues, 'but I've learned to live with my imperfections. And I have this innate – or maybe misjudged–ability to always see the best in people. Much to my detriment.' She pauses. 'I would never do anyone any harm.' She gives a low grunt. 'Only myself.'

Mac turns away and appears to be studying his shoes. 'I get that. I really do.' He grips the bench on either side of his legs and hangs his head. 'Ruth, I've been worried sick about you.' He turns to look at her. 'You know, from the very first day that I met you, I could tell you were innocent. I was assigned as your FLO because of the road traffic collision. Once you became part of a criminal investigation I had to be moved. But I suspect my superiors could see that wasn't the only reason it made sense for me to step down. A perceived conflict of interest. An inability to be impartial. A feeling that I wanted to get closer to you. As I got to know more about you through Val it only convinced me further of your innocence. That's why I was taken off your case.'

Ruth stands up and regards him accusingly. 'It didn't stop you arresting me, for fuck's sake.' Her eyes prickle.

'Ruth, I was just obeying orders. Being taken off the investigation allowed me to make my own enquiries.' His hands move from the bench, and he laces his fingers in front of his chest, as if preparing to defend himself. 'Anyway, it's not just me who believes in your innocence. The Court does too.'

Ruth absorbs the words slowly. 'What do you mean?'

Mac holds out his arm, motioning for her to sit down, but she remains standing.

'Varsha tried to contact you, Ruth. Many times. There was even a press statement released so the public could keep an eye out for you.'

Ruth shudders. She zips her fleece and moves towards Mac, blocking him from the sun. 'What do you mean? Tell me!' She is surprised how her breath escapes in a strangulated cry.

Mac stands up, bringing himself to her eye level. 'The hearing. It was yesterday. It was brought forward. The Judge ruled that, because at least three serious attempts had been made to contact you unsuccessfully, it would go ahead without your presence.'

Ruth grabs Mac's sleeves. Brought forward? Innocent? She shakes him but he remains resolute. Unmoving. 'What happened? TELL ME!'

Mac's voice is barely audible. 'There's so much to tell you, Ruth. But there's something you should know first.' He swallows and looks at her with an unflinching stare. 'David Morgan has been awarded custody of Bella.'

She glares back, not blinking. 'Wait,' she says, tightening the grip on his arm. 'Let me get this straight. David Morgan? Bella's uncle? But he lives in Australia.' There's a ripple of movement which starts in her toes and fingers. It spreads up her legs and arms and crests across her body in a tsunami of despair. 'No!' She screams, as a roost of birds take flight from nearby trees.

She breaks away from him and starts running but her legs feel like sponge. The faster she runs the harder the ground feels. The vibrations hammer into her body and her breath wheezes free of her chest. Taking the footpath further up the hill she heads towards the wood. When she gets to the clootie well she collapses onto the ground and her sobs emerge in unexpurgated gulps.

How could Bella ever forgive her? Bella, dear Bella. She'd failed to protect her. She'd breached the very safeguards that were there to keep her from harm. And now she might never see her again. It's too awful to contemplate. The cold ground torments her body, as the damp seeps through her clothes. She sits up and brushes her matted hair away from her eyes. Mac is sitting on a nearby tree stump watching her.

'Take me home,' she says.

59

RUTH

Mac has everything organised, from the return of the hire car in Harbour Road to the overnight accommodation just south of Berwick–upon–Tweed.

'It's a long way home,' he says, handing Ruth her room keys at the hotel reception 'and I reckoned you could do with a decent night's sleep before you face the barrage of questions.' As soon as he says this it's obvious he's trying to retract his words. 'There's no hurry, after all,' he adds hastily, but Ruth knows he's right. She needs to feel ready.

The porter opens the door to her room and places her black canvass holdall on the floor. A single bed, a television on the far wall, a floor-length mirror, a small en-suite bathroom. Simple but comfortable. She thanks him and flops on the bed. Fifteen minutes Mac suggested, before meeting her for coffee in the bar. She had dozed off during the car journey south, her dreams punctuated by stilted conversation. Now she feels nervous about facing Mac again.

When she walks into the tartan-heavy sitting room, having rearranged her hair and applied more concealer to the dull half-moons under her eyes, he is sitting by the log fire which crackles and spits. He looks up and smiles, then shuffles some papers under his newspaper. A waitress is dispatched with their order and Mac leans back in his chair and looks around the deserted bar area.

'I have a confession to make,' he says, with a grin, but his expression changes to one of concern when Ruth frowns. 'Oh no, no, it's nothing serious. How tactless of me.' He leans towards her. 'What I should have said is that I know this part of the country pretty well.' There's a softness to his voice and Ruth knows he is trying to distract her with trivial conversation, but she can't stop dwelling on Bella. It's all she could think about during their silences in the car.

'I grew up in Kelso,' Mac continues. 'A small market town in the Borders, not far from here. I used to come here on holiday as a child. Not *here* exactly. A caravan park near the cliffs. Probably long since gone.

Maybe we can take a walk along the shore later, if you feel up to it.'

'What were those papers, Mac?' asks Ruth.

Mac looks confused but follows her eye-line to the pile of crumpled newspaper on the coffee table.

'I know you're trying to distract me with small talk but you're hiding something from me.' She grabs at the papers but Mac is too quick for her. He snatches them just as a young girl appears bearing a cafetiere and two cups on a tray. The sheaves land on the floor. The waitress sets down the tray and, in a soft lilting accent, asks them if they'd like anything else, before disappearing. The sitting room is deserted. Ruth pounces forward, grabbing the stapled sheets and her eyes scan the pages.

'Well-presented two bedroom cottage for sale. Sitting in an elevated position with commanding views over the Moray Firth. Grants Estate Agents, Inverness. And a photo of Alt-na-Beinn.' She shakes her head. 'Why?'

'Curiosity,' says Mac, with a shrug of his shoulders. 'Nothing more, nothing less. Read it if you like. I've nothing to hide.'

Ruth picks up the heavy cafetiere. 'Did you go to the hearing?' she says, casting Mac a sideways glance. The blurb on Alt-na–Beinn has unsettled her but she has so many more important questions. As she fills the cups she tries not to splash coffee over the saucers.

'No, it was a closed case. Varsha briefed me afterwards. She knows I'm here. So does Val and … I'm not sure about Mike.'

Ruth nods.

'Your statements-the one you sent with a sample of Dominic's handwriting, and your e mail with the drug information-both were considered, as were statements from Viviane Zuckerman, David Morgan, plus the Local Authority reports-you know, the psychiatrist, Social Services and the hospital paediatrician.' He looks puzzled. 'There was one more, I think, but I can't for the life of me remember who it was from.'

Ruth bristles at the mention of Viviane Zuckerman. It's a name that had completely fallen off her radar. 'Dominic's mother?'

'Yes.' Mac has turned his head and is stroking his chin. He doesn't look at her and it makes her feel uncomfortable.

'What is it, Mac? Please tell me.'

'You met Viviane Zuckerman, didn't you?' he says, turning towards her.

'Yes. She arrived in the UK shortly after Dominic … soon after the accident. We met in the hospital, maybe a couple of times.'

'Presumably you knew about his childhood accident?'

'Dominic told me about it. His mother was in an

abusive relationship with his father. The night of his accident he tried to protect her from being strangled and he fell through a window shattering his arm and spleen.'

Mac leans forward again and this time he places his hand gently on her knee. Her sharp outline is reflected in his eyes.

'He was a pathological liar, Ruth. And a psychopath. Mrs. Zuckerman provided a lengthy statement which was no doubt pivotal in the Crown Prosecution Service deciding not to pursue a criminal case against you.'

'Wait, wait,' says Ruth. There's too much information coming at her all at once.

'The CPS are not taking this further? So DS Bailey is off my back now, too?' Mac grips her knee.

'Viviane Zuckerman provided extensive details about Dominic's childhood in her statement,' Mac continues. 'He was a bright kid at school, but he was always a bit of a troublemaker. A bully. A cheat. A liar. He got into trouble for peddling cannabis. One day he truanted with a friend and they were found by the police hours later, having fallen through the roof of a disused warehouse. He sustained life-threatening injuries. The doctors said that if he'd been found sooner and had treatment earlier his arm would have healed properly.'

Ruth tries to digest this information. So that explains the Volkmann's ischaemic contracture. He'd convinced her it happened while he was protecting his mother. He lied. She sits in stunned silence as Mac proceeds.

'He spent weeks in hospital with his injuries, then years attending hospital outpatient appointments. His father was a pilot and was frequently absent from home, then became ill and died of cancer, leaving Dominic and his mother. Not long after his father's death his mother remarried. There was never any history of domestic violence in either of their marriages. According to Dominic's psychiatrist the accident and the months Dominic spent in hospital reinforced his attention-seeking behaviour.'

Ruth sits back compelling Mac to do the same. She lifts her cup to her lips and takes a sip of lukewarm coffee, spilling some of it down her top.

'His last contact with the psychiatric service was about ten years ago when he was graded a score of thirty one out of forty on the Hare Psychopathy Revised Checklist.'

Ruth's coffee cup clashes down on the saucer. Her cheeks feel hot. The coffee tastes bitter. 'Thirty one? That high?'

Mac nods.

'My God,' she says, considering this. In her head she goes through Dominic's traits like a ready reckoner. 'And to think I had confused the mood swings, the attention-seeking behaviour and the lack of empathy with a bereavement reaction.'

'Don't be hard on yourself. I can see why you did.'

'The smooth-talking compulsive liar. The juvenile delinquency.' Ruth tries to recall the diagnostic criteria.

'The promiscuity.' Mac darts her a look and she feels her cheeks colour.

'It's okay,' she says, 'Val told me.'

Mac's eyes widen. 'About Courtney? When?'

'No, about Val. Wait, we may be talking at cross purposes here.'

Mac stands up and paces round the room. He stops and looks at her. 'You first.'

'Val told me she had an affair with Dominic. About six years ago. She said she regretted it and that Mike knew all about it.'

'Ah, yes. I see.'

'Why did you mention Courtney?'

Mac turns his back to her. He looks out the window.

'Mac, answer me, please. What did you mean?'

Mac turns round. 'Dominic had an affair with Courtney too.'

Ruth reels back in her seat. She feels sick. 'Oh, my God. No. When was this?'

Mac advances towards the sofa and sits down. 'Courtney used to be a care worker. She was employed by Dominic to look after Madeleine when she was very ill. The affair started then. After Madeleine's death Courtney thought she and Dominic might get closer. She became a teaching assistant at Bella's school. And then you came along.'

'But I had no idea. How do you know this?'

'She was taken in for questioning when we discovered that she was the instigator of the abusive online posts about you. It was easy for her to get access to Dominic's computer. She was often alone in the house with Bella and she even had her own key.'

'And the derogatory posts?'

'Not only was she jealous of you but she has a deep resentment of the medical profession. Doctors accused her sister Bridget of harming her own baby and had it taken into care. It took months of legal wrangling and the belief of a psychiatrist that she was innocent to get Bridget acquitted.'

'Niall Freeman. I read about it.'

'She was trying to discredit you. She was seeking revenge, not only for being usurped as Dominic's lover, but for the wrong-doing meted out to her sister.'

Mac, his eyes like enamel, has adopted his sleuthing persona. 'The Crown Prosecution Service has no interest in pursuing a case against you. Even the computer sheets and the earring they found in the box of drugs was deemed inadmissible. Everything was taken into account.'

He smiles, but it's a fleeting expression, the kind that Ruth recognises is reserved as a preamble for breaking more bad news. She pinches the flesh on her legs.

'Ruth, this could be so much worse for you. You've been through a hell of a lot but your innocence has been proven.' He hesitates. 'There's something else you should know, though.'

Ruth snorts. 'Something else? Now what? Nothing you tell me now will surprise me. Go on, try me.'

Mac is studying her face, and the smile has left his eyes. 'The police have been asked to open an investigation into the death of Madeleine Peterson.'

'What?'

'Now that Dominic is dead there's some things we may never know, but Courtney will need to be part of the investigation.'

The tartan wallpaper takes on a kaleidoscopic appearance as Mac's voice dwindles then grows.

'Ruth? Ruth? Are you okay?'

Dominic had tried to kill her. And Bella. He had been so close to succeeding, until fate intervened. Her eyes refocus. Mac looks anxious.

'This is all too much,' says Ruth. 'I'm feeling a bit hot and faint. Do you mind if we go for a walk?'

60
RUTH

They turn left outside the hotel and follow the signpost to the Promenade. The amusement arcade on the corner is empty, save for a woman who is smoking in a cash booth and a few men playing the slot machines. The sound of carousel music dissipates behind them as they continue along the front, past the boarded up charity shops, the bookies and the chip shop. Ruth pulls up the collar of her fleece as the wind whips round her ears. She should have worn a thicker jacket. As Mac digs his hands deeper into his pockets she links arms with him, warmed by the draught-proofing effect. She tries not to think about Madeleine Peterson but she can't help it. How could Dominic be implicated in his wife's death? Madeleine was known to have a genuine chronic illness. Was Mac suggesting that Dominic might have hastened it? If that was the case, what was his motive? Control? Financial gain? A complete lack of empathy?

They pick up their stride and Mac guides her in the direction of the Venetian pavilion. They walk past it and up to the iron rail that separates the Promenade from the beach. Part of her wants to suggest to Mac that they head back up north, to avoid this tangled web of hurt back home.

'You see over there?' says Mac pointing in the direction of the lighthouse. 'Straven Caravan Park. Just before the promontory. Memories of sand in our ice creams, and playing dominoes in the caravan while the rain lashed the windows.' He laughs. 'Fancy a walk on the beach?'

Ruth nods and they follow the stone steps down on to the sand.

'I feel much better now,' she says, gripping his arm, 'now that we're outside. I was nervous of eavesdropping ears when we were in the hotel, but I don't mind talking about the hearing when we're out here. No one can hear us, not even the gulls.'

'Only if you want to,' says Mac. 'There's no hurry.'

'No, I want to know exactly what went on in my absence.' The tide has receded and she sidesteps a pile of rotting seaweed. 'The social worker. The paediatrician. Niall Freeman. I want to know what they said.'

'Well Brenda Madingley was convinced by your story initially, that Bella had a legitimate illness. Then she felt you had hoodwinked her by persuading her to close the safeguarding file. The same was true for the paediatric team. It seems that the hospital team were the ones who had suspicions about you. They got the police involved. But it was Bella that disclosed that her daddy was giving her pink Smarties and white tablets as a treat for being a good girl. Apparently she made quite a lot of helpful disclosures during her play therapy sessions.'

Ruth's feet are submerged in the sand, which is as soft as muscavado sugar. She feels weighted down by these last revelations and it's becoming more of an effort to lift her feet. 'Shall we walk nearer the water's edge?' she asks, tugging on Mac's sleeve. 'Only I feel like I'm sinking.'

They change direction and move towards the water which breaks into lacy cuffs of foam. The wet sand is firmer and it's much easier to walk over its velour surface.

'The one person who had your back,' Mac continues, 'was Niall Freeman.'

Ruth clings onto Mac's arm.

'He dismissed all the allegations as unsubstantiated.

He described you as a conscientious doctor. A perfectionist. Hard-working. Always willing to go the extra mile for your patients.'

'What else did he say about me?' Ruth shudders at the lack of privacy probably afforded to her by the court.

'It was all positive, Ruth,' says Mac, as if reading her mind.

'All?'

'There was some mention of your history of anxiety, apparently. But, you know, that is easy to put into context, given the nature of your job.'

Ruth brushes wisps of hair away from her face. She must learn to cast off this self-doubt. They get as far as the RNLI slipway and decide to turn round. They pass a family on their way back – a couple with a young girl and boy who are chasing a briny-haired dog in and out of the waves. Ruth walks on in silence, not sure how to broach the subject of Bella's future. The parade of shops has come into view and she knows if she doesn't speak up now it will be harder to address the issue when back at the hotel. She tenses her grip on Mac's arm.

'And what about Bella? Where is she now? Still in foster care? Where's her Uncle? When will he take her to Australia?' She's desperate to know but isn't she acknowledging the inevitability of Bella's departure just by asking these questions?

Mac takes his hand out of his pocket and interlocks his fingers with Ruth's. 'Val suggested I take you to stay with her for a few days, so you're not on your own. Varsha has said she will come out to see you and she'll fill you in with all the updates. She will be able to tell you about Bella.'

'But will I ever see Bella again?' She can't bear the thought of not being able to say good-bye.

'Let's talk to Varsha. Honestly, I don't know, but I can't see why not.'

'And please take me back to my house. I'll be fine on my own.'

Mac clears his throat. 'There's another reason why Val made that suggestion. You'd be keeping her company as well.'

'What do you mean?'

'Mike has left.'

'Sorry?' says Ruth. She tries to unpick her thoughts. What is Mac trying to tell her?'

'I'm not party to all the details,' he says. 'Val will explain. But I know you'd be doing her a massive favour if you went to stay with her.'

He lets go of her hand and they head up the stone steps to the Prom. Ruth feels dazed by all these disclosures.

'Oh,' says Mac, 'I've just remembered the name of the person who gave you a good character reference.'

Ruth stops. 'Who?'

'Alan Tremayne.'

Seagulls circle high above Ruth's head, their raucous cries distracting her train of thought. Alan Tremayne. His son Elliott. Elliott's grandmother Margaret. She moistens the cracks in her lips, tasting the tang of salt which has been whipped up by the breeze.

Truth above all, Niall Freeman had said in her dream. He was right.

61
RUTH

'When did he leave?' asks Ruth.

Val stops checking the 'use by' dates of her fridge contents and looks at her. She seems to chew over her words. 'Over a week ago.'

'I'm sorry.'

'Don't be. God knows, Mike and I have both made mistakes.' She hesitates. 'We need time. Space. Need to consider what comes next.' She looks down at Ollie, who is lying on an activity mat on the floor. He's mesmerised by a swirling disc, his chubby arms and legs mirroring its movement. 'I'm supposed to be going back to work at the end of the month,' she continues. Her features crumple. 'Don't know how I'm going to cope.'

Ruth moves towards her and gives her a hug. Ironic how their roles have been reversed. 'It will all work out in the end,' she mumbles into Val's shoulder. She moves back. 'You know, I still have so many questions,' she says, switching the conversation to safer ground. 'Varsha filled me in on the details of the hearing. She's arranging for me to see Bella next week.' She falters, rehearsing what she is going to say next. 'But I don't think I've got the full story. It worries me that you and Mike may be the missing bits in the jigsaw.' She thinks back to that day on the towpath, when Val confessed to her affair with Dominic. Why has Mike walked out? Surely there must be something else going on? Unease grips her and she wants to understand why.

The shadows in the kitchen lengthen. Through the window the sun sinks in a contusion of pink, purple and orange. Val lifts Ollie up and places him in a travel cot, amongst a mountain of soft toys. His eyelids seem to be battling against gravity and he lies down and closes his eyes. Val flicks on the worktop light and draws a chair up to the breakfast bar.

'I told you about my indiscretion with Dom,' says Val.

'Your affair?' Ruth is not inclined to make this easy for her. Varsha's meeting this afternoon has left her emboldened. Val looks flushed.

'It was six years ago,' adds Val, as if this somehow

made it more acceptable. 'I told Mike everything shortly after it ended. He forgave me. Or so it appeared. Seems he always held a grudge towards Dominic. He may have excused me but he didn't forgive Dom.'

Ruth's skin prickles. 'Did he confront Dom about it?'

'No. Dom never found out that Mike knew. In fact Dominic was so arrogant, that when Madeleine died he thought he could take advantage of Mike.'

'What do you mean?'

'Prevail upon him for financial advice. He even tried to inveigle insider tips on share deals from him. Even though he knew that was illegal. I now know that Mike saw that as his opportunity for revenge.'

Ruth can't help but notice the fine tremor in Val's hands as she speaks. 'What happened?'

'By coincidence Mike ran into a former friend and colleague of them both soon after Madeleine's funeral. They got talking and Mike discovered that his friend also had an axe to grind with Dominic.'

Ruth feels light-headed. She has an ominous feeling about the direction of this conversation.

'Do you remember that evening way back in May when the four of us had a take-away at our house?' asks Val

'I think so.' How could Ruth forget? It was the evening when Dom left without saying goodbye.

'Mike and Dom had been to a meeting that day. It was carefully orchestrated by Mike. They met the mutual friend who took Dominic into his confidence and convinced Dom he could make a financial killing by investing in the Chinese telecoms business, Lucky Pagoda.'

'Oh my God. Gary Sharp.'

'Yes. What made you say him?'

Ruth thinks back to the evening when she went on the internet date in the Rose and Crown. Gary Sharp came to her rescue when she sprained her ankle. She had made Mike promise not to tell Dom he had seen her in the pub. So they had been scheming against Dom all along. She looks out the window. It's dark outside now.

'You know me. I have a good memory for names. He cropped up in conversation that evening.'

'It transpires that Gary knew about Lucky Pagoda's association with the Chinese State Tobacco Enterprise. He gave Dominic the wrong advice. On purpose.'

'When did you find this out?'

'Not until last week. Mike had been bottling things up but he hasn't been behaving normally since the inquest. He was deeply affected by Dominic's accident. But his emotions seemed disproportionate. Do you know what I mean?'

Ruth nods. His behaviour at the Coroner's Court had seemed at odds with the stoical person she knew.

'After the verdict I remember him constantly seeking reassurance from me that the Coroner had said it was an accident. It wasn't like him at all. But now I know it was guilt. He felt partly responsible for what happened, the accident coming so soon after Dom lost his money. He confessed everything to me about ten days ago. We decided a trial separation was the best thing. He left nine days ago. Nine days. Eight nights. I've been so worried about him that I've spoken to him every day. I don't want him to do anything stupid.' Her eyes look teary. 'Hell, I just didn't see this coming.'

'Tell me about it,' says Ruth, immediately regretting her coldness.

Val looks up and offers a weak smile. 'I'm sorry. I wasn't trying to be facetious.'

'That's okay. I'm sorry too.' Ruth reaches her hand out over the worktop. A gesture of conciliation. 'But you said Mike told you everything?' she says after a protracted pause. 'I still don't understand how Gary Sharp fits into the picture.'

'It transpires Gary's girlfriend, Courtney, had a grievance against Dominic.'

Ruth's gut twists at hearing this name. 'Courtney? The same Courtney that posted the online abuse about me?'

'Yes. I told you about the on-line posts, didn't I? Did Mac fill you in on her association with Dom?'

'He mentioned that Dominic had an affair with

her while Madeleine was ill. He told me she's currently helping the police with their enquiries.' She wags her forefingers in the air, gesturing quotation marks.

'You could say that. Shortly after the affair ended she took up with Gary Sharp. After hearing Courtney's sob story about how she was treated by Dom, Gary was only too pleased to exact revenge on her behalf, as well as Mike's.'

'My God,' says Ruth, pondering the significance of this latest revelation. 'Mac didn't mention Gary Sharp.'

'I always knew Gary Sharp was trouble. Seems I was right,' says Val.

'You know Courtney had a double grievance against me, don't you?'

'A double grievance?'

Ruth gives a derisory snort. 'Oh yes. Not only was I the other woman in this love triangle, but she also had a deep resentment of doctors.'

'Why?'

'Do you remember a few years ago we stopped prescribing Absorbix?'

Val looks blank.

'Absorbix,' continues Ruth, 'the anti-reflux drug? It was banned because of its cardiac side-effects.'

'And?'

'Courtney Weaver's sister Bridget had it prescribed

legitimately for her nine-week-old baby. The baby suffered recurrent arrhythmias and was admitted to hospital twice after it stopped breathing.'

Val's eyes widen. 'Oh my God. Did it survive?'

'Yes, but Bridget was falsely accused of inducing the attacks and had her baby taken into care. Niall Ferguson, my psychiatrist, was instrumental in proving Bridget's innocence. He was able to prove that the baby's symptoms were due to the side effects of Absorbix. It left Courtney with a deep distrust of doctors.'

'A double whammy.' Val shakes her head. 'Incredible. Oh what a tangled web and all that. Let's hope she gets her come-uppance now that the police are involved.'

They sit in silence, their heads bowed. Ruth wonders what to say next but it's Val who speaks first.

'At the risk of sounding disingenuous I owe you a huge apology, Ruth. I've been such a shit friend. I hope you'll forgive me.'

Ruth bites her lip. 'Of course I bloody forgive you.' She smiles. 'You were there when I needed you, weren't you?' She reaches over to Val's hand and squeezes it. 'Just remember I'm here for you too.'

There's a stirring coming from the travel cot and a babbling noise. Ruth looks at the clock on the oven. 'Shouldn't Alice be back from her party by now?'

Val features soften. 'Don't look so worried. She's

having a sleep-over at Chloe Maitland's house. I know her mother, Carla, from the mother and toddler group. She was only too happy to help.'

'Well, in that case,' says Ruth, her chair grating over the pine floorboards, 'let me make supper while you put Ollie to bed.'

'That would be great,' says Val. Standing up, she opens the fridge and takes out a bottle of baby milk. 'I'll give him his bottle upstairs. I was going to do a stir-fry later. The ingredients are all here. Thank you.' She taps on a green bottle in the fridge door. 'And don't forget this. Sauvignon Blanc. Pour yourself a glass.' She fills a bowl with hot water and bobs the baby-bottle in it. Then she scoops Ollie up in her arms, waves the bottle out of its bowl and disappears.

Alone in the kitchen Ruth hangs her head, deep in thought. After Mac's thorough commentary about Bella's hearing, Val's disclosures about Mike had not really surprised her. Saddened her? Yes. Disconcerted her? A little. But not astounded her. Will she look back on this unhappy chapter one day and be grateful that she's had the chance to move on? She hopes so. At least Varsha had promised her a meeting with Bella next week to say goodbye.

She selects a wine glass from the kitchen cabinet and pours herself a drink. Better go easy. Just one glass. Anymore and Val might find her asleep at the table, their supper still in the fridge.

Above the sound of kitchen clatter there's the bang of a door and muffled voices. Ruth strains to hear what's being said but can only conclude that the conversation is measured and calm. It startles her then to see Mike stride into the room, and sweep up to her to deliver a kiss on her cheek.

They stand for a moment, before Mike ventures an awkward gambit. 'Val will be down in a minute. I've been such a bloody fool, Ruth. I hope you'll forgive me.'

62

RUTH

OCTOBER 2005

The last time Ruth visited Windridge dragon-flies hovered in columns of warm air, the park throbbed with day-trippers and Dominic had a migraine. There's a hesitation in Ruth's step today returning with such ambivalent memories, coupled with a nervous anticipation.

Today there are no boats out on the lake and the kiddies' train is operating a reduced service. A couple of pensioners have braved the chill to sit in the café's outside seating area and enjoy the Autumn sunshine. At the edge of the playground an elderly woman, a grandmother perhaps, bends down to fasten a child's coat before the youngster runs off to join her friends on the climbing frames.

Ruth's gut does somersaults. Thankfully she didn't have breakfast. The handles of the carrier bag stick to her palm, and she fiddles in her pocket with her other hand to check she has her handkerchief.

'At least the rain held off,' says Mac.

He props his rolled umbrella against the cast iron armrest of a park bench, takes off his jacket and adjusts the sleeves of his Ralph Lauren high neck jumper. He's managed to swing another day off work to come with her and now he's trying to fill the gaps in their conversation with awkward repartee.

A figure waves at them from a bench at the far side of the play area. The woman stands up and walks towards them.

'There's Sally,' says Mac, changing their trajectory to walk over the coarse grass and on to the rubber-tiled enclosure.

'Hi, lovely to see you,' says the woman, holding her hand out as she approaches. Cropped orange hair with a turquoise head band, a long canvas jacket, and striped leggings. 'I'm Sally Watkins, Byefield Social Services.' The piercings on her face regroup sympathetically when she smiles. She babbles on in pleasantries but Ruth is unable to compute what she says above the sound of children playing and the thumping of her own heartbeat.

Playful shrieks reverberate around Ruth as she scans the playground for signs of Bella. Some of the kids are wearing sunhats, others sunglasses. Adults apply sunscreen to their charges, one woman bends over a child, moistens a tissue with her tongue then wipes the face of the child who is crying. The social worker turns and projects her voice towards the climbing frame.

'Bella, can you come over here a minute, my love?'

A little girl with sherbet-lemon hair hesitates at the top of the slide then launches herself forward, landing on the bouncy tiles.

Ruth catches her breath. She'd failed to recognise Bella at first. She's taller, the sallow complexion replaced by a bloom in her cheeks. Her hair glints in the sun. Bella runs towards them then stops short when she looks at Ruth.

'Look who's come to see you,' says Sally.

Bella lowers her head but casts her eyes up at Ruth through her fringe.

Mac's hand is on Ruth's back. 'Sally and I will be in the café when you're ready,' he says. Ruth nods and they disappear, Sally's chatter tinkling like broken china.

'Hello, Bella,' says Ruth. A kiddie's squeal pierces the silence between them.

Bella regards her, unblinking. 'Where's Tilly?' she asks.

Ruth laughs, completely disarmed. 'She's at home.' Holding her breath she extends her hand towards Bella, hesitates, then starts walking. Her steps feel light, her breath floats away from her. She turns in the direction of the banana boats. 'Would you like me to push you on the swings?' She keeps walking. Little fingers curl round hers, warm and sticky. Ruth doesn't want to let go. She slows down, anxious to prolong the moment for as long as possible.

'Do you remember the last time we came here?' says Ruth. The words *with your daddy* almost escape from her mouth but she clamps her lips.

'You gave me bubbles,' Bella pipes up.

'So I did.' Ruth laughs, amazed at Bella's recall. 'And it was a very hot day and we had ice cream'

'Uncle David says "eat your ice cream, Bella, or it will melt."'

'Uncle David?' Ruth's throat constricts.

'I'm going to live with him in Stralia,' says Bella, taking a hop and a skip as she pulls on Ruth's hand.

'Australia? That's nice. I've been there.' Bella's grasp slips and Ruth tightens her grip. 'Do you remember me telling you about it?' Ruth pictures the two of them standing in Dominic's bathroom the day Bella asked her if Australia was further away than heaven. 'In fact I've brought you something to take to Australia.'

Bella sees the carrier bag and tugs on Ruth's arm,

dragging her away from the swings and towards the park bench. As they approach the seat a young woman stands up. Ruth's eye-line is drawn to the swell of the woman's belly. She must be nearly term. The woman smiles at Ruth then, placing a hand in the small of her back, she stoops over a buggy, and says something to the toddler strapped within it, before moving away. Ruth gives a weak smile in return and plonks down on the wooden seat with Bella, who swings her legs. In the distance a figure is taking down the parasols on the café tables. It must be nearly closing time. Not much time left. Can Mac see her from here? Will the Social worker have Bella in her sight at all times?

'What's in your bag?' says Bella, pulling at the sides of the carrier bag.

'Wait, wait,' says Ruth laughing. 'You must be patient. I don't want you to open them all at once. There's some surprises.' She delves into the carrier bag and pulls out a bulky object wrapped in tissue paper. Bella's eyes widen as she takes it and pulls off the wrapping to reveal a fluffy toy.

'He's a koala, Bella. He lives in Australia too.'

Bella's mouth forms a perfect O. 'He's lovely.'

'I thought he could keep Roo company,' says Ruth, swallowing hard. The lump in her throat takes on the consistency of a plum stone. 'Do you like him?'

'Yes.'

'I'm glad.'

'Thank you, Ruth.'

'You're very welcome.' Her voice wavers 'Every time you look at him I want you to think of me.' Her eyes prickle. She looks away for a second. In the distance the low afternoon sun casts moving shadows across the glass doors of the café. Mac will be patient. She turns back, taking in Bella's sunny expression. They squeeze each other tightly and Ruth closes her eyes, breathing in the jelly-bean scent. How she longs to tell Bella that she loves her so much it hurts. She bites her lip. Enough. Bella will be fine.

'Come on,' says Ruth, stroking Bella's silky head and releasing her from her grasp, 'time to have a go on those swings.'

ACKNOWLEDGEMENTS

This novel would never have seen the light of day were it not for the encouragement and support of my writing buddies on the Bath Spa MA in Creative Writing: Amanda, Anita, Charlotte, Clare, Grace, Jo, Karla, Nicola, Robynne, Ruby and Trenna. Thank you for the constructive critique, the wine, tea and chocolate.

Thanks also to the following:
Dr Alistair Hay, Consultant Forensic Psychiatrist
Detective Sergeant Debi Ellender and Inspector Matthew Armstrong
Fiona Farquhar, Barrister in Child Law
Elleni Ross, Social worker and Senior Practitioner in Child Protection
Shaun Baskett for advice on the Stock Exchange
Nathan Filer, Lucy English and Philip Hensher, my tutors on the Bath Spa MA in Creative Writing
BJFB and SNKG for your patience and support

This is a work of fiction and any inaccuracies in procedure are entirely my own.

Finally, thank you to Chris Simms of the Murder Squad and to David Grogan for giving me a timely prod in the right direction!

Printed in Poland
by Amazon Fulfillment
Poland Sp. z o.o., Wrocław